CW01496369

In my father's memory.

"Remember that what matters in life
is not what you take,
but what you leave behind."

(Goffredo De Matteis)

ADRIANO DE MATTEIS

THE WOUNDED EAGLE

A NOVEL

DISCLAIMER

The author has chosen to write a novel based on events that happened to himself, his friends, and his family, weaving them into a plot of fictional characters and events.

Any similarity with and any reference to anyone living or deceased is accidental and unintentional, except where explicitly mentioned.

The days, times, and magnitudes of the various earthquakes mentioned in the novel are faithfully reported. However, the effects of the tremors on the novel's characters are fictional. The damage to the dam of Campotosto, located near the fault line in the Laga Mountains, is entirely fictitious.

The book mentioned in the last part of the novel does exist. It was published in 1964 in English and translated into Italian in 1990. But I disclose neither the title nor the author so that the readers may discover it by going on a personal treasure hunt, establishing which parts of the novel are factual and which are invented. Good luck, reader!

This work is not intended to assess the events that make up the background or to describe them accurately and completely. Please refer to other sources such as newspapers, documentaries, and reports since 2009.

The Wounded Eagle © 2020 Adriano De Matteis.
ISBN: 9798353441472

ACKNOWLEDGMENTS

Many people helped me to write the book you are now holding in your hands.

First, I want to thank my patient wife, who has listened to these stories countless times and for so many years as I, my father, mother, uncles, and aunts told them endlessly.

You wouldn't have been able to read an English version of this novel if it wasn't for the generous help of the writer John Stewart. He edited the book and advised me on how to improve my amateurish translation. All mistakes are solely mine since I reviewed the text again and again after his excellent job. His wife, the fabulous designer Marjorie Farnsworth Stewart, has created a cover that I love and beautifully expresses the novel's spirit. I owe this splendid couple a full Abruzzese dinner.

This book is partly the result of my spiritual journey. I'm sincerely grateful to Ali Dedé of the Khwajagan. Dedé has guided me for many years, and my debt to him is immense.

The writer and savant Idries Shah taught me how to look more closely into myself and the traditions of my region to discover timeless truths. He unlocked in me a way to look at history, architecture and traditional stories that opened many routes, which is just one of the countless reasons I feel profound gratitude for him. His books are fundamental, and his contribution to the evolution of humanity is invaluable.

Finally, I want to thank his son, the fantastic writer Tahir Shah. Tahir warmly encouraged me to write before even reading a single line of my book, thus initiating me into the Salinger's brigade.

Later in the novel, I will reveal why the word 'brigade' is so meaningful.

PLACES MENTIONED IN THE NOVEL

The empty map of the province of L'Aquila is courtesy of: https://d-maps.com/m/europa/italia/laquila/laquila20.pdf

Adding the names of places and towns mentioned in the novel is the author's responsibility.

Their location on the map is approximate.

1. THE FAIR

Milan, 11 May 2008 – Sunday

Federico had already come to terms with it: for some men, it's hard to ask a favor. It's like admitting defeat in the covert war they are fighting. They seem to have embedded in their character the will to solve everything by themselves, under penalty of public humiliation and shameful exposure. Federico was reluctant to ask for help. But while he knew that he felt that pain even more than others, he also wanted to offer a unique experience to his son Manfredi. He had no choice but to do one of the things he hated the most: soliciting his boss to invite them to his house in the city and watch the explosion together.

The fair was, in fact, only a hundred and fifty meters away from Giorgio's balcony: the minimum distance to watch the event indoors. A crowd had already rushed into Domodossola Square, with Security keeping everybody back at the prescribed safety distance of three hundred meters for those outdoors. They were all exalted to attend the most significant demolition ever in Italy. A ton of explosives was set to blow up the Pavilion 20 of the Fiera Campionaria: the equivalent of eight hundred three-room apartments.

Federico was even more elated looking to the North: the San Siro Stadium stood up, fronting a line of white-capped mountains biting their teeth into a strip of clouds. Above them, the spring sky.

His attention was taken aback by the building as the countdown began: "Three, two, one, go!"

The roar of three cannon blasts swept away all other sound waves in the city.

At 10:07 a.m., the base of the construction crumbled, and the rest fell like a drunken giant whose legs had given way. But the colossus didn't get up; what rose in its place was a cloud of smoke and rubble that darkened the stadium, the mountains, and the sky, while the smell of gelignite saturated the air.

Federico felt the adrenaline rush from detonations coursing through his body and turning into worry. The explosion's shock wave made Manfredi gasp for breath and cling to his father's leg.

Ten seconds, and only debris was left of the pavilion. In its place, the curved skyscraper designed by Daniel Libeskind would be built in the new area to be called City Life.

They went back into the house. Giorgio started brewing coffee while Manfredi regained his breath and resumed the drawing he was coloring. He tilted his head as if trying to perceive its depth: "Papi, I like the sky so much. Can you please pass me the color of the sky?"

Federico passed the blue crayon to Manfredi and turned to Giorgio: "A nice way to celebrate our last success."

Giorgio didn't answer, but Federico smiled at him and put on a CD that he had brought to play for his boss. He laughed when he heard the lyrics of the song. He explained its meaning to his Managing Director, who didn't know the Abruzzese dialect.

"Why is this music so funny?" Manfredi asked.

"It's a song from Abruzzo; the words make me smile."

"And what is it talking about?"

"It's about a hut that reminds me of a stone building made by your great-grandfather. I used to hide there when I was a boy."

He started the song again and sipped the coffee, cursing silently: Giorgio had let the Moka pot boil. Federico hated the taste of burnt rubber in the coffee. He masked an expression of disgust, but he didn't comment. He realized he hadn't thoroughly enjoyed the song, not even this second time. So, he took the remote control and started it again.

He looked at Giorgio, who walked into his home office next to the living room. Federico gulped his coffee and followed him.

Giorgio was looking out the window. The cloud of dust was still hiding the view of the mountains: "My friend, the world is changing. Faster than we think."

Federico hated when he called him 'my friend' but avoided to start being argumentative. He knew his sarcasm would have only caused him more trouble: "What do you mean? What's the problem? My production plants are doing well. That's why I wanted to celebrate."

"Sometimes things are bad for everyone, but good for you. Other times, they are bad for you, but good for everyone else."

Federico's mobile vibrated. Stefania texted to remind him not to feed Manfredi meat or cheese, but only fruit and vegetables—plus a thousand other recommendations. And to 'remember to send the alimony check and to cover the medical expenses of last month.'

"What's up?" Giorgio asked.

Federico put the phone back in his pocket and returned to the earlier discussion: "Will you tell me how we are doing?"

"I guess you haven't seen the latest oil prices."

"No, I had to take care of a personal matter."

"So, relax for now. We can't do anything today. It's Sunday. Come to my office tomorrow at nine, and I'll show you the numbers. I'll get them tonight. There could also be important updates for you. But now, let's get back to your son, who has been drawing for a while all by himself."

Federico already knew about what Giorgio called "updates." He hoped he wouldn't have to justify himself again for not having accepted the secondment to Germany. He had refused, so he didn't have to move away from his son, but even if his boss understood the reason, Giorgio had changed his attitude towards him. They were on good terms and continued to see each other outside of work. But Federico had noticed that Giorgio was trusting him less and less, although Federico had turned a disastrous situation around. He applied his logic and mathematical knowledge to such an extent that the plants he was responsible for were now profitable and efficient. That had helped Giorgio's career, even if the Managing Director had always been skeptical about numbers. He never congratulated Federico, who now looked Giorgio in the eyes and felt the same bitterness in his throat as when he refused the ex-pat's proposal.

Giorgio shook his head and then nodded: "I'll tell you more tomorrow. Take it easy."

"'Take-it-easy' died, stabbed in the back by 'trust-me.'"

Giorgio smiled as he pursed his lips and patted him on the shoulder, while he motioned with his other hand for Federico to return to his son.

2. A WORLD OF COLORS

Milan, 11 May 2008 – Sunday

Manfredi stood up to close the curtains, dimming the light in the living room. He sat down and returned to his coloring:

"I like the sun so much. Would you pass me the color of the sun, Papi?"

"Sure, Manfredi, here it is."

He always called him Manfredi, without diminutives. When people asked him about that, he said that if he wanted to call him Freddie or Manfry—as Stefania did—he would have named him so.

"What are you drawing?"

"I am working on a story. The teacher asked us to draw a treasure we may have heard about. I chose the bandit's treasure; the story of my great-grandfather."

Federico had told Manfredi how his grandfather once let it slip that, 'one of these days,' he would look for that 'little paper' that had instructions on where to locate the treasure. He had put the note in the cellar and had hidden it so well that the last time he looked for it, he could not find it anymore. Federico had searched for it several times among the piles of tools, sawdust, screws, and nails. To no avail. After his grandfather died, everyone agreed that the 'little paper' was just a story made up by a loving grandfather to entertain his grandchildren.

Manfredi continued with his homework: "Papi, would you pass me the color of the golden eagle's feathers?"

He said 'eagle' with emphasis, swelling his chest and mimicking a flight with spread wings. Manfredi had drawn the mountains, a boot full of gold coins, and a flying eagle. Then he took the blue crayon from the box and colored another part of the sky.

"Papi, when are you taking me to Abruzzo?"

"One day, I will."

"You always say that, but then you never do it."

Federico hoped to put off explaining why until Manfredi was old enough to understand. However, he suspected that it was he who had to grow up and find the courage to tell his son the cause of his hesitation—a reason he had hated for almost thirty years.

Federico unclenched his jaw while looking over at Giorgio, who was staring at him as if he were reading his mind.

Manfredi continued: "Papi, the teacher said that many hidden treasures are found every year. I would like us to be the ones who uncover the bandits' treasure."

Federico caressed his son's head, messing up his hair. He would love to go back and become a child again like Manfredi and be able to lose himself in such wild daydreaming. For Federico, these stories were a way to fantasize about a world that no longer existed: hidden caves, chests of gold, ferocious bandits.

"And are we going back to see the hawks again?"

Giorgio was surprised: "What?"

Federico clarified: "Yes, we have been watching the urban nesting of hawks for eight years now. In Bologna, a pair of peregrine falcons have a nest on the thirteenth floor of one of the Kenzō towers in the Fair district."

"Dad once saved one of them. He saw it in the high grass. We took it to the hotel. We gave it food and water. It stayed on the balcony for the night, and then he flew away".

Giorgio shook his head: "Who knows if they will ever come to Milan?"

For Giorgio, Milan was the center of the world. Relevant things happened only in Milan. He would have had to wait another nine years before the renovation of the Pirelli skyscraper revealed, at its top, a nest with two peregrine falcons, Giulia and Giò.

Manfredi asked for another color:

"Papi, I want to work on the grass of the hill. Would you pass me the green, please?"

While he was texting his reply to Stefania, Federico passed Manfredi the crayon. Manfredi colored the grass and then showed his father the drawing: "Papi, look: how is it coming along?"

Federico took the picture and examined it with his own eyes. The sky was a cloudless blue, with a shining sun. On the hill sat a boot full of gold coins. But when he looked down, his eyes widened, and when he saw the grass, his jaw fell. The drawing made no sense; it seemed that blood was pouring out all over the hill: "Manfredi, what crayon did you use to color the grass?"

"The green one, Papi. The grass is green; what kind of questions are you asking me?"

Federico realized that, distracted by his cell phone, he had accidentally passed him the red crayon and that Manfredi had used it thinking it was green. He looked at his son and held his breath. He remembered how Manfredi had taken only the blue from the box. And that was after he had already used it. He had then always asked him for the other colors. Federico kept his cool and put his suspicion to the test:

"And what color do we make the car?"

"Yellow, of course. Like New York cabs."

Federico deliberately passed him the green, and Manfredi, without hesitation, used it to color the car. The confirmation he was looking for made him wince; he stood up and pushed his chair behind him, bringing his hand to his mouth while he leaned his other hand against the edge of the table.

"What's wrong, Papi?"

Federico looked at Manfredi and felt the weight of his discovery sink onto his shoulders. He let his chest fall, together with all of himself, and sank into the armchair.

"I hoped that by now it was over."

Giorgio came closer: "What are you talking about?"

"The family curse. It has just found its next victim."

"A curse?"

"I can't believe I didn't see it coming. What kind of father am I?"

"Federico, what do you mean?"

"My son. He is losing his eyesight."

3. A CRUMBLING CASTLE

Federico had brought Manfredi back to Stefania after the weekend. He had not yet told her anything about his vision problems, but only that he would schedule a routine eye examination. He went to bed with Giorgio's words, 'there is important news, also for you,' and thoughts of Manfredi's illness, which turned and twisted his mind and body all night.

The following morning, he woke up only after his third coffee. He took another one in the bar outside his office building, where he had stopped to read selected articles carefully from the newspapers. He read about the explosion they had witnessed the day before. A new neighborhood would take place, including three skyscrapers by Isozaki, Hadid, and Libeskind. The journalist reported that the last tower had been much debated, and so they decided that they would reduce its curvature.

Another article discussed the need to fire 'lazy employees'; it said that new rules were already available, just waiting to be applied.

He went to the stock exchange. Last Friday, oil broke through at $126.59 per barrel and closed at $125.64. In January, it was quoted at 91.6. Almost a 40% increase in less than five months. A crazy race.

That's why Giorgio was so worried.

Federico tried vainly to put aside his concern for Manfredi and climbed the steps into the building. Federico entered his boss's office when the second hand touched the minute hand. At 9 o'clock, sharp.

He was annoyed by the presence of the human resources manager and stopped halfway between the door and Giorgio's desk. The boss remained serious and blinked only once before speaking: "Have a seat. Coffee?"

"Yes. Black, please."

Giorgio called the secretary, ordered coffee, and continued:

"Yesterday, you asked me how we were doing. Were you able to look at the stock exchange this morning?"

"Yes. Oil's price broke through at one hundred and twenty-six dollars a barrel. As my model predicted, I believe it will reach almost one hundred fifty, and then it will fall back."

"But meanwhile, we are paying it far too much. The processing costs us even more, so the products we sell are too expensive."

Federico smiled. "That's why we have included those clauses that allow us to adjust our prices to the increase in the cost of oil and fuel."

"You may remember that we have accepted a special condition with some customers. It provides that they can terminate the contract if the oil price goes above one hundred and twenty-five dollars."

"I didn't know about this clause. Who granted it?"

"I didn't remember it, either. Our largest customers refreshed my memory on Friday night. And the other two clients have already left us. We lost a hundred million in revenues."

"Wasn't the Contracts' office the super smart department we were supposed to emulate? How could you have accepted such a clause?"

After he spoke, Federico rubbed the four fingers of his left hand along the scar on his left cheek, where he could feel his tongue pushing it out.

"Don't be the usual argumentative know-it-all. They convinced me that oil would never reach that price. A chain reaction has been triggered. We must reduce our costs."

"Then let's cut the Contracts office, and with the saved money, give me a bonus since I predicted what would have happened. I also deserve a promotion since I suggested you put in those safety clauses."

"You don't seem to understand that the situation is much more serious. It's a domino effect. Other customers will exercise the option, and even those who don't have it will still not be able to sell products that have become unaffordable. Our parent company has decided to reduce fixed costs to be more competitive. It is the law of the market. These things are bigger than us; we can't do anything about it."

"What does it mean specifically?"

At that point, Giorgio was brutal: "They are closing half the factories. The ones assigned to you. Your position is eliminated. You are liberated, along with all the members of your department."

Federico turned his head as if he had taken a slap, put his thumbnail between his teeth, and looked out the window. The Milan cathedral appeared white, as if sprinkled with salt dust. He saw the spires turn into tongues of fire; he imagined himself taking the golden halberd of the Holy Mother and pitching it into Giorgio's chest.

Instead, he stood up, combed his hair with his hand, and turned back towards his boss, raising his voice: "Liberated? What kind of word is that? Come on; I can't believe it. It can't possibly be true. You have pushed us for years with that story of quality and processes. I have improved the operation of all my plants. I have put in the right clauses to absorb the impact of adverse scenarios. And now I'm hearing that the smart-asses, who have always claimed to be the model of how everybody had to work, have accepted clauses that can make us close the shop. And you support them and fire me?"

"The consequences will be there for them as well, as for everyone. I'm sorry, it's not my decision."

Federico raised his voice even louder; the HR manager pressed herself against the back of the chair she had pushed against the wall with her feet.

"All excuses. Don't they know that in Italy, you can't dismiss people so easily?"

In the face of Federico's angry cries, Giorgio maintained his composure: "Do you know how many companies went bankrupt in Italy in the first quarter of 2008? One thousand per month. The worst results since 2000. And fewer new companies are forming, evidently discouraged by the business climate and the fact that banks are beginning to grant credit with much mistrust. And do you know how many jobs have been lost? Did you think you were immune to it? You, the only genius who, during the job interview, was able to answer the question: 'how many ping pong balls can fit in a Boeing 747?'"

"In Lombardy, companies don't go bankrupt that easily."

"Then learn to deal with the real world, not just abstruse intellectual challenges. In the first quarter of this year, more than seven thousand people in Lombardy had been laid off. In each of those companies, there were people like you and me, and each had a low probability of losing their job. Let's say two out of a thousand; maybe you don't know even one of them. What do you say? Is it a low number? But what if you are one of those two? Think of the stadium during the last game. One hundred sixty people watching it will lose their jobs within three months. These are the current, actual numbers.

Federico understood that he couldn't do anything; he had nothing more to say. He had always seen Giorgio as an ally, perhaps even a friend.

"We were at your place just yesterday. You already knew everything. You saw that my son is going blind. And you dump me like this?"

"I couldn't tell you in advance. Nothing personal."

It's always personal.

Federico looked at the human resources manager.

"So why don't you call your department 'in-human resources' from now on?"

And at that, words stopped in his throat. He felt the taste of the coffee coming up in his mouth, pushed by his heartbeat. He tried to swallow and dropped. Unconscious.

When he recovered his senses, he saw Giorgio's secretary checking his blood pressure. Giorgio continued, and his voice was dry, like a morsel of stale bread, although the words were meant to be comforting.

"Federico, it's a difficult moment; we do realize it. We are in a crisis. We have to prepare ourselves for a new era. But you have to keep calm."

"Calm? I am ruined. I need my job; I have a small child, a debt on my shoulders bigger than the house I bought it with, and an alimony check to pay."

"We are sorry."

Giorgio put everything on the table, almost as if he enjoyed diving into the muddy waters of reality.

"You asked for an advance from the pension fund, almost all of it, to buy your house. And in these cases, there are no additional severance payments."

"What? Nothing at all? Have we become so immoral?"

"Did you believe that severance payments are given out of a sense of honor? Big companies treated those they sent away well because they would rather not discourage those who came after, since they would expect at least the same guarantees. Here, however, we are shaken at our foundations; we don't even know if there will be an 'after.' However, I got one week's salary for every year you worked with us."

"But I've only been here for three years. I won't even make it to the end of the month. You are killing me."

The human resources manager tried to reassure him:

"With your skills, you will find a new job. We will support you with an outplacement company."

Federico didn't feel any relief at those words. He only felt the taste of coffee, the weight on his chest choking him, and the grip of despair in his gut. He put his things away in a few boxes. They had already prepared them; he wrote his address on them in handwriting that looked like the report of a seismograph. They would have these sent to him. He went to get his coat in the closet near the reception, and when he saw the gray locker where Giorgio kept his gym bag, he punched it. The metal resonated throughout the office and took the shape of his knuckles. The secretary looked away, returning to file her nails.

Stefania reacted with resentment:

"And your best response was to hurt your hand?"

"What else could I have done? They have eliminated the role. The crisis, which started in America last summer, is spreading worldwide. First, with unpaid mortgages, now with oil. The worst recession in decades is expected."

"And are you telling me you didn't have any clues?"

"I knew it, but I didn't consider it serious."

"And now, what do we do? You are so selfish."

"What does being selfish have to do with it?"

"If you had not been so self-centered, you would have been more careful; you would have done something; you would have pushed them back. And instead, you are being slapped by everyone. You couldn't even fight for your son. Manfredi needs you, and what do you do? You get yourself fired like the last of the fools."

"It's not that 'I got myself fired.' THEY fired me."

"Because THEY know that you are weak. You should have been smarter."

"What is that supposed to mean? I don't have a handbook for that."

"These are not things you learn in a manual."

"So, where do you learn them?"

"These are things that a man knows. Especially a father."

Federico returned home on trembling legs. He sat down and had a mental review of the situation. Among the few savings, the alimony he owed Stefania every month, and the mortgage to pay, he had enough to last about three months. He felt his bowels tighten again.

He would have to look for a fallback job.

He had to move fast.

Meanwhile, he may have been lucky enough to sell the house before the crisis hit other sectors. Maybe from the sale, he would have had something left to move forward. With little strength, he immediately set appointments with the ophthalmologist, a real estate agency, and a headhunter.

When he hung up after the last call, he tried to encourage himself: *while there's life, there is hope.*

But life had become more concrete than a sidewalk on which that hope had just slammed its face after stumbling.

4. DYSTROPHY

They went to the ophthalmologist, and Federico's hand still hurt and aching. He felt like an idiot and was ashamed of those self-made bandages that he didn't know how to hide.

He should have known better from his family's past. Once, when his grandfather's donkey, Giulia, didn't want to move, his grandfather tried to urge her in every way. It was as if she were stuck, standing on all four legs and looking at him expressionlessly. He would pull on her halter, give her a thrashing on her back, and try putting the famous carrot in front of her. Nothing.

It took an hour of such attempts before Nonno completely lost patience and punched her in the face with all the force of exasperation. The donkey still didn't move, but his hand remained swollen for two weeks, making working the land and looking after the animals an even greater effort.

Giorgio's cabinet had been softer and more flexible. It had not moved, but at least it changed shape with the blow, absorbing the shock.

After visiting Manfredi and sending him to a side room full of plastic toys, the ophthalmologist was direct: "Macular dystrophy. It modifies the central part of the retina, the macula, and causes a progressive deterioration of vision. Once involved, the cells of the retina cannot regenerate and die progressively. As in your child's case, people affected may have difficulty distinguishing colors. In addition, they may have a certain intolerance to light. It will worsen until he becomes almost blind, although complete blindness is rare since lateral vision is not impaired."

Stefania put her hands over her eyes: "How is it possible that he didn't tell us anything?"

"Not all kids want to share their difficulties. Some hide them so as not to be mocked or feel inferior or 'wrong.' They somehow hope to get by and never have to run the risk of being excluded from the group. Have you never noticed any other problems?"

Federico replied: "No, never. The routine eye examinations have all gone well. We always draw together, only on Sunday I realized that he could no longer distinguish colors."

At that point, Stefania snapped: "Sunday? And you didn't tell me anything? Who knows how often it happened, and you didn't notice anything!"

She continued with a sprint of insults, probably thinking that the doctor was on her side, or maybe she had chosen him as a paid audience, witnessing her outburst. The doctor interrupted her: "Do you have anyone in your family with a similar disorder?"

Federico confirmed: "Yes, my parents told me that there was one per generation. In mine, it's my cousin Vincenzo."

The doctor raised an eyebrow: "And how is he now?"

Federico realized how much time had passed: "I haven't seen him for about thirty years. As a boy, he saw little, even less at night, but I don't know how much. We realized this by the strange way he rotated his head to catch the ball when we played. He, too, had managed to fool the eye doctor for a while."

"The symptoms correspond. After months, or even years, you can begin to see objects in a deformed way, the curvature of the lines is altered, and a spot may appear in the center of the visual field. The lateral vision, however, remains intact."

"You mean that when he looks at me, he will see the ears but not the nose?"

"That's right. Stargardt's disease is the most common form of juvenile macular dystrophy. From what I understand, there is already an episode in the family. However, I must clarify that there must be a unique condition for it to be of genetic origin."

Federico looked at Stefania for a moment: "That is?"

"It is transmitted only when both father and mother are healthy carriers of the disease. The risk, therefore, increases in the case of marriage between relatives or within closed communities. Are you consanguineous?"

"No, please. Un-sanguineous, I would say. Not even a drop in common."

"So, either one of you is not the parent of your child, or I would lean towards an autoimmune disease, perhaps of psychosomatic origin. Even those often manifest themselves in the same family, not because of the genes, but because of the type of environment, the atmosphere the child lives in, and the air they breathe in the family."

"Psychosomatic? The environment in which they live? What does it mean? And above all, what can we do?"

"These are pathologies that arise in mind and manifest themselves through the body."

"I get it," Federico replied, still irritated by the previous innuendo.

The doctor raised an eyebrow and looked at Federico right between the eyes: "Don't be a braggart. The immune system believes that some body parts are dangerous and phagocytize them. We don't have a cure. Not in Italy, at least."

"Why am I not surprised?"

"But in Cuba, there is a clinic that combines different treatments: sun exposure, ozone therapy, and surgery."

"And what kind of success do they have?"

"We don't have much feedback yet. Few people go there because it's expensive and few people can afford it. But for the ones who go, we have heard the results are positive."

Federico had no money left, given the divorce from Stefania and the mortgage for the new house.

"Can't you ask your bank for a loan? They know you," Stefania urged him.

"They fired me. I am unemployed. Who would grant me a loan right now?"

The mobile vibrated, and Federico looked at the message: "The company considers you an interesting candidate, but we don't have suitable open positions." He had already received dozens of similar messages. Federico apologized as he began typing the answer.

"He's always on that phone."

The doctor continued: "I know a specialist who deals with psychosomatics. Maybe he can help you while you think about the Cuban clinic. Be prepared, however, because he asks special questions."

"What types of questions?"

"As you know, this disease reduces central vision but not peripheral vision. It is as if the brain wants to exclude what is in front of it, to focus on what is around it."

"And so, what could he ask us?"

The doctor gave an example:

"What is happening in front of him that Manfredi does not want to see?"

Stefania and Federico turned to each other.

He continued with the same style: "What imminent danger does he perceive around him, on which he must keep a close watch?

5. THE TEACHER

Milan, 3 April 2009 – Friday

Federico was sitting, holding his breath. The teacher had requested the meeting. He was still staring at her when she asked the first question: "Manfredi told me that you are going through difficult times."

"We have some financial issues, and, as his mother told you, he has a vision problem that we don't know how to deal with. There are promising treatments in Cuba that we can't afford."

"Often in these moments, when life becomes stressful, kids take refuge in fantasy. Manfredi tells stories in the classroom. I would just like to make sure that he is not going too far with his imagination and that he is not disconnected from reality."

Federico became even more severe at her words and moved to the edge of his seat: "What kind of stories?"

The teacher continued: "He says that when you were a child, you used to fly eagles in Mongolia."

Federico squared his shoulders, leaned against the backrest, and breathed again: "Oh my, you scared me. Sure, yes. My father's company was looking for metals there, and we moved in with him. We met some falconers who taught us the basics of falconry."

The teacher apologized for the intrusiveness: "You know, it is rather unusual. I'm sorry to have made you worry. But now I am curious. It seems like a fascinating story."

"I don't practice it anymore, and I don't talk much about it."

"Too bad. A fantasy that becomes a reality would be beneficial for Manfredi."

"I don't have an eagle and wouldn't know where to fly it."

"He told us that you had taken it with you to Italy."

"We left it in Abruzzo, like all the animals that passed through our house."

The teacher smiled: "At least there it has free and immense skies."

Federico turned towards the window: "I don't even know if she is still alive. Almost thirty years have passed."

They had left the eagle to the family of his childhood friend, Eleonora. They had been dedicated to falconry for generations, the eagle stayed with them, and when Federico returned on vacation from Milan, he would fly it. It had been almost thirty years since he last saw them all.

Federico also had a question for the teacher: "Speaking of fantasy, Manfredi told me that you are researching treasures found recently. How recently do you mean?"

"Like a year ago, for example. Two Englishmen located, with a simple metal detector, a pile of Iron Age gold coins buried in a field. A value of half a million euros. It's the most important find in England in the last hundred years."

"Who would have thought of it?"

"Also, a metal detector found a stack of gold and silver coins two years ago. It had sunk with a Spanish frigate off the Portuguese coast. It was valued at five hundred million euros."

"Impressive. And why are you interested in these things?"

"When I was a girl, I wanted to be an archaeologist. I found plenty of gold coins in Sicily with a metal detector and Greek terracotta vases."

"With the metal detector?"

The teacher laughed: "As I was saying the sentence, I felt you would ask me that. The terracotta pieces weren't, of course, located with a detector. When you look in the ground, you often find pieces of Greek pottery, simply digging with your hands."

"And did you keep them? Isn't it illegal?"

"Selling them is difficult. I tried to become a tomb raider, but failed. So yes, I kept them for myself."

Federico took a moment to digest the information while she showed him some pictures: "These are from where I found a coin and pieces of Greek ceramics. Moreover, a nest of tarantulas. And while I was running away from the spiders, a bright black snake chased me."

The teacher paused and looked Federico in the eyes: "My favorites, however, are the treasures found in moments of misfortune and destruction."

Federico put his head back, and the teacher approached him, whispering: "Hurricane Katrina has torn apart, among all the other things, a centuries-old oak tree. Among its roots, there was a pile of gold and silver coins. Hidden, as in children's stories, by pirates who had a nest near New Orleans."

Federico's curiosity was satisfied: "I thought by now all the treasures had been discovered."

He promised to bring her some books on the history of the Abruzzo bandits, who were said to have left much loot buried and still not found. The teacher liked the idea: "Traditions are important. Excuse me for daring to say so, but you should cherish them and make them known to Manfredi."

Federico smiled at that advice. *All psychologists, all counselors. Always experts on the problems of others.*

"Yes, perhaps. Now I have to go. I have an appointment with a real estate agency. When I pick up Manfredi, I will bring you the books in the afternoon."

Federico discovered that he felt better. That moment had pleasantly distracted him. He always liked to learn something new. As a child, he was passionate about the weekly Puzzler magazine. He loved the section "Not everyone knows that…," and he would immediately go and read it when his mother came home with the weekly. Afterward, he would devote himself to various puzzles and rebuses. He wasn't as good as Mom, but he learned new ways to solve problems weekly by playing with letters and numbers.

He went to check the status of his home with the real estate agent, a young man dressed in a suit one size too small for him and with hair that looked like a cow had licked it: "The whole market is down. Banks stopped granting mortgages, so people aren't buying houses."

Federico knew the story all too well.

"And since nobody buys, houses don't sell, and prices go down."

After the oil crisis came the real estate market and then the financial crisis. The practice of granting loans to those who couldn't afford them to sell more and more had become a house of cards that collapsed on itself. People stopped paying installments, the banks didn't receive the money, and so they seized the houses, only to discover they were worth less than the mortgage they had granted.

The best-known company linked to that disaster was Lehman Brothers. On September 15, 2008, Federico could relate to the employees who lost their jobs that day, all at once. He had seen them on TV holding boxes as they walked down Seventh Avenue in New York. All in suits and ties. Just like him when he had been fired.

And, as it occurred to him, with no notice. Until the last day, everything was usual for the more than 26,000 employees. Then a cold email, dried out by the network's electricity, had cut all their ties with the company.

One of the workers, being escorted out of the building by security, said they would probably not receive either their September salary or severance pay. Like him.

The largest bankruptcy in the history of the United States.

When America sneezes, the world catches a cold.

The crisis spread all over the world and affected all sectors. Production and orders fell to a minimum.

A damn vicious circle. Everyone was afraid to sell, buy, lend and borrow money: the virus of distrust had infected the world.

Even today, after nearly a year, no offer for his house or a job. He had done dozens of interviews with all his contacts thanks to his previous position and the employment agencies. The answers were always the same: "Nice resume. You must be good; I never understood anything about mathematics."

But then no job turned up. The truth was that, with the crisis and in just a few months, his work had no more reason to exist, abolished by the failure of giant multinationals, collapsing on themselves like buildings crumbled by uncontrollable vibrations. And Federico's skill set was not transferable; it was too specific. And he was not even suitable for a waiter or bartender job at his age, mainly because he had no experience in that field. Working as a receptionist at a few euros per hour and with some manual labor, he had only managed to slow down the inexorable decline.

The installments of the apartment and the alimony check crushed his bank account, and it dried up. 'Trouble shared is a trouble halved' apparently didn't count with debts. He hadn't paid his mortgage for more than six months, considering that he also had a monthly check due to his ex-wife. And he wasn't employed by a large multinational corporation anymore. So, the bank snapped its claw and foreclosed on his house.

Federico took the letter out of the envelope. He looked at it every day, hoping it would disappear. But it had not gone away while he was trying to think about something else. It was still there, in all its concreteness and violence.

He read the date of the eviction: Friday, April 3, 11:30 am.

He raised his eyes to the Burgundy-colored wall and swallowed:

It's today.

6. HOME SWEET HOME

Milan, 3 April 2009 – Friday

Federico didn't know how to react, what to say, not even where to put himself. The appraiser and his helper took measurements, sealed windows, and packed. He felt both criminal and robbed: "What will happen now?"

"Your house will be auctioned off. If you are lucky, you will repay the debt, break even and draw. But most likely, you will not be able to pay off the full loan and remain in debt with the bank."

"And what can I do without a home, without a job, and overwhelmed with debt?"

"Look, it's not my fault. I'm just doing my job. I'm struggling to make ends meet, too."

"But I have a son and an alimony to pay."

"I didn't advise you to split. My wife and I don't get along well, but we keep together. Divorce is for rich people."

The helper cut back in the conversation, with a marked Venetian accent: "Do like those fathers who sleep in the car and go to eat at the soup kitchen. In Padua, I know that there are several cases. They are found in the industrial area south of the city. There must be similar communities in Milan too. If you tell them your story, maybe you can join them."

"There must be another way."

"We told you the way; it is what it is. There are major league parents, like mothers, and minor league parents, like you and all fathers. It's the same with credit score; how do you say, 'prime'? And 'subprime,' sub. Doesn't it mean 'under'? You seem to have been relegated to a minor league. We are sorry. We really are. You may be promoted back to the major league, but you must fight for it."

"Don't you have a grandparents' country house or something like that?" suggested the helper.

"Yes, I would have one, but it's been closed for thirty years. And a restraining order prevents me from returning to Abruzzo."

When he felt the jamb vibrate after the crash of the door that locked him out of his house, his legs gave way, his head began to spin, and he had to lie down.

He temporarily placed some selected objects and the hundred books he still had left in his friend's garage. Antonio let him and Manfredi stay with him while his wife was away on a trip. The other books he had sold to raise some money. He looked at them and remembered his father's voice: 'If you have the feeling that you've read enough, then you haven't read enough.'

In the evening, he put Manfredi to bed and told Antonio his fears about the future. The discouragement gave way to an aggressive disappointment that became anger: "Yes, there must also be fathers who sleep under bridges. In Milan, where our parents came, instead of staying in the South or going overseas, to America."

"As the saying goes: turn your back to Milan, and you'll turn it to daily bread."

"Milan, our little America, where you work hard and can afford a good lifestyle."

Antonio echoed him by exaggerating the Milanese accent: "I work, I earn, I pay, I demand!"

Then he mentioned that he was training for a triathlon. He said that it indeed required physical training, but that mental training was perhaps even more critical. The difference between them, Federico thought, was that while Antonio succeeded in everything he did, there would now always be a minus sign next to Federico. Maybe several minus signs: a father with a moral debt to his son that he wouldn't be able to pay off; a financial obligation to the bank that would make him destitute; an unreliable person, someone to stay away from.

Antonio went to bed, and Federico made himself another coffee while drawing diagrams and notes that he already knew would be of no use to him. Like the presentations in the office: they didn't describe reality, but rather how everybody wanted it to be. And reality had not followed the predictions of Federico's parents, nor his own. He scribbled on those sheets of paper, but each jotting led to nothing but one conclusion: he was desperate from every standpoint.

He imagined going to live in Abruzzo and reopening his parents' house. Who knew what condition it was in? What renovations would have to be done? His father had had to go abroad to work; how could he think he would be able to find a job there? And even worse, he remembered what prevented him from going back. He thought about it every day, and, as he did every day, he chased the thought away.

He turned on the TV and found nothing interesting. So, he switched to the internet and came across a boxing documentary. It showed intense training and explained the various techniques, all followed by an overview of historical knockouts. There was the famous reference to an interviewer asking Mike Tyson whether he was worried about Holyfield and his fight plan. He answered: "Everyone has a plan until they get punched in the mouth." A boxing version of military strategist Helmuth von Moltke: "No battle plan survives contact with the enemy."

And that enemy, whose fierce face he could not even see, had punched him in the beginning, liver, kidneys, and knocked him out, shattering all his plans.

He wondered if he would even hear the bell, or if he would be able to get up before the referee counted him out.

One. He had to find a way to survive. Soon.

Two. How did those separated fathers, who slept in the car under that bridge that his mother always talked about, live? He heard time slowing down to the sound of his mother's voice, which scolded him: 'Study, or you will end up under a bridge.'

Three. He had studied. Elementary, middle school, high school, and university. He had put together all those signs, the strokes, the dots, the numbers, the letters. Yet, that bridge was inexorably closer and closer.

Four. Or maybe that bridge would have been like the one in Brooklyn. With those Italian immigrants who arrived there with just two cardboard suitcases. As his relatives who had made it.

Five. He went over the idea of sleeping in his car under that bridge. He felt like he was in a dream, alienated, devoid of energy. He imagined pulling down the car seat and looking out the windows at the moon and the stars.

Six. A part of himself hoped to fall asleep and wake up as if nothing had happened. Another part reminded him that it was all true and would soon hurt even more, as when the dentist's anesthesia ends.

Seven. He thought about everything that had happened to him in the last year. Time slowed down even more.

Eight. The divorce, the loss of his job, the new house taken away, the debt left to be paid, Manfredi, who would go blind. His legs could no longer find the strength to support all that weight.

Nine. He couldn't believe it, no matter how hard he tried. Putting all the pieces together seemed more and more absurd. As in a dream he had when he was a child and had a high fever.

Ten. He didn't get up. And at half past three in the morning, the clanging of the ring bell made him fall into the same sleep that the prisoners sleep on death row.

7. NIGHT ATTACK

L'Aquila, 6 April 2009 – 3:32 a.m.

Eleonora was sleeping six hundred and sixty-six kilometers away, measured by Federico's father's Alfa Romeo during a Milan-L'Aquila trip. She dreamed of riding a wave when her forty-four kilos were thrown from the bed as if the mattress's springs had all fired at once. The closet fell in front of her and smashed to the floor, waking her not from a nightmare, but *in* a nightmare.

She was already rolling on the ground when she heard a deafening roar that disintegrated the windows into thousands of fragments. She covered her belly with her hands and smelled the dust from the rubble. She got up, but the floor changed inclination, and she dropped again. The closet tipped over her side, and she scratched her right ear. She touched where it hurt and tried to get up again, but felt the furniture weighing on her leg.

Still on the ground, wrapped in the darkness, she raised her hand higher on the wall to find the light switch. Thrown by another blow from the floor, the closet moved, freeing her leg. She tried to stand up but fell again, banging her left eyebrow on the crib's edge, which was rocking a lonely piece of masonry chopped from the ceiling. Holding her belly, she managed to find her balance in the dark; then she felt what she could only describe as a haunting underground wind that passed below her and through the walls.

She shrugged her hair out of her mouth and leaped to where she knew the door was. Breathing, she realized that what entered her lungs was not the hoped-for pure mountain air, but a mist of white powder. She coughed while managing to lower the handle and pushed it while trying to throw herself out the door, but she slammed into it and was thrown backward by the recoil.

The door was blocked: a pile of stones and wood prevented any escape. The wall to her right fell, taking part of the roof with it, and in the open sky, she saw flashes of light and luminous spheres, as she had already noticed in the previous months, followed by electric shocks that reached the ground.

She was imprisoned in blackness. Surrounded by dust, her feet trampled on debris as the floor snapped, again changing angles like a surfboard on an angry sea.

Feeling the bitterness of the rubble from her tongue, she cried with despair, as superhuman as the breath of the earth that had rushed through her.

And then everything stopped.

As if that same earth had listened to her.

The dust fell to the ground, dancing with no hurry, and the air began to fill the space again. Her eyes, adapted to the darkness and the little light of the not-yet-full moon, showed her a hundred versions of herself reflected in the splinters of the wall mirror. With dusty hair and blood coming down from her ear, her grainy eyes attempted to make sense of what they were seeing while her breath continued to accelerate.

Twenty-three seconds in total.

For the first time in her life, she had perceived each of those seconds passing in their entirety—one by one. Inside every second, she felt every tenth, every hundredth, every thousandth.

And for each fraction of a second, a wall was moving; another one was torn apart, and a stone was separating from those it had been stuck for centuries. Another fraction passed, and this time it was a pillar crumbling; a hundredth second more, and there was one less piece of roof.

There, and throughout the basin of L'Aquila, for every house in the city and lower Aterno Valley, those same twenty-three seconds.

And then silence.

Eleonora smelled a new smell for the first time.

Fear. The primordial one.

Her senses were alert, and she listened attentively.

And her ears also heard something new.

Something they had never heard before.

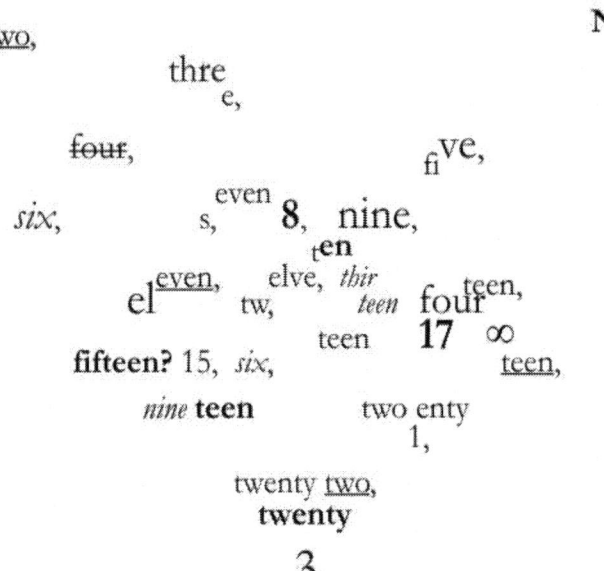

two,

O
NE,

thre
e,

four,

fi ve,

six,

even
s, **8**, nine,

ten

el even, elve, *thir* four teen,
tw, *teen*

teen **17** ∞

fifteen? 15, *six*, teen,

nine **teen** two enty
1,

twenty two,
twenty

3.

The silence.

Not the usual, customary silence.

It had an ultimate quality, the deafness of nothingness.

With a twenty-three-second eternal blow, the earthquake took every sound with it.

8. GROUND ZERO

Federico was watching the Moka coffee pot, keeping the lid open while he started pouring the freshly brewed coffee. When the sound changed from 'khuuu' to 'kheeeee', he closed the lid. The little coffee that came out afterward found its way into the sink. *'A bit of waste for a rounder taste.'* Sipping the third coffee of the morning, he turned on the TV.

He felt his eyes pressing on his orbits and eyelids in an attempt to let in the enormity of dismay. Like a great bird of prey in flight, a helicopter looked over the villages affected by the earthquake during the night. Under the aircraft, the view was that of a bombing. One by one, the camera framed what was left of the places of his childhood. The TV showed his father's village, Villa Sant'Angelo, made into a pile of crumbled stones. No experts were needed to offer hyperbolic descriptions: he had them all in front of his eyes.

Earthquake? At Villa Sant'Angelo? No way.

The camera overviewed the village, and Federico hoped to see some houses still standing. Instead, the school, church, and grocery stores had all returned to dust.

There were victims; it was not yet known how many; some had already been found during the night.

Federico wished that Balthazar had died in the rubble of one of his villas, but while he realized what he had just hoped for, he felt ashamed of himself. The camera went from one village to another. He knew them all; in each of them, something had happened during the endless summers of his childhood. In each, there was a particular point he was fond of. A square where festivals were held, a carousel, and a rugby field.

Federico was appalled: *Even Vallecupa? Onna? Paganica?* Rhetorical questions. The seat of the Prefecture of L'Aquila was gutted. The dome of the Church of the Anime Sante had collapsed. The apse and transept of the Cathedral and the Basilica of Santa Maria di Collemaggio were a pile of rubble. The House of the Student also collapsed. The Department of Letters and History and the Center of Engineering and Economics of the University of L'Aquila in Roio were severely damaged, as were tens of thousands of houses.

It was calculated that the earthquake that hit the area had the same destructive power as the bomb dropped on Hiroshima. As if fifteen thousand tons of TNT had been placed along the Aterno Valley and detonated at 3:32 a.m.

From the camera's perspective, Federico could see the strip of destruction snaking on the ground all along the shattered valley.

He felt his childhood leaving his body, squeezed out of his heart, and dissolving into the sky. And to that heaven, he lifted his head for an infinite moment. Then he bowed, his eyes closed in his hands, and cried.

9. MILAN AND VINCENZO

Milan, 6 April 2009 – 8:30 a.m.

His cousin Vincenzo had called Federico half an hour before to tell him they needed to talk. With Uncle Maurilio, they were headed down to Abruzzo. They wanted to bring Aunt Cesidia with them to spare her the stress of the earthquake recovery.

Before going down the street to meet him, Federico went to the bathroom and again dismissed the idea of cutting his beard off. While working for a multinational, he used to shave every day, and if he went out in the evening, he would shave again; he didn't skip the ritual, even on weekends. Now that amount of care seemed pointless to him, and he didn't even understand how he could have wasted all that time over the years only to shave. He was beginning to look like a ruffled version of his father, who kept his beard relatively short and well-tended. A nice by-product was that the scar on his left cheek could hardly be seen, covered by some hair that leaned over it.

He left Manfredi inside, took to the street, and saw Vincenzo in front of him. The same faces as when they were children. He recognized him immediately. Both with grainy eyes, although for different reasons. Vincenzo almost didn't greet him before speaking, as if he had seen Federico every day they had been apart for the last twenty-eight years. He began to talk in gusts, coming close to Federico's face, forcing him to pull his head away and even to take a step back:

"You have to help us."

Federico felt powerless: "And how? I am left with nothing. No wife, no home, no job, and no money."

Vincenzo stared at him as if he might attack him at any time, although his gaze seemed to look beyond, as if he was looking at someone else behind Federico. Perhaps the ghost of his childhood that had left him the day before was still visible behind him. Or maybe it was an effect of the family eyesight curse.

His way of speaking kept changing, coming in jerks, and pauses. Then sudden accelerations: "Come down. Everything is destroyed; we must help our people. Give a hand. Like everyone else. You must do it now."

The words came out of his mouth, clashing against each other as terrified people ran away from an explosion. Federico pushed him back forcefully when he came close to his face again. His words burst out: "I can't do it. I can't do it. And I have Manfredi with me. His mother is away, and I am staying with a friend. Where would we go? The houses are all damaged or collapsed."

Vincenzo came even closer. If someone had put a nut between their foreheads, it wouldn't have fallen: "Your son can come with us. It will be like camping with the Boy Scouts. We set up the tents and cook with the stove we use for the truffle festival."

"I have seen the news. It's an apocalypse. I cannot take Manfredi there."

And then Vincenzo fell into a sudden silence in which he seemed to cower within himself, as if he had short absences from the reality that had been a remote possibility until yesterday and was now concretely true. And then he resumed, persistent. The disconnected rhythm took Federico's breath away, he tried to swallow, yearning for the saliva he no longer had. Vincenzo lowered his voice, looking down at him: "Tell me the truth, is it because you are still afraid of Balthazar? Do you think he would kill you if you came back?"

Federico denied: "Of course not. I remind you, however, that I have a legal warning that prevents me from entering Abruzzo."

Vincenzo spread his arms and began to speak out loud again: "And who will find it in that mess? Federico, we promised each other that if one of us ever needed anything, the other would be there for him."

"Vincenzo, we were just kids. You're not going to pull some crap like that on me!"

"And so, the promise is no longer valid? Federico, you are a coward. Your fear made you avoid everyone, including your childhood friends and relatives. The last time we saw each other, you didn't even know what it felt like to have hair on your cheeks. How long has it been since you heard about Tonino?"

Federico had cut off all contact with Abruzzo, including the few people left in his extended family. He had postponed that reckoning day after day, and three decades of notches had run out of space on the handle of his rifle: *Where have all these years gone?*

"Why? What happened to Tonino?"

"He is nowhere to be found. His house hadn't been damaged; maybe he was somewhere else when the blow came. He hasn't been well for some years, and he told me he would have been sorry to die without seeing you again."

Federico closed his eyes, lifted his head, and opened his lips, cursing with narrow teeth. This was a shot below the belt. He knew he was Tonino's favorite nephew. Federico owed him a great deal. Tonino made his childhood a fantastic period of joy, magic, and learning. He felt immensely grateful for him, and the guilt for letting thirty years go by became remorse. His past was now clutching him by his ankles and wrists, staring him straight in the eye, sucking him into the bonds of blood and the debts of gratitude. In addition, an unprecedented disaster was underway; help was already coming from all over Italy and the world. How could he be so coward as to refuse?

He couldn't say no. Not to both.

Yet, he was about to repeat it: *I'm sorry, I can't make it.*

Federico assessed the choices he had. None. What would Father have done? He would have gone, of course. If there were people in need of him, he wouldn't have given it a moment's thought. And he certainly wouldn't have been afraid of Balthazar. Federico could remember that it wasn't Father who feared others; it was the others who feared Father. Of course, his father had never had these problems—an ex-wife, the loss of a home, and a sick son. And what would Stefania say? She would berate him, all the more so when thinking of Manfredi. Every choice he made in his mind terrified him. He had only questions and no answers.

But reality didn't leave room to escape. With no home, no job, and no money, with Manfredi in need of expensive care—and fast—he could do no better than accept, even though he felt as if he were going to the gallows.

He agreed with Vincenzo that he would go into hiding to avoid facing the threat of Balthazar's retaliation or territorial restriction. And he would see for himself how, once again, fate had decided to rage against him and his childhood.

10. THE CHAMPIONS

It had been twelve years. Twelve years of nerve-wracking wait. Federico was with the other fans in a scrum in the stands while the players were doing it on the field.

L'Aquila was first in the league standings. Winning today meant clinching the championship a week early and triumphing at home. Already the winner of seventeen out of twenty games, the team was at the top of the league, undisputed; if it had not been that day, the 'Scudetto', the championship, would have come the following week in Livorno. But winning at the Tommaso Fattori stadium would bring further glory to the event and add the soundtrack of epic deeds. Giving the passionate and faithful L'Aquila's fans the final victory that would secure the Scudetto was the dream of every team player.

The public was the sixteenth man on the field, with whom all the teams visiting L'Aquila had to reckon with. And the reckonings for the guests that year had been heavy. They all had still in their eyes the match versus Petrarca, the "game of the heart," played only with the willpower left in their nerves. Someone even proposed doping the players, who refused and demonstrated that giving drugs to wild boars was useless: they still won, even when they were struggling.

Federico's father considered those young guys lucky and brave because, while keeping their jobs, they lived an extraordinary adventure rather than having to travel the world to earn a living. He came back whenever he could. Every vacation, every break between one job and another, often separated by different continents, with dramatic school changes for Federico. Being present as the team won the Scudetto would be a beautiful gift.

That day was also Federico's mother's birthday. Another reason to make that party unforgettable.

Federico's father took him a few times to the bar that had become the meeting place of the rugby players and a city landmark: '*See you in front of Scataglini.*' Under the arcades of the city of L'Aquila, it became the quintessential bar. Everyone went there to see the players who had become not only stars but heroes. Those young men were builders, carpenters, and municipal employees that worked during the day; at night, they trained, and on Saturday, players like Mascioletti would hang out with Ghizzoni and Ponzi at Scataglini's. They welcomed their supporters with joy and big hearts, surrounded by young girls looking forward to meeting these brave and smiling young athletes: the beauty and the simplicity of small-town life in Italy.

This was back when L'Aquila was a team that won epic games, brought home championships, and had several players representing it on the national team. But Antonio di Zitti, another L'Aquila rugby legend, wanted reinforcements. He called a fellow villager who had emigrated to South Africa and asked him who was the best player there. The friend replied that it was Robert Louw, who was then persuaded by a South African girl working in Italy to move to Abruzzo. Robert Louw was tall and blue-eyed; everyone loved him and his even blonder wife, Azille.

Federico had met them both when they had come to his classroom to lecture on rugby two months earlier than the match.

Federico was still not interested in women, and as far as male role models were concerned, he didn't desire to be tall, blond, and blue-eyed. He wanted to be like SuperMas: quick, elegant, and soft-spoken. Always able to set the pace of the game. Curly hair, neatly trimmed stubble, dreamy look but an indomitable warrior.

Massimo Mascioletti—SuperMas—was a legend. He never left L'Aquila Rugby or his job as a municipal employee. They offered him money and glory, but how could they think he would have left his friends? They would go to the bar together; they had known each other since they were babies.

But SuperMas was not on the pitch on that day. He was injured. During a challenge in Fiji, Massimo's arm popped out of his shoulder socket after an off-timed tackle. The doctor put it back in place, so even though he was in pain, Mascioletti decided to continue. But another tackle took his shoulder out again: joint dislocation, surgery, and a year off.

Of opposite temperaments, Mascioletti—more introverted—and Serafino Ghizzoni—more exuberant—were 'goal twins'. Two wings that made The Eagle, L'Aquila, fly over the Gran Sasso above all of Italy. Like Federico and Vincenzo dreamt of becoming one day. Mascioletti and Ghizzoni had broken the classical rugby schemes and introduced the concept of total rugby, and they fit everywhere in the game, complementing each other.

And Ghizzoni had the guts to attempt the impossible from the center of the field. He remembered that he was also a ski instructor, and with the ball under his arm began a Stenmark-style slalom. While he seemed to go downhill, the opponents appeared to run uphill. He first left one opponent on his right and the next on his left. Then, when he was right in front of the third adversary, and could no longer avoid crashing against him, just a millimeter before colliding, he passed the ball to Giancarlo Morelli on his right. Morelli was already so fast that he ended in the in-goal by his momentum.

Die-hard Abruzzesi, Mascioletti, and Ghizzoni had never been separated from the black-and-green L'Aquila jersey.

As the game proceeded, L'Aquila's black and green jerseys turned out to be the fastest on the field. Federico was impressed to see that a couple of players were on the field with their heads bandaged; the father told him: "They have an Abruzzese's head; they don't break easily," his father told him, "and rugby players are fearless and know how to ignore pain."

The match was well underway when they waved away a throw-in, the 'plum' not even falling to the ground; it was sent over to Ennio Ponzi. Ennio received it as he saw a space between two opposing players and dove into it with sprinter-like strides. He waited until the two opponents were on him, and right on the attack, he stretched the ball and his hands toward Lucio Pelliccione. The two opponents instinctively moved toward Lucio as well, but Ennio brought the ball back to his body; the stadium began to murmur about the splendid feint, while he avoided them by dribbling to the right. After two strides, he repeated the same maneuver, but this time, the players pounced on him, but he passed the 'plum' to Lucio, a runaway train destined for the end of the line. And Lucio did carry his mustache and the ball over the goal line. The stadium exploded on that dizzying action, witnessing a selflessness on the field that seemed taken from the novels of the three musketeers, an exchange that reveals a perfect understanding and an unwavering trust among teammates.

The stadium exploded at the sight of their dizzying actions, the roar beating on the eardrums as if in a war.

And so, it finally happened.

With their hands peeled raw by applause and their voices hoarse by the screams, spectators from all over Abruzzo overwhelmed the safety net and invaded the pitch at the eightieth minute.

The city was all in celebration and the flags, black and green and the Italian tricolor, waved throughout L'Aquila and the province.

The players were carried in triumph. South African Rob Louw, affectionately elected by the fans as the team's symbol, looked like someone who couldn't believe his eyes.

The prizes for the winners would be sheep, hams, and tires: all the things it takes to survive on those barren mountains.

Federico, too, was overwhelmed by adrenaline, excitement, and the insane desire to challenge Balthazar.

11. BOYS WILL BE BOYS

L'Aquila, 3rd May 1981

Everyone in the town and the countryside celebrated with flags and honking horns. The energy was too much for the boys' bodies to contain. It gushed into their eyes and charged their legs. Trying to emulate their idols the same afternoon of the victory, they went crazy on the local pitches.

Federico, Vincenzo, Balthazar, Crocko, and the others had been playing for over an hour, and the sun was about to set. Balthazar was agile on his ankles; he could make two or three body feints within a second and jump over anyone. He held the ball close to his body and ran with his head high. When a collision with an opponent seemed inevitable, he would turn to the left and spin back to the right. But he could also do the opposite when he wanted to, or instead of one fake, he would make two or even three. He was unpredictable and unstoppable.

Balthazar had already been selected by L'Aquila Rugby Club and would have had a future as a champion; his skill and demeanor made it natural for his mates to shorten his name and refer to him as: "the Tzar".

Crocko was his wingman on the field, taking out tacklers. They called him "The Crusher" because of his rugby style of play. And everybody knew that he hoped to follow the Tzar to the Rugby Club.

With Balthazar running towards him, Federico approached him at a trot, prepared to bend and take the blow as best he could. The Tzar lowered his head and accelerated straight at him. Federico imagined his opponent's nostrils widening, his eyes on fire, and, on his frowning forehead, two bulls ready to crash. Balthazar made his classic moves, but Federico had already decided his strategy. He ignored the fake and threw himself to the opposite side so that his right shoulder crashed against the right shoulder of the Tzar as he turned, twisting him back on himself and bringing him flat to the ground. The collision made the ball slip out of his hands; Vincenzo grabbed it and started running the other way, just as Federico's mother shouted to announce dinner: "Federicoooo! Vincenzo!"

Vincenzo stopped and smiled at his companions: "Have you noticed that the best day is the one that ends with dirty clothes?"

Federico extended his hand to the Tzar while he was massaging his burning shoulder. He refused it by slapping it and got up on his own. He stormed toward Federico and glowered over him. Federico felt his neck stiffen, thinking he could give him a header at any moment. At the same time, he sensed that he didn't have to back down.

"It's the last time in your life that you stop me. I promise."

They set out on their way home; Vincenzo took via Capo la Terra towards his home. When he was far enough away not to see them, Balthazar kicked Federico from behind as if trying to boot his oval ass towards an imaginary goal twenty meters away. Federico's head snapped back in reaction, and just then, Balthazar slapped him on the back of the head. Federico folded forward, and so his ass was ready to take another kick. Between kicks and slaps, Balthazar drove him almost to his home. No one was in the street, and the sun had already set, leaving the scene at dusk.

"So, you're still trying to stop the Tzar?"

More slaps and kicks. Federico didn't answer, and Balthazar got even angrier.

Balthazar saw it when they arrived in front of Federico's grandparents' house. The puppy dog.

It had once fallen from the balcony of their house in Milan. Its pelvis and jaws were smashed. It survived but had remained lame, had difficulty eating, and barked as if he was instead catching breath. It walked in such a way that everybody called him Merengue. The family decided to leave it there in Abruzzo because they often traveled, and it was difficult to look after animals.

Balthazar took it by the scruff of the neck. "Should I hurl it down the ravine?"

Federico begged him: "Don't".

Balthazar grinned as if he were waiting for that very answer. As if he were bowling, he stretched his arm backward and then threw the puppy forwards flat, making it tumble for about ten meters. The dog rolled downhill and banged its head several times, clumsily trying to parry the falls. It stopped against a stone, avoiding ending up in the ravine beyond the road. Federico ran towards it and took it in his arms. Blood came out of its nose; it was whining in pain and blinking its eyes rapidly.

Federico caressed its head and laid him on a slight grassy stretch, far from the side of the road and closer to the house. Then he felt his pectoral muscles tighten, and he sprang towards Balthazar, who, probably for the first time in his life, fled. Federico reached him at the top of the hill, under the house of Armando, and began to punch him in the stomach until Federico felt pain in his shoulders and chest. Balthazar broke down, screamed in pain, and began to cough because of the spasms.

Federico walked away while keeping an eye on him. "What's going on?" shouted Armando.

"I'll kill him," replied Balthazar, coughing even louder.

"Who?"

Balthazar raised his cry by an octave: "Federicooooo!"

When he bent over to wrap his arms over his belly, he must have noticed the ax on his right stuck in a wooden log. Federico, who had followed his gaze, understood his intentions. He ran away just as Balthazar grabbed the ax and threw it at Federico, who heard it hissing toward him. When he slammed the garden door behind him, he heard it stick with a sharp noise into the beaten-up wood. Federico breathed a sigh of relief as he leaned against the door, only to feel it smashed into him by a kick from Balthazar. Federico, exhausted from running and fear, thought he was suffocating: the Tzar clutched his throat; he could neither breathe nor move Balthazar's hands. They were as strong as Uncle Tonino's pincers.

Armando broke through the remaining part of the door without wasting time opening it. Snatched Balthazar away from Federico, who, on the evening of the legendary Scudetto and his mother's birthday, fell unconscious in the garden among the new tomato seedlings.

12. BALTHAZAR

L'Aquila, 6 April 2009

The TV interviewer asked about the extraordinary disaster response. Balthazar, standing as a column of a Greek temple, with a calm and deep voice, proclaimed: "We have organized the first responders, shelter, and hot food."

"How many tents are there already?"

"Not enough. Some people are camping with their tents or with makeshift protection. We expect to have many more thanks to the Civil Protection. Help is coming from all over Italy."

"Are you still digging?"

"Many people are still under the rubble; the work is coordinated to free people and give them assistance."

"What message do you want to send to those affected by this calamity?"

Balthazar took a deep breath, and the tricolor rosette, which he had pinned on his jacket, stood up and entered the frame: "The strength of the people of Abruzzo is enormous. If we remain united, we will be able to face the emergency and rebuild L'Aquila and our villages."

Seeing the confidence and ease in the speech delivery, Federico, watching the news, felt his spine stiffen and his legs soften. He swallowed, thinking that The Tzar was outstanding. A part of himself admired him.

Since childhood, he has been the most confident. He was sure of his father's money, assertive with girls, and reliant on his physique. He was the strongest, the tallest, and the best conditioned. In rugby matches, he was the fastest. The girls liked Balthazar, and he wanted them.

He was the son of the lawyer from L'Aquila, Don Cesare. His father told him a thousand tricks on behaving, which none of the other kids knew.

It was said that Don Cesare became rich on the backs of the pensioners in the area. One example was when the arrears of pensions for the elderly of the villages were paid. He sent his French wife to solicit a fee because, he claimed, the arrears had been obtained thanks to his support of the case with the Ministry in Rome. He had many friends in the institutions, so he asked for compensation of one million liras from each pensioner. And guess what? Did anyone object? No one. Did any complaints come? None. Nothing. All the elders of the country paid in cash. No fees, no traces, and no taxes. All were afraid to go against the lawyer because, 'you never know, maybe one day we will need him', so people paid the fee.

With these stratagems, the lawyer had bought himself ten houses in the whole area, including some apartments in L'Aquila.

Federico also remembered his mother telling him that Balthazar's grandfather seduced and impregnated a minor girl. When it was discovered, he threatened the young woman and asked her to confess that the priest had to be blamed for it. It took a little investigation to find out the truth, and her family begged him to marry her. He accepted, but asked for the family's land outside the village. On that land, he built the mansion where he segregated the girl, whom no one ever saw again. That palace later became the summer residence of the family. Meanwhile, he continued his gallant raids. He even married a second time, although no one knew how he managed to get around the law and the Catholic Church.

Balthazar received his name because Don Cesare's wife was French, and they wanted to give him a transalpine name: "*C'est plus international.*"

Don Cesare didn't love that name, but out of love, he gave in. This happened just the year before French director Jean-Louis Bresson directed a film in which the donkey's name was precisely Balthazar.

13. THE END OF A SCHOOL DAY

Villa Sant'Angelo, June 1980

When his parents took a break between two trips, Federico attended the last year of Middle School at Villa Sant'Angelo. During the week, his father used to go to Rome, where the company was based, and returned on Friday evenings. Every so often, he also came for dinner on Wednesday and left on Thursday morning. At the end of the lessons on that Thursday, the classroom had emptied, and only Federico, Vincenzo, and Giovanna remained. Federico didn't want to go out; Balthazar was waiting for him outside. The janitor shouted from downstairs: "Guys, come on, we are about to close. We can't stay here until midnight."

They looked out and saw Balthazar surrounded by his friends and embracing his girlfriend, Eleonora. Balthazar was older than they. Like them, he was attending the eighth grade, but had failed twice.

Giovanna was the first to break the silence: "What do we do? Do you want me to talk to him?"

"He wouldn't listen."

"Let's then warn the janitor."

"I want to avoid being called a troublemaker."

"We can talk to him; come on. It's just a misunderstanding."

In the end, they were forced to go out; Balthazar was pounding his fists in his hands, alternating left and right, and now and then, he would do a few jumps on the spot. When he saw Federico come out as slow as a turtle, he smiled at him as you would with a friend you meet on the street: "At last!"

When Balthazar smiled, his mouth widened in a horrible grimace. He approached Federico and wrapped his arm around his neck. Federico smelled him and felt like throwing up. He hunched his shoulders and lowered his head, and began to walk, guided by Balthazar's arm, who kept smiling:

"We are friends, aren't we? What has been, has been."

"Of course, we are friends: what has been, has been."

"And you would never make a fool of the Tzar."

"Never."

"And do you like Eleonora?"

"She is your girlfriend."

"So, do you like her or not?"

"I don't know; she is your girlfriend."

"Ah, so she's ugly."

"I didn't say that."

"So, she is beautiful."

Federico felt he had to give in at some point, but he did it with a positive remark: "Yes, of course."

"So, it's true that you like her and looked at her today. You just said she's beautiful. How do you know she's beautiful if you haven't looked at her?"

"She was sitting on your bike's seat; everyone saw her."

"The Tzar is your friend, and this time he wants to give you only a friendly warning."

Meanwhile, they had been walking, and they had turned the corner of the school's railing and arrived under a large alder tree that hid the view from the square. Checcótt, a friend of Balthazar's, had blocked everyone, including Vincenzo and Eleonora: "He said he just wants to talk to him, don't worry."

Giovanna gave Eleonora an angry look, who raised her chin and turned her head the other way. Federico thought that maybe Balthazar just wanted to talk to him, that he was his friend, and felt a sense of relief. He did like Eleonora, but considered her out of his reach: "Thank you, Tzar."

At those words, Balthazar moved behind Federico as though returning to the others, but instead took Federico's head and slammed his face against the grating. Federico couldn't even scream. His nose broke, and he started bleeding. Balthazar locked his arms behind his back with one hand and, with the base of his other hand, kept hitting the back of Federico's head so that his face crashed against the railing. Balthazar repeated the blow every time that Federico's nose bounced on the irons.

At that scene, Giovanna and Vincenzo wriggled away from Checcótt and ran towards Federico.

Balthazar turned towards them. With his nose curled, eyebrows furrowed, and upper lip raised, he threw Federico on the ground, where he passed out in the pool made by his own blood.

14. THE VEGETABLE GARDEN

Milan, 6 April 2009

Federico had already taken some of his stuff to Ranieri's garden hut. Ranieri was a man born in Apulia who had emigrated to Milan. Federico had helped him with manual labor. In exchange, the man gave him vegetables and tomatoes and treated him to endless laughter when he spoke to him in the Apulian dialect. Once a man passed by with his bike roaring, with no helmet on, and Ranieri came out with: "That one has the face of the three of clubs."

And what does the 'three of clubs' look like?

Federico went to buy a deck of Neapolitan playing cards just to check. He had not seen them for years and was fascinated by their symbolism: gold, swords, tree branches, cups, jacks, kings, and queens. He wondered if they didn't hide some secret code in addition to the game. The images arrived in Naples from the Arabs, thanks to the Spanish, but what the cards represented was a mystery. Federico thought that if there was a way to hide something in plain sight, it was to make it a game. In passing them through his hands, he felt like he was touching the supernatural, scratching the surface of an alchemy that combines numbers, thousand-year-old symbols, and occult forces. The gold, the wealth; the swords, the power; the cups, the vices; the branches, the vigor.

Shuffling through the cards, he came to the one he was looking for. A card different from all the others. The face of a laughing monster-man, a grotesque mask with a large mustache: The Mammon, one of popular culture's most mysterious horror characters. In the New Testament, the term Mammon is used as a personification of material wealth, understood negatively when idolized since it may divert from sticking to a spiritual path. Jesus says in the Gospel: 'You cannot serve God and Mammon".

The origin of the term Mammon, probably from the Aramaic or Syriac language, can also be traced back to the idea of a 'buried treasure. The reason for the presence of this face in Neapolitan cards is perhaps linked to the City Guard. They patrolled in groups of three, carrying sticks and decorating their jackets with a red cockade. Big mustaches and mocking smiles completed their menacing image. It reminded him of his great-grandfather Carlantonio; he, too, had that grim look and those mustaches that extended beyond his face.

Ranieri had been dead for some time, but Federico imagined an impossible conversation with him speaking proverbs in Apulia's dialect:

"How is it possible that Giorgio fired me like that? We had a good relationship."

"To the best friend goes the best stone."

"What will I do now? I am out of work."

"If you want to work, America is here, and America is there."

Opportunities are everywhere for those prepared to do the work. Ranieri says. And popular wisdom agrees.

He had gone to see what had become of the shed before he lost his house. No one was looking after it anymore, and no one, he hoped, would have noticed his presence. There was tall grass and weeds everywhere. He decided that once Antonio's wife returned, he would move from his friend's apartment to the shed. Stefania would criticize him, as always, and, as always, without giving him solutions or alternatives. He had already started to fix it up. He had brought with him what he had left of his camping equipment and the few things he had managed to keep: the outdoor solar shower, binoculars, a sleeping bag, and the gas stove. Furthermore, he had put a new lock on the door.

Before leaving Milan, Vincenzo accompanied him to the shed: "What is this? Are you cultivating vegetables?"

Federico didn't want to give explanations: "Forget about it, Vince. Shall I take the camping tent?"

"No need, I know where to sleep."

"And where is that?"

"It's a surprise."

"One of your gimmicks, I guess. But I'll take hunting binoculars. And also, this military flashlight that I bought in Texas."

He went through the toolbox and took some other tools he thought could be useful: screwdrivers, pliers, and a hammer.

He opened the small drawer under the worktable and took out the nine-millimeter gun that Ranieri had left him. Federico sighed and thought to himself: *It can't be that serious.* He loaded it and weighed the nine hundred fifty grams with his hand while his mind weighed something else. Could I use it if needed? *Perhaps it is more dangerous to take it with me than to leave it here.*

Vincenzo rushed into the hut: "Your uncle is waiting."

He looked at the only two suits he had kept, the few ties and the hanging shirts. He felt sad thinking about when he might wear them again. But now was no time for unproductive reflections. He packed his suitcase with the heaviest clothes he had.

Meanwhile, the words Ranieri said to him when he gave him the weapon began to turn around in his head: 'I hope you will never have to use it. But remember—better a bad trial than a nice funeral'.

15. SOUTHBOUND

Uncle Maurilio was waiting in the car. He was a man of few words and even fewer thoughts. They greeted each other, got in, and left. Vincenzo continued to speak in jerks, sometimes agitated, sometimes whispering, and then shutting up. Since his uncle was becoming half deaf, he didn't understand them, so he made the mistake of saying: "You have to scream, or I won't hear."

"Put the hearing aid in, then."

"These devices don't work."

And so on, everyone was trying to impose their opinion. Federico realized they were all screaming and cut them off: "Why don't you put on a fake but flashy device; people will instinctively start talking louder when they see it."

They burst out laughing and laughed until they cried.

Even if the reason for the trip was due to a catastrophic event, Federico felt excited about leaving for Abruzzo. It was as if he were returning to his most intimate essence, which he could not demonstrate in the city social environment and that, indeed, seemed to disadvantage him there.

Manfredi observed them in silence, smiling. Since early childhood, he had had the look of a child who understood things that adults didn't perceive; now Federico knew he had that expression because he was struggling with his eyesight. A bit like Rodolfo Valentino, who was said to have a magnetic look but, in reality, was cross-eyed. In Vincenzo, the same family curse had produced a look of a paranoid in perennial anxiety. After a few hours, they passed San Benedetto del Tronto, and Federico saw the sign delineating the border between the regions:

"Wait, let's stop for a moment; I have to get out."

Federico pretended to pee. He got out to watch that sign. He thought about the warning and the almost thirty years of absence from his region. The diagonal bar on the 'MARCHE' sign that signified leaving Marche also seemed to give a refreshing brushstroke to his entire journey to this point and what he was leaving behind, erasing his hesitation. He looked down at the other sign that said 'ABRUZZO', took a deep breath and got back into the car.

"I'll take over; I'll drive."

As soon as they crossed the border, Maurilio could not resist: "Open the windows and let in that good fresh Abruzzese air," but after a few gear changes, he fell asleep. Federico and his uncle were taking turns driving. Vincenzo didn't. Due to his eyesight problem, they had not renewed his license. Federico didn't comment, and, above all, he didn't make any mention of Manfredi's illness. After twenty minutes, the passengers were all sleeping, so Federico grimaced in the rearview mirror. He gathered his eyebrows, squinted his eyes, lowered the corners of his mouth, and put out his chin. He was looking for the scariest possible expression that he would need to face Balthazar.

As they approached their destination, they saw more and more mountains. Federico remembered what the Renaissance writer Boccaccio had one of his characters say in the Decameron: 'It must be further off than Abruzzi.' The reference had stayed in his mind because it was uncommon to hear or read a reference to Abruzzo. It gave a sense of a remote region, a secluded place, a land of fairy tales. Among the many hypotheses about the origin of the name Abruzzo, Federico liked the etymology; aper—wild boar—therefore Aperuzio—the land of the wild boar—which, with the classic substitution of 'b' for 'p', became Abruzzo. He saw a confirmation of this in the ancient coat of arms of Abruzzo Citeriore (Hither Abruzzo). A shield with a boar's head.

The section of highway between Assergi and West L'Aquila was closed in both directions to facilitate rescue. They decided then to exit the highway and pass through the villages. The road became winding, and they had to slow down to let hundreds of sheep cross. People were watching them, wondering who they were. The speed of time altered; the seconds and minutes of the typical hurry in a large city broke against centuries of unchanged rhythm from the Middle Ages to the present day.

To drive in those mountains, one had to learn how to declutch, and before a hairpin bend, a double-declutch is recommended. Federico had learned them from his father, who had taken part in the uphill race of the Popoli turns. Even though they were still in elementary school, he and his buddies were already driving, especially the Fiat Cinquecento, which was manageable even for kids, given its small size. With the synchronized gearboxes of today, the 'one-two' was no longer needed, but Federico loved to do it anyway, honoring his father, who seemed to be sitting at his side teaching him how to do it:

'Listen to the sound of the engine as you watch the speed of the car relative to the road. Hear the vibration of its body and seat; note when all is synchronized. It takes some practice.'

'When you feel the speed is right, press the clutch and put the gear down. Then give it a second throttle to keep the revs up, and finally release the clutch.'

Every so often, the gear would scratch; other times, the engine would scream or go soft. All because either he accelerated too much or too little, or the car was too fast or too slow. They were also trying to get the gears out without pressing the clutch. If the engine and the wheels spun at the same speed, a tap was enough, and the gear shift came out without any resistance: 'When the gear comes out easily by itself, listen to the engine, look at the speed of the road out of the corner of your eye, and feel how the car moves under the seat. Send all these details to your mind and memorize them.'

He practiced so much that he developed a particular feeling, and now, with any car, it was enough for him to make two or three attempts to recreate that relationship with the vehicle.

They left the city of L'Aquila to their right, deciding to avoid the SS17, where they would have seen the devastation of Onna and Paganica. They passed just south of Onna, through Monticchio, since they had heard from the news that it had not suffered significant damage. Furthermore, they were afraid that the bottleneck between the houses where they would have to drive might be closed by some debris fall, but they were able to pass, leaving behind the blue sign: ONNA 2. Only two kilometers had made the difference between an almost intact village and another razed to the ground.

And at 6:30 p.m., just as the Great Risks Commission's press conference was taking place, a magnitude four quake shook the earth, the people above it, and those below who were still imprisoned inside it.

16. THE CRIPPLE

Abruzzo, 6 April 2009

Leaving Monticchio, they followed the foothill route that connects the villages halfway up: Fossa, Casentino, Tussillo, and Stiffe. The illusion of avoiding the sight of the catastrophe was destroyed by reality. They looked around, and it was as if they had been teleported into an alien landscape.

There were crashed cars covered by rubble, the shape of the houses looked like a Picasso painting, and Federico could not imagine how such a disaster could ever be repaired. Water sprayed from a cracked tube, and while Federico saw another broken pipe, he felt the smell of gas reaching him in the car. When he breathed, dust entered his lungs. He coughed, almost crushing himself against the steering wheel, and turned to look at Manfredi. He took another breath, this time of relief: he had not awakened him. At least he wouldn't witness that terrible view. He adjusted himself on the seat, exhaled his anxiety, and set off again, bypassing a fire truck.

On the mountain to their right, he saw the medieval convent of Sant'Angelo d'Ocre, built on a rocky spur of Monte Circolo, above the church of Santa Maria ad Cryptas, in Fossa. His father called it 'the eagle's nest of the Franciscans'. He once brought Federico there to see the result of the fourteen years of restoration made necessary after the Nazis burned the furniture and the one thousand and five hundred rare volumes of the library. Looking at it from the street, it seemed intact, but who knew if it had been damaged. Federico prayed that it had been spared, at least this time.

He wanted to stop and see the church. They left the dairy shop on their right, where his family had always bought mozzarella and mixed pecorino cheese, and climbed just above to see the place of worship.

They remained silent as they viewed the whole valley and the Gran Sasso. Santa Maria was torn on the external walls, the vaults, and the part between the nave and the apse. The plaster of the frescoes had detached in many places. It seemed that their surfaces were about to fall flat to the ground. Federico saw the images of the Last Judgment—with St. Michael the Archangel weighing souls to assess their degree of purity—and pictures of Hell with the torture of demons. The Resurrection was depicted with the dead coming out of their graves.

"Let's go before something falls on our heads. Didn't you feel the shock earlier?"

And so, they arrived in the village where Aunt Cesidia lived. Federico could glimpse her house. Vincenzo commented: "She still lives there; the house has not been damaged."

Further on, the Genoese man's house appeared, furrowed like an ancient turtle. The wrinkles of the earthquake intertwined with those of time. His mother used to tell him that, on that little terrace, Umberto tried to communicate his sense of infinity to his sister: 'Listen, Anita: stars are talking.' And her: 'Umberto, and how is it? I can't hear anything. I must ask Nino why.' And they laughed until their bellies hurt.

Federico noticed another house, which he had never seen inhabited, with its roof broken. It was said to be the home of what was believed to be the witch Melinda, who died at more than a hundred years of age. The woman was seduced and abandoned by a young man from Penne. Melinda then prepared her first spell as a woman in the village taught her: with a lock of her hair, a button from her bodice, and a piece of cloth soaked in her menstrual blood. Then she left it on the bed, waiting for her seducer's return from the war front. The spell struck the young man, who was left without any hope. Later, Melinda learned other magical techniques from the sorcerers of Frocella and Montepradone and made a living thanks to the spells she made on commission. According to the ancient local witchcraft code, Melinda would be free of her curse only if someone pierced the roof of her home after her death, leaving her soul free to escape. Now, with the top of the bedroom upstairs torn open, perhaps she had managed to fly away, finally finding peace.

Vincenzo interrupted Federico's thoughts: "That hole reminds me of something; have you ever told Manfredi about The Cripple?"

"Yes, of course, but tell it to him again if you'd like to."

It was a classic in Abruzzo. Telling the same stories several times was acceptable since, depending on the situation, it always took on a different shade. Even his father claimed that to understand if a story is good, you had to repeat it on many other occasions. If it improved over time, as wine, then it was intrinsically valid.

Vincenzo prepared Manfredi: "Your Dad was scared to death every time your grandfather told this story."

Federico didn't react, and Vincenzo started: "In a stone house called Snirr Thool, in the hamlet of Siamt Betel, just above Firri, once lived The Cripple. The house was tall but had a tiny door, which he didn't need because he could enter from above. At night, he wandered around the villages, and when he knew a naughty boy was inside a house, he would sneak in through the chimney."

Manfredi knew the story but played along: "And how did he do it?"

"Thanks to his long leg, he would reach up to the roof and lean on it with the shorter one. Then he would pull up the other leg and climb. He hypnotized the children with the sound of an ancient instrument, the 'Faoram', and kidnapped the bad ones. And you, have you been a naughty boy?"

"No, I am good; I don't have to be afraid."

"So, was your daddy afraid because he was bad?"

"My dad is good too, and he's not afraid."

Federico sketched a smile.

"And did he also tell you about the treasure?"

"Yes, of course. I also made a drawing for the school."

"Did he tell you where it is?"

"Nobody knows. It is written on a small piece of paper that can no longer be retrieved."

"You're right; in fact, it was never found. Maybe it's one of your great-grandfather's many tricks?"

Vincenzo continued: "According to the story, a part of a fragmented treasure had been hidden by a bandit on the run, who abandoned a boot full of gold coins on the inaccessible 'Goats' Drop", in front of Fontecchio. It is hidden under two rocks that cross each other, the only ones between which you can see the church bell tower. More details were written on the lost note. The Goats' Drop is an impassable place that only goats and some reckless bandit with the physique of a Roman gladiator were able to walk through. The bandit Franco was sighted, and he had bare feet when he came down at night and was arrested by the forest ranger, who was waiting for him.

"The forest ranger was none other than Carlantonio, your father's great-grandfather, and Franco confessed everything to him in exchange for his freedom. Since there was no more news of Franco at a certain point, people suspected that the ranger had helped him escape in exchange for that treasure. But since Carlantonio never became rich, that story, too, was forgotten."

Manfredi listened with his mouth open and eyes wide. The story made him fantasize, just as Federico had done when he was a child and spent his summers in Abruzzo. Vincenzo caressed Manfredi's head and smiled at Federico: "The kid likes Abruzzo. You should bring him here more often."

Federico smiled back, and Vincenzo changed his voice to a sweeter tone: "Maybe your parents' house is still habitable; perhaps you could move here. Come on; you can find a job in a bank. You are good with numbers."

"What I was doing is not a bank job. I'd need a branch of a large company, preferably in the oil sector. How many are there in the area?"

"Whatever. You understand numbers and money; how difficult can it be to find a new job with those skills?"

He couldn't explain the difference, nor precisely what he did for a living. Federico had thought many times about leaving the city and changing his life. Maybe he could find a solution right there. He thought about it for a second; then he shook his head: "Let's go. I need to see something."

Federico drove just in front of the most impressive building in the whole village. It was isolated from the huddled stone houses by a hundred and fifty meters long driveway. Surrounded by three-meter-high walls, it was built in concrete blocks, interrupted only to support the ancient black wrought-iron gate that closed the entrance.

The lawyer's home was an impenetrable fortress.

And it was also the summer residence of Balthazar.

17. THE DANCE IN THE SKY

The Altai Mountains, province of Bayan Ulgii, Mongolia, 1980

As a child, Federico often went to the mountains with his father. In the Altai Mountains, eight thousand kilometers away from Italy, the landscape was almost identical to the Gran Sasso upland. Immense highlands surrounded by mountain peaks that stood out towards the blue.

Federico's father was there for work. The area was sparsely populated and with few access roads. This was because, without mineral resources, it had not aroused great interest, unlike other parts of Mongolia. The city of Edernet, for example, was built in 1974 to exploit the largest copper field in Asia. And the largest coal field in the world, although still unexploited, was located in the Gobi Desert. But nothing had been found in this area yet. So, the father had joined an expedition of geologists, engineers, and miners looking for metals: copper, iron, and zinc.

They were walking when his father looked at the sky through binoculars. He then passed them to Federico and pointed to a dot in the vast blue: "Look." Federico watched through the powerful lenses while his father continued: "They call it the 'dance in the sky'. Eagles mate for life, so the ritual is complex. They prefer to avoid mistakes."

The father took other binoculars from the backpack and looked through them: "They are flying in the sky, as if they were dancing. The one that is flying upside down is the female."

Federico saw her flying belly up as when he swam on his back to look at the light of the sky; then the male swooped down on her, and they went around together.

"Papi, are they fighting?"

The father smiled again: "They are courting each other." Then he winked: "Almost the same thing."

Then the male dived to the ground, spread his wings like the flaps of an airplane to slow down, and, without even stopping, grabbed a little mouse. Clutching the prey, he climbed towards the female, tilted horizontally, and dropped the mouse behind him, as if it had escaped. Immediately after, he swooped on it and grabbed it in his talons again, still in flight, about twenty meters below. An undeniable display of skill that culminated in passing the mouse to the female with a single magnificent bow.

"They exchange prey in flight as if they want to communicate that they will take care of each other. Even in the nest building and in the care of the eaglets, they are loving."

The two birds of prey then hooked one leg and held each other in free fall with somersaults and loops of death; they seemed to be two trapeze artists playing with air.

To Federico, flying was like a dream, as it had been for humanity for millennia. His father changed the subject: "In two or three months, we'll be back to get an eaglet."

"And how do we do it, Papi?"

"We get help from our Berkutchi friends."

The father referred to the Kazakh community, a minority of the Muslim religion that had managed to preserve their traditions in those mountains almost one thousand and five hundred kilometers from the capital, Ulaanbaatar. Together with the nomadic life spent in the company of goats and cattle, they had preserved a wonderful tradition for more than six thousand years: hunting with eagles.

"We must take a female and young."

Because eagles are fiercely independent, they need to be trained early to create that bond of trust between hunter and eagle, which can grow deep and robust. Federico's father had made friends with a colleague searching for underground minerals, Bikbolat. He gave Federico's father the nickname 'the gold digger' because he was searching for metals, and even though he said he was looking for something else, everyone was convinced he was there to look for gold.

Bikbolat had given him the first directive: "Better to train young eagles. They won't harm either the children or the animals. Females are the best hunters; they are more aggressive and heavier than males."

"Can Federico make it at his age?"

"Here, kids have been doing it for millennia. Only one person must do the training to develop the right bond between master and eagle. The eagle lives up to forty years; it's like having an extra child in the family. It is quite an experience for a boy, but he must be assisted and supported."

"Must he also learn to ride?"

"Yes, the horse is an integral part of life here. Riding it's a skill that every eagle hunter must master. We always hunt on horseback because you either go on horseback in these areas or don't go anywhere. How else do you go after the eagle? With the car?"

He burst into laughter in the face of their naivety: "You city people are killing me."

And so, before the eaglets began their first experiments with flying and were still unable to leave the nest, his father took Federico to the mountains with Bikbolat and his daughter, Zhuldyz. They walked the way to the top of the chosen mountain. There were difficult passages, and Federico felt his ass melting from fear. Instead, Zhuldyz smiled, covering her mouth with her hand.

"Why do the eagles come so high?"

Bikbolat smiled: "They love neither crowded places nor people. Just like me".

They arrived at the ridge above the nest. The time had come: "Federico, now I tie you at the waist and let you go down. When you get close to the eaglets, put this bag over the head of the one you prefer. Give a tug on the rope to tell me you have it, and I'll bring you back up."

There was no way: Federico was paralyzed by terror and didn't move. He sat down on a rock, wrapped his knees around it, and put his head between them. Zhuldyz was lighter and not afraid of heights. She proposed to go. Her father tied the rope to a rock spike, secured her, and let her slowly down. When she arrived at the nest, Zhuldyz put the sack on the eaglet with a single gesture. Federico would have imagined a deadly hand-to-hand with a lot of pecking and claws scratching. Instead, nothing. His father had told him: "When they are so small, they are also tame."

When they went back, Zhuldyz looked at Federico. He had his arms folded, his eyelashes wrinkled, and his lower lip stretched and protruding. He didn't say a word as they began their descent.

Federico's father wanted to congratulate her: "You are brave, Zhuldyz. You have confidence in yourself."

Zhuldyz didn't take the credit: "I was confident because my father was holding me."

Federico was ashamed and blushed. He didn't trust anyone or anything—neither the rope, his father, or himself.

After about half an hour, Bikbolat proposed: "There is another nest nearby; let's go see it. Maybe there is an eaglet for you too. Let's not take them all from the same nest."

Then he turned to Federico: "Now that you have seen her do it, it will be easier."

At the next nest, after some jokes by Zhuldyz's father, a thousand explanations, and ten thousand reassurances, Federico experienced what it means to trust someone. With his eyes closed. Literally. Yes, because he didn't open his eyes the whole time as his father lowered him. And when he put the sack on the eaglet, he even turned his head not to see the ground so far below.

They came down happy that the kids had one eaglet each. The fathers smiled and exchanged hugs, as if they had always been friends: miracles of the mountains. Federico started smiling too.

"We will call you Arystan."

"And what does it mean?"

"Lion."

Federico was surprised; terror had paralyzed him. He had undoubtedly not behaved like a lion.

"Although many things do scare you."

"Then why Lion?"

"Because even though you were uncomfortable, you went down. It's easy when you're not afraid. But in life, sooner or later, something, or someone, will surely come along that will terrify us. Better to know that fear can be overcome."

"It was Papi who held me. Without him, I would never have made it."

His father caressed his forelock. Bikbolat continued: "There is a story about Queen Alungo, an ancestor of Genghis Khan and therefore part of what we call the 'golden lineage'. Alungo had five children who didn't get along well. One day, she called them into the big white family tent and gave each of them an arrow to break. They all succeeded easily. Alungo then gave five arrows to each of them and asked them again to break them. No one succeeded: 'My children, you are like an arrow. Alone you could break, but united you are invincible.'"

Zhuldyz's father asked the meaning of Federico's name. His father explained that it derived from the Germanic Frithurik: rich ('rik'), peace and security ('Frithu'). He named him in honor of Frederick II of Swabia, whom he referred to as 'Frederick the Second to None'.

And the Swabian sovereign had linked his name to the foundation of the city of L'Aquila, where both Federico and his father were born. The castle, which later gave its name to the town, was called Santa Maria de Acquilis because it was close to numerous water springs. The assonance, which is not preserved in other languages, between 'aqua' (water) and 'aquila' (eagle), which also appears in the imperial insignia of Frederick II and which flies over the peaks of the Gran Sasso mountain, did the rest. The choice was 'Aquila', since it summarized many concepts in a single name.

A further coincidence was that the sovereign wrote a treatise on falconry in which he described the systems of breeding, training, and employing birds of prey in hunting. He also studied a text written by the mysterious Syrian falconer, Hunayn Ibn Ishàq, while learning Arabic with his master and advisor, Theodore of Antioch, also Syrian.

Frederick II was an expert in achieving multiple goals with a single activity that acted at different levels simultaneously. He saw in falconry a manifestation of personal power. A person could demonstrate worthiness to be a sovereign after developing self-control that would allow a falcon to rest on their arm. The ability to develop the noble part within himself was symbolized by the care given to the falcon, the symbol of nobility.

In his treatise, "De Arte Venandi cum Avibus", he wrote: "A day without falconry is a useless day."

His father asked: "What would you name the eagle?"
Federico showed no hesitation: "Maya."
Zhuldyz asked: "Why Maya?"

He loved Maya, the elephant from the movie. Direct and peaceful. But if you hurt it, it would never forget it, and you would pay for it: "She is a fantastic female elephant who defended her baby from three tigers."

Federico's father smiled when he saw his son so attentive and impressed by the film: "I also like Maya; it reminds me of a legend from our parts about another Maia, which is written differently but pronounced in the same way."

Federico and Zhuldyz were both fascinated by stories and wanted to listen to them: "We like stories about mountains."

He cleared his voice and announced: "The legend of Maia and the Gran Sasso."

Then the story began: "Legend has it that Maia was the most beautiful nymph of the Pleiades. From her relationship with Zeus was born the warrior Hermes, who was wounded in battle in Phrygia. Maia sought a place where she could take care of her son and passed through Abruzzo. There she found a cave on the Gran Sasso mountain, where she hoped to cure Hermes. But she realized she needed a special medicine, a healing herb, and a flower. She looked for it everywhere but didn't find it, so her son died. Maia wept for many days over his body, and then she buried him on top of the mountain, creating the two Horns of the Gran Sasso."

"Is that what you call the 'Sleeping Giant' when we see them coming from Milan?"

"Yes, Federico."

"Even here, the mountains have people's faces," said Zhuldyz, "Daddy and I always play a game: 'Who reminds you of that mountain?'"

"The story continues. Maia, disconsolate, abandoned herself on the mountain next to the Gran Sasso, dying of heartbreak. She, too, was buried by the gods with all honors and became Maiella. And when we return on vacation to Abruzzo, we will go there, and you will also see the shape of the body of a woman resting while lying with her arms on her chest."

They resumed the path toward the valley. Federico walked down with his sack on his shoulder next to Zhuldyz. She was constantly staring at him, and Federico lowered his head, feeling his cheeks warming up. When he turned his eyes towards her, Zhuldyz was still there, staring at him and smiling. He seemed to lose himself in a reverie every time that he looked at her: large, elongated eyes as the almonds of Sulmona's confetti, smooth skin, white teeth that, every time she smiled, seemed to send light first to her whole face and then all around her. He saw her almost wrapped in a shaded outline, just like in dreams.

Federico found the courage to ask her a question, too:

"And your name, Zhuldyz, what does it mean?"

"Star. It means Star."

18. THE HUT

Castellana, 6 April 2009

Vincenzo took Federico to the stone hut. They left the car hidden at the base of the hill known by locals as 'Castellana'. They walked in the middle of the woods; Federico knew the road well, having walked it thousands of times as a child.

"Where are we going, Papi?" Manfredi asked.

"To the hut. The one you know from the song."

"How nice; I finally got to see it."

The hut was technically a tholos, although no one would call it that way besides a professor or perhaps in a book. It was a round structure made of dry, stacked stones with a small door, originally built by shepherds and woodcutters to rest in the coolness.

They are an extraordinary example of architecture connected with the life of mountaineers. They took the stones called *maceri*, piles of rocks taken out of the fields, and built dry stone walls without mortar. In this way, the marked property boundaries indicate and protect water sources and create archaic shelters. The huts recalled the Apulian Trulli that the shepherds were indeed familiar with from the seasonal moving of their flocks. Federico noticed how a waste element, hostile to agriculture, was repurposed as an element for shelter.

For Federico, the idea of seeing childhood friends was again chasing away all other thoughts. He didn't know what to think. How would they welcome him? Would they despise him? Or would it be like a friendly reunion before trekking in the mountains?

When they arrived, he was surprised to see that the stone hut looked the same. No collapse, not even minimal. Then he saw Eleonora and Giovanna preparing the food, along with Eleonora's brother, Giulio. His cousins, the twins, were coming up with bundles of wood in their hands. Vincenzo referred to the girls the way Federico's father always did, claiming it was a Mongolian saying: "It's a wonderful day: 'Yowl gow sams'; here come the two suns".

They hadn't seen each other for almost three decades. But after a few exchanges of greetings and updating questions, it seemed as if nothing had changed. Same faces, same gestures, same ways of doing things. The twins kept grumbling about everything, echoing each other. Giovanna had become an engineer. He had already seen that Vincenzo hadn't changed at all. Indeed, they still nicknamed him '*Ju Zellus*', the Capricious. And he, Federico, was the one in the group who never knew the right thing to do. For this reason, Eleonora often called him my Hamlet.

They greeted each other as if time had never passed. Federico both felt and wished that those thirty years had been canceled. Perhaps they had never really existed? It was like he had been living on a planet and returned to earth in the company of a little boy from that distant world, Manfredi.

Eleonora hugged him: "Maybe my magic Hamlet is coming back. Thank goodness Vincenzo found you."

Federico had always loved it when Eleonora pronounced the 'm', five times in her first sentence. Her nose would go down, the tip would pull, and it seemed to light up just before coming back up. Her embrace froze him, and he didn't know how to react: how long had it been since he received a manifestation of affection like that?

He realized that only Manfredi loved him. All the others seemed to want something from him or wanted him to be different from who he was. He realized it was only a matter of time before Manfredi would become a contentious teenager and lose his warm bursts of affection. Maybe being half-blind would soften that. Or perhaps, on the contrary, make him more aggressive. Federico felt ashamed of having desired the infirmity of his son to keep him docile and even more so for having taken that blindness for granted, even if partial. He understood that he had already resigned himself. He hated himself. Meanwhile, Eleonora's arms were still around him: *React, Federico, react. At least try.*

He looked at her and remembered another time when they had been watching the clouds in the sky just outside this same hut. This was after Balthazar broke Federico's nose, and Eleonora didn't want to deal with him anymore. They played at making the clouds disappear with their thoughts:

"Let's start with that little one over Stiffe."

They both looked at it, concentrated, struggled, and the cloud disappeared.

"Now, you choose one."

"I don't know which one."

Eleonora mocked him: 'How come my Hamlet always has all these doubts?'

Then she would choose a bigger one, and Federico would say: "This one is difficult. Are you sure?"

Eleonora laughed at those hesitations: "Federico, I can't believe you are fearful."

Then she moved on to one with an even more extensive or elongated shape. If they could not make it melt, Eleonora would look around, turning her head while lying on the ground and pointing her finger towards a new one: "Look at that beautiful cloud."

Federico searched the sky: "Which one?"

Eleonora had her eyes on the horizon: "The cat above Tussillo, there, look."

After they had made it disappear, they returned to the previous, more difficult one. It had meanwhile changed shape, perhaps becoming less thick and easier to dissolve.

"But in this way, we will always succeed."

Eleonora always laughed first, and Federico followed her.

He was brought back to the present reality by the news, about the earthquake and common acquaintances—who had married or died—and by Balthazar's growing power in politics. Eleonora told him that she had been delighted to learn that the earthquake had damaged almost all the lawyer's houses, some even destroyed. Her delight was of short duration, though, because: "He has friends and knows shortcuts. His houses will be the first to be rebuilt. Even if he doesn't need them."

The radio said that looting had begun. Reports were that thugs had started robbing houses immediately after the 3:32 a.m. quake. Federico was shocked: "Not only in L'Aquila but also in our villages?"

No one commented. Federico looked at them in silence, grave, surprised by that lack of reaction.

The embarrassment was broken by Giulio, Eleonora's brother, who called for dinner. He had managed the fire, carefully making as little smoke as possible and dispersing it as best he could so as not to be seen: "The chops are ready."

"Couldn't we eat something without making a fire? I understood that we had to stay hidden. Wasn't it supposed to be a Top Secret Mission?"

The twins said that, at this point, nothing more could be done.

So, it looks like an actual reunion, thought Federico.

For a moment, he wanted to believe that Eleonora had insisted so much and that she had taken advantage of Vincenzo's determination to bring him back after all these years.

The thought first cheered him up; then he thought he was being naïve.

It's my imagination. We were just friends, then. Maybe not even that now.

He bit a rib and returned to the main reason he thought he was there: "So where is Tonino? How is he?"

19. TRAINING

Altai Mountains, Mongolia, 1980

In Mongolia, Federico learned how to train a raptor to hunt. While it's not common to use the eagle in falconry, the Kazakhs tradition is one of the few to favor them over the falcon. The eagle has a more independent character, making it more challenging to train. Moreover, if forced to stay in a highly populated environment, it can become nervous and react by pecking and scratching even human beings, leaving deep and indelible scars. But it is also the only raptor that can hunt prey like foxes and hares, which are too big for hawks.

During the one Sunday a month that his father was free from work, they went to the mountains to see how eagles behave. Federico saw one catch a fish underwater and another swoop down and take a hare with its talons without even stopping.

Hare hunting with a rifle is impossible in the Central Asian steppes. The prey can see the hunter from afar, as there is no vegetation, and even more so if there is snow. A white bed, several kilometers square, reveals the human presence at distances impossible to cover with a rifle. That's why the art of eagle hunting was born right there, at least six thousand years earlier, and then changed into falconry in the Persian and the Arab deserts. The eagle, or falcon, sees its prey miles away and is a more refined hunting instrument than the rifle. With a gun, you are ready; you aim and then shoot. If you miss the target, even by a millimeter, it's gone. The eagle is launched before you aim. The aim comes after. As the prey moves, the eagle adjusts its flight path, first in broad strokes and then increasing precision until it reaches its target. Impossible to miss.

Federico also witnessed a battle between an eagle and a wolf contending for prey. It was a chaotic fight with clawing, biting, and pecking, which in the end, the eagle won. Federico watched the scene with his hands in front of his eyes, widening his fingers to peek through and close them again when the scene became brutal.

Their trainer was Zhuldyz's grandfather. The two youths listened to him in awe when he stopped to give them brief explanations. He spoke rudimentary English, and even Federico, who started to learn it, could understand his simple and direct instructions: "Eagle is strong. Powerful wings. It can lift three times its weight. A hare, a fox: easy. Look what happens now. See how it attacks big animals."

He pointed out some chamois on the ridge of the mountain. The incredibly steep mountain was not a problem for their stability. Already that was a miracle to be observed, the chamois balancing its weight towards the hill and its tiny hooves finding protrusions on which to stand. Just looking at how precarious it was, made Federico's buttocks tremble. The eagle began to approach and then descend faster and faster. Federico couldn't believe that the eagle would attack.

"It's not going to try to lift a chamois, is it?"

His father repeated the instruction: "Look."

The eagle swooped down on the back of the chamois, three kilos against sixty. While holding on with its talons, it started flapping its wings as if it wanted to take off again and take the chamois with it. But it was too close to the mountain itself to fly and would have ended up against it. Federico then understood: "It doesn't intend to take off. It's pushing the chamois. It wants to make it fall."

The prey struggled to climb the ridge, looking for better holds, while the eagle remained on its back. When it found the right spot, the chamois planted its front hooves and started kicking like a rodeo horse while the eagle held on with its talons as if riding it. Then the raptor turned towards the valley, flapping its wings faster. The chamois' hooves couldn't hold any more; the animal started to slide down until it had no more ground under its feet and fell into the precipice. Only then did the eagle free its claws so as not to be carried down by that enormous weight. The falling animal waved its legs and neck, desperate to see something around it to place its hooves until it crashed into the rocks. The eagle swooped down and began to tear its flesh. The other chamois rolled their eyes wide open in all directions.

Federico brought his hands to his mouth, and his father looked at him, shrugging his shoulders: "Mors tua vita mea. Kill or be killed. The law of nature."

Their parents stayed with them when they had Sunday off and were resting from mining. Zhuldyz's grandfather continued to transmit to them the basics of falconry. He taught them to put on and remove the eagle's hood: "The hood covers the head. Not the beak. It leaves some room at the sides. The eyes are free to move. It's needed to avoid stress. Eagles react to everything they see, to every detail."

Federico's father had already learned something: "It is not a problem outdoors. But in the narrow spaces where man lives, there are too many things to see, and the eagle becomes aggressive."

"They calm down in the dark. If they don't see 'something', they don't get stressed by that 'something'."

His father commented: "Out of sight, out of mind."

"Now you try. Put the hood on it. Keep your head back, don't stop, and keep calm. Leave it some meat so that it feels: 'hood is good'."

Federico gave it a try, and the eagle pulled its neck back. Then Zhuldyz's grandfather gave him a direct order: "Go!" Federico put the hood on it with a single gesture. The eagle calmed down. Federico smiled when he realized that he had succeeded.

The man showed him how to put the anklets on the legs, just above the talons. And how to hold the longer leather stripes, the jesses, to keep the eagle on the glove until the falconer decides to let it fly. Federico liked the feeling of leather to the touch. He would sniff it and get intoxicated with that perfume while Zhuldyz and her grandfather would shake their heads. The objects they used were not only beautiful but also robust and functional, like so many things he had seen artisans make in Abruzzo. Federico's father added: "It was your friend *Frederick the second to none*, who introduced the use of the tranquilizing effect of the hood, which he learned from the Arabs. Before in Europe, the eyelids of birds of prey were sewn shut, and the sutures were gradually loosened as the level of training progressed."

Zhuldyz's grandfather was tireless: "You can't control the eagle. You need to create a strong bond with it. Now we learn how to make the eagle jump on the glove."

The first time the eaglet jumped on his arm, Federico felt the claws tighten around his skin and was afraid.

"Relax hand and arm," said the grandfather.

Federico resisted: "It hurts."

"Take a deep breath and relax your arm."

Federico did it, and the more he relaxed, the more he felt the eaglet soften his grip.

"See? The art of falconry is foremost the ability to control emotions. Never anger. Never hurry. Never sadness. The eagle has an exceptional vision. From tiny changes in face and body, it feels how you feel more than you do. We cannot pretend with them as we do with other human beings. Or with ourselves."

20. MAYA

Altai Mountains, Mongolia, 1980

As Maya grew, her feathers became shades of brown, while on her head, she had golden streaks, hence the name of *Aquila Chrysaetos*, or Golden Eagle. When she learned how to fly from the glove they started practicing with the bait.

"Be careful because she will try to train you. Instead, you must train her. Remember that it is the eagle that must wait for you. You must never be waiting for her."

"And how is it done?"

Grandfather smiled: "With hunger. The right amount. Neither too much nor too little."

He had built a fake prey, consisting of hare fur, and tied it to a rope a few meters long: the threadbare. He put some raw meat secured by two leather straps over the simulacrum. Zhuldyz got on her horse and pulled the rope. She was already far away when she began to gallop at her grandfather's sign. The prey seemed to move as if it were alive, jumping here and there depending on the roughness of the terrain. Federico moved his arm towards the hare, taking a step forward in the same direction. Maya took off in flight, looked around, saw the prey, and swooped in as if she had always done so forever. Zhuldyz pulled the reins and braked the horse while Maya devoured the meat.

To this association between hunting and reward, reinforced every day thanks to the animal's predatory instinct, were added a whistle and a gesture of recall. The grandfather continued with the instructions: "Every day, talk to her. Sing also. She will get used to the sound of your voice. Create a close relationship, and she will follow you. She will see you when she is flying, even if you don't know where she is."

One evening in the big tent, a cousin of Zhuldyz, dressed in a thousand colors, sang in a way neither Federico nor his parents had ever heard. She made several sounds simultaneously, swaying as if she were gliding on the wind. Federico and his parents looked around to see where those musical notes, which seemed to be played by a celestial instrument, came from. He had never heard anything so wonderful.

Zhuldyz knew the basics of that art. She taught Federico how first to roll up his tongue and push it back to create two cavities, one in the mouth and one in the throat. Then how to move the tongue to produce high-pitched sounds while a lower note could still be heard in the background. Seeing the light appearing on Zhuldyz's face, and listening to those sounds of paradise, enthralled Federico, who wondered what fairy world he had ended up in.

But they all had to laugh at Federico's funny attempts to reproduce those sounds by widening his eyeballs: "You don't make sound with eyes." Or when he pulled up his shoulders: "You don't sing with your neck."

After a few weeks, Federico mastered the technique enough to call Maya. She got so used to it that all he had to do was utter that '*eeeeeuuuuu*' and modulate the sound with his tongue. The eagle became attentive, turned, and flew to him.

The grandfather used a thousand tricks for training. Federico could not believe how many things he knew: "Give her satisfaction without following any pattern. Let her take the bait right away. That's how she'll always work hard. When she takes it, let her take it. Always make it unpredictable. If the eagle gets bored, you lose her attention, and bye-bye."

Grandpa also insisted on cleanliness for hygiene and mindset: "Where dirt, shame."

He mixed words with practical demonstrations. For example, he told him that the best food was quail, but only when he had it. He passed one on to Federico, who fed it to Maya. In the same way, he showed how to grease the two leather strips by taking Federico's hand and inviting him to caress them: "Smooth, soft."

He said it was necessary never to frighten the eagle while getting used to external stimuli. A scare could mark her for a long time, even forever. "Better wait than make a mistake. If you are angry, better not to fly a raptor."

He insisted on developing a relationship—a communication without words. Federico repeated inside himself: *Never get angry with her, never scold her. Express love and dedication.*

"Feed her when she comes closer. Talk to her."

"Even if she doesn't understand?"

"She doesn't understand words. But she feels the sound. Sound is important. And she understands food for sure."

And on those last words, he smiled. Then he became more serious: "You quiet, she quiet. You nervous, she nervous. Learn tranquility."

He offered Federico some meat on his glove to give the eagle: "See? This is love."

Federico admired that ancient tradition. Seeing the majesty of a horse and a noble Kazakh on the saddle with an eagle on his arm reached something deep inside him without even thinking about it.

Grandfather said that the following Sunday, "when your daddy is not searching for gold," they would go and free Zhuldyz's father's eagle. The Kazakh falconers live together with their eagles for ten years at most. Afterward, they leave them at liberty. This way, the eagle can reproduce and continue the life cycle.

On Sunday, they mounted the horses and took the eagle to the mountains. When they reached the slopes before the peak, Bikbolat, Zhuldyz's father, uttered the day's first words.

He recited a short prayer and spoke to the eagle: "Everything has a beginning and an end. It is the life cycle."

Then he walked to the top alone: "I have to do it."

After removing the leather strips and the hood, he fed the eagle with lamb meat, the best prize. He left it on the peak while it was still eating, turned to the valley, and began to descend. While Bikbolat was leaving the eagle, it remained still, without turning around, as if it didn't understand or didn't want to believe it. Then, without warning, it spread its wings and soared up into the sky.

"It still has at least twenty years of freedom," said Zhuldyz.

And also, for Federico and his father, it was time to leave and return to Italy. But Federico stood his ground; he didn't want to leave Maya.

"By now, a strong bond," said Zhuldyz's grandfather.

His father had to agree to take her to Italy. Federico saw him give lots of paper money to somebody at the airport, who then passed them on.

"As a sign of gratitude," said his father.

At the end of that summer, they left Maya in Abruzzo; it would have been impossible to take her to Milan. Federico accepted this only because they entrusted her to Eleonora's family. Growing up, she would take care of her as if she were her own. And every time Federico returned on vacation, he would take her with him for hunting and training flights.

When they were in the car on their way to Milan, his father asked him:

"Do you miss Xhurthyx, your friend?"

"Her name is Zhuldyz, Papi."

"So, you do miss her," his father answered for him.

21. IN THE PIG PEN

Villa Sant'Angelo, July 1981

The following summer, when Federico was back in Abruzzo for some vacation, Balthazar and Checcótt surprised him as he walked home.

Federico began to stretch his step and run, but Balthazar reached him and wrapped his hands around his arms, lifting him off the ground: "You deserve a lesson. We will lock you up in the pig pen and watch you being eaten alive."

"They leave only the teeth," grinned Checcótt. Balthazar dragged him to the gate of the pigsty, pushed him inside the fence, and then closed the door. The beasts approached Federico, who, terrified, froze. They smelled him, weighing six hundred kilos each as if they were guard dogs. He still didn't weigh a fifth of them.

Balthazar opened the door and peeked in. As soon as he saw the door opening, Federico threw himself out and, thrusting his hands and arms, made Balthazar fall inside while cutting himself on his left cheek with a nail sticking out of the door. Now alone in the enclosure with the mud and the pigs, Balthazar plodded towards the exit. Federico has the time to hear the nearest beast grunt and then Balthazar screaming while trying to escape. He saw the pig attacking him by biting his ankle, pulling off a shoe with his hoof, and eating three toes of his naked foot. Balthazar curled up on the ground, which brought his face closer to the snout of another pig, who bit him, scratching his face. Federico looked him right between the eyes and slammed the door, leaving him at the mercy of the animals.

Then he saw Armando running from the street towards them, rushing into the pigpen, beating the pigs with a stick, and letting the boy out. Balthazar came out of the enclosure, limping and bleeding from one ear. When his gaze met Federico's, he tried to wriggle himself out of Armando's hold and screamed like an All Blacks rugby player during the Haka: "Don't ever come back, or I'll kill you."

In the end, no one filed a complaint; Federico feared the repercussions and Balthazar because he had caused the episode. In the emergency room, they said it had been an accident. Federico had his cheek cut, and Balthazar had his foot mangled, which proved the accidental nature of the event. They confirmed that they had entered the fence to pull a stunt that had gone wrong.

Later, Balthazar's father managed to obtain from the judge a territorial prohibition. Federico wouldn't be able to enter the region under penalty of a fine or even arrest. His father could not get around it since Federico wasn't prepared to disclose how things actually went.

He felt that his father was trying to reassure him: "It will pass. And you will play again with your friend when we return next summer."

Federico stopped talking for days. He remained locked in his room, hoping to leave for Milan as soon as possible, and praying every day that he would never have to return to Abruzzo.

22. HONOR KILLING

Villa Sant'Angelo, 19 July 1981

A few days after the pig incident, Armando played cards at Erminio's bar. He had served in the Carabinieri for over twenty-five years, always flawless, the 'adorable corporal' as Uncle Tonino jokingly called him. He rarely played cards because he saw gambling and the illegality that could result from it as a risk. Since, in the village, the stakes were nothing more than beer and soda, he occasionally allowed himself to participate.

While they were playing trumps, a quarrel broke out with Giovanni, the builder, because of an incorrect count of points. As Armando lost his temper, Balthazar's father whispered in his ear as he looked at Giovanni out of the corner of his eyes: "While we are here playing cards, your wife is sleeping with Riccardo."

Armando looked at Don Cesare, who nodded two or three times, with eyebrows raised and lips pressed against his teeth, confirming that he was not joking.

My wife is sleeping with Riccardo.

Armando threw the chair behind him and ran home in anger. He saw his wife with Riccardo, Federico's father, took out his service pistol and shot him first, causing him to fall beside the sofa, and then he shot her. Then he went to the command, handed over his weapon, badge, and uniform, and turned himself in.

Holed up at home, Federico watched a documentary about the moon landing twelve years earlier, on July 20, 1969. 'The Eagle' was the name of the lunar module used in the mission. At that moment, Balthazar's mother knocked on the door, and his mother let her in. She spoke in a soft voice, with a long face, and then his mother brought her hands to her face before collapsing on the armchair.

Federico's mother was sure that her husband was not having an affair. She had always accompanied her husband on every trip; to Mongolia, Nigeria, and Peru. To build dams in isolated places or to excavate land to extract metals. They had married in Africa. Riccardo was there for work and wrote her a telegram announcing the date of the marriage: February 21, 1965. He would send her a plane ticket to a place she had never heard of.

She talked about it at home with her family and answered: "My father doesn't think it's a good idea."

Riccardo replied with an even more laconic telegram: "Marry your father."

They had been through a lot together, including being terrorized on their honeymoon by baboons throwing stones at the car, making it look like a wreck. His mother had seen him work under intense pressure, knowing his strengths and weaknesses. She did not doubt that if he was at Armando's house, he had a good reason for it apart from an affair. However, she could not find out what it was.

When Armando was interrogated, he said he was unable to remember anything. At the trial, he was defended by Balthazar's father, who invoked, by reading it aloud, the article about honor killing: "Criminal Code, Art. 587. Whoever causes the death of his spouse, daughter, or sister in the act in which he discovers their illegitimate carnal relationship and in the state of anger caused by the offense done to their honor or that of the family is punished with imprisonment from three to seven years. The same sentence applies to anyone who, in the above circumstances, causes the death of a person in an illegitimate carnal relationship with his spouse, daughter, or sister."

He followed the text with the harangue: "If you don't absolve him and spare him three years of prison, it means that you believe in dishonor. And if dishonor is allowed, chaos reigns. And in chaos, there is anarchy and malpractice; you can no longer trust your brother and are reduced to beasts. There can be harmful consequences when a man sneaks into a woman's house. For thousands of years, honor could only be defended with blood, eliminating all that is dishonorable. Otherwise, how else could one show one's face and walk in the street? Armando acted with conscience, both for his good and that of the community. Share in this man's drama, empathize with his pain, feel the tears of the terrible shame he had to face, and absolve him. Absolve him. Absolve him!"

And so, Armando returned home three weeks later. There was total silence in the house. He called his wife, then realized how stupid he had been. The noise of silence became unbearable; he took his hands to cover his ears and turned on the TV. He breathed a breath of relief when he heard the news theme song, which drove out that emptiness, filling it with the usual roundup of negative news in which journalism specializes. A report on the law regarding honor killing began, and Armando increased the volume. The journalist commented: "The provisions on honor killing have been repealed, with the law n. 442, as of today, August 10, 1981."

He looked around, turned off the TV, and came back to his senses. From that day on, he realized that an act like his would bring life imprisonment. He had been acquitted thanks to that law, which allowed murder if committed in a state of rage caused by the threat of losing honor that would result in being mentally incapacitated by what was considered legitimate anger.

He relived the scene inside himself, as he had done many times. At home, the details came back to memory. Now he remembered why Riccardo was there. That day he had forgotten why because his rage blinded him, ignited by the suspicion that the lawyer's comment planted into his head. Now, the scene changed its meaning. He had killed his wife and a close friend.

He felt life slipping from his heart. He climbed on the chair, took the belt off, and fastened it to the hook for hanging hams from the ceiling. Then he put his head into it, kicked the backrest, and fell, hanging himself.

23. THE DECEPTION

Tonino's illness had been an exaggeration by Vincenzo to bring Federico back to Abruzzo, along with the aggravating circumstance of the earthquake. Federico felt betrayed and manipulated at a time when his life was already rolling along the ridge of the highest mountain he had ever seen.

He attacked him: "So you convinced me to come here by lying to me?"

"Don't make it worse than it is. I'm doing you a favor. Tonino is sick and did want to see you."

"One lie and one truth added together don't make two truths. A favor is if and when I ask you for it. I feel as if we've gone back in time. You 'doing it for me', and me ending up in trouble."

"Federico, by helping me, you're helping yourself. Do you remember what your grandfather used to say? There are treasures hidden around here. We must hurry. They will find them before us if they move the stones or dig."

"First, it is illegal to keep archeological discoveries. We will end up in jail."

"Illegal? Archeological? Who cares? Do you think the law will help you when you need it? Do you think they will rebuild your house? Who treated my retinopathy? I am now almost blind; I have to use a thousand tricks to orient myself in space."

"These are not reasons to break the law."

"And tell me, what's the amount of taxes you have paid so far? Are any of them returning to you now that you need help?"

Federico could not resist and started adding up the taxes he had paid in recent years. He was getting frustrated about that, too, when Vincenzo resumed: "If we rely on the law, then it's game over. We wouldn't even reach retirement age. We have to do everything on our own."

"Vincenzo, the second most important reason is that they are just legends. Stories that our grandfather used to tell us. For fun. It was just entertainment. Nobody has ever found anything."

"Why, have we ever looked? Have we ever gone down the Goats' Drop?"

"Well, no."

"Then how do you know they are not true?"

"Someone will have tried."

"Someone? Someone who? Who is this 'someone' whom we always refer to? Do you know, Federico, 'someone' who has tried?"

"You know they are stories. Rural legends, hoaxes."

"You know, you know'. As everyone used to 'know' the earth was flat. And if you told someone that a preserved mammoth fossil was found just fifty years ago in the province of L'Aquila, who would believe you? It had been there for more than four thousand years, before the Ancient Egyptians, before the Greeks and Romans, who dug and built everywhere around here. It was still there throughout the Middle Ages, the Renaissance, and two world wars. Yet no one had ever found it until 1954. If you could not see it now, standing at the National Museum of Abruzzo, you, Federico knows-it-all, might not even believe it yet."

Federico didn't know what to argue. He sighed, and Vincenzo pressed him: "Federico, come on! We will hide, and Balthazar will not find out. We'll sleep in your grandfather's hut and organize ourselves. Take your share, go back to Milan, and solve all your problems."

"A treasure? The hut? Vincenzo, the area is a pile of rubble. And you and I put us up to look for a treasure as two fools?"

Vincenzo interrupted Federico: "What choice do you have? Do you think you can find a job so quickly? Do you think you can soon repay your debts?"

"So instead, you would have you and me against the world, as Butch Cassidy and the Sundance Kid, and we will recover thirty years of bad luck?"

Vincenzo played his ace: "And who told you that we are alone? I have already assembled a team; didn't you notice yet?"

"Oh my, did you convince them, too? Vince, are you kidding? We are adults; life is not a children's tale."

"Really? Hasn't anyone ever told you how many treasures are found each year? And do you know that most of them are found after natural disasters as if the earth would give them back to the world by taking them from its bowels?"

Federico recalled the examples of the found treasures that Manfredi's teacher had told him about.

"Yes, I have heard something about it. But there is no evidence of treasures around here. Only tales, anecdotes, stories."

"Absence of evidence is not evidence of absence."

Vincenzo came out with that sentence, which hit Federico as a punch to the liver. Logical reasoning always killed him.

When you hear about an earthquake, a hidden treasure is not the first thing you think of. But Vincenzo had considered the possibility and, in the absurdity of that thought, he could even be right. If there was a good time to look for a buried treasure, it was right after an earthquake, a hurricane, or a tsunami. Federico had also seen evidence of recent examples. And since there are no tsunamis and hurricanes in Abruzzo, the only natural catastrophic upheaval could be an earthquake. What the hell was he thinking? He, a mathematician, a chief financial officer—'ex' a little voice inside told him—who was now fancying the absurd existence of a treasure.

The others also arrived at the hut, and he faced them: "In a few words, all of you dragged me here, knowing that I have a legal injunction against entering Abruzzo, that if Balthazar sees me, he will kill me. All while trying to find a job, I'm left with nothing. And you told me that Uncle Tonino needs me because he is ill while, in reality, you want to look for a treasure that exists only in fairy tales?"

Eleonora replied: "In a few words, yes. Actually, you used too many of them."

"Why did you think of me?"

"Because now that you are homeless, without a job, without any protection, and a sick son, you have the right state of mind to start considering an impossible endeavor. Just like all of us."

24. KLUTZ

Castellana, 6 April 2009

The twins looked at each other, raised their eyebrows, smiled, and then spoke together: "Those stories about the treasure. It's all crap."

Federico liked how the twins, despite being quite cynical, were always present, helped each other, and got busy. His father always told him: "Do not listen to what people say. Look at what they do. Like in the parable of the two sons, as told by Jesus."

Federico had thought it was a comment referring to bigotry and hypocrisy, but now he realized there was another level of meaning. An order of priority, of depth, between saying and doing.

"The other reason we called you is that we are all old hands, and you are a klutz," said Vincenzo.

"Ah, thank you. And what kind of reason is this?"

The first time someone called him 'klutz' was when he boated with Stefania and her parents. Federico had made a mistake that had caused them to approach the cliffs. She started screaming with fear, and her father had to intervene to adjust the sails. Her mother said: "With a wimp and a klutz, where will we end up?"

He didn't reply. On the contrary, he kept to himself that he felt even more scared than clumsy.

Eleonora articulated Vincenzo's argument: "First, you were the only one missing from our group. Didn't you want us to include you? And then, as a child, you always knew everything. You had a theory for everything, a solution for every problem. What happened? You don't know anything anymore?"

The twins added even more flesh to the bone: "You have been studying the mysteries and history of Abruzzo. You like codes and puzzles."

Federico became irritated: "How do you know this?"

The twins winked at each other: "We have our snitches."

The spirit of polemics broke out in him: "And what would be the plan? Thanks to an unexpected stroke of genius, the exile discovers what no one has guessed for a hundred years, and we all become millionaires?"

"Ooh, what a beautiful Milanese accent you've got," the twins made fun of him.

Vincenzo became straightforward: "Federico, seriously. Focus. The treasure could be there. We just have to understand where to look. Did you notice that we equipped the hut to hide you from your enemy? We are leaving nothing to chance."

Giulio had remained silent until then. One head taller than Federico, he was a rugby fan who played in the youth teams of L'Aquila. He was big and hairy like a bear. He had long hair and a long beard; when he had shaken Federico's hand, he looked straight into his eyes, lifting his nostrils, and behind that hand was the strength of a tractor.

"They told me that you are good at rugby."

"Who told you this?"

"My sister, Eleonora."

Federico didn't want to throw himself into a challenge, physical or verbal, that would only leave him with broken bones: "I'm not as good as you. I see you are pretty sturdy."

Giulio was satisfied to close the first half in the lead and started doing something else, muttering: "I knew that my sister doesn't understand anything about rugby; this guy seems a chicken to me."

Federico imagined the following days unfolding. He could stay there for a while, maybe until the end of the Easter vacation. Then Manfredi would have to return to school, Stefania would come back, and he would sink again into the same depression he had left in Milan.

Eleonora hadn't said much, but she had been twisting her lips and hands for some time until she turned to Federico: "Federico, I was left homeless. The only thing I feel is that wind beneath the ground every time there is a shake. And here, there are hundreds of them every day. When one comes, I never know if it will be small or if another piece of home, history, or life will fall. Everything is collapsing, everything. I don't know if I will ever get my house back, or even just a house. I'm even too scared to fall asleep. If nobody helps us, we have to help ourselves. And here you are, still living your life with the memories and fears of a child."

Federico felt the energy of Eleonora taking his breath away. His eyes tightened, and he paused for a moment: "I want to think about it. But first, I have to meet with Aunt Cesidia."

"She is still at home; it has not suffered any damage, as I told you," commented Vincenzo.

"Tomorrow morning, I'm going there. Now I am too tired."

Federico helped Manfredi to get into a sleeping bag in the hut, then he took another one for himself and slipped into it. Manfredi smiled at him: "In the end, you managed to bring me here, Papi. I can't wait to find the treasure."

Those words made him feel like a hero in his son's eyes. An imaginary hero, though, coward to become a real one. The enthusiasm of Manfredi's smiling eyes was the last thing he saw before dawn.

25. AUNT CESIDIA

Abruzzo, 7 April 2009

Federico was preparing coffee while the mountains still covered the sun. He could see the incoming dawn by looking at the pink color of the snow on the Gran Sasso. It advanced slower than he remembered when he was a child.

Vincenzo came to pick them up. Federico shared coffee with him, and they left. There was no one in the street, so Federico asked to pass by his parents' house first while staying hidden from Balthazar and the notorious warning. He and Manfredi crushed each other in the back seat while Vincenzo was driving up the hill, even if he wasn't supposed to, given his low eyesight that cost him his driving license.

"Papi, it's like in the movies; it must then be true."

The old house was still standing, the facade wrinkled with cracks like a zombie. It had been there, closed for almost thirty years. On the ground beside it, with its entire frame smashed, was the window from which his grandmother used to call them for lunch while they were scattered somewhere in the country: "Federicoooo. It's ready!" And everyone running as fast as possible not to get yelled at.

Vincenzo showed him a bunch of keys: "I used to go in there now and then to let in some fresh air."

"We'll come back tomorrow. Too many memories for today."

His grandfather once pointed out to him that memories are like trains; they travel in coaches, and if you hear the distant sound of the engine, it means that a whole convoy is stretching on the rails to smash into you all at once. Federico had just been hit by a high-speed Frecciarossa train that his inner protests had failed to stop.

Grandpa didn't talk much. He would hint at things and then let the listener complete their meaning. Once, while he was building a floor, Federico watched him for half an hour before asking him what that wire mesh he put on the floor was for. He answered after a few minutes: "Mamma mia, how many questions. You sound like Giulio." Eleonora's little brother was in the phase of asking "why?" all the time.

So, he watched him in silence all morning. He had designed the whole house and even built the furniture himself, showing everyone great pride whenever they visited the place. His grandfather was a mechanic, bricklayer, tiler, carpenter: everything. And his father had learned everything from him.

Federico remembered the time when they renovated the small bathroom. They needed expanded clay to mix with cement; they did the math and went to buy twenty bags. When they returned, his grandfather saw them: "Riccardo, aren't they too many?"

Federico's father was sure: "No, no. I did all the calculations."

They kneaded the lime on the bathroom floor, and when they opened the fifth bag, they already had a mountain of cement and clay in the center of the bathroom. They had misplaced a zero in their calculations, so they had ten times as much as required. Federico was fascinated by what a small zero could do. For example, imagine adding a zero at the end of your salary; go ahead, imagine it for real. You are happier, aren't you? That is what a simple zero can do.

Apart from that accidental miscalculation, with the only consequence being the effort of bringing out all that pile of clay and cement, his grandfather and his father always did their construction work with great care. And, except for some damaged external elements, the house they renovated and reinforced many years before seemed to stand in decent condition overall.

Interrupting the memories, they returned to the car and went to see Aunt Cesidia. Now the sun was higher in the sky and appeared between the ridges to warm the whole valley.

When they arrived, Vincenzo took Manfredi to see the horses and told Federico: "Go, talk to her alone. I will take Manfredi for a ride."

He turned the key, left out of the door, as he had done a thousand times as a child, and entered. His aunt didn't understand who the stranger was until he greeted her by raising his voice a little: "Hi, Aunt, it's Federico."

She jumped in her chair, opened her eyes wide, stretched out her arms, and took his cheeks with both hands: "Federico, my treasure!"

They, too, had not seen each other for twenty-eight years, and Federico felt he was losing a few heartbeats. When she took her hands off his cheeks, Federico saw his tears running down her wrinkles and hoped she didn't notice them.

Federico was thrown again into the past and realized how sometimes holding back tears can do more harm than letting them go. Aunt Cesidia would turn one hundred years old, and Federico remembered that, since there wasn't room for everyone in his grandparents' house when they came from Milan for visits, he would sleep over at her house. She was always moved when his parents came to get him in the morning before returning to Milan. Federico would see her from the window, bending down, pretending to take care of the flowers she cultivated to take to the cemetery. In his childish naivety, Federico asked his father why she cried: "You know, she's old and thinks that maybe she won't see us for Christmas."

"Why, Papi? Aren't we coming back for Christmas this year?"

He remembered seeing that scene countless times until Aunt Cesidia stopped crying. Perhaps because, in the end, she didn't die and Federico returned on vacation once or twice a year, and they continued to see each other.

But this time, it was different. The earthquake had been a harrowing experience. She had already lived almost a hundred years, and everyone was worried that she might not survive such a shock.

Aunt Cesidia wasn't Federico's biological aunt. Still, his parents had always called her 'aunt' as a respectful custom in central and southern Italy, reserved for less close relatives. She was good at sewing and embroidering; she always wanted Federico to take her to 'Mani di Fata' in Milan, a sacred temple for crochet and kneading lovers. She always told him they would go there together when she was older. As a child, she asked him to draw a Japanese woman wearing a beautiful kimono. When he returned the following summer, she showed him the brocade she had woven based on that model. She was so good that the 'Madonna della Libera' statue in Villa Sant'Angelo church wore a dress embroidered by her.

When she was left without anyone except Uncle Tonino, who lived as a hermit, she decided not to live in Vallecupa or Villa Sant'Angelo because, in those villages, she had too many sad memories of her family.

"Aunt, Vincenzo has gone mad. He wants us to find the brigands' treasure. He asked me to help him, but I don't know how. It seems absurd to me that there could still be treasures to be found in two thousand and nine."

"What do you find so absurd?"

"They will have already found them. And the little things I know, everyone knows."

"It is not enough to know. One must believe. One must believe that one can do. And then one must do. And you have forgotten that. You fled in terror, and out of fear, you have adapted yourself to doing what you believe everyone does."

"I wish you were right, and I was wrong."

"Do you hear yourself when you speak? You desire to be right so much that you'd rather suffer a negative outcome than be wrong. That's the real problem."

"That's not true; in this case, I'd like to be wrong instead."

"No, because if you say the treasure is not there, then you don't look for it, and you don't find it. And you can say you were right. If you looked for it and found it, you would have been wrong to think it was not there."

Federico objected: "What if I don't find it, even if I look for it?"

The aunt concluded: "You would have been proven wrong to look for it since it wasn't there."

The nephew tried to bounce to the conclusion: "So...?"

Cesidia summarized it: "So the only case in which you would be right is by not looking at all. That is exactly what you are trying to do. You prefer to be right and stay poor and alone. You prefer to avoid an experience with your childhood friend in exchange for being right. Hence, the saying: 'Being right is the booby prize.' It's the lowest stakes. A leftover for losers."

Once again, logic had destroyed Federico's attempt to escape action. He sighed: "Then what should I do? Put the pieces of the stories back together according to the little information available. Maybe even search for some evidence?"

"Do you still remember some of those clues? I am too ignorant to decipher them, but you can do it if you let all the memories come naturally. Do not block your thoughts by judging them, as you continue to do every second."

Although Federico was now beginning to trust his aunt's intuitions, he wanted to understand more: "And how do you know I do that?"

She smiled: "Ignorant does not mean stupid, Federico. And I have lived my first hundred years: do you know how many observations you can make in a century? You studied a lot; as a child, you asked a thousand questions to which we often had no answers. Did you continue?"

"Yes, of course. They always made fun of me because of it. And now I am convinced that they were right. I have become what is called a good-for-nothing."

"You should talk to your Uncle Tonino."

"They told me he is nowhere to be found."

"If you make an effort, you will know where to look for him."

"Vincenzo has already told the whole gang about the treasure. It seems that he has gone mad."

"He has always been crazy, ever since his brother died. What a tragedy."

Aunt Cesidia's voice changed into the sound of an enchanted flute; she looked into his eyes while holding his cheeks with her hands: "Federico, you must lead your old friends. No one else can. Vincenzo is too emotional; Giovanna is an intellectual. Not even Eleonora and your cousins can do it. What are you waiting for?"

Federico felt helpless: "I just don't know how to do it."

The aunt threw her head backward, stared at him, then leaned towards him again: "So you're waiting to know how to do it? Are you waiting to hear from someone else about how to live? There is no 'how'; the how will come from the doing itself."

Federico was perplexed: "But I never know how to counter Vincenzo, he is too strong for me, and even the twins seem to say intelligent things, as does Eleonora. Giovanna, also, is a well of science."

"Then, don't argue. That's not the point. You don't have to be better than any of them; you don't have to be right. Listen to them all. Each of them will give you a different perspective, and then you put everything together. Listen, think, and then suggest an action. If you leave them alone, they will only grope confused. Start by putting into practice what comes from them, and you will see that they will listen to you. Maybe some will protest, others will complain, accuse you, and whatever, but they will follow you. Perhaps a little late, but they will. Be patient. You cannot control people, as you can't control your eagle."

Federico asked himself about Maya. *Who knows what became of her?* And then remembered what Zhuldyz's grandfather used to tell him in Mongolia. *'You can't control the eagle.' You must establish a strong bond with it, and it will follow you.*

Aunt Cesidia continued as if reading his mind: "With your friends, it's the same thing. Weren't they the ones who first looked for you? Doesn't this mean they need your guidance?"

Then she got up, opened a cupboard door, and handed him a box: "Do you remember?"

Federico looked inside; there were photographs, newspapers, and even a copy of the "Il Corriere della Sera" of May 4, 1981. Federico remembered it well: the day after the Scudetto victory by L'Aquila Rugby.

Twenty-eight years earlier, he had sought the newspaper with the excitement of being able to read about an important event in which he had participated. Maybe there was a picture of him and his father together.

He began to scan the pages of the old newspaper, and after a few pages, he saw a big headline: THE LEGENDARY FEDERICO; for a moment, he felt he was the protagonist, then just above, and smaller: A BIOGRAPHY OF THE SUEVIAN SOVEREIGN. Despite the vanity he had felt, it was not referring to him but to the much more famous Federico: Frederick II.

And then, in the sports section, after pages and pages of soccer and motor racing, after golf, after horse racing, lower than the article that said 'Former Swiss letter carrier in Zurich beats the aces of cycling', he saw the headline: 'L'Aquila—The Eagle—wins the Rugby Scudetto after twelve years', followed by just a few lines.

26. LOOKING FOR TONINO

Abruzzo, 7 April 2009

They had all agreed to meet back at the hut, and on the way there with Vincenzo and Manfredi, Federico felt his butt tightening as when he was at altitude and looked down below. Was there anything he wouldn't do for his son? How would he raise him in his condition? He gave himself a week. Then he would have to take Manfredi back to Milan. Since he was here, though, he might as well try.

When they regathered, he found the strength to announce: "All right, I'm going to talk to Tonino. I think I know where to find him. And I will also do my best to find the treasure, even though I don't think it exists."

Eleonora put her arms around his neck while the twins joked: "Federico with a vengeance," and Manfredi began to clap his hands. Vincenzo gave him a big push: "We'll show him where the mutton has its balls", as the Abruzzese saying goes.

Giovanna smiled sarcastically: "We're good, then."

When Federico was a boy, Tonino used to disappear occasionally and wouldn't show up more or less for a month. Federico's father knew where he was hiding and sometimes took Federico to see him. They would stay there for a few hours; Tonino and his father would talk, have a coffee, eat some dried fruit, and then leave again.

They divided into two groups and got into the cars, taking the road to Sulmona. Meanwhile, there was news of a member of the Fire Brigade of Bergamo who had come to Abruzzo to help. After an exhausting effort to recover people buried under the rubble, he died because of the extraordinary physical effort. He left a wife and two children.

Starting today's journey made Federico remember when he had walked with his father on the so-called "Path of the Spirit." About seventy kilometers long, it connects the main hermitage places of worship on the Maiella massif that borders L'Aquila, Chieti, and Pescara. It would take an adult four days to walk it, but his father slowed down, and together they did it in a whole week. His father had been on the trail of Pietro del Morrone, the future Pope Celestino V, who chose the most remote places in the area to deepen his faith.

They visited the hermitage of S. Onofrio, perched on the rocks, and also stopped for a break to enjoy the thermal village of Caramanico Terme. They walked through the valley of Orfento, with the panoramic cliff close to the deep gorge carved by the river's waters. They climbed a series of narrow steps cut into the rock. The foliage of the trees filtered the sunlight, which gave the river water its emerald green color, while in the clearings, there were flowers of anemones, primroses, and cyclamens. They crossed many wooden bridges built over the roar of the rivers. There were dry stone huts in the thick beech woods, similar to the one in Castellana.

From time to time, his father gave him brief explanations: "In Abruzzo, going back to distant times, people have hunted down solitary places such as caves, gorges, and caverns. They transformed these into numerous hermitages, sanctuaries, and chapels with mystical charm. They are difficult to reach because of their locations in the wild and are so immersed in the mountains that they create considerable problems for those who decide to visit them. The hermitages are inserted in the landscape, almost without changing it, merging sacred buildings and nature to symbolize the union between the inner world of man and God."

Federico hoped that Tonino had not changed his habits in the last thirty years, which he thought unlikely. Abruzzo is the area with the highest concentration of hermitages, comparable only to Tibet. If Federico's intuition was wrong, they could be looking for Tonino for thirty times thirty years.

27. THE MINE OF THE HOLY SPIRIT

Abruzzo, 7 April 2009

The mine of Santo Spirito—Holy Spirit—in the locality Ripa Rossa is close to the hermitage that bears the same name. Entering the abandoned mine and knowing where to turn, you can leave the marked path and find yourself in an incredible cave. Federico knew the way by heart thanks to all the times he had walked it with his father. In the cave, hidden by the woods and the ravines of the National Park, there were remains of wolf, bear, goat, and deer. It had been a hideout for wild animals, perhaps even during prehistoric times.

Tonino was right there, immersed in meditation. He had his arms crossed, his hands resting on his shoulders. He looked like a holy man. Federico seemed to notice a bright shiny wet line on his cheeks. He turned towards the others, putting his index finger in front of his mouth, and sat down on the floor, followed by the group. Even with his father, it was like this; sometimes, they waited even until Federico's tummy rumbled before Tonino noticed them. This time, after about half an hour, Tonino opened his eyes, saw them, and smiled. When he noticed Federico, he widened his eyes, mouth, and arms, reached backward and then, and threw his arms around him. He crushed him with his powerful hug, and Federico's face got lost in the thickness of his eighty-year-old beard.

"You're back then; your ass is not twitching anymore?"

Tonino mimed it with both hands, smiling with raised eyebrows while looking at Federico. And then another fat laugh, with the beard rising and lowering.

It was peculiar how, even though twenty-eight springs had passed, Tonino treated him as when he used to visit him as a child. He mocked him with affection, only now Federico noticed the effect that mockery had on him. It kept him awake and made him see his shortcomings or character characteristics that might have to be reconsidered. But he did it with humor, almost as if providing, together with feedback, the necessary fluid to make that suggestion flow to the right place.

Federico smiled and thought he was an idiot.

Tonino saw Manfredi: "And who is this little kid?"

Federico answered, swelling his chest: "My son, Manfredi."

Tonino went to a hollow in the rock, where he took a box of chocolates and candies, offering them to Manfredi and the others. Everyone looked at each other as if to say: *Is he keeping sweets in the cave?*

Manfredi turned to the remains of bones on one side of the cave, and Tonino noticed it.

"What is it? Have you never been in the cave of an ogre? Those are the bad children I ate. But you are good, aren't you?"

Then he widened his eyes and whispered to him: "I always say that there are no good or bad children; there are only good children and good children to eat."

Manfredi hid behind Federico's legs, who reassured him: "Uncle Tonino is joking."

They sat down, and Federico told Tonino of Vincenzo's deception and the fake terminal illness.

"I had just a few aches, but I understand that Vincenzo had even fewer ways to make you move your ass of stone. He may have exaggerated things a bit."

"So, the treasure does exist?"

"*It* does not exist."

"See, Vince?"

"It is more accurate to say that *they* exist."

"And how many are out there? Have you ever found any?"

"Quiet, quiet. I never looked for them."

"Why not?"

"What should I do with them? They would only bring me trouble. I don't need more of them. And if there were a necessity, you could always find them. The brigands hid them everywhere. This region contains ravines, mountains, caves, ruins, and abandoned and inaccessible places. For example, even this old mine alone, closed for years, would be a perfect hiding place."

He stopped, paused, looked at Federico, and reached down to smooth his beard: "I understand that you want to find them instead."

"No. I mean, yes. Well, I believe that they don't exist and are just stories for children."

Tonino straightened up, slowed down, and continued, almost as if he were whispering a secret: "The strongest deception is the one where you are told that there is nothing to look for. For this reason, you don't even start. And even worse, people don't look for anything unconventional in life. Perhaps out of fear, but also because they think there is 'nothing to look for'. Or maybe they think that if there is someone who will find it or succeed in an enterprise, it won't be them. And so, also in these cases, they don't even start."

Vincenzo nodded; the others, including Manfredi, listened enchanted. Tonino continued: "You have no idea how many teachings are hidden in children's stories. You are both afraid and don't believe in fairy tales. If you remain like that, you are lost."

He jumped up, with the agility of a much younger: "And now let's go back to Villa Sant'Angelo: there is something that has been waiting for you for almost thirty years."

28. VOLA, VOLA, VOLA

Abruzzo, 7 April 2009

As they approached Villa Sant'Angelo, Federico saw, above the cemetery, the hamlet of Tussillo lying under the first cliffs of Mount Saint Peter. The Saint whom the mountain refers to is Saint Peter from Morrone, or Pope Celestino V. Federico kept his gaze fixed in the distance just above the pine forest and a little to the left of the village. As if he were afraid that it might run away, he looked at the stone house built on the ridge of the hill and on the edge of the *sgrimone*, the ravine that cuts the mountain: *Saint Peter,* he murmured to himself.

When they arrived at the cemetery, Federico wanted to get out of the car. His ancestors had been buried in that cemetery for generations. He regarded the place with a reverence he didn't grant to anything else. He looked at the warnings on the cemetery wall: the grounds were unsafe. Built during the first half of the nineteenth century with dry stone, the division had collapsed in several places. It looked as if a shark had bitten it. He could see many fallen gravestones, the fractured walls of numerous tombs, and the chapel. Federico imagined the cemetery at night, with the open-air coffins, the uncovered burial niches, and the dead who came out to talk to each other, as in Totò's poem, A Livella', the ultimate level. His grandfather had used a level to build straight walls, but the earthquake had now leveled those walls, just as death had done its leveling in the poem.

Death.

In his mind, he had already asked that question many times but had not yet dared to voice it. He swallowed his saliva and asked Eleonora, who had joined him: "Is Maya still alive?"

Eleonora turned towards Tonino, who nodded, "Let's go to Saint Peter."

They set out for the coastal side of the mountain, outside the village, where Eleonora kept her birds of prey for falconry.

Immersed in that part of the landscape, Federico was reminded of the flights with Maya, his childhood with Eleonora, and the song that had become an anthem for Abruzzo: "Vola, Vola, Vola"—"Fly, Fly, Fly". The song was rejected at the Lanciano competition in 1922, but today no one remembers who the winner was or who were the other participants.

The author of the music didn't give up and sent the mayor of Lanciano a telegram: "'Vola, Vola, Vola' will fly! Guido Albanese."

Federico collected the stories of the critiques of all the songs that then turned out to be a great success. He had a big notebook in which he wrote them all down. "Vola, Vola, Vola" is a rare example of a popular song in an Italian dialect that is not Neapolitan and of international popularity. Albanese was right: thirty years later, and two thousand kilometers further north, "Vola, Vola, Vola" won at the 1953 Paris Festival.

"Eleonora, do you remember when we used to play Vola, Vola?"

"Sure," she answered, smiling.

Federico sang the first verse, with the short breath of the mountain fatigue:

"I would like the beautiful time of contentment,
to come back for one hour only
when we used to play Vola, Vola."

"Vola, Vola, Vola"—Fly, Fly, Fly—was a childhood Abruzzese game before it became a song. The kids gather around a companion and place their index fingers on their knees. The game leader says: "Fly, fly, fly ...", pauses, then tells the name of an animal of their choice. If the chosen animal is a bird, the players must 'fly', i.e., lift their finger; otherwise, they stand still and keep their finger on the knee. Whoever makes a mistake is forced to pay a lien. For example, a pawn is paid by those who, by mistake, make a donkey fly and not a hawk. The pawned object—a handkerchief—could then be redeemed with penance as embarrassing as possible. In the fourth verse, the song references this part of the game:

"Once, to return the handkerchief,
I was condemned to kiss you.
You blushed and told me
to kneel first and hug you."

Once it happened that to retrieve his handkerchief, Federico was 'condemned' to kiss Eleonora. She didn't miss the opportunity to add to his embarrassment, raising her chin and putting her hands on her hips, saying: "Before kissing me, you have to kneel, as in the song."

Federico turned red, knelt, and kissed her on the cheek that Eleonora lowered to him while she looked upwards.

"And it flies, flies, flies, flies,
and flies the goldfinch,
for such a wonderful time
I would like to sink."

When it was Eleonora's turn to be the leader, everyone put their finger on her knee. Even Federico, who blushed again while everyone started making fun of him. He felt the same heat on his cheeks as the flames of his grandfather's fireplace when he got too close in winter. Eleonora began: "Fly, Fly, Fly ...," she paused, held her breath, and then exclaimed as she lifted her nose: "The donkey, Federico!"

Nobody lifted their finger—nobody except Federico.

The song was sung at every party, and every time Federico thought about that episode, he always turned red, even if everyone had forgotten it by now.

He was shaken by those memories but decided to pretend to be excited at the thought of Maya in case Eleonora had noticed his redness. Furthermore, she had not yet answered his question, and Federico began to feel the first symptoms of anxiety.

"Of course, she is alive. A bit old, but alive."

"Have you taken her hunting in all these years?"

"Did you have doubts?"

He didn't have any doubts, except for one:

"Do you think she will recognize me?"

Eleonora didn't answer: "It hasn't been easy. She has become aggressive, and the separation from you didn't help her well-being because of the symbiotic relationship you had."

"Yes, it didn't help me either."

"The danger is that she may now perceive you as a predator in her territory and attack you. Behave."

Federico swallowed more saliva.

They arrived in Saint Peter, and Manfredi recognized the place, even though he had never seen it before, thanks to the stories handed down from his grandfather to his father and from his father to him: "Look, Papi, it's the house of the Cripple."

It had not suffered any damage from the earthquake. Federico mocked Eleonora: "Since you need a house, you can live here."

Eleonora smiled, shaking her head: "This is just the right place to raise little children. Just an hour's walk from the nearest train station."

It was a house built of stone, much taller than average, with a small door. *The Cripple doesn't need it; he enters through the chimney on the roof.* However, they had to lower their heads and enter through that tiny hole.

The inside space was almost empty, and one of the house's four walls consisted of the mountain's rock face. There were some aviaries with raptors, Harris's Hawks, and peregrine falcons. On one wall hung the materials necessary for the activity. It was an exhibition of high-quality craftsmanship, making Federico's mouth open wide with wonder. He loved hoods, leather laces, and bags to hold bait. He approached, reached out his hand to grab a hood, and smelt the scent of leather when out of the corner of his eye, he caught a movement above and to his left.

Maya.

She had rearranged herself inside a nest housed in a recess in the mountain wall. She was not looking towards him but tilting her neck to one side and looking out of the windows. Federico didn't turn around; Eleonora must have noticed it and whispered to him: "We let her nest, every year, she rearranges it with new leaves and branches. This is the right time."

Federico was insecure about what to do: "How do we do it?"

Eleonora opened the refrigerator, took some pieces of meat, and put them in the leather bag she passed him with a glove his size: "Go out, turn to your right, and stand in the middle of the courtyard. I'll make her fly; then you call her back. If it pleases her, she will come."

"What if she does not want to?"

Eleonora ignored the question: "Go before Maya sees you in here."

Federico went out, standing around the corner of the house, and Eleonora left Maya free to fly. Federico admired her as an ascending current lifted her over the hill. He moved, putting himself well in sight in the courtyard's center. He vocalized the characteristic sound of the singers of Mongolia; he continued to practice every time he was alone in the car. He placed a piece of meat on his glove, and the eagle saw him from afar. She dived, almost swooping with an arched trajectory, always looking at the meat. When she was a few meters away, she turned her wings, almost embracing the air, imprisoning it, to brake and claw the glove, landing on Federico's arm. Federico closed his eyes and went back one step to absorb the impact. Maya locked herself in her feathered cloak and tore the meal to pieces with her beak.

Federico looked at her while eating and realized that he had recognized her. Even if the eagles all look the same, standing close to them, you can notice the small details, the little differences that make them unique. The curve of the eye, the design and the shades of the colors of the feathers, the small plumage around the beak, almost a mustache. It seemed strange to him to notice how even animals age and, while understanding that they are still the same, we also see on them the paths of time that dig wrinkles in humans and color with white.

Maya adjusted her legs on the glove to keep her balance. He looked into her eyes. He felt she recognized him, too—the same two faces as thirty years earlier. Like him, Vincenzo, and all the others. The same childhood profiles were warped by the action of time as if they had been immersed in a field of forces that pulled them in unpredictable directions.

Maya was now about thirty years old. Although eagles can have a longer life in captivity, she wouldn't have lived much longer. Meanwhile, Federico noticed that the rooster, who had been chasing the hens in the front yard when they arrived, was now strutting in front of the house, moving away to keep a safe distance. It seemed to be like him, knowing that Balthazar might be nearby. The thought immobilized and paralyzed him, making him stiff like a chimney stump.

He looked at Maya but spoke to Eleonora: "Do you think she is happy to see me?"

"Eagles are independent. If they feel affection, they don't show it as a dog would."

"And how would they show it?"

"By landing on your arm."

29. CARLANTONIO

Villa Sant'Angelo, 1937

Carlantonio served in the Carabinieri Corps, spending countless nights in the wilderness to surprise the criminals who hid in the bush. One of those times, while he was sleeping under a blanket of stars, a tarantula bit his eyelid. The village doctor operated on him, but his eye remained half closed for the rest of his life. Because of that malformation, he was discharged by the Carabinieri and became a forest ranger. His main task was preventing people from stealing wood from public property. He patrolled, with a rifle on his shoulder and a gun on his belt, the forests on the hillside above Villa Sant'Angelo.

During one of those inspections, a man introduced himself to him as the murderer of his own wife. He wanted to turn himself in. He approached the ranger to be arrested, but when he was less than a meter away, the killer pulled out a sickle, such as those used to reap wheat. The weapon cut the air a few millimeters from Carlantonio's neck. He had dodged just in time. The criminal chased him, getting closer and closer, threatening him with the slashes of the peasant weapon, thus forcing him to retreat, one step after the other, towards the precipice behind him.

At that point, Carlantonio had no choice; he pulled out his gun and pointed it at the man: "Put it away." His hands were outstretched like dried tomatoes, and his shaking index finger may have induced the bandit to think he had pulled the trigger several times without shooting. Perhaps he had assumed that the gun was unloaded or fake, so he went for Carlantonio again, who shot him in the chest. The bandit fell to the ground and lost consciousness. The ranger loaded him on his shoulders, carried him from the woods to the village, and took him to the doctor, who requested his immediate hospitalization.

In a report, concealed in a sealed envelope to be delivered to the hospital, the doctor wrote: "Carlantonio, to test his new weapon, shot this unfortunate man in the back." The Carabinieri arrived, arrested their former colleague, and kept him in jail.

The prosecutor examined the papers and the case. Carlantonio had a past of honorable service with the Corps, and he had also been impeccable as a forest ranger. Indeed, the scrupulousness of his work had always distinguished him.

Meanwhile, in those few hours he spent in jail, he met an old acquaintance of his, the famous brigand Franco, whom he had arrested years earlier. When he saw him accompanied by the guards, Franco told them that he knew Carlantonio well and that it was impossible that he had committed anything vile. This spontaneous gesture of the convict persuaded the judge to review the case, and when the murderer recovered, he interrogated him.

Unaware of what the doctor had written, the murderer admitted that he considered himself blessed: "I was lucky that he hit me here"—pointing to his lower right side—"because if it had hit me here"—pointing to the heart—"I would be dead now."

The prosecutor understood that there had been no attack from behind and freed Carlantonio, who received a commendation for arresting the criminal.

No one bothered to investigate the work of the doctor who wrote that report. He belonged to Balthazar's family and bore the same surname.

The paths of Carlantonio and the bandit Franco, who with his generous gesture had saved him, had intertwined in the mountains many years before. While still serving in the Carabinieri, he was on Franco's trail when he saw him disappearing behind a wall of stones. He pulled out his gun and jumped after him, but Franco had already turned around, kicked the weapon out of his hand, and brandished his knife. Carlantonio, who had bent to one knee to retrieve his gun, raised his left arm, parried the blade, and, pushing himself up with his leg, hit Franco's chin with the butt of the weapon. While the brigand was still fumbling, he was already handcuffed at his hands and feet. Carlantonio pushed him, step by step, until they arrived under the shadow of an alder tree.

He let the bandit sit down, opened the saddlebag, and took out a piece of bread and half a salami. He broke the bread and offered it to Franco, who, with his hands tied behind his back, leaned forward like a moray eel and bit it. Carlantonio also provided him with some slices of salami. The bandit ate them and admitted his surprise: "You don't even know me, and you spared my life. They would have perhaps even given you a prize if you killed me. I am one of the bad guys for people like you."

"I don't know who is supposed to be like me. And I don't know what is good and evil, nor who is bad and who is not. No one can read another man's heart."

"I reckon that you are also a philosopher."

Carlantonio smiled at the mockery in that typical Abruzzese way of never taking anything too seriously.

"You treated me well; you offered me food, even though you are skin and bones. I want to reward you."

"It won't help you. I'm going to take you to the homeland's jail. Don't try to bribe me."

"I will tell you where I hid my loot. You can do with it as you wish."

"Awards don't interest me, and poverty can also be an asset. It gives you freedom. Exactly what you are losing as a wealthy man. The truly rich is the one who is happy with what he has."

He would come up with these maxims, and it was unclear if they had a profound meaning or if they were clumsy attempts to imitate more famous aphorisms. But when he perceived that philosophical side, Franco let himself go and revealed that he believed in defense of the weak, the search for justice, and truth. He made a distinction between justice and law, considered the latter a surrogate for the former, and said that if it ended up in the hands of the powerful, it would become persecution. They spoke at length, and although opposed from society's point of view, they had many points in common in their vision of life.

Franco also revealed some funny tricks of the trade. One of these consisted of lengthening his beard with some plumber hemp, which he blackened with coal. At night, he would light it up and open his eyes wide, laughing loudly at the terror of the unfortunate man in front of him. He also revealed to Carlantonio the location of a part of a treasure that he had hidden and what its origin was.

For years, Carlantonio went for walks in the woods, constantly checking if someone was following him as if you could read in his face that he was keeping a secret. He would go to the place where the treasure was hidden. Every time he wondered if he should have taken it, he always hesitated, as if giving in to that temptation meant giving in to a dark force and losing his self-respect. The idea of taking something that was not his own and a result of robbery and extortion, even if the victims were always wealthy people, kept him from taking hold of it.

One day, he read that Franco had escaped during the night. The newspaper warned the population: that he was a dangerous killer. It was recommended to stay alert.

Carlantonio went to the treasure site and saw an empty hole: the treasure had disappeared.

In his place, a note: "Thank you for seeing the man behind the bandit and the brigand inside the man. You are born a man, but you die a brigand. Decipher the card I leave behind: it indicates the place of three other treasures. Look for them in case of extreme need; otherwise, leave them as a gift to your posterity. Farewell, my Good Cousin."

30. THE BRIGANDS

Abruzzo, 7 April 2009

During the journey from the hermitage to Villa Sant'Angelo, they updated each other on the most important events. After the detour to Saint Peter, they went to the village and Tonino's house. He had built it out of wood. He said he didn't like to sleep under the stone and had plenty of time for that when he was in the cemetery. They called his house "the Barack", but Tonino was proud of it. He said that with stone, gravestones are made. And then wood costs much less. So, by chance or prudence, the house had not suffered any damage from the earthquake.

"Tonino, you are not going to tell me that you predicted the tremors?" asked Vincenzo.

"You are confusing predicting and preventing, or rather, preventing the consequences of an event, not the event itself. Of course, you can't predict if and when it will rain, nor prevent it. But meanwhile, you can buy an umbrella. If it rains, it rains. But at least you don't get wet."

Tonino then resumed his speech with Federico:

"I guess you've studied the history of brigands."

"Yes, I read some fascinating books."

"Do you know what Antonio Gramsci wrote in the *New Order* newspaper? It was 1920; I know it by heart: 'The Italian State was a ferocious dictatorship that put to fire and sword southern Italy and the islands, robbing, shooting, burying alive the poor peasants, while paid writers slandered them by calling them brigands.'

"As Francesco Saverio Sipari wrote: 'Brigandage is nothing but poverty, it is extreme poverty, desperate.' The brigands could be common bandits or paladins of the people, who revolted against the current power that was always exercised among tears and blood."

"Even when his bosses changed, my father would say: 'New master, same donkey.'"

"To fight against a succession of kings, dictators, and unscrupulous invaders, they needed to turn to delinquency and ally themselves with criminals they would have otherwise avoided. They adopted the same methods as those who held power and raged against them with ferocity to defend themselves."

According to Tonino, some brigands weren't criminals at all but mystics. And in the saying "You are born a man, you die a brigand'—'*Omo se nasce, Brigante se more*'—Tonino saw a spiritual path. One is born a man, but to become a 'brigand', in the sense that Tonino gave to it, one must die to earthly desires and free oneself from the chains of materiality. One must dedicate one's life to a higher purpose. It requires strength. And in fact, 'briga', from which brigand derives, in the Celtic language, means strong. The same etymology explains the military term 'brigade' and 'brigadier', the rank of the Carabinieri.

"You may be born a man, but to evolve, you have to be strong; you have to become a brigand," said Tonino. "They were heroes, helping the poor and defenseless, risking being arrested as criminals." And even on this, Tonino had his idea: "History is not only what men have recognized as significant, but also what they have not considered at all. The latter does not end up in history books, but that doesn't mean it didn't happen or wasn't relevant."

Federico liked to read about these men's adventures and mysteries, erased from school books. Men forged by the flames of coal and steel, who lived hidden and hungry, and who knew how to celebrate until dawn after sharing the loot. Men who walked for days on the highlands and mountains to look for a new cave, a new ravine, a new hiding place not perceivable from the outside.

The most extraordinary episode in their life was escaping from prison. They hid treasures in inaccessible places and then hoped to evade and live to spend their wealth once out of jail. Meanwhile, they had a tough life, often of hardship.

He had read with excitement the story of the bandit Domenico Trabassi, nicknamed 'Stornello'. Stornello was detained in the prison of Sant'Agostino in Teramo. He never confessed. He was tortured, but he didn't speak. He was guillotined in Teramo in the Piazza della Cittadella, 'Anno Dominis 1816, die vero 5 Aprilis'. But the day before his execution, he revealed to one of his cellmates a place where he had hidden two hundred pieces of gold. And told him that he had dispersed the rest in different hiding places, of course, difficult to find.

Federico admired that desire to break the chains of materiality and slavery. He desired to be freer, like a bandit on the mountain, master of himself and his destiny. But the thought of that freedom also scared him.

Is there a difference between those who don't respect the law because they seek the justice that it is not guaranteeing and those who steal for their benefit? Or worse, those who exploit people's ignorance and abuse their power?

His family had always been on the side of legality. Carlantonio arrested the brigands. Federico had uncles who served in the Carabinieri; his grandfather had even been the queen's guard. He remembered that once he had said, "It must be nice to be a king or a queen," but his grandfather replied: "Be careful what you wish for. I have seen the cooks and servants—who prepared and served the queen's soup—spit, piss and blow their noses into it. The freedom to do things by yourself is priceless."

Tonino continued: "Many of them were defenders of the rights of the poor, the peasants, the workers: humble, deceived, and exploited. Among the heroes of this resistance, the criminals were infiltrated. The powerful used the same word in the plural—brigands—for the thugs and the warriors to be seen as the same. A label can mislead perception. The real villains are others, dear Federico, and maybe they don't resemble what we imagine a criminal. If you want to know who the new criminals are, go to Aunt Cesidia and ask her to tell you about the letter."

31. THE LETTER

Abruzzo, 7 April 2009

Federico had read about a gentleman in Veneto who, after five years waiting to receive his pension, had discovered that the file had been stuck in the office of a lawyer, a Social Security officer. The lawyer said he would unblock the annuity in exchange for a percentage of the arrears that had been accumulating. But the experienced man was cunning. He agreed, and when the money arrived, he told the lawyer to stop by his house so he could hand it over discreetly. When the official showed up to collect his share, it was a miracle that he was not kicked. The lawyer threatened the man in various ways until the retired man denounced him to the Carabinieri, and the story ended.

However, Balthazar's father, also a lawyer, was not so naive. When the opportunity arose, he spread the rumor that a new law had been approved that would guarantee, for some people, the payment of pension arrears. Thanks to the new, revised formula, they could amount to considerable sums. Along with that rumor, he let it leak that he had worked to unblock the paperwork and that, out of his incredible generosity, he wouldn't issue invoices for his efforts but would accept voluntary offerings. The lawyer told Aunt Cesidia that she wouldn't be entitled to anything since her situation "wasn't included in this law."

When they received the arrears, the pensioners talked about it and decided that a thousand euros each were an adequate sum to donate to the lawyer. However, there must have been a mistake since Aunt Cesidia also received many arrears. The difference was that she didn't feel obliged to compensate anyone since Don Cesare had told her that she wouldn't be entitled to anything.

When Balthazar heard that Cesidia had received the money, he wanted to prove that he, too, was worthy of the family tradition and that he knew how to do his job. At least, what he believed his job to be: taking advantage of his power and getting rich on the backs of poor people. And so, he took a step longer than his battered leg. Not having the finesse of his father, he wrote and signed a letter with the name and address of the law firm. He reproached Aunt Cesidia for being ungrateful: "We would have liked to see some more tangible gratitude, such as we have received from all your fellow villagers, who are much more thankful than you." Balthazar was so accustomed to this kind of attitude that it may have seemed normal to him to write what had always happened before his eyes since he was a child.

However, he had not noticed a minor detail. Everything had always taken place without witnesses and without committing anything to paper. According to the twins, who were also lawyers, this was a glaring naivety. They did not doubt that this letter was proof of the dishonesty and the family's vexatious attitude towards the village and, in any case, the abuse of the profession. That letter was documentary evidence, almost a signed confession, of extortion.

"I'll report him to the police," said Aunt Cesidia.

"Shut up," responded her irritated son, Maurilio.

"Why? Are you afraid, Mauri?"

"These people are powerful. What if he had been able to let you get those fat arrears after all? What do you know about it? Do you understand anything about laws? It's better not to fight against them; one day, they could be useful to defend us."

"To defend us? And from whom? From themselves? They are the vultures. You are still not getting it?"

Although Aunt Cesidia was against it, Maurilio went to the bank in San Demetrio and withdrew a thousand euros. He then put the money in an envelope and sent his wife to deliver it to Balthazar's father. When the lawyer's French wife, who already knew everything from the rumors in the village, met Maurilio's wife at the door, she felt her face bleaching. She gestures to her husband, swinging her head side-to-side and squinting her eyes. And Don Cesare, although unaware of the facts, refused the envelope, saying nothing was due to him. After the lady left, with a thousand euros more than she expected, the wife confided to her husband what she had heard, and he slapped their son: "Have you gone mad?"

"But Dad, you always did it; I thought it was right."

"You're an idiot. Have you noticed that we never put anything in writing? And if someone refuses to show gratitude, we don't do anything; we don't put any pressure. Now they have a piece of evidence in their hands that can get us into serious trouble."

When they referred to her as the 'great refusal', Aunt Cesidia understood the importance of the letter and crammed it in a hidden place. Her son insisted that she entrust it to him, but she didn't give it up. Maurilio returned to work in Varese, no one said anything more, and the letter was forgotten. But not even the blow he received from his father could put out of Balthazar's head that Aunt Cesidia had evidence against him.

"Why did you never report it?" asked Federico.

"Because I wanted time to think about the pros and cons. I don't know who their allies are, and I don't know if they would receive the punishment they deserve. Remember that they managed to get your father's murderer acquitted."

In remembering that event, Federico was thrown into the dark well he had managed to drain until then. But now he felt as if it was filling up again with muddy waters at each step he took in what was once his land. A land that had decided to shake so hard that it could make him slip. A misstep now and he may drown; or would he be able to climb those smashed walls and get out of that dark pit?

Aunt Cesidia continued: "On the wave of my anger, I still would have denounced him. Now I understand that I have to find a better way, even if I don't know which one yet. Maybe you can help me."

When Federico later told him about the letter, Vincenzo smiled: "I thought about a way to make him pay for all his heinous crimes, once and for all. And we don't need to wait. Not even a second."

32. THE TZAR'S CROWN

For Vincenzo, revenge was a dish best served hot, and for his taste, this particular plate was already turning too cold: "In the attic of the lawyer's house, there are stolen valuables. If we take them, they will not protest because they are there illegally. We rip them off with their weapons."

Federico reacted: "Are you proposing to go and steal from the house of those who exiled me and threatened me if I came back? You wanted this from the beginning, didn't you?"

"No, the idea just came to me now. No one lives there at the moment. Balthazar sometimes goes there to wash his car on Sundays. Come on, let's practice a bit."

"By stealing from the most powerful lawyers in the area, right?"

Vincenzo ignored the sarcasm: "We have to walk there. We take the loot out of the house and hide it in the woods. Then we pick it up in the next few days."

"That's what the bandits did not to slow down their escape. The greediest ones were often captured because they hesitated to separate from the loot," Eleonora added.

Federico chided Vincenzo again: "So, you make me come here to visit Tonino, to look for ancient treasures, buried who knows where, but first, just to be sure we live an even more absurd story, we are arrested and put on trial."

Vincenzo became impatient: "Federico, if you don't want to come, then don't. I am going by myself."

Federico knew that Vincenzo could not see well. Who knew what he might encounter on his own? He sighed and, as always after protesting, accepted: "All right, I'm coming. But promise me we will return if we see someone on the road."

"Promise. You don't want to get caught on the first day, do you?" he said, giving Federico a pat on the back.

And so, by nightfall, they went to the lawyer's house. All around was wilderness. You could hear the cicadas' sounds and see fireflies' lights. Federico moved as if the Secret Service was chasing him. But no one saw them. They arrived in front of the immense black wrought iron gate.

That same gate was identical for over a hundred years, except now it was controlled electronically.

"How is it possible that I have just arrived and already feel as if I'm doomed?" commented Federico.

"Don't worry, Federico; the lawyer comes here as often as a mayor dies to wash the car or to bring some girl he is hiding from his wife."

Federico had no more arguments. Classic Vincenzo: they had already performed many similar deeds as children. It was always Vincenzo pulling him into situations that he couldn't avoid. He knew it was wrong, but he followed him. He consoled himself by thinking they wouldn't find anything and that at least it would get that idea out of Vincenzo's head.

They knew the house well, as they had spent many summers playing table tennis in the cool basement, sheltered from the hot sun. There was one room where they had never been before. The attic. It was always defended by Balthazar's mother: "C'est interdit!"—"It's forbidden,"—she warned the children who approached it. She wouldn't let anyone in, not even her son.

Vincenzo put a ladder on the wall and climbed over it. He then pulled it up with a rope and placed it on the inner wall. They went down, leaving the ladder there as Vincenzo winked at Federico: "We also have to get out of here."

In his backpack, he had burglary tools, and they managed to get in through the garage: "See what kind of an Arsenio Lupin you have as a friend?"

They turned on the flashlights and looked around. They saw Balthazar's large gray rubber boat, parked as if it was ready to take flight: "I'm going to punch a hole in this raft."

Federico took him by the arm: "Let's not waste our time. Forget about stupid revenge."

The house didn't seem to have suffered any damage: "They always have the most beautiful and best-built houses."

They reached up to the loft. With his lips up as if to kiss his nose, Vincenzo approached the door and imitated the French accent: "Sett-un-ter-dee," and placed a cutter on the lock.

"Double burglary," muttered Federico.

"We are like Robin Hood, Federico. We steal from the rich to give to the poor: us."

"It seems that we are just thieves. I wonder why I ever follow you."

Vincenzo pressed the handles of the cutter, and the lock broke. At that precise moment, Balthazar's phone vibrated, and a camera began recording the scene: Vincenzo and Federico examining every place, closet, and cupboard.

On the walls were their pictures as kids: at the river, at the stadium, Federico and Balthazar competing for the oval ball. In one photo, Balthazar was hugging Eleonora while bringing her hair to her mouth, both leaning against his bike. Federico wanted to smash it and throw it out the window, but he held back. His father had taken many pictures, and there were only a few after 1981: the graduation and the wedding of Balthazar, his mom and dad celebrating their 25th anniversary, and Balthazar with his son.

Federico was surprised that his enemy had kept the Lima electric model train—H0 gauge, 1:87. All railroads were in place, running and turning among the tiny houses, the trees, and the crossings. All were standing on a large plywood base. He swallowed, smiled, and turned it on. The beautiful 77 steam locomotive started to move and disappeared in the first tunnel to re-emerge on the other side of the papier-mache mountain. Everything was exactly as his father had built it with Don Cesare, under their kids' wide-open eyes and fast-beating hearts. The only difference is that all these carriages with their amusing labels, like RESIDENZA MILANO or OFF VICENZA, now looked smaller. But everything worked so smoothly; it was evident that Balthazar had kept the whole mechanism in fantastic condition with thirty years of careful maintenance. Federico turned it off, being mindful to leave everything as he had found it, and joined Vincenzo again in searching the loft.

They couldn't find any stolen items, jewels, or precious pearls.

Vincenzo gave up: "That damned gimp took everything away."

"Or maybe they never had all those treasures, hidden amphorae, valuable paintings, and ancient artifacts. Wasn't there supposed to be a golden crown too?"

"Yes, he always said that when he named himself Tzar."

Federico pointed his finger up: "Look."

They saw the camera light; they didn't even have time to swear before hearing the entrance gate squeak and a large car roaring on the pavement growl. They went to the window and saw Balthazar stepping out of the vehicle with Ceccótt and pointing his rifle towards the house, moving it as if he was looking for someone to shoot:

"Come out with your hands up."

Federico and Vincenzo looked at each other and then descended the stairs four steps at a time. They reached the ground floor in less than ten seconds. Balthazar operated the remote control and lit the streetlamps in the garden, illuminating it like the Tommaso Fattori stadium when there was an evening game. A cat jumped out of a bush, and Balthazar fired without even assessing who or what it was. The cat—bad luck for it since it was not black and therefore pretty visible—was thrown a few meters away by the bullet's impact.

Federico looked at Vincenzo: "Let's surrender. He will kill us."

Vincenzo escaped from the door towards the back of the house. He went by memory and paused, trying to stay in the shadows: "He who surrenders is lost. Follow me."

He slammed into some wire nets, a noise that Balthazar would have heard for sure. When Vincenzo arrived at the wall, he climbed the ladder's steps, put his hands on the wall, and jumped in the direction of the woods. Balthazar fired, and Federico saw Vincenzo dive and disappear into the dark silence of the forest.

Still, on the edge of the garage door, Federico went up the stairs, returned to the attic, opened the dormer window, and climbed on the roof. He closed the skylight and lay down between the tiles in the exact middle of the top. He hoped they wouldn't be looking for him if they had seen Vincenzo and could not spot him from the ground. He heard them coming up to the attic and then going down again. The engine noise and the gate clanging as it closed made him sigh with relief. Federico decided to remain still, however, at least for the length of time of a rugby match, plus the break.

Better to be safe than sorry.

He wanted to ensure that Balthazar didn't see him in case he came back, had second thoughts about some detail, or left Checcótt lurking inside the house. He didn't hear Balthazar looking for Vincenzo outside the fence. Perhaps he had missed him then. His phone vibrated several times but he resisted answering or reading the messages. Even though he had put the phone in silent mode, he didn't want to risk them seeing the light from the screen.

In that first half of his imaginary rugby match, he thought about Manfredi in the hut. He worried about Eleonora, who was taking care of him, and about the excuses she would be telling him to explain why daddy hadn't returned yet.

He assessed the situation: *how the heck did I ever end up on this roof—and how would I get down?* And he had put himself in this predicament only to find that the mysterious attic contained nothing magical or valuable. Maybe Balthazar's mother put there tomatoes, or chickpeas, to dry.

He decided to come down to the darkest side of the house. He hung himself from the roof ledge, swung once backward, and on the way back forwards, he let himself fall onto the balcony below. He was not used to that kind of jumping, and when his feet touched the floor, his legs bent, his chin snapped down against his knee, and he heard the sound of his teeth banging against each other. *"The head weighs more than anything else,"* his grandfather used to say.

He repeated the same procedure from the second-floor balcony, carefully controlling more of his legs' cushioning effect. He swung and let himself fall while thinking about softening the blow and keeping his head up. But this time, his left foot landed on something he had not seen, and his ankle twisted and gave in. He found himself lying in the grass, with his hands around his sore ankle and a scream that exploded deep and dumb into his throat.

He looked around. The garden was no longer floodlit. The mountains did not cover the moon anymore, and his vision had meanwhile adjusted to its light. He limped over to the wall—*who took the ladder?* Thanks to a large bin used to collect rainwater, he pushed off on his right foot, the one that didn't hurt, and managed to pull himself to the top of the wall. He fell into the cornfield, and because of the pain in his foot, he lay face up again. At that moment, he felt the weight of a man on his body and found himself, face to face, with a mocking grin.

"I never had so much fun in all the last thirty years."

"You are mad, Vince," said Federico with relief mixed with anger.

"Come on, admit that you feel younger. It must be the air of the mountains; what do you think?"

"He could have killed us, and you are laughing?"

"Instead, he killed a curious cat."

"There was nothing in the attic. It was just a fake story like all your others about the treasures of the bandits. I wonder why I still believed you."

"This is the gratitude I get for waiting for you here for an hour?"

"And how did you know I would have come down after just one hour?"

"I didn't know it, Federico. I would have waited for you until you had arrived."

33. HAMLET

Castellana, 7 April 2009

They returned to the hut, and Federico railed against everyone:

"Are you happy now? There was nothing in the attic."

"Then let's move on to the next plan."

"The super mega backup plan? The grandfather's stories?"

The twins nodded: "He's right; they're just fables for children."

Vincenzo wouldn't let go: "If we look at the clues, we can do it. The province is in turmoil. It's now or never; let's take advantage of the confusion and search."

"And how? Do we start again as we did with Balthazar's loft? In fact, who knows if he has already recognized us through the cameras."

"Cameras?" asked Eleonora, surprised.

"Yes, they were in the house," confirmed Federico.

"They didn't see us. It was dark; we used flashlights in front of our faces."

"Come on guys, can you believe those lawyers leaving the treasures to you? And even those of the brigands? Somebody would have already found them if they had ever been there." It seemed apparent to the twins.

Vincenzo didn't give in: "And I say instead that we don't lose anything in trying. If there is nothing: oh, well. But if they are there as I believe, I solve my problems, and you solve yours, Federico."

"But we don't know anything about anything," noted Federico.

"So, let's start with anything," replied Vincenzo.

Eleonora took a banana. She put one end to her ear and another one near her mouth. She imitated Federico's Milanese accent: "Hello, this is Federico. Who is it?"

She continued, now mocking the more rustic accent of Vincenzo: "Hello, Vincenzo here. Come, there's a treasure to dig."

Then she grabbed another banana: "Ring-ring," and put it to her other ear: "Hello, this is Stefania; where is Manfry? You kidnapped my son; you brought him into the apocalypse!"

And on the other ear, again imitating Vincenzo: "Whom are you talking to? Hurry up."

While Eleonora acted out the scene of uncertainty and of being pulled from one side and the other, Federico felt at least understood, even if lampooned.

"And now, what will my Hamlet do?"

He tried to resist, but then he gave in and smiled. Then he looked at her: "You're holding the phones upside down; they need to be reversed. Even monkeys know you have turned the bananas the other way around!"

Eleonora also puffed out a laugh, and the others joined in.

Tonino arrived at the hut. His face was dark, and everyone stopped laughing and kept silent: "So you tried to rob the house of the most powerful man in the area. I don't like him either, but if you think you can do something like that, I wonder what kind of sawdust you have in your head. Chipboard, perhaps?"

Federico replied: "I didn't know …," but Tonino cut him off. "You are right; you don't know. Between acting without having all the information and acting without knowing anything, there is a bit of a difference."

Federico looked down. When Vincenzo got him in trouble, he felt he was the real culprit.

Vincenzo didn't give up, though: "If there is any clue, it is in your old house, Federico. Let's go there."

Federico reiterated: "I have already looked everywhere."

Vincenzo's enthusiasm rebounded: "I don't think so, you were a child, and there were always people around. Don't you want to check if, by chance, you could come back and live there?"

After getting used again to his homeland, Federico was more open to the idea: "At least I want to see it."

Eleonora replied in a low voice: "Maybe, in the end, you will be happy to live in Abruzzo again."

"I don't think so. They say that you go back to where you have been happy and well, and in this place, I have been worse than everywhere else."

Vincenzo let a bite of truth escape him: "Did you do so well in Milano lately?"

34. THE GROTTO

Vallecupa, 8 April 2009

They let the night pass and then went to Vallecupa. The house of his grandparents, then of his parents, and now his, was nestled between other houses. It had an irregular shape, running both uphill and downhill compared to the nearby streets and houses. In addition, the mountain embraced one side of the house, excavated inside the rock. It had three entrances. One that gave onto the road above, where once there was a barn; one onto the roadway that descended towards the center of the village; and a third gave access to the cellar via a narrow and more sheltered alley.

Since he had lost everything, Federico had thought of coming and living there. Perhaps he could have sought employment in L'Aquila if everything had worked out. After seeing the window frame on the ground, he understood that hope was remote; the house had been damaged, and the repair time would have been too long. Not to mention the distance from Manfredi, who would stay with Stefania. Still, as they approached the house, he held a faint hope, along with his breath.

They had to enter through the cellar door on the lower street because the other two entrances were blocked by the rubble that had fallen inside. Federico sighed away that last hope lingering in his lungs: "First the window of the room, now the blocked doors: It will be difficult to live here in the short term."

The cellar had no windows, and the power had been disconnected for decades, so they lit the flashlights to illuminate the entrance. Federico noticed the sink built by his grandfather with an old semicircular salad bowl that he had buried, along with other objects, so that the Nazis wouldn't steal it. In recovering it, digging with a pickaxe, they had pierced it. Through that hole, the grandfather passed a tap connected to a water pipe. It seemed to have been built that way by a modern interior architect. Only in this case, it was useful and functional.

They went through the door, down three more steps, and entered the cellar. Federico's flashlight illuminated pieces of iron, drawers, and various containers. The objects of his childhood: pipes, wrenches, and T-shape pipe connectors. "Same stuff; there is nothing special here."

Vincenzo noticed some debris on the floor: "I think that if the earth is still shaking, this roof will fall on our heads."

Federico pointed the flashlight at the ceiling and then moved it around a bit, and when the light beam flashed high on the wall, just above the debris, it revealed a black hole as big as a rugby ball.

"And what is this?"

"We always thought it was a foundation wall in the cellar, a supporting wall," observed Vincenzo.

"And instead, there is something behind it," said Tonino, who had also brought a ten-pound sledgehammer.

"What do you need the hammer for, Ton?" asked Vincenzo.

"A good hammer is always useful, as well as a good rifle."

He picked up a piece of iron from a box full of screws and nails and scratched an X on the wall. Then he handed the hammer to Federico: "Hit with all your strength; I am too old."

"What? It's already semi-destroyed; do you want me to give it the *coup de grace?*"

Meanwhile, after having parked the car where it could not be seen, Eleonora arrived with her brother Giulio, who had heard the last exchange of words.

He came forward: "Give it to me."

Federico was about to protest that this was his house when Tonino banged on the wall and then leaned towards Federico: "Do you hear it rumbling? It is empty behind. It seems to be leaning against the mountain, but no, there must be a room behind it."

Giulio took the hammer and unloaded his biceps and triceps against the wall. A sound of thunder filled the room.

"Let me have a couple of hits," Vincenzo said, taking his chance with the hammer. Then a final bang by Giulio, and the light of the flashlight was absorbed by the darkness of the gap that had opened.

Federico approached to look inside: "It's a cave."

Eleonora looked at Federico and smiled: "Your grandfather always told us about a grotto, remember? I didn't even know it existed; I thought he made it up just to entertain us."

Federico returned her smile, but for a different reason, or perhaps, in a kind of way, it was the same reason.

They continued to smash the bricks, and what was once a wall became a pile of rubble, this time caused by man. They moved a mixture of stones, concrete blocks, and more enormous boulders to increase the space and enter the cave. As the rocks came away, more and more light entered the cave, which was then seen in its entirety.

Manfredi exclaimed: "Papi, it's like the cave of Ali Baba and the forty thieves."

"Open sesame," smiled Tonino: "See, two words are enough."

The earthquake had shouted open sesame, thought Federico, but he kept that to himself.

While removing stones and rubble, Tonino resumed his speech: "Do you remember that your great-grandfather had a construction company? While he was building some houses, he discovered several caves. Many years ago, when this was a hill without a village."

"I also remember that a cave led to the pine forest. Because of the terrain, it could not be seen from the village, so my grandfather brought his family there in secret to hide them from the German soldiers during the war. They also had hidden food there, like cheese and salami."

Tonino knew the history of those places as his beard: "These caves were common, and from them comes the name of the village: Vallecupa."

"Ah, is it not because it is a 'gloomy and sad valley'?"

"When have you ever been sad here?" asked Eleonora.

"Ah, before the earthquake, never, but now..." continued Vincenzo sarcastically.

"Smart aleck."

Tonino continued: "The ground below is full of caves, and the bricklayers, when they beat it with hammers and mallets, heard the earth respond with a gloomy sound: the response of the caves."

Vallecupa, the Valley of Caves.

Federico also remembered his father telling him that his great-grandfather Carlantonio had managed to avoid the Nazi searches thanks to a grotto next to a spring, which cannot be seen from the outside.

After some work, the opening was large enough, and Federico entered it feeling a sort of reverence, followed by the procession of the others. The flashlights began to blaze in every direction, bringing surprises. The scent of the grotto took Federico back to our primitive roots just before he noticed several tools, including an ax, hoes, shovels, and a pickaxe. Other objects were resting on the shelves; they were unusual and didn't seem to be standard furnishings. Federico recognized only the oil lamps.

"They look like digging tools," said Tonino.

"With metal detectors included in the offer?" the twins joked.

And in the cave, there was also a metal detector, one of the first built in Italy in the 40s.

"I wonder if it still works?" asked Vincenzo.

"Everything here has been sealed for decades," remarked Giovanna, "with no humans inside. And since most of the dust in a house is old skin, nail fragments, and clothing fibers. It still may."

"Ew, ew, ew," Eleonora snapped.

There was also an altar, and Federico searched the tabernacle. When he opened it, he seemed hypnotized by its contents. It looked like an antique wooden chest carved manually: "What do you say, shall we open it?"

They all looked at each other as if they were about to open Pandora's box.

"It is your legacy, go ahead," Vincenzo urged him.

Federico opened it as if it could explode and then took the lid off once he caught a glimpse of its contents. There were papers, photographs, ink, an inkwell, and wax seals. Federico stared at the objects with eyes of desire. He could resist almost anything except stationery, such as paper and writing tools.

"Isn't there a treasure?" said Vincenzo mockingly.

"It does not seem so. They are paper. Let's take them with us; I want to examine them in a quiet place."

He checked that the casket didn't have a double bottom and then put it back, empty, into the tabernacle. They closed the cellar and drove back to Tonino's house.

Stefania, meanwhile, called every day, many times. Federico had the excuse that there was no phone signal or lied, saying he was engaged in some rescue operation. When the phone rang this time, he cut it short, saying that he was driving, and passed the phone to Manfredi: "Mom, Mom, there is also Maya, Dad's eagle! And we found Alibaba's cave!"

And then she started the usual bullshit with Federico: "What possessed you to bring him where there's been an earthquake? Are you sleeping in a hut? Are you serious?"

"Ask him how it is," handing the phone to Manfredi again.

"Mom, it's beautiful; it's like camping in a stone hut. The shepherds and woodcutters built it. Sometimes everything shakes, but on the ground, there are so many building pieces that you can use to build entire houses."

Federico took the phone back to hear Stefania shouting: "Excuse me? Did you just say that everything is shaking?"

And then, as often happens in that area surrounded by mountains, the call dropped.

35. IN TONINO'S LIBRARY

Villa Sant'Angelo, 8 April 2009

Returning to Tonino's house, he invited them all downstairs: "Come on, underneath, we will have more space, we'll work better, and nobody will see us."

Tonino guided them through a narrow staircase dug into the stone and completed with marble steps.

"Aren't you afraid to live here, given the earthquake?"

"No, not here. The earth has been compacted over the centuries and has already absorbed all possible blows."

The staircase wasn't illuminated; Vincenzo placed his feet, making sure of each step, always keeping one hand on the handrail and the other touching the wall. Manfredi stopped in front of what may have looked like a hole in the floor: "Papi, can you please give me your hand? The staircase is narrow".

Federico passed in front of him and went down the stairs backward while holding his son's hands. In the end, he met Eleonora's eyes, who turned as soon as Federico noticed.

"Papi, do you know I can go down the stairs backward, too?"

Federico smiled at him: "Of course, I know that."

It was an underground library with wall cabinets and shelves carved in stone. There were all kinds of musical instruments: wind, string, and percussion. It looked like a lutherie store that you might have seen inside "The Library of Babel" story by Borges.

Tonino made room on one of the four tables on which books, maps, pens, and sheets of paper of various sizes were placed. Federico began to pass his fingers over the documents they had found. He could not keep his thoughts straight as Tonino smiled under his beard, seeing that intense interest. They were handwritten, a masterpiece of style drawn with sepia, black ink, on paper of yesteryear quality, held together by a leather lace: "It's a wonder, look how each letter is written."

Federico was ecstatic at the presence of those documents. He caressed their weaving; he could smell the fragrance, his eyes danced on the inscriptions, and he turned them all around following the ancient letters' embellishments. "It seems just like Carlantonio's style of writing."

Tonino tapped his index finger on his right nostril several times: "I bet you never even looked at your wife or caressed her and smelled her like that."

Federico blushed at that comment. For a moment, he felt guilty for not having been an attentive husband. He found refuge again in reading through the papers, moving his eyes from side to side, dwelling on the passages that seemed most dense with meaning. There were references to the Gospel, sages of the past, and even some poetry in a forgotten language.

He decided to return to these later when he was calmer. He was looking for something else now. He kept turning the pages until he came to one that stopped his breathing.

He had no doubt: *the 'Note'*. It was different from the rest of the papers in format and writing. It was even more elegant and artistic in black ink and partly in red. Federico looked at it, focused away from it, and brought it closer, tilting his head as if he couldn't see it well. Awed by the writing, he was confused by what he was trying in vain to decipher: "I can't understand it. It is a strange language. I will read it to you, even if I don't know what it means."

Federico held it in front of his eyes and spoke out loud, with the solemn tone of someone who knew what she was saying:

> *"Cooth gousams revt de toors vol you to use*
> *ipofe de logq dit sbrat de sholes am twams,*
> *perow de towel dit heifems sethuge,*
> *pesathes de witel srobamc wad de wamths.*
>
> *mew rame wad de romc eye imth dem wad ess,*
> *de rettels amto vacules tulm you warr,*
> *thafame de brige imth dem ats sun you cuess,*
> *de sine dit haththem lests om nijol Harr.*
>
> *de Ome imth Omry dit heilts gim ravt*
> *qmowm py dose dit rofeth imth cife de cavt."*

After a few seconds of silence, the first comment was by Vincenzo: "What is this? A child rhymes in a language between Sardinian and Croatian?"

"It sounds Hungarian to me," said Giovanna.

"And what do you know about Hungary?" Vincenzo mocked her.

"I'm always Hungary. Don't you always say, 'speak as you eat'? And you, what did you eat, Vince? A pig with all its pigskin?"

Federico stayed focused: "I hope we can find some clues in some of these books."

Giovanna preferred technology: "Wait, I'll put a few words in Google Translator."

Federico said a few words of the poem, and Giovanna pressed them on the telephone keyboard and pressed send.

"How can you use the cell phone without a connection here?"

"Tonino has Wi-Fi here, moron."

Google Translator replied: "Language detected: Esperanto."

"Did you see?" Vincenzo was satisfied. He felt he was right whenever someone else was wrong, even if he never got one right.

"But it's not even Croatian; you are wrong as well. And in any case, it doesn't translate the words, look. It doesn't work."

Eleonora rubbed her hands, hunched her back like a crone, and imitated a shrill voice: "It is an ancient secret recipe of witches. We must find all the listed plants and magic ingredients and then go to a 'café'. That's what it says."

"And all the rest?"

Tonino searched the shelves and found an Esperanto book: "I have always been fascinated by this language. It was born at the end of the nineteenth century in an attempt to create an international language and thus promote understanding and relationships between people."

"And what does it sound like?" Federico asked, becoming curious.

"Mi fartas bone."

"Was it not a language to create peace and understanding?"

"It means 'I am doing well'," Tonino reassured him.

"However, I would point out that we now have a real, actual clue," said Vincenzo. "I was right, men and women of little faith."

"Wait before you claim victory," Giovanna warned him.

"So much for the idea that I could have put together the pieces of the various stories and tales. If we hadn't found these papers, we would still be at square one," Federico remarked.

Vincenzo spoke as a wise man: "At last, you now understand the saying, 'He who seeks, finds.' This is the truth."

But searching both in the Esperanto book and in Google Translator, they could not find anything. The words were similar to some translated words, but none corresponded to a good translation of the poem.

"One step up and two steps back," said the twins.

Vincenzo ignored the comment and insisted: "Federico, now comes the interesting part. We have to start putting the pieces together right now. Come on, let's see what your years of study and reflections have been good for."

Federico was dismayed: "Not a word of this 'note' is easy to understand."

They searched the library of Tonino but found nothing. They read about 'Caesar's Cipher' and the 'Enigma Code' deciphered by Alan Turing. They were fascinating reads, but nothing that resembled what was bewildering them. More than just a codified text, it seemed to be written in a foreign or ancient language.

Giovanna made one of her scientific observations: "Manfredi, did you know that squirrels hide their nuts so well that they forget where they put them, and in the end, they find only half of them?"

"I didn't know that. What fools."

Vincenzo didn't understand: "So what?"

"So, when you write something with a code, you should at least leave a few elements to give you a key. Otherwise, you lose everything trying to hide it."

Tonino still looked for the clue on the paper: "Giovanna is right; let's look at all the documents we found. Maybe there are indications about the code used."

They took the pages in their hands again, each in turn so that everyone could see them with different eyes. They seemed to hold in their hands an ancient crystal vase worth millions. They turned each page over, held them to the light, superimposed them, and read them backward.

Nothing.

They applied all the most absurd approaches but couldn't get to the bottom of it: "The more we go on in this research, the more absurd it seems," sighed the disappointed twins.

Tonino turned to Federico: "There is no indication of how to decipher this note, so we have to start all over again with different methods. Choose another angle because something is eluding us. We also have little time, maybe only a few hours, before Balthazar finds out that you are in the area and comes looking for you."

"No worries, I know how to hide."

"Be careful not to overestimate yourself. Here, even collapsed walls have eyes and ears."

Then he looked at everyone and encouraged them: "Come on, we don't know it yet, but it is clear that by analyzing that language in another way, the clues will become clearer. Let's think better; Giovanna is right; if it is written like this, it means that we can decipher it with the elements we have."

"It depends. If those who hid the treasures reasoned like squirrels, then they wrote the poem in such a way that nothing will ever be found again," said Giovanna.

"Didn't you say that at least half of them are found?" quipped Vincenzo.

He snatched a smile from everyone. It seemed like they were children again when Tonino would submit riddles to everyone and then reveal an unexpected solution.

There was only one difference. This time Tonino had no idea how to solve it.

36. THE VIDEOS

Balthazar thought he recognized him: "I'm sure it was Vincenzo; let's check the recordings."

They saw him opening the door and entering the room, always with the flashlight that, dazzling the cameras, didn't show his face, thus preventing a secure identification.

"It was him; I can tell you. I recognized his agility and hesitation due to his vision problem."

"He's a monkey. Do you remember how he climbed as a kid?"

"I should have shot him instead of that cat."

"You will have time to take revenge."

A detail attracted Balthazar in the video:

"Stop, go back. What is that?"

"It's his shadow."

"Caused by what light source? The moon?"

"Go back with the recording, don't be silly."

Behind Vincenzo, another person covered his back. Balthazar's anger exploded: "Damn it, there were two of them."

They watched the few minutes of the video, looking for some clues that could direct them to a trail. In one frame, there was something that made them both jump. You could see the light hitting the other man's face, and under his cheekbone, there was a small sign: "Zoom in, Checcótt."

Vincenzo's flashlight moved upwards for a tenth of a second; the beam of light illuminated his mate's cheek, thus revealing the shadow of a scar.

"I know one guy with that cut. The mark left on him that day. I still have a limp from that accident."

"That bandit has returned."

"But why did they enter here? What were they looking for?"

"Weren't there some ancient amphorae, Tzar?"

"What are you talking about?"

"Why, then, did your mother keep that room locked and keep us away, saying 'sett-unter-dee'?"

"She would put her things there when you guys came to play and, to prevent us from breaking them, she would lock it. She wouldn't let me in either."

"And why keep it locked today?"

"Just a habit; now the attic is full of memories. The key is in the cabinet right in the hallway. If they had seen it, they wouldn't even have had to break the lock."

"What about the Tzar's crown you were always talking about?"

"I made it up to have some fun. There are neither amphorae, stolen paintings, jewels, or crowns. Did you really believe those jokes?"

"Well, actually."

"He can't be here just for that. What is he looking for?"

"No idea, but I will find out. And we will make them pay. Rather, how do you feel knowing that he's back?"

Balthazar squeezed his eyes, paused, and then nodded several times: "I have been looking forward to it."

"Meaning?"

"I was missing a rival, an enemy in this disaster."

Checcótt rubbed his hands and grinned: "Then we have to find him. I'm looking forward to it as well now."

"And not only that. I already thought about a way to make all of this useful for our plans."

37. THE SECRET ALPHABET

Villa Sant'Angelo, 8 April 2009

Giovanna proposed a less linguistic and more empirical method: "Since we don't do well with the subtleties of language, let's solve it the old-school way."

"And how, without a key?" Eleonora wondered.

"And what does 'old-school' mean?" asked Vincenzo.

"Instead of looking for a key, we try to understand the structure rather than its meaning. We can observe and analyze the basics of language. The shape of articles, verbs, conjunctions; they have rather predictable lengths and positions."

"And which language do we choose?" Vincenzo seemed reluctant to give up the possibility that the text was in Croatian.

Giovanna wanted to move on to some and avoid getting bogged down in useless discussions: "Let's start with one hypothesis. We may later discard it. But let's start; otherwise, we will look at this 'note' forever and never play it."

"Can't we search the internet for phrases like 'how to decipher messages hidden in a cave in Vallecupa'?" joked Eleonora.

"Tonino's Wi-Fi has stopped working. The line is broken; maybe one too many shakes."

Federico took the cell phone. No signal either.

"There is zero reception here; you have to go up to the corner of Aunt Dorentina's house."

Federico moved to go out, but Eleonora stopped him: "Don't go outside, don't let them see you."

He smiled at her: "Whom do you expect to be around at this time of night?"

Federico got out and went up the stairs behind Tonino's house. To its right, Aunt Dorentina's house had been left without the entire facade, opened like a dollhouse. The streetlight in front of it was at the height of the second floor and illuminated an intact room, even though it lacked the fourth wall. The bed with the iron backrest was still there; next to it, the bedside table and, leaning against the opposite wall, a closet with the classic mirror door, like the one in his grandmother's house. He had to climb the pile of stones that once were walls to search for a signal. As he climbed, he heard Stefania's messages piling up. He texted back, lying:

"Everything is fine. Manfredi is asleep. Reception here is weak. We will call you tomorrow."

Federico was still dazed by the mixture of sadness for the devastation he had seen and excitement for the stunning discoveries. The Internet gave him some answers, so the annoyance of Stefania's messages mixed with his enthusiasm for the new findings. And in the distraction of those conflicting emotions, which he didn't know and could not handle, he didn't notice that Checcótt, Balthazar's henchman, saw him from the street.

Federico reread what he had found and ran back to Tonino's house. When he went down the stairs, they all stood up: "I didn't find much, but there is perhaps a trail: the frequency analysis to break ciphers. Al-Kindi first studied them in the ninth century. This was the most important cryptanalysis discovery until World War Two."

Giovanna was surprised: "What an idiot, it's true. How could it have escaped me? I have even seen a documentary. So, if the message was written before the war, we could break it with normal tools."

"Tools? What tools? Those of the cave?" asked Vincenzo.

"I meant pen and paper. We know that the most frequent letter in a text is the letter E. We check which is the most frequent letter in the ciphertext and replace it with E. Then we continue in the same way with the other, less frequent, letters."

"In this way, we have a chance to solve it 'the old school' way," said Tonino ironically.
"I didn't understand anything: to me, you are speaking Arabic," had to admit Vincenzo.

"Let them do it, Vince because we'll never understand what those engineers and mathematicians are saying," sighed Eleonora.

The inventor of Morse code was one of the first to use this principle to give the simplest codes to the most frequent letters. The most frequent letters he came up with were first E, then T, and, after them, a group of other letters, O, S, A, I, N, and H.

Federico counted the most frequent letters of the poem. As he did, he looked at Eleonora with a smile. Certain letters appeared many times: it seemed the right trail. But when he put them in order, he had to swallow a morsel with a taste bitter than he had expected: the most frequent letter of the ciphertext was E, then T. The complete frequency list was as follows:

Letter	E	T	H	O	S
Frequency	46	43	28	26	25

Giovanna was the first to get it: "We have a problem: the most frequent letters in the poem are the most frequent letters in the language."

Tonino, who had been more hopeful than anyone else, was disappointed: "You are saying that because of that, a substitution would produce the same text, word by word?"

"That's right. I don't understand how this is possible," Federico said, dropping his arms to his side: "These guys were smarter than we thought. There is also a message in those frequencies: ETHOS, character. They were familiar with the Morse Code and suspected we would have tried this way."

Vincenzo understood less and less: "Can you explain it to a mortal like me?"

But Giovanna was already thinking of something alternative: "Wait for a second, Vince. Let me think."

They tried other possible solutions. But there was always a piece missing. Working with the other elements of the language, they always found something interesting but never conclusive."

"We may have used paper and pen as tools, but they still make us look like fools," huffed Vincenzo.

Meanwhile, Checcótt, too, had found a signal for his phone: "I thought to check around Tonino's house, and I saw Federico."

"Excellent," replied Balthazar, his smile could be felt through the phone. "He has always been careless. I want someone to keep an eye on him. I want to know where he goes and what he does until the moment he delivers himself into my hands."

"I can arrange that."

38. MANFREDI

Villa Sant'Angelo, 8 April 2009

They turned on the radio to hear the latest news and take a break to refresh their minds before getting back to the task, as when you start a new card game by shuffling the deck. The bulletin reported criminal incidents. Two thieves had been arrested in Onna with loot worth eighty thousand euros, obtained by rummaging through the rubble of abandoned houses.

Vincenzo could not resist: "Since we have not yet understood anything about the 'note', I think that looting is the most profitable business. If you don't get caught, of course."

Federico was about to blurt out a response when Manfredi came out with a sentence that pierced the air: "Papi, the poem seems written in the strange language of Nonno."

Federico turned: "What do you mean?"

Manfredi explained: "Nonno said '*yowl gow sams*' every time the twins arrived, as Vincenzo said. And you sometimes told me that he used weird words instead of the right ones."

The twins confirmed that was the case, and Federico weighed the affirmation: "'yowl gow sams', 'here are my two suns'; he always translated like that; maybe we have a trail."

Giovanna replaced the corresponding letters, but no particular meaning emerged.

"Wait," exclaimed Federico, "what if it wasn't, 'here are my two suns,' but, 'here are your cousins?'"

Giovanna followed the logical thread: "'Yowl gowsams', 'your cousins'; I can see how 'G' becomes 'C', and 'N' becomes M."

A memory took wing in Federico's mind:

"Do you miss Xhurthyx, your friend?"
"Her name is Zhuldyz, Papi."

"Xhurthyx instead of Zhuldyz," Federico continued, remembering how his father misspelled some names: "I think you're right, Manfredi. Your grandfather didn't distort names at random; he was giving us the key to a code."

The excitement accelerated Federico's heartbeat and refined his senses as if in battle. He continued with greater ease: "Listening to the sound, I can hear 'L' naturally becoming 'R', and 'Z' becoming 'X'."

"How couldn't we notice that the substitution letters are similar in sound? With this trick, the poem seems to be written by ancient or foreign lyricists. That language doesn't exist, however. But it sounds like it does. Pure Genius."

"Yes, when they spoke this way, they seemed to be doing so in an actual language, which some perhaps mistook for a northern dialect."

"And even the awkward phrases of The Cripple are perhaps invented with the same system: Siamt Betel, Snirr Thool, Farri."

"Yes, Saint Peter is in the hamlet above Villa Sant'Angelo, Tussillo. Then 'Siamt Betel' is Saint Peter, and 'Farri' is 'Villa'."

"Yes, 'L' becomes 'R' again, then 'F' in place of 'V'; 'A' and 'T' are exchanged as well."

"'R' and 'L' are both liquid consonants, and 'F' and 'V' are velar consonants. They are articulated with the back part of the tongue against the soft palate. They are voiced similarly and so can be exchanged. Same for 'A' and 'T'," Eleonora said.

"And how do you know these things?"

"I learned it from the speech therapist."

"The litmus test is 'Snirr Thool', which is the small door."

"So, the sounds of the letters resemble each other, a vowel with a vowel, consonant with a consonant."

"Yes, and some letters remain unchanged, such as E, T, H, O, S, as we suspected, to keep the text difficult to crack. And maybe send an implicit message as well."

"It's too easy; I understood it this time, too," Vincenzo said, shaking his head.

"Now that we have discovered it, it does seem easy," said Eleonora.

"I wonder how it never occurred to me that my father was talking in that code." Federico still couldn't believe that he was never the least suspicious.

"It is a variation on the previous point; it seems obvious when you know it. A famous scientific law also known as: 'Hindsight is 20/20'," offered Giovanna.

"I knew I was too old for these things," said Tonino. "We needed all of you, much younger and fresher."

Federico smiled and looked at his son: "And without Manfredi, the youngest of us all, we would never have gotten there."

Giovanna summed it up: "So, letters are exchanged based on similarity of sound and the way they are voiced: lip, palatal, dental consonants. B and P, F, and V, D and T. Same with vowels with similar openings A and I, for example. E, T, H, O, and S are not substituted to make the text harder to crack with frequency analysis."

"How well articulated you are, my dear engineer," Eleonora teased. Giovanna smiled and further simplified the scheme, building a table of substitutions:

B	C	F	L	M	U	Z	Y	J	A	Q	D	E	T	H	O	S
P	G	V	R	N	W	X	Y	J	I	K	TH	E	T	H	O	S

She replaced the letters of the poem one by one, copied them all, and passed the paper to Federico: "Here it is. Ready. To you, the honor and privilege of reading it out loud."

Federico squinted his eyes, cleared his voice, and began to recite.

39. THE POEM

"Good cousins left the tools for you to use
above the rock that split the shores in twins,
below the tower that heavens seduce,
besides the water sloping with the winds.

New line with the long eye and then with ess,
the letters into figures turn you will,
divine the place and then its sum you guess,
the same that hidden rests on Major Hill.

The One and Only that hearts can lift
known by those that loved and gave the gift."

Federico was spellbound: "It's beautiful."

Vincenzo was slightly less convinced: "I could almost understand it better before it had been deciphered."

Tonino was even more ecstatic than Federico: "The Carbonari—'the charcoal makers'—were a secret order, and they referred to themselves as Good Cousins. Making charcoal in a stove refines and purifies the wood. This process was symbolic of their 'ethos', their character. This is why there were objects such as salt, coal, and ladders in the cave. Those are all Carbonari symbols. We could be on the brink of a sensational discovery."

"Then forgive us if we point out that it was thanks to us, 'your cousins', that the cooker piece has been deciphered," said the twins, echoing each other.

"Cooker piece? What are you talking about?" asked Vincenzo.

"Yes, that was the name of the Carbonari compositions and speeches," confirmed Tonino: "Well done, you are well-prepared."

"Thank you, thank you all. You are wonderful," and the twins bowed as if they had received a standing ovation.

"You should then prepare a nice carbonara with those cookers, dear cousins," replied Vincenzo, licking his lips.

Tonino smiled but didn't divert from the wonder: "Did you know that, according to some scholars, the Carbonari were born here, in

Abruzzo? It started as a society of mutual aid, motivated by religious faith. Each of those objects has a precise and deep symbolic meaning."

Federico wanted to satisfy a curiosity that he had put aside: "And what are those rust stains?"

"They are those left by a small ax used to open and close the meetings."

"I don't like hatchets."

"Your great-grandfather Carlantonio, at a certain point, began to study the history of brigands and charcoal burners. He spoke about them for hours to your father and me. He told us how a core group of people—the Carbonari—were considered brigands but worked secretly for humanity's future."

"In Abruzzo? The future of humanity?" laughed Federico dismissively.

"Why, what's wrong?"

Federico remembered his father saying to him one day: "People often think that important events are taking place elsewhere or have happened at other times in history. Could you recognize if something fundamental was happening right before you now?"

He had once again fallen into the trap, so he shook his head and turned his attention back to Tonino, who resumed his memories: "Carlantonio said many times that he had seen a piece of paper, what we all know now as the 'note', in which there were written the instructions to find a treasure, but that he had never understood anything about it. It was never clear if he hid it or if it had never existed. I feel guilty of not having believed him to the end."

"I think, however, that we have found it and even deciphered it," Giovanna countered and read it out loud again.

The twins raised their eyebrows: "It may have been deciphered, but we don't seem to understand it any better. Even the civil procedural law exam at the university was easier. Vincenzo is right."

40. THE BROTHERHOOD

Carlantonio ripped the thigh from the quail's body and put it on the glove. The eagle flew down from the hill, swaying on the force of gravity, always keeping his eyes on the prey. It braked by rotating a two-meter wingspan and controlling the airflow with the ends of the wings, as if they were fingers, to slow down without stalling. It landed on his arm, tearing the quail flesh to pieces with its beak.

He took its leather laces—the jesses—to make sure it wouldn't fly off and put the hood on it: "That's enough for today." He adjusted the shoulder strap of the rifle and resumed climbing his path. He took off his hat to feel some air on his forehead and, putting it back on, looked up towards the village. The sunset light was reflected unusually, and Carlantonio sensed something wasn't right. He squinted his eyes and noticed the helmets of the German soldiers who had come to rake the village and commandeer donkeys and horses. He tightened his jaw while felt his fist clenching inside the glove.

The German army had taken advantage of the disorientation following the removal of Mussolini and the armistice signed by the new Italian government in 1943 by invading the country. With "Operation Oak", the German paratroopers freed Benito Mussolini from where he was held prisoner by the Italian government on the Gran Sasso. In a matter of days, the German army got the better of the Italian armed forces and created the Gustav Line in Abruzzo. The Germans began the retreat when the allies broke through that defensive barrier. Onna was identified as the seat of a supply company for the withdrawing troops, and the headquarters was located in the Pica Alfieri Palace. Every day dozens of soldiers passed by to refresh themselves and resume the march.

When some of these soldiers seized two horses, their owners went to the palace to protest. A brawl ensued, and the young owner of one of the horses escaped, taking refuge on Mount Archetto, the hideout of a group of partisans. However, the seventeen-year-old daughter of the family that owned the other horse was captured. Since she refused to answer questions, she was beaten and then killed by the military.

Nine days later, the 114 Jäger-Division led by General Hans Boelsen arrived to complete the reprisal. The soldiers gathered about thirty people, asking for information about the fugitive's family. Some women handed the man's widowed mother and sister to the Germans, hoping to obtain clemency. The military dragged the two women and fourteen other men—between fifteen and thirty-eight—into a house belonging to the family of the young runaway, shooting all those present and then blowing it up. Ten other places were mined, and others were looted and damaged.

Carlantonio turned to retrace his steps down the path when he heard a squad arriving right below him. He braked with his boots, turned around again, and, quickening his walk, took off the eagle's hood, released the jesses, and threw it towards the sky. He hoped the military would have been distracted by the sight of the raptor.

I hope they won't shoot at it or that if they do, they will miss it.

And then he ran to the fountain. He realized he could still make it without being seen since the hill had hidden both him and the eagle. Meanwhile, the other soldiers in the village were seizing cows, farm animals, and objects considered valuable, such as pots, shovels, and picks.

The arch-shaped fountain leaned against the hill and provided water to the village. Four spouts came out from its wall, with water flowing into a pool one meter wide and five meters long. From it extended a stone table, made smooth by centuries of clothes rubbing against it by generations of washerwomen. To the right, a smaller arch allowed the water to flow downstream to join the Aterno river. It was almost all walled up except for an opening down low, about forty centimeters high.

He went to the opening, turned away from the wall, and lay on his back, with his head towards the dark entrance. Then he emptied half of his lungs, held his breath, closed his eyes, and pushed himself inside with his heels slipping on the bed of aquatic plants and slime while keeping his rifle as high as possible so as not to get it wet. Once his feet disappeared under the wall, he resumed normal breathing and paused for a few seconds looking into the gap between his two shoes. The field was still clear.

They didn't see me. And they didn't shoot.

He then stood up in a cavern twice as high as himself and took a long, relieved breath. He walked away from the water and sat down on a rock. He was still counting, and when he reached thirty, he heard the voices of the military and the barking of the dogs muffled by the flow of the underground stream. He imagined them dominated by their anger, walking on the wet stones outside the spring, which over the years, had caressed the bare feet of the village girls. Even though his mind went mad, and he didn't want to believe what was happening, he knew they would neither see nor hear him. From the outside, you could not detect the presence of the hidden space, and he, passing through the water, had left neither traces nor smells that the dogs could have perceived. Inside the cave, there was the roar of the waterfall of the stream coming out of the mountain, and it covered the noises of his breath and the heart that thundered in his chest.

In another cave two hundred meters higher up, hidden under his house, a ritual was taking place that had to begin even if he was missing.

The Grand Master used a hatchet as a gavel, calling the meeting to order, and began: "To the Glory of the Grand Master of the Universe, and our Protector, St. Cesidio, and under the auspices of the High Order of L'Aquila, the Respectable Lodge of the Order of the Laurel opens its work to seal the Chamber of Honor and go to the Mountain."

He continued solemnly: "The task that awaits us is grave. We will face it with sincerity of heart and with the usual contempt for danger".

They had a precise purpose for the meeting: "Here is the writing in which secret places are shown, where the donations of our brothers are hidden. We propose to leave these as a future recourse to ourselves or our progeny, and only in case of extreme need".

The Grand Master deposited the poem inside a casket and closed it into the tabernacle on the altar. Then he recited the other passages of the Rite: "May knowledge reach us through the spirit and essence of Socrates, who passed on to us the philosophy of continuous learning. As well as through the glorious chain of transmission: the Egyptian priests, Zoroaster, Osiris, Thales, Plato, the numbers of Pythagoras, and Cicero's oratory. And since the Sun no longer illuminates our Forests, it is time to close our work. To the Order, and standing".

The Grand Master struck the hatchet three times, and all rose: "To the Glory of the Grand Master of the Universe, and under the auspices of the High Order of L'Aquila—the Eagle— the Respectable Lodge of the Laurel closes the works. We swear secrecy and to meet at the first opportunity, with greater fervor, even if decades should pass".

All raised their hands: "I swear".

They left in the cave shovels, pickaxes, and a metal detector. They took the mason's tools, went out, and completed the brick wall, the same as the adjoining cellar wall; they sealed the entrance to the cave and, with it, the gate to a world that would never return. They washed their hands at the pipe from the wall and broke up the meeting. They went out thinking to disperse in every direction, but instead, they were intercepted by a German raiding team. They were not deported, they were not tried, but lined up along a wall and, while they were saying in unison: "In virtute vera Felicitas"—"True happiness is found in virtue"—they were shot with machine guns.

Carlantonio saw the light of dawn filter three times through the access slot to the cavern of the fountain. When he left, he ran home. His wife came to him with a baby in her arms, a few months old.

Thank God they are all right.

He went around the house to go to the cave. He opened the door and closed it behind him. He went under the stairs, down the three steps, and entered the cellar. The entrance to the cave was no longer there; in its place was a wall that sealed it.

He felt relieved: *They made it just in time.*

He would never see his Carbonari brothers, nor the eagle, again.

41. THE NUMBER

Villa Sant'Angelo, 8 April 2009

Vincenzo took stock of the situation: "Well, the summary is simple: now that we have the whole text, we have no clue about what's next."

Federico smiled when he noticed the rhymes in septenaries.

"Yes, when you think you have arrived, you discover that there is another level. In the spiritual search, you have never 'arrived'," Tonino philosophized.

"Oh, has this search now become spiritual?"

Giovanna wanted action, not philosophy, and focused on the text instead of the comments: "There are some clear instructions and some obscure ones."

Tonino already had an idea: "You are right; the poem refers to numerical divination, as seen from the word 'divine'."

Eleonora seemed to know nothing about it: "And what is this practice?"

"An ancient science of numbers. Each letter corresponds to a digit: 'letters into figures'. For example, the 'A', the first letter, corresponds to 1. Adding together the values of the letters that make up a word gives a number associated with that word. Same thing for a sentence."

Eleonora asked: "And what numerical values do letters have?"

"It depends on the language: in Greek, it's different than in Hebrew or Arabic."

Giovanna continued: "Not only that, but that value must be equal, as the penultimate verse says, to 'the same that hidden rests on Major Hill', but who knows what that number is. As Eleonora said, we never heard about it."

"At least we can say what Major Hill is. 'Colle' is a hill, and 'Major' means maggiore: Collemaggiore, or Collemaggio, where the church that is the symbol of L'Aquila stands."

Tonino was about to continue, but Federico interrupted him: "Wait, Tonì. Do you remember when we went, on the first day of summer, to see the labyrinth of Collemaggio? Six wonderful circles were on the floor, illuminated by the sun filtering from the rose window. And you told me they were not six circles but three 'eights', or the number 888".

"And 888 corresponds, in Greek sacred numerology, to the name of Jesus, Iēsôus. Here you are; you have been served the number and the alphabet."

Giovanna wasn't sure: "The poem says, 'long eye', which we can take as a 'long I', the J, as it is sometimes called. It cannot be the Greek alphabet, however. J in Greek is called 'jota'. They would never have made such a mistake. They were sophisticated enough."

Tonino tried to resume talking, but Federico interrupted him again: "Just a minute, Tonì, I have another idea. They wouldn't have quoted the J if it hadn't been necessary. And if it is not Greek, maybe it is the Latin Renaissance alphabet, which includes the J. Latin was used for solemn occasions, and here we are facing something sacred. They wouldn't have placed the poem in the tabernacle otherwise. And if it says, 'new line', let's go there: how many letters are there before the J?"

Manfredi counted: "A, B, C, D, E, F, G, H, I. Nine."

"Fascinating, the number of all digits. And from J before S? We all agree that 'ess' is S, right?"

Manfredi enjoyed himself: "J, K, L, M, N, O, P, Q, R. Nine."

"What a coincidence, again all the digits," and he filled in a grid:

1	2	3	4	5	6	7	8	9
A	B	C	D	E	F	G	H	I
J	K	L	M	N	O	P	Q	R
S	T	U	V	X	Y	W	Z	

"Here is the new line with J and S. They start each line when the digits are over. We have the correspondence between numbers and letters."

"Do you see how the many years of study have been useful? And now, what's next?" Vincenzo was even more impatient.

Giovanna, too, was getting excited: "Looking at the table, we see that the letters of the village of Stiffe, for example, are S = 1, T = 2, I = 9, F = 6, E = 5. The sum gives 29. So, the value of the word 'Stiffe' is 29."

Vincenzo was beginning to understand but wanted to move on to some form of action: "And what words do we need to translate into numbers?"

Federico completed: "Those of the places whose corresponding value is equal to the number associated with Collemaggio."

Tonino broke in: "Which is the second thing I know about this enigma."

They looked at him with surprise: "And you are only saying that now?"

"I was trying to, but Federico's impatience kept interrupting me."

42. THE QUATRE DE CHIFFRES

Villa Sant'Angelo, 8 April 2009

Tonino loved to tell stories about the history of L'Aquila. Everyone hoped this time it would be shorter than usual: "The Basilica of Santa Maria di Collemaggio is the most famous religious building in L'Aquila. It's considered the highest expression of Abruzzo's architecture as well as the symbol of the city. Pietro da Morrone was crowned Pope right there, with the name of Celestino V, and was buried there afterward. It was the first time in history that a pope was crowned outside Rome. The church is home to an annual jubilee, the oldest in history: the Celestine Perdonanza, or 'Forgiveness'. Celestino V instituted it on the same day he was elected, with which plenary indulgence was granted to anyone who, confessed and communicated, would have entered the basilica of Santa Maria di Collemaggio from August twenty-eight to August twenty-nine's vespers of any given year. The event is a precursor of the Universal Jubilee of the Catholic Church established by Pope Boniface VIII, which occurs every fiftieth year."

Giovanna completed: "And the motto of the event is: 'The first jubilee in history.'"

"That must be why sin is accepted with a certain degree of humor here in Abruzzo. Because every year, we have much to be forgiven for and restart from scratch," said Eleonora.

"If you are cheating stealthy, it means that you are healthy, as the man in the song says, forgiving his cheating wife," quipped Vincenzo.

And everyone laughed; everyone except Federico: "My father, however, has been killed for allegedly cheating."

"Sorry, I didn't mean..."

"It's okay. The song makes me laugh too."

Eleonora was not smiling: "It seems that today it is easier to live in conformity, let's call it morality, than to live in beauty and full realization. We have existed for years, living with minor sins of which we are perhaps even proud, all while committing the greatest, tremendous sin: not living life to the fullest, in beauty and love. Minor sins can be forgiven every year, Celestino teaches us. But the greatest sin of all is to waste an entire life conducting an existence that is not ours. You may be forgiven, but you'll never recover."

Federico swallowed and felt a grip on his guts.

"That's why Celestino V returned the pontifical insignia and renounced the office. He must have realized that it wasn't what his soul was longing for."

Tonino let them reflect for a few seconds, then stood up: "The three 'eights' story is fascinating, and we need to understand it. Federico, do you remember that we also visited the octagonal tower?"

"Yes, of course. The base of what used to be the bell tower."

"Right. In the Basilica, the number eight can be found many times. Eight is also a reference to infinity, as the symbol of infinity is an '8' placed horizontally: ∞. So, on a spiritual level, the octagon represents man's attempt to rise to infinity. Christianity used the octagon as the shape for baptismal fonts. The meaning is that, through baptism, human beings acquire the potential for spiritual elevation."

"Then the hidden number is eight. We have it!" exulted Vincenzo.

"Nope. Eight is also associated with many other monuments. The octagonal plan, for example, is found in several buildings: the convent of the Order of Christ in Portugal, the Micalet in Valencia, the Castel del Monte of Federico in Apulia, the Qubbat al-Sakkra, the Dome of the Rock in Jerusalem; just to name a few."

"And we want to find a number that is only associated with Collemaggio," Federico completed.

Tonino nodded: "And what about that particular symbol, which looked like a four with a circle near it, that we saw on the basilica floor? We moved the benches to take a picture of it."

"And we were also yelled at."

Even Vincenzo seemed to remember: "The *quatre de chiffre*? We still have the photos at home, buried somewhere."

Vincenzo drew it: "Let's see if I remember it."

Eleonora squinted her eyes: "It looks like the key to an ancient door."

Vincenzo laughed: "To me, it always seemed like the rat trap that Grandpa used to make with the wooden sticks and the brick on top."

"I know what it means," interrupted Giovanna. "There is the cross and the four that symbolize it; in fact, the cross has four points; and then there is the triangle that means the trinity, and the circle represents the infinite. Have I been good, Toni?"

"Fantastic. It's a part of the whole explanation. Let's follow another trail instead. That of the mark of Mastery, of the Great Work. And let's start from the magic square."

"Magic square?" Manfredi raised his eyebrows.

"This is fun, look."

8	3	4
1	5	9
6	7	2

"The sum along the rows, columns, and diagonals is always 15. All digits from 1 to 9 are being used without repetitions."

"Cool!" Enthused Manfredi.

"Now rotate the symbol of the *quatre* by ninety degrees to the left, point the cross on the nine of the magic square and note how another nine is formed upwards."

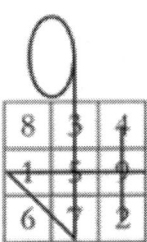

"The figure crosses all the squares except the eight. Federico, your father told me that this can be interpreted as 'the eight is the way to the nine.' He had read it in a book he worshiped. The pillars that support Collemaggio are, in fact, octagonal. The 'eight' supports the 'nine'. The nine is the arrival, and it's no accident that it's also the last digit.

They were all in silence. The air had changed.

"Many churches in Europe have their own *quatre de chiffre*. Each sign, in addition to the *quatre*, is different to give a precise signal on the symbolic meaning of that place. You can understand what message is hidden in a basilica using the magic square. In the same way, Collemaggio has its own. Note that the superimposition has revealed two 9's. The one where you center the *quatre de chiffre* in the magic square and the 9 of the key handle."

"Twice 9? That is 99?"

"That's right. The eight represents balance; it's associated with baptism, a symbol of initiation, the beginning of the search, or 'the way to nine'. Whereas nine has the meaning of hidden, occult, secret knowledge. Secret knowledge means that it's not apparent; it's not material but is connected to divinity. It is spiritual."

Manfredi asked about the magic square: "How beautiful; in addition to the fifteen, is there also the 99-magic square?"

"Of course, Manfredi, I'll write it out for you."

36	31	32
29	33	37
34	35	30

"If you add columns, rows, or diagonals, you always get 99."

Federico summarized: "Therefore, the number associated with Collemaggio would be the same one associated with L'Aquila?"

"That's right."

"Why didn't they write 'the number of L'Aquila', then?"

"It would have been too obvious."

"Since it is not obvious, how can we be certain? We should find at least one other way to prove our theory."

Tonino was just waiting for that moment: "And indeed, there is one. And I promise that it will fascinate you."

43. THE GORGES OF CELANO

24 August 1937

The gigantic gate of the lawyer's house was so famous that his grandfather, Don Mimì, was nicknamed "Black Gate". They were a noble family, possessed extensive lands, and no one could remember the last time they needed to work. People like them were the favorite targets of the brigands. To Franco, these families were synonymous with the abuses against the peasants. He considered them, above all, the real obstacle to the creation of the republic.

So, he kidnapped the younger son of Don Mimì. The request was a ransom in family jewels; among them was a specific request for a golden chimney pendulum. At first, the gendarmerie said they were already on the bandit's trail, knew where he was hiding, and would capture him. Strengthened by that confidence, Don Mimì rejected Franco, sending him a message: "I won't give in to any blackmail."

Franco threatened him: if Don Mimì didn't pay, he would cut his son's ear off. The father still resisted, and just when the gendarme admitted they had not found the bandit, Don Mimì received a jewelry box. A short note asked him: "What is the most precious thing in your life?" Don Mimì opened it and fainted on the floor, dropping a piece of bleeding ear.

When he came to his senses, he felt guilty, cursed himself, and gave in. He was instructed to show up alone along Rio La Force, before the Gorges of Celano, with a donkey and the required ransom. He collected all the necklaces, rings, and bracelets, and just before putting the pendulum in the bag, he called his servant and told him: "Engrave these words on it: 'Black Gate'."

"But it's a nickname; I didn't even know you knew about it, Sir."

"Of course, I know about it; do you think I'm unaware of what people say? Even if it's a nickname, it's all the same. Indeed, it's even better."

He went to the appointment, following the instructions to the smallest detail. Franco made him wait for hours until, from the bottlenecks dug by the stream in the gorge, between the 200-meter-high rock walls, he materialized in person: Franco himself, the ferocious bandit. He rode a steed while Don Mimì's son was hooded on the back of a donkey. He brought the boy down, and the father saw his son running toward him when he removed the hood. They hugged each other for more than a minute, and when he regained his composure, Don Mimì thought of the mutilation; he checked his son's ears and saw that they were intact.

Franco laughed: "It was a cut of a pig's ear."

Don Mimì seemed relieved: "This is the happiest day of my life."

"Interesting," replied Franco, "and above all, stupid."

"How dare you still taunt me? Isn't the pain you caused us enough?"

"You have had your son under your eyes for eleven years. You have been able to hold him as tightly as you are holding him now for more than four thousand days. How many times have you done it? Yet only today do you say it is the happiest day of your life. Isn't it stupid?"

Don Mimì remained silent after that observation. Franco continued: "What matters is not what a person has or what he doesn't have. What matters is what he is terrified of losing."

Don Mimì rallied and responded: "And you, brigand, what are you afraid of losing?"

"I wouldn't call it fear, but the thing that would bother me to lose is my freedom."

Franco took Don Mimì's loaded donkey and exchanged it for his: "Go home, but first let's play hide and seek: put these hoods on and count until ninety-nine. Then take them off."

His laughter dissolved among the thousand echoes of the serpentine paths of the Gorges of Celano.

44. THE CROSS OF COLLEMAGGIO

Villa Sant'Angelo, 8 April 2009

Tonino showed them a book with a picture of Santa Maria di Collemaggio: "Let me show you what your father had discovered. We have observed that we can get numbers from letters and from numbers, architectural models. First, are you aware of any other church with a similar facade?"

"Not that I know. Its design is unique. Even the cross motif is so particular that it is called the 'Croce Aquilana', The Cross of L'Aquila."

"Collemaggio is extraordinary," commented Vincenzo, "one of those monuments that make you proud to be Italian."

"I cried when I saw the apse of the Basilica on the ground," admitted Federico.

Tonino regained control of the conversation: "And do you know how the facade hides a specific number?"

"I didn't even know that there was one."

"What do you see on this book cover? Anything that might have something to do with a number?"

They started to count every element on the book cover: The number of white squares and red squares, the number of crosses, and the number of elements in the rosettes. After five minutes, Giovanna reported to Tonino: "We are confident that we have two numbers, not just one: the rose window wheel is formed by thirty-six spokes, with each spoke forking at the end, so double that to seventy-two."

"You are maybe beginning to understand. But these things are not unique. They also occur in other churches. I want something that can be associated unequivocally with Santa Maria di Collemaggio. Let's set aside the two numbers that you have found. We will need them. What about the drawing itself on the facade? Do you see a number?"

No answer. Tonino turned to Manfredi: "Please write down the times table."

"There is a beautiful lamp. Will you put it on the table? So that I will do a better job?" asked Manfredi.

Federico saw on Tonino's face the exact look that Eleonora had when she noticed Manfredi going down the stairs with hesitation.

Tonino didn't comment; he took the lamp and tightened its base to the table: "Sure, here it is."

Manfredi adjusted himself on the chair and began to write the table that we all, except Vincenzo, had studied at school:

1	2	3	4	5	6	7	8	9
2	4	6	8	10	12	14	16	18
3	6	9	12	15	18	21	24	27
4	8	12	16	20	24	28	32	36
5	10	15	20	25	30	35	40	45
6	12	18	24	30	36	42	48	54
7	14	21	28	35	42	49	56	63
8	16	24	32	40	48	56	64	72
9	18	27	36	45	54	63	72	81

Federico took Tonino aside, his arm around his shoulder, and whispered in his ear, squeezing the words between his teeth: "Wouldn't it be better if you told us what you know? Let's hurry because as soon as Balthazar knows I'm here, he will hunt me. In addition, I am homeless and jobless."

Tonino smiled at him but turned around, the movement causing Federico's arm to drop, and continued, with rising intensity in his words: "Come on, don't be lazy. Think about the effort that the builders of the Basilica have made, foremost mental and moral. You have to live up to being Italian. And, by the way, that wouldn't even be enough for you to be worthy of the works you inherited; you should aspire to what their purpose means for humanity."

Vincenzo brought his hands forward: "Let's calm down a bit."

"People make me laugh when they boast about the wonders we have on our territory. But you: What have you created of those beauties? You can't boast of anything. Indeed, I tell you that if it had been you who created them, you wouldn't boast about them at all."

Tonino sat next to Manfredi, and everyone else turned toward them: "Fill in a new table by putting the sum of the digits of the times table's numbers in the respective box. For example, twelve becomes one plus two equals three."

Manfredi did it: "Here it is."

1	2	3	4	5	6	7	8	9
2	4	6	8	1	3	5	7	9
3	6	9	3	6	9	3	6	9
4	8	3	7	2	6	1	5	9
5	1	6	2	7	3	8	4	9
6	3	9	6	3	9	6	3	9
7	5	3	1	8	6	4	2	9
8	7	6	5	4	3	2	1	9
9	9	9	9	9	9	9	9	9

Since Tonino was blocking everyone from getting close to the table, Federico began to prepare the coffee pot. He pressed the ground powder into the Moka. The correct pressure was the key. Too much, and it would have come out burned. Too little, and it would have been dirty water. He carefully kept the water level below the valve to intensify the coffee. He felt he needed it even more than usual.

Meanwhile, he heard Tonino continuing with the instructions:

"Let's go back to thirty-six and seventy-two, the numbers you found in the rosettes. The sum of their digits always equals nine. From this perspective, thirty-six and seventy-two, as well as sixty-three and twenty-seven, are both equivalent to nine."

Tonino passed Manfredi a sheet of large squares, such as those used in elementary schools: "Now use this information to keep only the rows and columns where 3 and 6 are close together. The same thing happens for the 7 and 2. Leave the edge of 9's since it's the sum of the two digits. You see how it will create a connection point: the keystone."

Manfredi kept writing as if under a spell, forced to follow the orders given by a higher consciousness:

9	3	6	9	9
3	7	2	6	9
6	2	7	3	9
9	6	3	9	9
9	9	9	9	9

Tonino then helped him by drawing a rhombus around the two and the seven: "I just rotated the square, where there are the seven and the two, to indicate that the nine can be formed in different ways; nine is seven plus two, but also three plus six. We have nine twice two. Double nine, or ninety-nine."

Manfredi was instructed to color the boxes with the threes and sixes and the box with the nine at the intersection of the rows of nines. He left the space inside the rhombus blank to signal the difference Tonino was referring to.

"This step is crucial because it gives you an idea of what Frederick II was trying to do: Building a bridge between two worlds, two traditions, and two spiritualities. We know that 'eight is the way to nine', and nine symbolizes the inner knowledge that leads to deep spirituality. Here we have two nines to suggest that the way to the nine is not unique. Different spiritual paths can lead to the same result: the perception of the divine."

Federico lowered the stove heat to the minimum so the coffee would have come out denser.

"Manfredi, now put four of those diagrams side by side."

Manfredi continued filling the sheet until he exclaimed: "Papi, it's like the cover photo on your Facebook profile."

Tonino smiled: "Manfredi, what'd you say? Can we show it?"

Manfredi nodded, and Tonino took the sheet and passed it to Federico: "Look now how, for those who can see, the number 99 is hidden in plain sight."

Federico took the paper, and everyone surrounded him, as when they scored a goal as children. The cup fell from his hands and shattered to the ground. They were all amazed. In front of them stood out the pattern that covers the facade of the Basilica of Collemaggio in the unique way for which it is known:

9	9	9	9	9	9	9	9	9	9	9
9	9	3	6	9	9	9	3	6	9	9
9	3	7	2	6	9	3	7	2	6	9
9	6	2	7	3	9	6	2	7	3	9
9	9	6	3	9	9	9	6	3	9	9
9	9	9	9	9	9	9	9	9	9	9
9	9	3	6	9	9	9	3	6	9	9
9	3	7	2	6	9	3	7	2	6	9
9	6	2	7	3	9	6	2	7	3	9
9	9	6	3	9	9	9	6	3	9	9
9	9	9	9	9	9	9	9	9	9	9

45. NEWS FROM ROME

L'Aquila, 9 April 2009

Federico saw Balthazar announcing on TV the first measures taken by the Council of Ministers. He reported them in the way he had learned from his father as if they had been his initiatives and merits. "We are talking to Rome"; "Rome listened to us"; "The Council told us"; "It was important for us that they gave us this and that". Using expressions of this kind, he made it seem as if the results were thanks to him, just as the arrears of pensions of the elderly had been.

"We know there is still fear; we are twenty-eight thousand homeless."

He said, "we are", so he communicated that he was like the others; he was one of them.

The interviewer continued: "How many people died?"

"The death toll has worsened. We have reached two hundred and eighty-one. Twenty of them were less than sixteen years old. The funeral of the victims will be held on April the tenth at eleven."

He wore a tricolor cockade, as those for official occasions, even if Federico didn't know what it represented.

"And the shocks?"

Balthazar continued: "The tremors didn't stop; there are dozens every day. We are happy to note that not all of them are strong. We will go on digging until Easter".

The interviewer was looking for some controversy: "We also know that at times like these, there are sly people who take advantage of the situation to plunder houses, churches, mansions."

Balthazar didn't miss the opportunity: "Yes, the government announced that the crime of looting would be reintroduced. Seven hundred soldiers and police patrol the earthquake zones to catch offenders. Specific rules will be set out in the 'Abruzzo Decree' that the Council of Ministers will discuss after Easter."

"And what about the economy? People can't work; they're in trouble."

"Sure, we know. We will suspend mortgages, electricity and gas bills, taxes, and other fees."

"We will; it seemed like he was the one providing all those possibilities; all he needed was to give some money to the people.

Federico wondered when that moment would arrive, too—and what he would ask in return.

Another service gave the news that the mayor of Pacentro praised the generosity of pop star Madonna. She had made a substantial donation to support the relief efforts in the village where her grandparents on her father's side, Michelina and Gaetano, lived before emigrating to America in 1919.

On a different channel, a journalist suspected that some buildings collapsed because they were built with "low consistency" concrete. To stay within the budget, after winning tenders at low prices, some builders would have tried to save money by using less cement than required by regulation, replacing it with material that didn't have the same adhesive capacity.

Federico argued, with his tendency to always see exceptions: "Are we convinced that the buildings would have resisted otherwise? Some dilapidated houses remained standing, while others that were well-built fell. It depends more on the ground they had underneath."

Giovanna reacted: "Although we cannot say that building with less cement is the cause of the collapses, neither can we deny it. If they had been built according to engineering practices and the law, they would have been, on average, more resistant."

"You have a point."

"There have often been many changes during the construction phase that have moved far away from the initial project specifications and have not always been up to standard."

Giovanna described to Federico how Balthazar and his father had specialized in requesting building amnesties for those who built small villas or other houses. In 1985 their firm helped people to submit applications to be pardoned for even the most egregious transgressions. Some people regularized irregular situations, perhaps even with good reasons, as in those cases where the owners had made changes that would have been compliant if they had been reported. Others, however, were able to get approval even for anti-ecological obscenities.

"The worst was that, later on, their firm started contacting people even before the work began, telling them not to worry if they wanted to introduce changes during construction. Balthazar's father would help them to obtain remission. And so, in 1996, those who went along with them obtained approvals for houses, apartment blocks, and various buildings, all of which may have had any possible construction defect, transgression of town planning regulations, or building plans. And they earned tens and tens of millions of old liras, which added up to hundreds of millions, so several million euros."

Vincenzo sighed: "Who knows how much money they will also be making with the reconstruction; those people are always in the middle."

Those comments seemed gossip to Federico, like the complaints of his ex-colleagues at the coffee machine: "Those who are without sin cast one of the battered stones they see around here. The State grants building amnesties to make money. So, in the end, we are all in agreement. One transgression here and there, then you get away with it by paying, and it's all over by drinking a good bottle of wine. However, I see that you have missed out on one more important detail for all of us and our new venture."

"And what would that be?" Giovanna didn't like to miss details.

Vincenzo mocked him: "Let's hear it; what would it be, professor?"

Federico took a breath and looked at them all: "We will be nine jackals on the run, hunted by the Carabinieri and seven hundred soldiers of the army."

46. FOUR QUARTERS

Villa Sant'Angelo, 9 April 2009 – Thursday

Ninety-nine.

The mystery hidden in the facade of Collemaggio was another confirmation of the number that had always been associated with L'Aquila: 99 churches, squares, and fountains; 99 spouts of the fountain near the river; and 99 chimes of the Cathedral bell. The widespread interpretation is that there were one hundred castles in the area that came together to find the city, but then one pulled back at the last moment: 'One hundred minus one'.

Later, each of the lords of the various castles contributed to the city with a square, a church, and a fountain. Each is remembered with a stone mask from whose mouth the water flows into the fountain of 99 spouts.

To tell the truth, they didn't add up. Federico had done much research and the castles around L'Aquila, including those that had been destroyed, were many, but they didn't reach 99. And even the fountain of the 99 spouts didn't really have 99 of them. The number of masks from which water gushes out is, in fact, 93. Afterward, 6 more taps were added under the parapet on the right side. It seemed as if they had been added just to support the legend of the 99.

Federico also understood that the faces of the masks didn't represent the founding kings. He counted them as a child, and when he reached number fourteen, he came across the figure of a man with a ram's head. His father told him that it was Baphomet, the satanic goat. He mentioned that it had an esoteric, positive meaning in reality and that he would reveal something more when he grew up.

Federico liked the idea of a series of gentlemen wanting to create a city that brought people together. To unite those who seemed to be in opposition was a gift of Frederick II. Federico had always admired that, even if he had never managed to make it happen in his own life.

Meanwhile, these different interpretations made him think. It seemed to him that these legends had more and more layers. One more credible, or more ordinary: ninety-nine castles founded L'Aquila. But when you check it out, it's never proven, almost as if someone wanted to tell you: 'look harder; there's more.' And then there was the more profound level, which rang true: 'eight is the way to nine; there are more ways to reach the Divine.' This more extraordinary level is less verifiable in the materiality of existence and, therefore, more difficult to believe.

Vincenzo had kept his enthusiasm: "Let's be optimistic; we have the number that the poem was referring to. We just have to look for names of places that, when coded into numbers according to the numerical table we built, add up to ninety-nine."

"Wait a minute more," Tonino warned him, "are you sure you have deciphered everything? In my opinion, there is still work to be done."

Giovanna joined him: "The poem reminds me of the symbols of the L'Aquila banner. Perhaps the treasures are hidden in the four quarters of the city."

"Explain a little more, please."

"The symbol of the quarter of Saint Peter: 'Blue sky with a bird on a tree planted on a grassy ground.' And birds are those 'that heavens seduce.' The quarter of Santa Giusta is where you find Santa Maria di Collemaggio; the symbol is the cross, the same one we find on the facade. I thought that the reference to 'the rock that split the shores in twins' was the baptismal font of Collemaggio, the blessed water in the rock stoup. The fountain of the ninety-nine spouts is in San Giovanni: 'the water sloping with the winds'; wind, in the sense of air, could represent the displacement of air caused by a waterfall."

"Fantastic, Giovanna," Tonino was proud of her knowledge of L'Aquila's traditions.

"And what about the flag of the quarter of Santa Maria, displaying a Moor's head? We are neither under the flag of Sardinia nor in Africa: what is it doing there?" asked Vincenzo.

Amid the symbols of those mountains of Abruzzo, what was the reason for a head of a North African or Middle Eastern person to be drawn on the banner? Federico reflected. That presence in the insignia of L'Aquila had always puzzled him.

"They say it's a representation of the prisoners captured during the Crusades," offered Giovanna.

Tonino invited them to look deeply: "Try again. The Moor's head here doesn't have the classic *tortiglione*, the headband around the forehead and the nape: instead, it has the laurel around the hair. In heraldry, laurel indicates nobility. It was used to crown the emperors of Rome, the victorious warriors, the poets, and the winners of the Olympic Games. We say 'laureate' to indicate somebody who deserves the highest honor."

"Like the one that Julius Caesar had?"

"And then the Moor has a rose in his mouth. The rose symbolizes beauty, purity, and recognized merit."

"Laurel is also a symbol of immortality and eternity since laurel is an evergreen plant. The great religions all speak of the immortality of the soul," Federico added: "Then the Moor of the banner can be a charcoal burner, and his face is made dark by working with coal."

"Even in the banner of L'Aquila, a coal man?"

Tonino seemed to favor that interpretation: "The banner is from nineteen thirty-seven. I wouldn't be surprised if our good cousins, the Carbonari, had influenced the adoption of certain symbols, even for our beloved city."

Giovanna observed: "By the way, have you noticed that the poem is made up of nine decasyllable—as in Shakespeare—except for the last line, which has nine syllables? So, ninety-nine syllables in total. This is further confirmation of the correctness of the number."

"There is also the rhyme in chained triplets. Three verses of thirty-three syllables, like the Divine Comedy, also formed by ninety-nine songs: three of thirty-three," Federico completed.

Giovanna joked about it:

"With two decasyllables, I will tell,
I can't see anything in it but hell."

Eleonora tilted her head:

"Ah, what an improvising poetess,
The decasyllable is your best dress."

Federico smiled and diverted the discussion: "It's unlikely that nobody would have already discovered these treasures if they were in the city. Assuming they were ever there, of course. With all the work and renovations done over the years, or even if the earthquake had brought to light some of them, as Vincenzo likes to think, we would have known about it."

There was total silence.

Tonino resumed speaking: "They left a metal detector in the cave, and most of the treasures have been found with similar tools. People searched the fields, first, to locate the mines and unexploded bombs after the Second World War, and then they found, by chance, buried coins or other valuables."

Giovanna followed his lead: "The bombardments in Abruzzo hit Sulmona and Pescara, both important railway and road junctions. Furthermore, Avezzano, in just a few months, underwent almost one hundred bombing raids by the allied air forces. They wanted to destroy Rome and Pescara's road and railway communication system. In this way, it would have been impossible to send a supply of weapons and ammunition to the German forces stationed between the Gustav and Caesar lines."

Tonino opened and closed his eyes with anger and barked between his clenched teeth: "In addition to killing ninety-four civilians in Avezzano, they destroyed three-quarters of the architectural heritage rebuilt after the earthquake of nineteen fifteen."

"And in fact, they still today find unexploded bombs in these areas from the Second World War," recalled Giovanna.

Federico, always looking for exceptions and equivalencies, found a counter-example: "You forget at least two episodes. The first is in Campana, where the Allies' objective was the tunnel and the railway station. A bomb destroyed a house, but it didn't explode. I think it's still there; I don't remember it ever being found. And then the twenty-seven planes, also of the Allies, which on the eighth of December blew up the train station in L'Aquila together with the '*Officine carte e valori della Banca d'Italia*'—known as the 'mint' by the citizens of L'Aquila—because it had become the coffer of the German armies in Italy. More than three hundred people were killed."

"Of course, I do remember. The gusts from the explosions dispersed hundreds of freshly printed banknotes in the area, and those who rushed to grab them became rich."

Vincenzo could not resist: "Do you see it, professor? Do you need another example of money jumping out of chests in the rubble, whether it's below the roar of planes or above the subterranean wind of the earthquake?"

Tonino invited Giovanna to finish the reasoning: "So what's your conclusion?"

"That there have not been too many bombings in this area, so no one has ever searched with a metal detector. This means that in this part of Abruzzo, no one has ever found, 'by chance,' buried treasures. In addition, the area is not a nerve center, nor are there many attractions that lead people here. If the treasures were here, they're probably still here."

"I don't understand why they didn't just put the treasures in the cave and let that be the end of it," said Vincenzo.

"Because houses change ownership, and if someone had found the treasure, it would have become theirs," the twins countered. Their preparation in jurisprudence made them hyper realistic.

Federico concluded that he was not sure it was a positive one: "So the 'note' indicates places almost certainly owned by the state?"

Tonino confirmed: "That's what I think, that they're not in L'Aquila. Despite the legends and indications, they are in the surrounding area, in natural places, where no one has ever looked for them. Where no one would do renovations or build new houses."

Meanwhile, the twins asked the group: "Have you thought about what to do when we discover treasures?"

They all looked at each other. Federico had not thought about it. Yes, they fancied vague riches, but the logistics of the smuggling, or the method of sale, had not yet entered their plans.

The twins discussed laws all the time, almost as if they had the Civil Code in their hands, but just to be specific, they took a copy from Tonino's library.

"No more codes, I pray," complained Vincenzo.

They solemnly read in turn. How they knew when to stop and leave words to each other was a mystery to everyone: "Part of the unavailable patrimony of the State are things of historical, archaeological, palethnological, paleontological and artistic interest, by anyone and in any way found underground."

"What should someone who finds 'something of interest' do?" Federico asked, almost more worried about the enterprise's success than its failure.

"Whoever fortuitously discovers immovable or movable things must within twenty-four hours notify the superintendent. The Carabinieri are also informed, by the superintendent, of the fortuitous discovery."

"And not even a small reward?" complained Vincenzo.

"Of course, there is one. According to article ninety-two of the Code, 'Prize for Discoveries', the Ministry shall pay a prize to the discoverer, not exceeding a quarter of the value of the things found or by giving part of the findings."

"We would only get twenty-five percent?" Federico was disappointed.

Giovanna joked about L'Aquila's city plan: "Of the four quarters, only one is due to us. It's true that if the value were several tens of millions, even a quarter wouldn't be bad."

"Unless we avoid getting caught," suggested Vincenzo.

"And we keep everything for ourselves," completed Federico.

47. STARTING TO SEE THE LIGHT

Villa Sant'Angelo, 9 April 2009 – Thursday

In the meantime, good news arrived. The shrine containing the remains of Pope Celestino V had been recovered under the debris and transferred to the tower next to the Basilica.

Federico was happy: "May it be a good omen for us and all of Abruzzo. If the saint does miracles, he may do one for us, too. And I don't say this with irreverence."

Tonino brought them back to the task, and Federico summarized: "It seems that the three places have to do with a tower, water, wind, rock, and the shores of a river."

Vincenzo smiled: "You're getting into it, huh? You are chewing on this like a dog with a bone."

"Or the shores of a lake," Giovanna pointed out.

"Great, we have twelve lakes and sixteen rivers in the province of L'Aquila alone, almost ninety-nine castles, each with eight or nine towers. Without mentioning the number of springs, underground streams, waterfalls, and so on," Eleonora remarked.

"It's an impossible undertaking," said the twins.

"I would rather say unlikely," Giovanna said. "Come on, let's get to work, which will be neither easy nor short."

Using the table they had created from the poem they began to calculate the numerical equivalents of all the names of natural places that they could think of, including articles, prepositions, and adverbs of place, for example: mount = M(4), O(6), U(3), N(5), T(2) = 20; castle = 15; river = 36; bridge = 36; on = 11; of = 12; below = 21; the = 15; roman = 25; tower = 27; waterfall = 35; a = 1; bell = 13; above = 18.

They collected hundreds of them and filled pages and sheets even with the numerical equivalents' sums in different combinations.

'Behind Stiffe's waterfall = 33 + 29 + 1 + 35 = 98' Or, 'On the old Roman bridge = 11 + 15 + 13 + 25 + 36 = 100'.

Getting to a meaningful ninety-nine didn't seem so obvious. Sometimes it was one hundred, other times ninety-eight or other close numbers. But never 99. It seemed almost like a game to prevent them from finding that exact number.

"I thought it would have been easier," commented Vincenzo.

"You always think that everything is easier," said Federico.

The twins interjected: "The Carbonari are making fun of us."

"Yes, in fact, it's that 'turn' of letters by which both the I and the R correspond to nine, which makes it difficult to guess the number associated with a word. So yes, it's almost as if they're doing it for spite," said Federico in frustration.

And then Manfredi shut everybody up by standing and reading from the thick sheet of numbers: "Fort eight on a bald hill, twenty-three plus thirty-one, plus eleven, plus one, plus ten, plus twenty-three equals ninety-nine."

"It's not that precise, far-fetched at best," Giovanna seemed skeptical.

Federico wanted to follow the hypothesis: "There are many bald hills in the area. Bald because they are rocky and nothing grows. But there is only one with a fort on top: Cerro hill. And the river Aterno comes against it and divides into two branches, reuniting further down the valley: the verse of the poem says, 'above the rock that split the shores in twins'. That's right."

Tonino smiled at Manfredi and caressed his head: "Extraordinary job."

"Yes, Sant'Eusanio Forconese's Fort. One of those that took part in the foundation of L'Aquila. It's one of the famous ninety-nine."

"I didn't know, however, that it had a number, and that number was eight," admitted Giovanna.

"Perhaps at the time, there was a numbering, or maybe it refers to the number of towers of the castle? There are eight," Eleonora hypothesized.

"Why did you look for the word eight, Manfredi?"

"You have mentioned it so many times that I thought I would calculate it with the diagram. It's the same trick you showed me with that game of passwords and numbers, Papi."

"Let's go right away," urged Vincenzo. "It's getting dark enough not to be seen, but still able to see the road."

"A night on the Bald Mountain: tonight, there is a full moon," observed Giovanna. "What a stroke of luck. It will help us to see better."

Eleonora exalted: "Fantastic! After the last few days now, these coincidences no longer surprise me."

Vincenzo put it on a more occult level: "Or maybe we are witches, devils and damned souls, who meet on top of the hill for the Great Sabbath and in the moonlight will dance wildly."

Federico focused on the work they would have to do: "We need some tools."

They went to the cave below Federico's house to get shovels and pickaxes. When they entered it, Tonino took the opportunity to contemplate the Carbonari objects arranged on the altar, each with its symbolic meaning: the white linen cloth and salt, the red fire, the black coal, the cross, and the green laurel leaves.

On the other hand, Giovanna was in love with the metal detector: "Ever since I saw it, I wanted to resurrect it."

After looking at it again, Vincenzo seemed perplexed: "It's a second world war wreck in sad shape: "It has been here for at least sixty years. Are you confident this thing works?"

"It doesn't. Yet," answered Giovanna. She took some batteries out of her backpack and connected them in series to a sort of transformer that she rolled around the device's handle. She pressed the power button, and the metal detector activated. Everyone looked at her, astonished. She moved it just above a box full of metal tools, and it started buzzing: "Now it does."

48. THE NIGHT ON THE BALD MOUNTAIN

They arrived at the mountain's base and walked along the path. Now that they had gone into action, Federico had second thoughts: "I can feel it. We will end up in jail."

"We are just hiking on a deserted mountain. We are not rummaging through the rubble to steal from old people; we are looking for treasure."

"It's illegal anyway."

"But it's not looting."

"Oh, then we're all set."

They had decided to climb the mountain on the side of the necropolis of Fossa, the less accessible side, without following an already existing path, at least at the beginning. The Fossa Necropolis, with its upright stones, or menhirs, was—with a bit of imagination—their Stonehenge, and bare Mount Cerro, looking like a hard mound of earth and stones, was—with more than a bit of creativity—their Ayers Rock. Of course, the mountain didn't extend for nine kilometers, only two, and it was not eight hundred meters high, only two hundred. Still, it was without any vegetation, just like its Australian counterpart.

Federico's father told him that the hill had sacred connotations too. The necropolis of Fossa is protected by its bulk, and there are still a Neolithic village's remains above it. The mountain seems to come out of the ground as if pushed upwards from the earth's bowels, splitting in two the plain of the Aterno and the river of the same name.

Several are the legends that it has listened to over the millennia and that Tonino and Gianantonio had passed on to their nephews. One that Federico remembered well tells that the mountain was a heap of wheat belonging to a greedy lord. He didn't distribute it to the farmers who worked in his service and who had harvested it. So, it was cursed and became a hard stone on which nothing would ever grow again, a barren hill standing out from the green landscape of the valley and the surrounding hills.

They arrived at the path. A strip made silvery by the moon's light was winding through the arid terrain. To Federico, it seemed they were back in the Middle Ages. They were moving on full moon nights when it was dark enough not to be seen in the distance but with enough light to see where to put their feet, as Vincenzo had remarked. Behind them, the fortress-monastery of Santo Spirito rose, and to their right, the remarkable convent of Sant'Angelo, built on the overhanging rock, watched over the valley.

Although it wasn't noticeable outside, Federico knew that the convent had been damaged. On the day of the earthquake, three friars had been living there. The prayers he said when passing by this night hadn't been heard; the friars had left the day after his arrival.

Dividing the two religious places was the village of Fossa, wrapped in a natural amphitheater formed by the mountain that opens in an almost perfect semicircle.

San Cesidio was born in Fossa. He was a Franciscan missionary who died in China, where he was burned alive, wrapped in a burning blanket, during the Boxer Rebellion. Federico remembered the story well.

"Papi, will you take my hand?"
"Of course, Manfredi. What's the matter? Can't you see well?"
"Of course, I can, Papi."
Federico took his son's left hand and saw Eleonora take his right as she lowered her head to smile at him.

They headed towards the Church of the Madonna, built over the fort's remains on top of the hill. From that position, it was possible to control the valley and the course of the river below. It was a visible connection to the other fortresses located in the strategic points of the territory: San Pio delle Camere, Ocre, and Barisciano. Having castles arranged at suitable distances and heights meant being able to supervise the transport network and the territory.

Federico had always been fascinated with how the watchtowers of the castles communicated with each other through coded messages transmitted with mirrors or with fires when there was no sun.

"How strong was the underground wind tonight? Did you feel it?" said Vincenzo. No one had mentioned the tremor before, almost as if they would have invoked it again by naming it.

"It was strong. The radio confirmed that it had a magnitude of three point six on the Richter scale."

"Will they ever end? Will I still have a home when they do? Or will the next one knock everything down?"

The castle of Sant'Eusanio itself was destroyed several times by earthquakes. In fourteen sixty-two, between the nights of twenty-six and twenty-seven November, there had been two violent tremors, two hours apart, striking many villages in the valley of the Aterno. There had been about one hundred and fifty victims, of which half were in L'Aquila and half in the towns around Sant'Eusanio, which alone mourned thirty victims. In the region's capital, a quarter of the buildings collapsed, and the rest were damaged. Almost all the belfries crumbled, and their bells fell, breaking through the roofs below.

Federico was reminded of a Sunday in August when his family saw a procession carrying the Virgin statue from the Basilica of Sant'Eusanio Martyr to the church on Monte Cerro, where they were heading. His grandmother, who was from Casentino, a rival village of Sant'Eusanio, recited the nursery rhyme suitable for the occasion:

"Sant'Eusanio Forconese, one day
Said it wanted water for the village.
Casentino replied: 'You need money
To buy such an outstanding privilege.'"

If you want water, you have to pay—a lot. An essential resource, is water.

They went around the mountain and, one by one, Fossa, the convent of Sant'Angelo d'Ocre, the monastery of Fortezza di Santo Spirito, Casentino, and Sant'Eusanio disappeared behind the curve. They arrived at the citadel's walls on the opposite side of the church and off the path to decrease the possibility of anyone seeing them, even by chance.

Vincenzo was right, at least on one point: the earthquake had stirred things up. One side of the castle had collapsed, showing a chasm. Giovanna, helped by Giulio, began to pass the metal detector over the ground around the towers. Federico and Vincenzo put themselves on the opposite side of the citadel perimeter to keep watch in case anyone arrived.

When the metal detector began to buzz, it sounded like a war klaxon. Federico and Vincenzo heard it even from their side of the castle. They dropped their tools and rushed around the walls toward Giovanna.

"It's not possible."

"Something's down here if we're lucky," said Giovanna.

"I can't believe it; it must be some old Neolithic metals that have remained underground," remarked Federico.

The shovel and pickaxes quivered to be used, so they began digging. Federico illuminated the spot with the military flashlight he had brought with him.

"What a futuristic torch, Federico."

"Yes, it's American. From Texas."

They dug, they moved stones, but nothing appeared. Federico was disappointed: "As I imagined, if there were something, someone would have already found it after all these years."

"This 'someone' must be the richest man in history," interjected Vincenzo.

Giovanna teased Federico: "Don't you want to see how it turns out? Let's dig and see."

And, even though he didn't yet believe it all the way, by now, Federico was as psyched up as before a match at the Tommaso Fattori stadium versus an aggressive opponent, and curiosity took over.

"All right, maybe it's just a little deeper. I'm going to get the shovel and the pick so that we can redouble our efforts. You can continue smashing the ground."

49. THE SHOVEL

Federico went back to where he and Vincenzo, in their excitement, had dropped their tools. Rounding the corner of a rickety tower, he froze: in front of him, he saw the last person in the world he wanted to meet. His breath stopped, and he felt specific hairs rising on his back that he didn't even know he had.

Balthazar had taken the shovel and was holding it with both hands. The Tzar reeking smell returned Federico's memory to the rugby pitch of their youth. Federico remained stunned, and when he searched for air again, Balthazar's stench sent a gagging wretch down his throat. With bated breath, he checked where the pickaxe was. It was still there on the ground, where he had left it. He raised his head and looked at his childhood enemy. He remembered him being taller. He had the same horrible grunt, though he hadn't seen it when he spoke on TV. Now he seemed to be wearing a mask distorted by the oblique rays of the moon.

Balthazar blew in his face: "What have you come back here for? You have a legal warning never to set foot in Abruzzo."

Federico curled his nose, moved his head backward, and coughed at the stench. Then he regained composure and replied: "I missed you and came to see you. Finally."

"Yes, finally. In fact, it's the end," replied Balthazar, raising the shovel above and behind his shoulder, poised to strike Federico's head.

"Go back to Milan. I warn you."

Federico stepped and reached the tower where the pickaxe was. He hoped to both take it and put himself in a narrower space, among the castle's ruins, where Balthazar's arms would have less room to swing, and hitting him would have been more difficult.

Seeing the shovel ready to split his skull reminded him of when his great-grandfather Carlantonio, already suffering from stomach cancer, was being fed broths and soups. He had a few weeks left to live, but that didn't prevent him from starting arguments if he thought he was right. He got into a dispute with his neighbors, Duilio and Cesira, about the shared border of their land. According to Carlantonio, they had moved the boundary stones to gain a few meters of property. He even pointed out the loose soil where the rocks were initially located. Cesira began to slap him while he was talking and in the end, the husband and wife, taking advantage of his weakness, attacked him.

Federico's grandfather, Nonno, heard his father's cries as he passed by with the cart pulled by the donkey Giulia. He stood up on the cart step, and when he saw the scene, he sent Giulia at a gallop, climbing the hill, breaking through the wooden fence, and driving into the field. Giulia had grainy eyes and dilated nostrils while his grandfather twirled the shovel, standing on the step of the cart with eyes wider than melons, looking for the best point of attack: "You bastards! You are killing a dead man!"

He threw the shovel at Cesira, the flat of it striking her head and causing her to stumble but not fall. Duilio grabbed Federico's grandfather by his jacket and dragged him off the cart, throwing him to the ground. While he was still down, Cesira kicked him in the face. Nonno got up and threw a straight punch that hit Duilio on his chin, knocking him flat in the stubble and putting an end to the fight.

Cesira and Duilio went to the village doctor, the same uncle of Balthazar who had accused Carlantonio of shooting the bandit in the back. The doctor certified the beating. However, when Nonno also asked for first aid treatment, he told him that the black eye and the broken shoulder were not from the fight. According to the doctor, they must have been caused by something else, and now Carlantonio was trying to blame the two innocents.

Nonno had to sell much land to pay for the damage he had caused to Duilio and Cesira, while Carlantonio didn't speak any more until the moment of his death, three weeks later.

The fiery passion for witty and aggressive remarks ran in the blood of Federico's family for generations, and seeing Balthazar with the shovel resurfaced the memory. He had already regretted his words when he realized that what he was hearing was not his own thoughts but his voice speaking up loud: "Do you know what is hilarious? That a donkey may think it's a horse, but, eventually, he's going to bray."

Balthazar roared, turned the shovel, and swung it down as if trying to hammer a spike into the ground. Federico covered his head with his arms and tilted to one side, causing the shovel to glance off his left forearm. It crashed down to hit his shoe, the blow partially absorbed by a stone next to the foot itself.

"Now you will limp, too, and you will know what it means."

Federico, trying not to show pain, as he had learned on the rugby pitch, increased the dose: "True, both of us crippled by pigs. The difference is that the pigs that attacked you smelled better."

Balthazar lifted the shovel again, and Federico turned to run away. He'd barely taken a step before feeling a blow on his back that crushed him. He looked around as he tried to suck breath back into his body; he saw the pickaxe resting on the wall, but it was closer to Balthazar, who grabbed it after discarding the shovel. Federico crawled into a corner of the unsafe wall, only to see Crocko arrive behind him with a fifteen-kilo mallet.

Balthazar brushed his hair back from his forehead and grinned: "You didn't think I would come here without a plan and weapons? It will look like a tragic accident, a leg mangled by the unexpected collapse of an already dangerous wall. 'We tried to save him, but he was too close to the wall.' Our word against yours. And then you will go away. Limping, sure, but you will leave. And I will know that there is justice in this world. If, perhaps, the wall should weigh a little too much, crushing your chest and other internal organs, and you lose your life, well, too bad. You know how it is; Crocko is not always precise in masonry work. I will say a toast at your funeral and remind everyone of your good heart."

Federico spat the little saliva he had left on his face: "I guess you will have one of your relatives sign a fake death certificate like your grandfather did, and then your father will defend you at the trial."

Those references set off Balthazar's wrath, and he threw himself at Federico. Which was what Federico was waiting for. He pressed a button on the Texas flashlight, which flashed a strobe light strong enough to give a Tibetan monk an epileptic seizure. At the same time, it made a sound as loud as a train approaching high speed in a tunnel. Balthazar first covered his face with his hands, then closed his eyes and covered his ears, dropping the pickaxe.

Federico squeezed the upper part of his vest between his teeth to resist the sound and leaned forward as his fingers changed the position of the sliding button under the flashlight. He then pushed a button with his thumb as he touched Balthazar's side with the flashlight. The strobe light and sound of the flashlight were replaced for half a second by a fifteen-thousand-volt discharge.

Balthazar first realized the moment of fear that made his muscles spasm, then felt his spine and bones disappear as if the skeleton had left his body, extracted by a magical entity. He collapsed on himself like a pile of clothes with nobody inside. No pain, no sensation of a shock. Just the feeling of an empty body yielding and muscles no longer responding to any command.

Federico had his momentary triumph and knelt close to Balthazar's ear: "And did you think that I, too, would descend among the pigs without a way to slaughter them?"

The flashlight taser that he had bought Stefania for self-defense and that she had never taken with her, had worked. However, Balthazar got up too soon, and Federico wished the effect had lasted at least a second or two more. Crocko had remained motionless, dazed by the lights and noise, not knowing what to do. Balthazar made a sign, tilting his head to the left to show where he wanted him to go. He advanced towards Federico, who triggered a safety catch at the end of the flashlight, causing a ten-centimeter dagger to appear. This time, however, Crocko didn't approach, so Balthazar retrieved the pickaxe and tossed it to him while he collected the mallet with his right hand and began twirling it.

Meanwhile, the noise had attracted all the others, who had come up from the lower part of the castle. Vincenzo raised the portable video camera and challenged Crocko: "Come on, do it. Do it! You will be on television tomorrow and broadcast worldwide the same evening."

Balthazar was still shaking from adrenaline and the electricity that had run through his bloodstream: "He has a warning. He must stay out of Abruzzo. And you stay out of it. This is none of your business."

"Or what?" replied Vincenzo. "And where do you think you can find that warning? In the rubble?"

Then, turning the camera back to Crocko: "Come on, beat him up. We've been waiting for years to get it over with between the two of you. Come on, hit him."

"You don't need to insist," Federico told Vincenzo as he took two steps backward, keeping his eyes on Crocko's hands.

Balthazar leaped towards Vincenzo and, in a single motion, took the video camera and smashed it to the ground: "Record this, Vince," and then pointed his finger at Federico: "I don't want to see you again."

He took a step forward while Federico continued to look him in the eyes. Vincenzo, a span taller than Balthazar, put the forehead against the Tzar's: "Come on, then."

"You don't know who I am. I will ruin you."

"Sure, but first, I'll crack you like a nut."

Crocko dropped the pickaxe, much happier to switch to fists, and approached to protect Balthazar, waving his arms and swearing.

Vincenzo turned and grabbed both of his waving wrists and jerked them downwards, closing them in his own hands:

"You think you are the only one who can swear?"

Crocko tried to free himself but was handcuffed by the strength of Vincenzo's hands and arms which, as Federico knew, could burst a rugby ball. Vincenzo looked Crocko in the eyes but didn't let go of his grip, holding his hands together at belt height.

Balthazar realized that from then on, the situation could only get worse. His political career was getting dragged into the game, and whatever side he played would be compromised.

"I'll leave you alone. This time," he said magnanimously.

Vincenzo waited a few seconds before releasing Crocko without ever having stopped staring him in the eyes.

"After you," Balthazar said, making way for Federico and the others, who began to descend the mountain without saying words, and without any treasure found. Federico did everything he could not to show that he was limping, leaning on the path.

Balthazar looked at him, sneering; Federico knew that, in the Tzar's evil mind, a movie was already unfolding about how he would carry out his revenge.

50. LEGENDARY CREATURES

They were walking down the path, and Federico trembled and limped. Crocko addressed him: "What was it like to see the Great Tzar again after all these years?"

"Awkward. For me, the Tzar has always been like a kind of legend," admitted Federico.

Crocko raised his voice: "You see, I told you, Tzar, he was crazy about you."

Balthazar grunted.

"Yes, he's like a legendary creature, like the Minotaur," Federico resumed, "He's different, though. He has the body of a man and the head of a …" he paused to release the punch line just as he saw electric flashes in the sky, signaling another tremor. Eleonora's eyes became as big as the moon before she clenched them closed, her nostrils flared as those of Giulia, the wild donkey, and she shouted: "The wind, the wind!" Then she curled up on the ground as the hill began to shake, like a giant alien spaceship about to take off with all of them on board.

It was 9:30 p.m. Federico felt the hill was enchanted, and magic was happening right before their eyes. Then he felt his temples shrinking and his hair standing up on the side of his head and realized the inhuman power of the shock. His neck grew cold, neither his legs nor Balthazar's could hold steady, and they both fell to the ground, one on top of the other. The smell of his enemy was almost like a physical presence itself; Federico shrugged Balthazar, and his stench, off of himself and ran limping towards his son: "Manfredi!" he shouted.

"I'm here, Papi. I kept my balance just like I do on my skateboard. It's easy."

He saw Balthazar get up and take a series of quick little steps as he tried to regain his balance before sliding back down the slope. He clung to Crocko, who remained motionless, holding him like a hundred-year-old oak tree. The vibrations also caused the metal detector to roll down the mountain, stopping against a boulder. Crocko saw it and, first making sure that Balthazar was stable, left him for a moment, picked up the object, and brought it to them: "What is this?" he asked Federico.

"A machine to measure the damage caused by the earthquake. We were testing it," replied Giovanna.

"It seems like a metal detector to me. Although a museum piece," said Crocko.

Meanwhile, Eleonora had brought her hands to her temples, and her breathing panicked: "Oh God, the wind, the wind: it will never end!"

It was at that moment, with his anger now gone, that Balthazar did look around. He must have taken stock of the situation, realizing that the scene was unusual, to say the least. The most normal thing about it had been the shock: "What were you doing up here with shovels and pickaxes?"

"Nothing, all right?" snapped Vincenzo while Federico tried to reassure Eleonora.

"No, it's not all right," Balthazar shot back. "I get it: you're trying the metal detector and then going to the ruins to look for gold, watches, jewelry, and to rob the poor people! Damn jackals."

Vincenzo threw himself at him: "Jackal is you, lawyer-destroyer." Vincenzo seemed satisfied with the assonance.

With his one hundred and twenty kilos, Crocko held Vincenzo still while Balthazar took the pickaxe he had been carrying as they descended. This time he swung it down on the metal detector, putting it out of action: "In three days, you won't be here anymore."

Crocko became cocky: "So Federico, did you think you could fool us? Balthazar is epic, didn't you say so? What were you saying? A legendary creature with a man's body and …."

"And a dick's head," completed Vincenzo.

51. THE COUNTERMOVE

On the way to Castellana, 9 April 2009 – Thursday

Eleonora voiced her anxiety: "What a shock. Thank goodness we were up there and not inside a house."

Federico agreed: "This tremble caused other buildings to collapse; let's hope it didn't cause other deaths."

"And how do we search for the treasure?" asked Giovanna.

Vincenzo looked at the smashed camera: "I have an idea. Our countermove: let's go on TV."

"What?" Federico feared another of those brilliant ideas that always turned into even worse trouble.

"Yes, let's reverse the situation. You thought you were hiding so that Balthazar wouldn't attack you. But now that he's seen you, we need to be even more visible instead of staying undercover."

"What do you mean?" Federico liked paradoxes.

"State that you have come here to help, and Balthazar can no longer touch you. Even the territorial warning will have to be put aside, at least for a while. If he alludes to it, he will refuse help, creating a national stir."

"And how do we search for the treasure on TV?" laughed Giovanna.

"We don't even know if there is one," the twins replied. "It's a bit like the mysterious territorial warning, by the way."

"We know where the treasure is now," retorted Vincenzo.

The twins played the Devil's advocates as they exchanged a look with their raised eyebrows: "Maybe there are just some old iron tools up there. Or some Neolithic metal scraps."

"Do you think Balthazar saw where we were digging?" Vincenzo interrupted.

"I don't think so. I met him far from there, on the other side of the castle."

"And, by the way, who told him where we were?" asked Giovanna.

"The moon," replied Vincenzo, feigning a dreamy look.

"All right, I have a friend who works in TV; I'll call her right away," said Eleonora, who, probably because she had something practical to do, seemed to have put aside her fear from the tremors.

"Federico, remember that to be good with bad people doesn't mean to be good; it means to be foolish," pronounced Vincenzo.

Eleonora called her friend, who told her that she would interview Federico. They would come the next day, around eight in the morning, with a camera, microphones, and the necessary equipment. They would meet just below the hill of the stone hut where the van could park.

"And so, after everyone sees you, you can mix with people, and you will no longer have to hide; you will be protected by people themselves," rejoiced Vincenzo.

"We're uncertain whether we understand this trick well. How does it work?" the twins said in unison.

"Nowadays, everything takes place in the media," Eleonora said, "Perception is truth. If you hide, it means that you are a criminal, a thief. If, instead, you advertise yourself as someone who has come to lend a hand, it's always more difficult to refuse your generosity at times like these."

Giovanna didn't let her guard down: "I bet Balthazar will also counteract by going on TV and telling his story. He goes on air every day."

Federico bit his lips: "We have to get there first."

52. THE WOLF

Thanks to the full moon, they could find their way to the hut without using the flashlights and risking being seen. They collapsed into sleep, exhausted. As tired as he was, adrenaline still flowing through his body, Federico slept alternating between fevered dreams and semi-wakefulness. Soon enough, his body sent another signal: he had to pee. Through half-open eyes, he could see out of the small door in the tholos that the moonlight still lit the clearing. *Fresh air may help.* He ducked through the door and stepped a few paces away on leaden legs, already starting to unbutton his pants. The night was still, and the leaves on the trees reflected the moonlight while dark shadows pooled beneath the branches. His hands froze where they were, as did his feet: from those shadows, two wolves emerged, their gleaming eyes and teeth pointed in Federico's direction.

Flight? Fight? Play dead?

He remembered his father telling him stories of when he would take sheep to graze as a boy and about wolves. "Wolves don't attack men," he would say. "But don't run away from a wolf. Its instinct will then be to chase you. Only prey runs away." Another unsolicited voice came to him, his grandmother's. "Make yourself a sheep, and the wolves will eat you."

He wouldn't run. But he couldn't fight two wolves, either. *I would have to be a bear*, he thought. Or an eagle. The wolves were moving closer. Federico dismissed fears and fancies from his head and started looking for a plan. The hut was just a few meters away, but so were the wolves. He decided to back up toward the door, keeping his eyes on the wolves. When he moved, so did they.

I'm leading them to my friends. He took two more steps backward but turned his ankle on a loose stone. He fell on his ass with his head reaching the doorless entrance of the hut. He used his arms to scramble toward the opening as he kicked with his legs. One of the wolves growled—odd, it sounded almost like Crocko's laughter—just as the other wolf lunged at him and sunk its teeth into his calf, just above where the shovel had struck him earlier. Federico gasped, and then as he looked at the head of the wolf that had his flesh between its teeth, he saw it turning into the face of Balthazar, licking his lips and smiling at him. He screamed. And woke up. He was in the hut. The others were stirring around him, calling out, wondering what was happening. Eleonora curled toward one wall, her face in her hands, moaning, "The wind! The wind!"

"It's fine! I'm fine!" Federico blurted. "It was just a bad dream."

Yet, it seemed so real. Even now, his leg hurt, and—it was wet. Was it blood?

He no longer needed to pee.

53. STOP THEM

10 April 2009 – Good Friday

At seven in the morning, Don Cesare would have strangled his son for the umpteenth time: "When will you get the basics? You are violating one of the sacred rules of our family: 'Do only what is convenient and advantageous for you. No anger, no revenge, no fights.'"

Although he was an unscrupulous politician and a ruthless lawyer, Balthazar didn't dare to counter his father's authority.

"The desire for revenge took me."

"We are not those who get revenge by fighting. Let them quarrel with each other. We solve their disputes, and we get paid for it. Don't you understand? What would happen if you hurt or, even worse, killed him? Do you have any idea what would have been unleashed?"

"What should I do now?"

"You have to keep on attacking. But follow the legal ways."

"Meaning?"

"Report him for looting."

An hour later, Balthazar had a coffee and croissant with the Carabinieri Marshal, the senior officer in the area: "You have to arrest them; we need to stop these robbers who get rich by stealing from the rubble. We must restore order. You should also involve the special anti-money laundering agents. Their leader even has a territorial warning; he's not allowed to enter Abruzzo."

"Their leader? Do you mean Federico, the son of Riccardo? Is he the boss? And anyway, where is this warning?"

"You should have a copy."

They searched everywhere for it, but half of the barracks was flat on the ground: "It's not here. Are you sure it was issued? Didn't you just want to frighten the boy? I don't remember this warning."

"Are you accusing me? Of course, there was one. Thirty years have passed; who knows where you filed it? Anyway, it doesn't matter. I'm telling you that they're jackals."

"Look for the warning. Check the old archives," the Marshal said to his men. "Although, I doubt that you would find anything.

On the Castellana hill, Federico went out of the hut to prepare coffee, unscrewed the Moka, and began to pour water into the lower end of the pot. Not a millimeter more than where the valve was. A few minutes before eight o'clock, he saw the television van arrive, parking at the bottom of the hill and turning to stay level. The crew got out with the windproof microphone, the camera, and a reflective panel in their hands. They climbed the hill and turned on the instruments as soon as they arrived. The operator began to give instructions: "Stand over here; the light is better. Frame the mountain and the stone hut. Zoom in on the coffee machine."

"Hurry, come and see this!" a voice called from the van. A mobile TV was in the truck to follow the news minute by minute. Everyone ran down to watch Balthazar being interviewed, expressing outrage, and making accusations: "These people say they're here for other reasons. But they're thieves, and I caught them in the act! One of them was even responsible for the injury to my foot, long ago; he has a legal warning against entering Abruzzo, but he still has the nerve to come back here to defile our ruins and steal from our people."

"What can we do?" asked the journalist.

"I am satisfied that people now know that the crime of looting is taking place. They must realize that people among us come from the North and pretend to help us. In reality, they're here to rob our citizens and come away with gold, watches, and even our artistic heritage. You have to report them as soon as you see them."

"We know looting is frequent after earthquakes," stressed the interviewer.

"Yes, be alert. Officers are already patrolling the area."

"As I said, I witnessed such an attempt. These are unscrupulous people. Some may even be from our land, so they know the territory and how to hide. They are traitors who steal from the poor old people."

And needless to say, just as Balthazar was talking on TV, the Carabinieri arrived at the hut: "Federico, you are arrested," said the Marshal.

"And on what charge?"

"You are violating a restraining order."

The Carabinieri took them to the barracks and questioned them. They searched them just as they had searched the hut.

"You can also sift through the dust that lurks in the rubble of our houses," said Vincenzo with a grin.

"Don't be ridiculous, Vince."

The beauty of small communities is that the Marshal knows everyone, including their children, grandparents, and parents. He had known Federico and his friends since they were children.

"Why are you hiding?" he asked them.

"We don't hide; we sleep in Federico's grandfather's hut because our houses are unusable," Eleonora answered.

"You can't; it's dangerous."

"But it's not considered uninhabitable."

"Of course not; it's not even a house."

"So, what law prohibits it?" Federico argued, happy to have a point on which to complain.

"Federico, I loved your father and mother, but I warn you that this attitude won't help you."

"Yet what good has your love done for them since no one saved them or saw justice done on their behalf?"

The twins joined the counterattack: "Marshal, you have no basis for an arrest, and a territorial warning doesn't seem plausible. We were unaware of this order; can you provide the relevant documentation?"

The Marshal grimaced, sticking out his lower lip and turning his face. He realized he had little reason to hold him. Meanwhile, the copy of the restraining order was still missing. The possibility of finding it in the L'Aquila public prosecutor's archives didn't seem feasible in a reasonable amount of time, even if the copy of it hadn't already disappeared under the rubble.

Eleonora intervened: "Federico came here to lend us a hand, to help us with this devastation. Vincenzo brought him from Milan. Would you want to send him back? Are we to the point of refusing the help of Abruzzo natives who return because they feel an attachment to their homeland?"

After consulting each other, the Marshal and the Carabinieri Brigadier decided on a sort of probation for the time being.

"We will not hold you. But you must leave the hut and stay in the tents to help the earthquake victims," the Marshal said. "If it's true that Federico is here with the genuine intention to help, you can prove it with your acts. We will check to see whether he's sticking to the purpose he says he came here for. And you all cannot use the car."

The situation became difficult. What had seemed like a stroke of genius, the television interview, no longer made sense. To tell the truth, the twins didn't even think it was a great idea from the beginning: "We told you it was better to mind your own business," even though Federico didn't seem to remember that they had said it.

Giovanna emphasized one positive development: "At least Balthazar can't do anything to you, and that's what we wanted."

Vincenzo seemed to have lost his enthusiasm: "Now that we have figured out where to dig, we have nothing in our hands. How can we look for treasure on the bald mountain when we live confined in tents, under the eyes of everyone, and in particular, the Carabinieri?"

54. STATE FUNERALS

10 April 2009 – Good Friday

At eleven o'clock in the morning, all the televisions in the tent camps were tuned to the same channel: the broadcast of the state funeral for the earthquake victims. A long line of cars was stuck on the roads leading to the courtyard of the Guardia di Finanza barracks, which could not contain either the crowd or its pain. The premises had been the last to receive the corpses for identification.

The camera could not frame all the coffins; it had to move, one row after the other, one casket after the other. And when it seemed like it had ended, it found yet another. Federico saw many tiny white coffins. Some were covered with arrangements of flowers, red roses, white daisies, and yellow gerberas; others had plushies and teddy bears on them, like pillows on which to rest children's heads in the last, eternal sleep. He looked at Manfredi; one casket was even smaller than him. A Civil Protection volunteer seemed to read his mind: "It's Antonio's; it's not even half a meter long. It's resting on top of his mother's coffin."

The youngest among the dead had not lived even half a year, the oldest almost a hundred.

Every face was lined with tears. Balthazar couldn't stop crying while trying to collect himself and regain a suitable composure. Federico heard that the Tzar had a close friendship with some victims. The L'Aquila Rugby team was standing, mourning the loss of their friend Lorenzo Sebastiani, twenty years old. Their number one, the pillar of the team. On his coffin, the National team jersey.

The Minister of the Interior declared, "Until Easter Day, the search for survivors will continue tirelessly". On TV, they confirmed that patrols kept their eyes on the places most affected by the earthquake. Uninterrupted, day and night, more than a thousand law enforcement officers were watching closely to deal with looting.

The Metropolitan Archbishop of L'Aquila, Monsignor Giuseppe Molinari, who survived the collapse of part of the Archiepiscopal Palace of L'Aquila, urged other believers to strengthen their faith in Christ: "Dear brothers and sisters, struck by our dearest affections, this is the moment of great faith. A faith stronger than pain, bewilderment, fear, doubt, and despair. It's faith in the words of Jesus: 'I am the resurrection and the life. He who believes in me will not die forever.' He who believes in You does not taste death even for an instant because from this poor, wounded, and fragile life, he passes into true, full, and dignified life. Lord, we believe in Thee. We believe in the power of Your love and the certainty of Your resurrection and that a new and luminous story of life and hope may be born from this unbearable and absurd death story."

Only the notes of the Miserere, sung by the choir accompanied by the melancholy of the organ, broke the silence spoken by ghosts.

While the majority who perished were Christians, some Muslims also died under the ruins. Federico heard the broadcast announce that the Union of Islamic Communities and Organizations in Italy (UCOII) president, Dr. Mohammed Nour Dachan, would also read a message in memory of the victims of the earthquake. He saw the Imam appear on stage and heard him say, "I will read in memory of all."

"In the name of the one and only merciful God, he who created heaven and earth, he who created men and women, uniting them into one great family that lives together the experience of life, and who in these days have lived together the tragedy of death. Like death and everything, life is part of the great divine plan. We find ourselves here today to share the pain for all those brothers and sisters, those young people, and those children who were victims of the earthquake that has wounded the heart of Abruzzo and all of Italy. In this same place, we want all to feel our solidarity and support for those who survived and those who will have to face the reconstruction with courage and dignity. We embrace them in a single supportive hug united in human brotherhood, united as religions, and united as citizens that experience tragedy together."

The voice of the news anchor of the broadcast took up the message and emphasized: "You have heard Dr. Nour say, 'I speak for all, I pray for all, without distinction of religion, in the name of the one God.'"

Federico appreciated those words, first Dr. Nour Dachan's and then the reporter's, that his throat tightened, and tears came down.

The Vatican Secretary of State, Cardinal Tarcisio Bertone, and the Archbishop blessed the coffins with holy water while the choir sang to Christ the Redeemer: "I believe, I will rise. My body will see the Savior."

Outside the barracks, the camera framed another endless line: that of the hearses.

Meanwhile, the volunteers had not stopped. They continued digging, many only with their bare hands, balancing themselves on the crumbling stones every time the tremors made the earth shake.

Eleonora hugged Federico: "I know it sounds weird in this surreal atmosphere, but I'm glad you're here."

55. THE RIFLE

10 April 2009 – Good Friday

"Nice idea to break the camera, Crocko, you donkey. Why do you take such initiatives? That's how they got the idea of going to the television. It's good I came to know about it and could think of a countermove."

"Sorry, I thought I'd remove the evidence."

"You're an idiot."

Balthazar took the rifle: "This time, I'm going to stop them once and for all, or else they won't go away."

"Be careful not to mess up your life; it's more valuable than his."

"He made the swine eat my foot."

The effects of the earthquake and the state funerals had changed people and their priorities and made the Tzar's harassment seem even more out of place. Crocko could not resist: "Yes, the pig ate your foot, but Federico was inside the fence in the first place because of you, Tzar."

The slap sounded like a giant stone falling in the mud. Crocko was taller, bigger, and heavier but didn't react. He could have crushed Balthazar like a chickpea that had been soaking all night, but instead shrugged: "All right, I'll go get the car."

When Federico came out of the tent, he was trying to find a way to reach Cerro hill and continue the excavations. Walking with the tools in hand was too long, and there was no way to get there without being noticed.

"Good morning," said Balthazar.

"Same to you," replied Federico.

He had learned it from Carlantonio. When they asked him: "Why do you always answer, 'same to you'?" He revealed his theory: "Because if he wants to wish me good morning, I wish him the same. But if his good morning is sarcastic, then so is mine."

Balthazar pointed down the hill toward the car where Crocko was waiting: "Let's talk."

"The last time you told me you wanted to talk, you smashed my face against an iron railing. Forgive me if I reserve myself the right not to believe you."

"This time, it's different; we're not kids anymore."

Federico followed Balthazar, staying a few meters away. They were now adults, and the man next to him had tried to shoot Vincenzo at night with a rifle and used his influence to cause the Carabinieri to kneecap him.

When they arrived near Crocko, the Tzar picked up a bolt-action rifle from the ground. Federico cursed himself for having just thought of the gun, almost as if he had attracted the weapon itself. He recognized the golden coat of arms and heard a bullet's bolt chamber. Balthazar adjusted his grip and aimed for the far road.

"Bet I hit the sign? Come on, let's have some fun."

On the road sign, there was the inscription: Stiffe. It must have been one kilometer, as the crow flies.

"This weapon is for boar hunting. They have thick skin. They don't die from the bullets of normal rifles."

Crocko passed a pair of binoculars to Federico: "Look at the sign. Can you see any holes in it?"

"No," said Federico, and on the 'no', he heard Balthazar's shot, while through the binoculars, he saw a hole appear, replacing the dot above the 'i' of Stiffe.

As the echo of the detonation ricocheted through the mountains of the valley, Balthazar was witty: "Excuse me if I like to dot the 'i's.' A perfectionist's occupational hazard."

Federico felt the skin on his neck prickle as if he had taken a shower with acid, which was now bubbling in his throat: "So, you have killed an innocent sign. By the way, is that legal?"

Balthazar raised his voice and gritted his teeth: "This rifle hits with precision from a kilometer, much further than you can detect. You die, and you don't even know how. No one will ever know where the shot came from in this uninhabited and wretched place."

Then he approached Federico, who took a step back; the Tzar's breath was even more disgusting than the smell of his sweat. He held back and answered: "My uncle had that rifle, too."

Balthazar laughed: "Yes, a model from forty years ago. Like that ridiculous metal detector."

The Tzar turned his head toward the road: "Do you remember the little dog you wanted so much to save? Look over there."

On the dirt road, two puppies were shambling toward their mother in front of them. Federico felt Crocko put his arms around his shoulders and then squeeze to hold him still. He struggled, first trying to kick the rifle with one foot and then throwing himself backward to try to make

Crocko fall. He wanted to scream, but what he heard, instead of his cry, were two shots. He then saw the two puppies crumble to the ground as the mother wheeled about and then, understanding what had happened, began a howl of desperation.

Balthazar approached him again: "Do you hear that bitch crying? I repeat, I don't want to see you here anymore; you must disappear. Stay a few days and pretend to help. Talk also to some relatives you haven't seen for thirty years. Then make an excuse and go back to Milan. And this is the last time I will tell you. I'm sure you don't want to increase the death count."

Balthazar walked towards the car and left Federico alone with Crocko, who set him free by pushing him away from himself: "Now it's our turn to talk about your future. Don't worry; it will be a short conversation."

56. TEMPTATION

10 April 2009 – Good Friday

Crocko led him away a few steps: "Maybe the Tzar would just like to hear you say you're sorry."

"You can see that he's a psychopath, right?"

"So, you want to make him angry? Why don't you just apologize to him?"

"Apologize for what? When we were kids, he wanted to kill me."

"Listen, I have an idea. Let's solve everything differently. Join us for the reconstruction. We already have excellent contacts. It's a lot of money, millions."

"Are you asking me to participate in a criminal activity?"

"Criminal? What are you saying? You offend me so. You know how to do business; you know how to do the math, right? Besides, you will not tell me they fired you because you've always been honest?"

"Maybe I lost my job because I was too honest. Too transparent."

"Make up your mind then. You just answered yourself. By now, you should have realized that honesty alone is useless. All that matters is making agreements with the right people and honoring them. I am proposing such an agreement. You are a decent person. You won't take part in the action; we take care of that. You just have to make the numbers add up. You are also well-liked in the area; if they do some audit, there will be opportunities for you to dodge the dangerous bullets."

"But the donkey just said that I have to disappear."

"Stop talking about him like that. I'll take care of him. Suppose you apologize to him and no longer behave like a rival, like someone who came to raid his territory. In that case, he will find words of gratitude and celebration: he will say something along the lines of 'as in the old days, 'united for the big reconstruction', 'the prodigal son of Abruzzo returns from Milan.' He's a wizard in this kind of thing."

"Raid? Why should I give a damn about his territory?"

"Then what were you doing in his house? We filmed everything."

They remained silent for a few seconds. Crocko had sunk his teeth at the right moment.

He resumed his speech: "Think about it, but not too long, say twenty-four hours, and let me know. Clear? The proposal is convenient, but it's not valid forever."

Federico summarized with a grimace: "Understood; I'll take care of the financial side of the reconstruction initiatives led by Balthazar. Limited time offer. Twenty-four hours."

"You shouldn't even need half of that." Crocko walked down the road to where Balthazar had already started the car.

Federico turned to go up to the tent, and when he raised his head, his eyes crossed those of Manfredi, who had been watching the scene from above.

57. REASSESSMENT

Federico thought about Crocko's proposal while preparing coffee. He could help to rebuild the country. After all, what had been said about Don Cesare and Balthazar could have just been motivated by envy and jealousy from others. Yes, all right, there was the letter. But even in that case, wasn't it the people who kept asking him: "When is the pension coming? Has the legal situation been unlocked?" Wasn't the attitude of the people, their greed, that had given Don Cesare that power? Federico didn't want to admit that, at last, he had realized something fundamental: when things were going well, he believed that it was thanks to him that he knew how to manage things. The studies, the career, the good money. Then, when he divorced, it was Stefania's fault. The loss of his job was caused by the rising price of oil and the multinationals that had become so crazy, and the earthquake obviously caused the destruction of the house in Abruzzo.

Now he realized that neither positive nor negative experiences had taught him anything because he had never understood what role his actions played and how much was due to circumstances, good luck, or even bad luck.

He remembered when the coach of the rugby team once gathered them all together. He had a video cassette in his hand: "This is the recording of the match we won on Sunday. Now let's watch it again as if we had lost it." He and his teammates were astonished. He made them review every action, every bounce, every mistake that, thanks to fate, had benefited them. They gladly remembered the fantastic goals but had conveniently forgotten the errors and the lucky breaks. A few chosen outcomes, positive or negative, don't say much about you and your skills. A prevalence of positive results does.

It had taken Federico thirty years to learn that lesson.

Meanwhile, they learned from the Carabinieri that the judge, that morning, had acquitted three of the four men arrested in San Quirico d'Ocre for attempted aggravated theft. It was the first trial against the presumed jackals, who had come to L'Aquila to loot after the earthquake. The story involved the Carabinieri discovering a woman who had been a caretaker at a house owned by an older man. The quake damaged the home, and the woman used the keys she still possessed to enter the house while three men waited outside. The suspicion was they were after one hundred thousand euros that the owner had hidden under a tile. The Carabinieri had arrived as the four were leaving, but the investigation showed that the money had not been touched. The judge condemned only one of them, who was found to have burglary tools in his car.

"See?" Vincenzo said: "Everyone here buries something. We are already late."

Giovanna pointed out, however, that one of the men had been arrested even before he had managed to steal anything. The Carabinieri had been alert and quick.

Federico was wrapped in his thoughts. He could not reconcile within himself with what was happening. On the one hand, his great-grandfather had set an example for observing the law irreproachably. He was a Carabiniere, like those of the episode that just happened. On the other hand, he was fascinated by the revolutionary bandits who fought for the people, living, by necessity, outside the law imposed by the authorities but longing for justice.

The charm of freedom as opposed to the torpor of conformism; could a passion for justice be so strong as to advocate defying unjust laws enforced by the powerful to oppress the weak?

Was illegality right if it was in the service of justice? And which side was he on? Was there still a side to be on? Was he not committing a criminal act himself? He had snuck into the lawyer's house. They thought they might be stealing items that had been stolen themselves, so perhaps stealing from thieves is not a crime?

And now, as a backup plan, he was trying to find a treasure that was itself the result of some illicit activity. What if they found treasures that brigands had amassed? Would it be correct to use it for himself and his son?

Yet this freedom that the bandits had, their search for an inner evolution that Tonino had mentioned, the liberation from the chains of material existence, fascinated Federico. But his heart stalled, and he could not decide. He remembered that, when you fly, stalling meant losing lift and, soon after, falling.

Eleonora entered the tent, greeted the twins, and Federico handed her a cup of coffee. She gave him a map: "Look what I got you. Maybe you can see some interesting names to convert into figures. I have already circled in pencil the names of some places that could be referred to in the poem."

Federico, however, felt exhausted: "That's enough; I'm fed up."

"How do you mean 'enough'?" Eleonora reacted in amazement.

The twins seemed to indulge him: "He's right. It's absurd. The treasure, the earthquake. It's all pure madness."

Eleonora was astonished: "Until a moment ago, it seemed as if you believed it."

Giovanna reinforced the doubt: "Without the metal detector, we can't find anything. We don't even know what was under the rock on Bald Hill. Maybe it was just an old pot buried before the war."

Federico sighed: "The problem is that water, earth, sky, and wind are everywhere around here. And so are the names of villages, boroughs, and towns—there are hundreds. It's an impossible task. And then I don't even know if it's right. I feel like a thief, a coward. We are stealing. We are not brigands who liberate an oppressed population; we are jackals. Perhaps we should just concentrate on reconstruction and lend a hand."

"Bah!" said Vincenzo with an explosive breath, waving his arms at Federico. "We needed a bold visionary, and we got a depressed philosopher instead."

Federico was about to answer, but Eleonora silenced him with an embrace: "I know we are hanging by a thread. Please don't be the one to break it."

58. THE TENTS' STORIES

10 April 2009 – Good Friday

During the evening, the tents seemed to become the crowded villages of the old days. Since you spend much time alone in Abruzzo, you have time to reflect and develop your ideas that may be quite different from those of others. Then you meet—or rather more often you clash—'at the square' and hear everyone's opinions, flavored with insults and shouts, and you even come to blows.

The earthquake had been like a rock dropped in a lake, and Federico felt as if the waves from the ordeal were the stories of his fellow homeless, breaking over him in the tent.: "And of all the tremors that began four months ago—what do we want to say? There were hundreds, always stronger, until the big shake at the end of March. You want to tell me that it couldn't be predicted?"

The fuse was triggered: "And if we knew it, what would you have done, huh? Would you have made everyone evacuate? Where would we have gone, and for how long? And even if someone had told you to do that, you know that you would still have stayed at home."

"This tent is more comfortable than my house," noted an old woman who had always lived in stone houses, and someone smiled.

The voices overlapped one on top of the other in Federico's ears, like the capsules of the lotto numbers mixed in the spinning urn: "I spent the night under the lintel of the door. They told me it was twenty-three seconds, but I think it must have lasted at least ten minutes. It's a miracle that the door didn't fall."

"I called the emergency number, but it was always busy."

"We heard it first like thunder and then the bed vibrating with the closet creaking. We were so afraid."

"Even my bed danced to everything, but it wasn't my husband who was shaking it, though he used to shake it well," laughed an old lady with no teeth.

"I can still rattle your old skinny bones and the whole of this tent," protested her husband.

Federico loved that way of being able to laugh even in misfortune while remaining somehow aware of the seriousness of the thing.

"This is a war without bombs."

"The question that comes to mind is always the same," Peppino, the bricklayer, said. "How do you build houses that crumple on themselves? Nothing has happened to my parent's house, not even a crack. I built it."

"It seemed light at first, but then the walls and furniture began to swing. Objects fell. I was nauseous. It lasted a long time, at least half an hour."

"I thought I was dreaming; I felt like jumping around on a dinghy on the rough sea. Then even the shells hanging on the wall began to clink. I realized that it wasn't a dream and that I wasn't on vacation by the sea when I saw the house dancing to the rhythm of castanets."

"At the funeral, I saw the rugby team; one of them also died."

"Yes, they were once again heroes. Even though they say they didn't do more than their duty," commented Eleonora's brother, Giulio, the young rugby player.

One of the players told the press that he had escaped from the collapse of his house and, while running out of it, had heard a woman's cries for help. He saw the stairwell collapse and rubble everywhere. Despite the confusion, the stench of gas from the broken pipes, and the wreckage, the player concentrated on one task: getting everyone to safety. He saw an elderly husband and wife; a stone and water pipes crushed the man. The young man lifted all the debris, and just as he carried them out, there was another tremor. The couple was even more terrified, but their rescuer knew that the real opponent was fear, and so, after saving the two elders, he also returned to bring out the oxygen tank the woman needed to breathe. Then he read on his phone a message directing him and his companions to rush to the hospital. And there, on the night of April 6, he met other players and managers of Eagle Rugby.

They had been summoned and didn't hesitate. Awakened by the scream of the earth, in front of the hospital, they exchanged a few glances and the minimum number of syllables necessary as if they were on the field: the game plan was arduous but clear. Still upset, dazed, and incredulous about what was happening, they entered the broken hospital, the walls lying on the ground instead of standing up. They saw the sick immobile in their beds, whitewashed by the dust and rubble.

Constantly threatened by the continuous tremors that followed the initial twenty-three seconds of shaking, the players evacuated the L'Aquila hospital. They secured eight wards, including the hardest ones to move, such as long-term care and geriatrics.

Balthazar entered the tent like a bull in a bullfight arena: "Now listen to the beautiful story I have to tell."

He kept his eyes on Federico as the people spread out and let him reach the center of the square. Balthazar addressed the crowd, rotating his face to speak to everyone: "It's the story of a jackal who came here pretending to help and who was caught stealing instead."

"And what evidence do you have?" Giovanna challenged him.

"You say that because when you were boys, Federico was best, and you won't let it rest," snarled Vincenzo.

Balthazar grunted: "I don't have the proof yet. But I'll have it soon, very soon. And I will throw you all in jail."

59. THE TORCH OF FORGIVENESS

Subequana Valley, 28 August 1980 – Thursday

Federico was in the group of runners from Fagnano Alto who would have brought the torch to the next town. Being the youngest of the group, they made him enter San Demetrio first, with the torch in his hand, followed by the others who ran behind him. Balthazar was not there that day, as the family was spending the month of August in France.

He was spellbound when he heard that the torch was lit on the morning and left on its journey from the hermitage of S. Onofrio to follow along the Peligna, Subequana, and the Aquilana Valley to the Basilica of Collemaggio.

Tonino told him that the path followed the procession route led by Pietro del Morrone, riding a donkey, who traveled from his isolated retreat to his triumphal entrance in L'Aquila. On twenty-nine August twelve ninety-four, he was crowned Pope with the name of Celestino V and, at the same time, issued the Bull of Forgiveness and the first jubilee of history.

The tradition of Celestinian Forgiveness had been abandoned for a long time but had a rebirth in the summer of nineteen eighty. It was reinstituted by the then Rector of the Basilica who, with the support of some friends and athletes of the Free Runners of Aquila, conceived the Fire of Morrone run.

When Federico received the torch from Claudia, he felt his saliva dry, and his legs falter, but he still took off like a rocket. Claudia ran alongside him, smiling: "Quiet. This is not a race. Slow down."

He relaxed and found a more appropriate rhythm with his breathing. He seemed to be the torchbearer about to enter the Olympic track in Athens, escorted by his group, the cyclists, the flagship car. And behind, all the region's vehicles honk like in the days of grand celebrations.

He entered San Demetrio with the crowd opening before him like the sea in front of Moses, hailing the torch of forgiveness and the resurrection of a thousand-year-old tradition. Those cheers hit Federico's nervous system as if the welcome were reserved for him. He felt the tears roll down his cheeks while his legs strained on the climb that led to the center of the village, where he would leave the torch in other trusted hands. Claudia smiled at him again and winked.

Passing from hand to hand and from village to village, the torch came to the square of Collemaggio at 18.00, guarded by the athletes of the Free Runners Aquilani, who were welcomed by the Fanfare of the Acqui Brigade. The tripod was lit on the Basilica tower, followed by the opening of the Holy Door, the Holy Mass, and the prayer vigil.

Federico saw his mother, father, and Tonino, together with the other faithful, cross the Holy Door, pray, and ask forgiveness for their sins. Thanks to Celestino V, they would have been absolved and made as clean as the waters of Tirino, the most transparent and most pure river in Europe.

On Sunday, August the thirtieth, Pope John Paul II himself would also arrive in L'Aquila, and everyone was in a state of throbbing anticipation, including Federico.

And also, on that Sunday, Balthazar would return from France.

60. ST. PETER

Mount St. Peter, 11 April 2009

Federico woke up remembering when he was training Maya. The eagle's feathers were turning brown; she was growing up. In Mongolia, they told him that the eagle is the noblest animal of all and that if you look with attention, you can read the Koran on their feathers. And Federico seemed to see shapes that resembled Arabic letters, although he didn't know their meaning.

Zhuldyz's grandfather taught him how to train the eagle to catch the fake hare. He tied raw meat on its back and pulled it with a galloping horse. As a joke, his father once told him, "I believe that if you'd put the meat on the money, it would learn to hunt for money. Like the thieving magpie that steals all the shiny objects, it can carry."

This caused Federico to remember when his mother, who would have been an Olympic-class slipper thrower, threw her shoe and hit a magpie that tried to snatch a ring she had just cleaned and placed on a windowsill. The same ring that Federico was now touching through his trousers pocket; he always carried it everywhere.

Federico got up; the dawn would arrive within an hour. He had thought of an absurd experiment to try. He began to prepare coffee as another memory came to him of the time he had taken Manfredi to see a falconry show just outside Milan. A caracara from Mexico interrupted its flying performance during the show to swoop down and steal two beautiful red shoes from a little girl whose mother had placed them next to the stroller.

And just a year earlier, he and his work colleagues had been awarded a business trip to Monterey, California. The company had taken them to the TED conference, where a man called Josh Klein demonstrated how he had trained crows to bring him coins they found on the ground in exchange for peanuts. He hoped to persuade the crows to learn how to do other activities, such as collecting litter, for example, after a big concert, and keeping the environment clean. The next day, the Chief Marketing Officer, picturing himself as a great motivator, spoke to Federico's group, reminding them of the demonstration and saying, "You don't want to tell me that crows are smarter than you, do you? Find me the money!"

An English colleague remarked: "Sure, we show you the money - and we get the peanuts."

Federico liked his English colleagues' irreverence, even though he could not make witty remarks in a foreign language. On the contrary, he felt anxiety about what might happen when his colleagues would throw themselves into these jokes about work, but they always did well.

He was fascinated by that trip to the United States, where you could drive for hours and still find yourself eating in places with the same name and items on the menu. In Abruzzo, all you had to do was move from one village to another, and you would hear a different dialect, and even bread types would have other names from the ones you knew.

Federico's mind returned to the conference and the puzzle he was now trying to solve: *Are eagles smarter than crows? And even if they are, would they have any interest in proving it?*

Federico moved the curtain to look out:

"Where are you going?"

"I have to pee; do you want to give me a hand?"

"Don't be a smart ass. What are you up to?"

"Come and see. But you have to pay."

"You're just stupid, then."

"Bring all the coins you have; I prefer the twenty cents. And some raw meat, whatever kind you find, but better if it's not salted."

Federico searched all the pockets of the backpack and his pants. Eleonora took all the coins she found in her purse.

"What is the money for? We no longer have a car that needs to be parked."

"Where we are going, there is no parking."

Eleonora found chicken breasts and mutton in the cooking tent. Federico said nothing more; he kept his eyes on the meat and cut it into irregular strips. She took a step back as if pushed by the shockwave of his precise and peremptory orders. Federico, however, was relaxed but showing the same focus as a feline observing the crack from which a mouse will come out; his mind picturing a caterpillar Federico about to become a butterfly.

They walked towards Saint Peter along a road through the middle of the woods, so they could not be seen. When they were a few hundred meters from the stone house, Federico began to drop the coins along the path and throw some in the surroundings. Eleonora asked: "Who are you, Hop-o'-My-Thumb? Must we find our way back?"

"Yes, we must find the right way."

"Remember, when Hop-o'-My-Thumb's Ogre comes back, he smells 'fresh meat', discovers the intruders, and tries to kill and eat them."

Upon reaching Saint Peter, they went into the house that had become an aviary. When Maya saw them, she began to get excited. Federico put on the glove and some meat on the coins. The eagle jumped to him and ate it. Then Federico went out and threw a coin down the hill; Maya flew out but returned with nothing. Federico gave her nothing to eat and threw another coin.

Patience. Federico said to himself. *Patience, it takes patience.*

Eleonora seemed to understand now what he was doing: "You are crazy, Federico; you are trying something impossible. She will never see a coin as prey; the coin has no hair; it's hard. Even if you put meat around it, she will ignore it".

"You are right. But I don't want her to see it as prey; I just want her to associate the idea of food with taking a coin. I want to get something in return for the meat she has been eating for thirty years."

"But the eagle does not understand such a thing."

"Then is it true that crows are smarter than they? So much for the eagle, that is called 'regal' and 'golden'?"

"Why, have you noticed that royals are smarter than others?"

"No, in fact. Touché."

"Even the magpie, the pica, is a corvid and, for example, can recognize itself in the mirror, like the chimpanzee. It has self-awareness. But not the eagle."

"Whatever. But even if we fail, we at least took a trip to Saint Peter and had a couple of flights with Maya."

"And made great fools of ourselves."

Federico nodded, then thought about it again and smiled at her: "And with whom would we make fools of ourselves?"

The eagle returned with nothing. Federico put a coin between her claws and gave her some meat while the eagle held the coin. Uninterested. Then he threw it again along the path they had climbed. Nothing. Federico declared the end of the test. "Let's go; soon, everyone in the tents will be on their feet."

Eleonora commented: "I knew it was madness. The pica steals objects, even the caracara. The raven can collect garbage."

"And there is the gardener bird who uses branches and blue objects to woo the female, for example, the plastic caps of water bottles," recalled Federico. "And the eagles, they don't do anything at all?"

"American bald eagles decorate their nests with bright objects. It's thought that it's to ward off other birds. However, that is the bald eagle, and Maya is a golden eagle. It does not stoop to such vulgar levels."

"Maybe it's not the hunting that is the key, but the courtship, for the decoration. We can try this another way. Let's put some coins in her nest."

"Right, for the decoration of the nest, not as prey. They are not like human beings who prey on money."

Federico felt encouraged: "It doesn't cost us anything to try, only that we look like fools in front of an imaginary crowd."

"We've already done it, so we're fine," Eleonora smiled.

"I realized that I was often right in life, but only when the stakes were low, and I didn't gain much from it. And the few times I was wrong, I lost everything. Now, the opposite could happen. If we are wrong, what do we lose? Nothing. But if we were right, we could become rich."

They looked at each other and laughed. It was between the comic and the tragic, but they laughed.

Back in Saint Peter, Eleonora kept Maya outside the house so that she could not see what was happening. Federico climbed on the rocks, using the easy holds until he reached the nest. He put some coins in it, the ones that most resembled the 'marenghi' currency of the past: the brass made twenty-cent euro pieces.

If Giovanna had been there, she would have cited the professor of engineering at the Faculty of Naples, Michele Pagano, who used to say, "The engineer knows what he does and does what he knows."

Federico had no idea what they were doing and even less what the Tzar was about to announce.

61. THE GIFT OF THE TZAR

As they returned to the tents, Federico's thoughts returned to speak about the poem: "The verse *'known by those who loved and gave the gift'* has stayed in my mind. Loved and gave. I keep thinking about it. They were generous people".

"Yes, it's nice to think that those who donated these treasures know about their highest meaning; to give without any thought of recognition or reward."

"They were not focused on material treasures; while those may serve to survive, to live it takes so much more."

"True, he who has just material wealth is the poorest in the world," commented Eleonora.

Federico felt guilty for thinking he wanted to keep the treasures if he discovered them. Perhaps he should have donated them, too, for love. Yes, he loved his son and wanted to provide for him, but would 'donating' the treasure for his care mask an act of selfishness? Of course, he didn't have any real treasure in his hand, so in reality, there was no decision to be made. It was just a fantasy, like contemplating whether it was right to eat unicorn meat.

Would I eat unicorn meat if I was hungry enough?

And he was hungry. His thoughts and stomach were in turmoil as they arrived at the tents. They saw Balthazar and Crocko leaving with shovels and pickaxes, followed by the TV van.

"Where are they going?" asked Federico.

"I have a terrible suspicion," Eleonora answered.

"Let's follow them."

Others had the same idea and were already following on foot and in cars on the narrow, rocky road. When the procession reached the ruins of the Sant'Eusanio castle on Monte Cerro and the Church of the Madonna, everyone followed the TV van behind the church in a column. Balthazar waited until a sizable crowd had gathered, and the cars had gone up as close as possible and couldn't find more parking places. Surrounded by the people, journalists, and anti-looting guards, Crocko dug for not even a quarter of an hour before the pickaxe hit a metal object.

"Move over," ordered Balthazar.

"Turn the camera on," he ordered the cameraman.

And so, framed by the cameras and surrounded by an audience, Balthazar removed all the dirt around the trunk, opened it, and then raised his hands full of gold coins and jewelry. There was also a gold pendulum. Balthazar knew the story and turned it upside down; underneath was written 'Black Gate': "Here is the treasure of my ancestor, who was robbed by the bandit Franco."

The crowd's excitement was like fireworks amid the devastation of the earthquake.

"Our land is always able to give us immense treasures, the fruit of the work of our ancestors," lyricized Balthazar.

The stories had always seemed impossible to everyone, and now a treasure was staring them in the eyes.

One of the elders who was there watching—the elders are always interested in excavations—had a doubt: "And how did he know there was treasure there?"

His friend answered: "He has a special intuition, like his father. They will always find the money." And they both nodded with their eyebrows raised as when hearing an irrefutable truth.

Balthazar donated the treasure to the reconstruction. Federico and the others bowed their heads in defeat.

Federico looked at Manfredi, who was staring back at him. He felt that he failed as a dad. He could feel it in his stomach; he could feel it on his shoulder. He hadn't been able to keep his job. He hadn't been able to keep Manfredi's mother. He hadn't even been able to keep his home. And now that he had the chance to make something extraordinary for his son, he had squandered it. While he clenched his fist and jaw, he heard Manfredi consoling him: "Papi, don't be angry. I know you found it first, but he took the credit."

But Federico's rage couldn't be assuaged.
Once again, the Tzar had struck a blow to get people to like him.
Once again, he carried the ball across the goal line.

62. ONE STEP UP

"We are cursed. He's always two steps ahead. Whenever we find out where things are, he claims them before we do and takes the credit." Vincenzo was furious.

"We must be smarter and act better in secret," Federico replied. "We cannot win a confrontation."

"Now it's even more difficult if we are stuck in the tents and in front of everyone's eyes," replied Giovanna.

Vincenzo's enthusiasm seemed to resurface with his anger: "We are still looking for combinations that add up to ninety-nine; we have not finished yet. One treasure was there, right where the instructions said. So maybe we can find the others. If they're as big as the one that Balthazar 'discovered', we are rich. Think about it; this finding is fantastic news. It means the stories are true."

Eleonora pulled Federico into a more secluded corner of the big tent: "What about the coins with Maya? What do we do?"

"We still don't know where to look. And the area around the Goats' Drop will have grown shrubs and weeds for decades, covering everything."

"We don't know that. It's mostly rocks up there and at such an altitude that nobody ever goes there. Let's try again; you don't have to believe it. If there are coins, there are coins; if there are not, we lose nothing. Easy."

"Sure, let's see how Maya reacts to the coins in the nest, and then we'll try again. For now, let's keep this to ourselves."

The earthquake had occurred early in the morning of April six; by that same night, there was already the idea of constructing a new town, built on the same plateau as the village of Coppito, and not on the hill 'where the Eagle—the town of L'Aquila—rises', since the latter was geologically unstable. The new town would be made of earthquake-proof apartments erected on reinforced concrete platforms.

Discussions in the tents turned to the possibility of replacing houses with tall multifamily buildings and what that might mean. Many criticized the idea since some architects said similar attempts in other parts of the world had ended badly. Without squares and piazzas, where do you go to hear 'what is being said'? Without a bar, without newspaper kiosks, the community disintegrates and manifests every kind of negative behavior.

"Man is a social animal."

"You have to let people choose where to live. There is something inside humans that can relate to a certain context, an environment, or the people with whom they're prepared to share their lives."

The new towns in other places had turned into dormitory neighborhoods with no social life—the opposite of the village mentality. At the same time, however, there was a real need to provide a roof over the heads of the people who had seen their old one fall on them. Looking at the stars in spring and summer can be romantic, but becoming an outdoor astronomer when the temperature can drop to minus fifteen degrees, is much less poetic.

Some had heard about a plan to build temporary houses, which would be much better than tents and—some admitted—much better than the stone houses in which they used to live. Others saw all these solutions as a retreat on all fronts and instead wanted to be proactive: "I want my house. Give it back to me. I can fix it myself."

The government would have put up prefabricated houses, called MAP for *"Modelli Abitativi Provvisori"*—Provisional Housing Modules. These could be constructed while the people awaited the complete reconstruction. Federico couldn't help but argue, as he did every time that things didn't go as he would have wanted: "I believe the abbreviation means something else."

"And what would that be, Professor?"

"It's in the letter P of MAP."

"What, you mean the 'P' for 'provisional'?"

"Given the state of things, the 'P' would rather stand for 'Permanent'."

Nobody laughed.

63. THE GOAT'S DROP

Pagliare di Fontecchio, 11 April 2009

Federico heard the voices of Balthazar and Crocko passing through the fabric of the tents: "We have to take a trip to L'Aquila. See you later."

Eleonora placed the cutlery on the plate and wiped her mouth: "This is the moment we've been waiting for; let's go."

Federico stopped her: "It's better if I go alone. The fewer there are of us, the less we risk being seen."

He had skipped lunch to calculate other numerical values of some places in the area and was going crazy trying to find a sum equaling ninety-nine. Eleonora offered a counter-argument: "On the contrary, it's better if we come too so that it will seem like a normal walk. We, too, need some distraction and fresh air."

The artificial city consisted of sixty tents of the Civil Protection Department. From there to Fontecchio was about an hour's walk. Federico remembered a story from grandpa, 'tatone', as they say in Abruzzo. A passerby wanted to go from Villa Sant'Angelo to Fontavignone, at the top of the mountain, after Saint Peter. He met a man peeling potatoes sitting on a chair:

"How long does it take to get to Fontavignone?"

"One hour. If you stroll."

The passerby seemed impatient: "What if I run then?"

"Then you'd need at least three hours."

They could not take the road most traveled, so they chose the one parallel to the main road and sheltered by the trees from unwanted eyes. Eleonora pointed to some menacing clouds over the village of Campana: "It's about to rain?"

Federico answered her with the proverb that he had always heard from his grandparents and came from years of experience with the meteorological dynamics of the area:

"When you see the clouds from Campana come,
You can take the long hoe and go irrigate.
If above Casentino, you see some,
Then let the hoe in the cellar await."

Federico smiled: "It won't rain then, don't worry."

Vincenzo mocked him as he turned to Manfredi: "Daddy is also a meteorologist; did you know that?"

Manfredi smiled and Vincenzo caressed his head.

They walked at a constant pace, mindful of Fontavignone's story, and got as close as possible to the Goats' Drop, always remaining at the foot of the mountain. Only Maya could have flown up there. Now and then, Federico slowed down to allow Manfredi and Eleonora, who were constantly chatting, to catch up. Vincenzo followed with Maya, who was hooded and secured to the glove with the jesses. After an hour's walk, they arrived at what seemed to him an appropriate distance and looked at Fontecchio's Clock Tower with the binoculars.

When the troops of the Kingdom of Naples had surrounded the fortified village of Fontecchio, it had been Marchioness Corvi who had taken the *spingarda* and had killed the leader of the attackers. Since then, the Clock Tower has been beating fifty chimes every evening, as many as the days of the siege. The clock is one of the oldest built in Italy and moves its only hand according to a refined weight mechanism. It beats the time 'Italian style', that is six hours in six hours.

Federico liked Fontecchio's symbol of the ancient *Civitella*: the fourteenth-century fountain. It was protected in the village corner; sitting there in the summer to enjoy the coolness was always one of his favorite moments.

Federico took the leather glove and Maya back from Vincenzo and removed her hood to continue training her with coins. They used twenty and fifty euro cent pieces, which most resembled the gold coins of the period before the war. Federico remembered the teachings of Zhuldyz's grandfather: "With the eagle, every time is different. You know little in advance. The variables are many: the weight, temperature, and humidity of the air, for example. Impossible to calculate everything. You have to be always alert and ready for the slightest change, even instantaneous, without ever expecting anything predefined. The problem lies in the human being who can't help but anticipate what will come. When you make plans, this is fine, but when you act, it's an obstacle."

Federico thought that a wild animal lives a new life every day. Deciding whether to act on a detail can determine its survival. For this reason, its senses and physical form are at their maximum. The diurnal birds of prey are spirited in temperament. They look everywhere and seem agitated, but in reality, they're receiving and sending millions of pieces of information they don't yet know how they will use.

Maya was reminding him how to live in the present.

He thought about the routine of his life in the big city. He had organized himself in such a way as to make it as predictable as possible and minimize the unexpected, an enormous and continuous effort to make everything 'normal'. Thus, he lived on a parallel track that gave him the illusion of flowing well. Only in the end had he realized that it was a dead-end track without a bumper to cushion the blows.

He shrugged off the thought, looked at Eleonora, and began with a few test runs, playing with the coins and Maya's beak. Sometimes she pinched the coin; other times, she bit it. Federico then decided to launch her towards the Goats' Drop. She flew in the right direction and seemed to know where to go, making some circles as if doing reconnaissance, and then swooped down, braking with her wings right near the ground, and, without even stopping, resumed the flight. Federico had followed everything with the binoculars: "She caught a mouse."

"Damn it, if Maya eats the mouse, it's over," Eleonora swore. "Let's move."

Federico was spellbound for a moment to observe the tip of Eleonora's nose as it lowered, showed a bright tip, and then rose at every 'm' she pronounced, four this time.

Maya returned to the call; the mouse had not enough to satiate her. Back on the glove, Federico let her find a coin under the meat he had prepared. The eagle caught the coin, squeezed it for a second, and let it fall. Federico picked it up and put it away, commenting: "I feel like a total fool. Indeed, I am one."

Yet in that nonsense, Federico perceived an unexpected hope. He had always relied on logic to anticipate results, but how much room did reason leave for experimentation and inspiration? When was the last time he had done something 'stupid'?

They made more attempts until it was time to return: "This is the last one, and then let's go, or they will notice our absence."

And so, with the sun still high in the sky, for the last time, Maya swelled her feathers, lowered her legs, and spread her wings towards the mountain. She took an ascending current and went up to altitude; it was fascinating to see how she was gliding and changing direction, tilting and taking advantage of the air currents. Then she swooped down to the ground. Federico didn't see her for a few seconds, not even with the binoculars. He called her back, and after ten seconds, she glided on the glove, saw the flesh, opened her beak to grab it, and dropped a coin that the pincers of her rostrum had clutched.

Eleonora hurried to pick it up and looked at it, holding it with her fingertips as if it were an alien find: "It's a golden *Marengo* of twenty liras. It says, 'coined in October 1923.' It's ridiculous."

She looked at Federico, who was holding his breath as he secured Maya's jesses: "I didn't know that eagles could do such a thing."

Federico breathed: "The eagles or Maya?"

Manfredi had an expression of joy and surprise impossible to describe: "Damn, Papi."

Vincenzo rejoiced: "Is this it? Is the 'the tower that heavens seduces' in Fontecchio? Have we found the second treasure?"

Federico said nothing. Immersed in silence, he was feeling something he had never perceived before. The past merged with the present, and the future came so close that the present became immense. A present so big that it excluded every other possible time, a single infinite moment in which everything was one: the man with the animal, the earth with the sky, destruction with creation, death with life, childhood friends with the whole of humanity. Just as the father with the son, and the grandfather with the great-grandfather, as if they had always been one entity.

He gave the coin to Manfredi: "Keep this in your pocket, and don't let anyone see it for any reason. Never brag about it. I command it."

Manfredi caressed the coin: "Okay, Papi."

Federico knelt to Manfredi's level, his eyes and mouth still wide open: "See, Papi? The treasure exists; Nonno didn't tell lies. You never trusted him, but I knew it."

Eleonora added a touch of philosophy: "It's true that in a haystack, you can always find a needle."

Vincenzo indulged her: "Even if you may need an eagle."

"Ah, also the rhyme," said Federico.

"But not in hendecasyllables," Eleonora smiled.

"Then let's fix it right away," he volunteered himself. He raised his hand in a poetic gesture, tilted his chin, and decried:

"If in a haystack you look for a needle,
make sure that your eyes are those of an eagle."

"It will be our motto," proposed Eleonora, and everyone laughed.

64. A TZAR IN THE NIGHT

That evening, Aunt Cesidia went to bed early. She felt tired, though she could not sleep. She was reflecting on what had happened. Federico's return had awakened many memories. She was reminded of his father, who had been killed, and his mother, who had died of shame and heartbreak. She turned in bed, worried about the earthquake and also the treasure. In the middle of that storm of thoughts, she heard a noise from the hall and got up to check. In the darkness, she saw the silhouette of Balthazar rummaging through the drawers of the cupboard.

He's searching for the letter.

Balthazar turned around, and she found him in front of her. He didn't hesitate to attack: "Where did you put it, hag?"

"It's no longer here. Did you think I was so stupid?"

Balthazar gave her a slap that knocked her to the ground: "And do you think I am so naive as to fall for the first trap you set for me? Tell me where it is."

Cesidia was infuriated, not intimidated, and got up from the floor with a verbal slap of her own: "Maybe you will fall in the second one, then: someone has it and is waiting for the right moment to expose it."

In response, the stench of Balthazar's breath exploded over her as he blustered: "Tell me where it is, or I'll throw you out the window."

Rather than recoiling, Cesidia drew closer to him, pulling his face down toward hers until their foreheads touched. Her eyes flashed, but her voice started as a whisper and then, with a crescendo, shouted at him: "*Suino*, swine! Armando's good soul should have let you die, mauled by pigs."

With a cry as tortured and mangled as his foot, Balthazar lifted her forty kilos of skin and bones off the ground. He shook Cesidia with a fury that, for a moment, felt like a supernatural force was jolting them both. Instead, at 9:53 p.m. and 53 seconds, an underground wind blew through the whole house; Balthazar dropped the woman, sliding on his injured foot as he tried to maintain his balance. Aunt Cesidia was thrown onto the couch while outside the people who still lived in the houses poured into the street.

Vincenzo arrived at his aunt's house just in time to bang his shoulder against Balthazar's on his way out: "You!" Balthazar ignored Vincenzo and walked towards the small square, slowing his pace, raising his chin, and buttoning his jacket, ready to address the crowd that had formed. He had already begun to speak, albeit exhausted, reassuring everyone: "Don't worry, it was a minor shock. I was checking the house of *donna* Cesidia; I don't think it's secure anymore."

Vincenzo joined the group, with Aunt Cesidia leaning on him, his arm over her shoulders. Balthazar stared at her, but Cesidia chose silence. She wanted a final, definitive victory or nothing at all. Balthazar was solicitous and kind: "Vincenzo, you'd better take her to the tents tonight. It's not safe here."

Vincenzo looked at Cesidia, who pressed her lips together and made a quick "shush" motion with her finger as she made eye contact. He frowned and knitted his eyebrows but turned towards Balthazar, controlling both his words and his hands: "Of course, this house is not at all free from danger. And the shocks don't seem to decrease. I will take her with us to the tents."

A woman in the crowd commented: "Balthazar is a good person since he cares about the good of his people."

"He's done us all many favors. What a pity for that terrible misfortune," said another. A third, who knew little about the village's past —she had married a local, but she was coming from a village on the Navelli plain—offered her opinion: "Yes, he's from here, not like that Federico, that individual from Milan. Who knows why he came back? I don't like him at all."

Yes, it seemed an altruistic gesture by the great protector. Balthazar was already planning to return. He had not taken the bait of Aunt Cesidia's fake. He was making sure that the house would be empty. Next time he would be alone. He would be able to look, undisturbed, for the letter that, he was sure, she had hidden somewhere inside her home.

65. THE INVISIBLE PATH

11 April 2009

They summarized the situation as soon as they had a moment when they could talk without having too many people around. First, Federico told Giovanna and the twins of the twenty-lira coin found by the eagle: "Now we have the third treasure to look for, and the second to recover," Federico continued. "Balthazar discovered the first one, and I heard it was valued at ten million euros."

Vincenzo rejoiced: "If the other two are also worth so much, we will have it made. And then, in my opinion, there are many more around here. I have had this feeling for years."

"Vince, don't start again, please," huffed Federico.

"Guys, let's focus," interjected Giovanna. "Never mind how many are here; we still have one to find and one to locate with more precision. And let's not forget that if we get caught, we risk ending up in jail. By the way, where is the coin?"

Federico told Manfredi to show it to everyone. They were fascinated by it. There, surrounded by the mountains, in the middle of that devastation, they felt as if they had somehow gone back in time before all that tragedy.

Giovanna looked up its market value on a numismatics site: "It depends on its gold content. It can vary between two hundred and two hundred and fifty euros per piece."

The first twin dampened the enthusiasm: "Excuse me, who says this is the second treasure since we haven't solved the rebus? Until we solve that puzzle, we can't know. Do we have the count that gives ninety-nine? This could be yet another treasure, as Vincenzo says, or maybe some coin dropped from the pocket of a brigand on the run. That same coin was minted between 1861 and 1878, long before the poem, the cave, and the metal detector."

"It matches Federico's grandfather's story; there must be a treasure on the Goats' Drop, whatever its origin. That's what matters. Not a correspondence with funny numbers" concluded Vincenzo.

The second twin poured more water on their flaming passion: "Be aware that these findings are in the public territory. We could be accused of stealing from the Italian State itself. I let you imagine how a trial would end: it wouldn't be pretty."

"They must take us first," Vincenzo retorted.

While they were arguing, Federico remembered reading about how Jean-Paul Sartre had never felt so free as when he worked for the French resistance and risked being arrested or killed at any moment. And so, it seemed the same for all of them. Just as they were homeless and under threat of arrest, Federico believed they could accomplish anything. And for the first time, he felt he was doing something special, something unique, for his son. Having lost so much as a boy, he had tried to play it safe, avoiding Abruzzo, his life, and his feelings to build a shelter from all the risks: a job, a marriage, a home.

Yet, he had lost everything and returned to the places of his childhood where it all began. To those places that he had tried to push down as deep as possible with his foot as if they had been rubbish in a garbage truck that he hoped would shred them forever. And instead of being safer, he was a centimeter away from the truck's claws that could hook his foot and then mangle his whole body one morsel at a time.

But now he knew what to look for and where. They were the only ones who knew. This time, no one could get there before them. They could come back with ease and locate the place with precision. His metal detector was a golden eagle, and the treasure, instead of being buried, was high up in the open sky where it had been seeing both stars and eclipses, ravaging storms and beautiful sunsets, for thousands of days.

But now he would reach the heavens by an invisible path on an inaccessible mountain. Up there, where only Maya could fly.

66. ZINGARELLI

A relative of Federico's mother had returned from Canada to spend some time in Abruzzo. They had just met him in Collemaggio after the mass celebrated by John Paul II. Balthazar and his family had also returned from France just to see the Pope and listen to his holy words. The relative was excited to be in Abruzzo. "This is a special vacation. I am so glad to be back and to have seen His Holiness. He even touched my hand when he leaned out of the Popemobile!"

After Mass, they went for a slice of pizza in the Pizzeria del Corso in front of the Cinema Massimo. His mother used to take him there often, and he loved those small rectangular pizza slices wrapped in food-grade greaseproof paper. He always ate a triple ration; he had a mouth bigger than the eyes of a child his age. His mother was proud of her son's appetite and progress in school and sports. "Did you know that this year they reintroduced the Race of Forgiveness, 'La Corsa della Perdonanza?'" she asked her relative. "The runners carried the flame by relay from the hermitage of Celestino to Collemaggio. Federico was chosen to be the one to enter with the torch in San Demetrio."

Federico's face became as red as the pizza stains on his shirt. The Canadian relative asked him: "Boy, do you like running?"

"Yes," replied Federico.

"Then you must participate in the Zingari's race."

And so, on the first Sunday of September 1980, they went to Pacentro, the medieval village between Mount Morrone, with the caves that were hermitages for Celestino V and the Maiella massif. When they arrived, the three square-based towers stood out twenty meters above the houses and caught his eyes. The castle was among those of the founders of L'Aquila, and, like Santo Stefano di Sessanio, Pacentro is known as one of the most beautiful villages in Italy.

Federico had no idea what the race of the Zingari was. When his parents were asked to sign a disclaimer in which they freed the organization from any responsibility for injury, he felt his neck tingling. The race was reserved for the village inhabitants; there were only three places for people from outside. Federico and Vincenzo had priority because they were relatives of a native of Pacentro, the Canadian, and

Balthazar managed to take the last remaining spot. Since they were kids, they would have run in the Zingarelli—little Zingari—competition, an introduction to the most important race.

The celebration was and still is, dedicated to Our Lady of Loreto, the Black Madonna. After the mass, a voice from the loudspeaker told about the tradition of the race, while outside the church, there fluttered the two flags of black cloth that would be the prize to the two winners. The announcer explained that the term 'Zingari', in Pacentro, refers to a person who possessed nothing, not even clothes. A destitute who had lost everything. In the imaginary description of such a person, naked are the feet, which are the part of the body always in touch with the earth. The gentleman at the microphone told of the different hypotheses about the origin of the race. Perhaps it was even born in Roman times to select the most vigorous, most resistant, and insensitive to physical pain to have them enlisted. Or maybe it was a training and initiation to adulthood through hunting. Even in this case, the exact origin was not known for sure.

Federico's mother added more details: "It must be said that in Roman times there were countless fights with the Marsi that had given them the reputation as fearless warriors. It was said that their name came from the Roman deity of war itself, Mars, from which the red planet was also named."

His father looked at Federico and concluded with a grave voice: "Later, they allied themselves with the Romans and fought side by side in the legions. They became proverbial: 'You can't win either without the Marsi or against them', or, 'To make a Marsican warrior, you need four Roman legionnaires."

He proclaimed the proverbs as if he wanted to tell Federico: 'Will you live up to your Marsican blood? Will you be as strong as four legionnaires? Did we do the right thing to sign the disclaimer?'

As soon as the statue of the Virgin came out of the church, the offerings of the faithful were pinned by the Lauretan monks on her robes. On the ribbons were attached paper money of various kinds of currency.

"Emigrants from America, Canada, and Australia send offerings every year," the relative told Federico while giving two hundred Canadian dollars to an altar boy who imitated the other monks and secured them on the statue.

Federico's mother explained: "Our Lady of Loreto feast is an opportunity to bring everyone back to our same deep roots."

Federico, Vincenzo, and Balthazar were among the children who entered the church, all with a handkerchief around their necks: "What is this for?" asked Federico.

Balthazar answered: "To squeeze it with your teeth when you feel the pain, you pussy".

T-shirts were taken off, and race numbers were drawn with a black marker pen on the backs of the kids. Barefoot, they gathered under the church altar and listened to the basic instructions of the race.

At 16:00, a boy rang the bell from the top of the tower, and Federico wished he were in that boy's place because then he wouldn't have to run. Just as he had that thought, Federico realized that the others had already taken off. Balthazar took the lead, ready to fight off any who would have tried to overtake him, while Vincenzo followed behind in the small group of kids that Balthazar had already left behind.

Federico started running and heard the sound of bare feet slapping the asphalt. They ran through the alleys, went up the stairs, and passed under the shadow of the arches of the streets as Federico's father, with the camera in his hand, ran beside him. Halfway through the race, Federico put his handkerchief between his teeth; he felt his feet frying as he heard shouting: "Come on, you can do it, don't stop, it's almost over." It was his father's voice.

Balthazar had let himself go while enjoying himself in France, but Federico was still in excellent condition, having prepared himself for the Celestinian Forgiveness run together with Claudia. The pain in his feet was holding him back but, incited by his father's energy; he was about to overtake his older companion on the left while Vincenzo was right behind him. Just as Federico arrived at Balthazar's side, the road bent to the left, almost turning back on itself and down a slope. Running downhill and in a curve, Federico was exposed on the side of the road where there was a drop-off. Vincenzo, from behind, guessed what the Tzar was thinking and shouted: "Federicoooooo, move!"

As he yelled, Vincenzo dived from the upper part of the road, cutting the curve and landing right between Federico and Balthazar, who was just about to hit Federico's shoulder, who managed to continue the race instead. Vincenzo tumbled down the road, breaking his arm. Federico and Balthazar arrived at the finish line at the threshold of the little church at the same time and crashed to the ground. Some people cooled them down by soaking their feet, and Federico felt his were so hot that he could see steam coming out of the basin.

When the Zingarelli competition was over, all three boys received a cup, and Federico helped Vincenzo lift his, because of his broken arm. Then the two cousins climbed on their fathers' shoulders to be carried in procession through the village to await the most important event, the race of the Zingari, the bloody scary one.

"You did a great run. When you're older, you'll run from the split stone," his father told him.

"Papi, if you weren't there to encourage Vincenzo and me to protect me, we wouldn't have succeeded."

"I will be there to encourage you even when you run the race of the Zingari, and Vincenzo will always be your best friend. Meanwhile, pay attention to what happens this afternoon."

67. BAREFOOT

Pacentro, first Sunday of September 1980

The young people who were going to challenge the mountain descended from the village along the path toward the valley. One of them said: "Either the mountain kills me, or I kill the mountain." Federico's father told him not to be impressed; it was a phrase taken from a novel by a writer from Abruzzo, Ignazio Silone.

The challengers walked single file up the Ardinghi hill until they reached a large stone painted with the three colors of the Italian flag, the Pietra Spaccata, or 'the split stone'. Then they looked down over the cliff's edge, made of stones, clay, and brambles.

It's reported that when their eyes are fixed on the void, their breathing accelerates, and they enter a state of competitive hypnosis. Someone already had a handkerchief between his teeth.

The announcer explained further: "The slope of the hill is deceptive; for those who look from the village, the Ardinghi seems to descend towards the Vella river gently. But its slope looks different from the vantage point of those about to begin the race. In a span of three hundred twenty meters of descent, they go from an altitude of seven hundred and fifty meters to an altitude of five hundred and eighty meters, with a gradient of sixty-three percent. Only by standing at the starting line is it possible to realize the terrifying test that awaits them. Only from the tricolor rock can the barefoot perceive the jump into the abyss ready to swallow them!"

Then the fireworks began, first a few scattered explosions, then a barrage of more and more bursts. A cloud of gray smoke rose from the valley, and with every blast, Federico's heart jumped; the explosions became machine guns in the sky and his chest.

When the bell rang, the runners rushed from the top of the rocky ridge into the cliff, scrambling down over brambles, stones, gravel, and sharp rocks. When they reached the stones, they sat down and let themselves be carried by gravity to the river with their legs stretched out on the ground, guiding the descent with their hands on the ground and braking with their bare feet. Splashing across the Vella, the runners ran up the village streets, reaching the church's altar dedicated to Our Lady of Loreto.

Federico saw the first runner arrive and fall on the ancient carpet of the church with a dazed look on his face. Some people ran up and washed his feet, from which they removed thorns, earth, splinters of wood, and tiny pebbles. A lady with scissors cut a few centimeters long piece of torn skin from his heel. The gaze of the other contestants as they arrived, exhausted, was always bewildered.

Little by little, they started smiling again, showing their feet covered with bloody bandages; others were proud to have their heels without skin. They gleamed with a new certainty: 'tried and tested, we are men, we are warriors.'

Their faces seemed to confirm the words coming over the loudspeaker: "The roots of this singular event remain shrouded in a mystery that gives the ritual of the barefoot race a lasting mythical aura."

The two winners came out of the church with a trophy cup in their hands and a cut of black cloth: symbolic prizes; in the past, they would have meant the possibility to wear precious robes. The crowd carried them in triumph, and Federico and the other kids followed behind them. The balconies were overflowing with excited young girls. Seeing the winners parading shirtless through the streets brought their hands to their mouths. One turned away so as not to have her face show what every pore of her skin had already expressed.

Families offered wine and sweets in the winners' houses to wish the whole country prosperity.

One of the runners was interviewed by a television reporter. His answer struck Federico: "I've already participated three times. Why? For the prize? The veneration of the Madonna? Yes, but there is also something inside me that goes beyond the prize and devotion. But I can't tell you what it is."

As the Abruzzo historian Franco Cercone said: "Today, the young people of Pacentro no longer run to have but to be."

68. THE EAGLE OF ABRUZZO

Villa Sant'Angelo, 1980

Federico, Eleonora, and Vincenzo spent their childhood days that September together on the mountain above Villa Sant'Angelo. Their base was Saint Peter, where Eleonora's family had kept eagles and falcons for generations.

Federico continued to build his bond with Maya. He enjoyed giving her the typical Abruzzo roasts. Occasionally he would take the cubes off the sticks and offer them to her. Other times he would hold the whole skewer on his glove and let Maya take them off. Eleonora would shake her head, smiling: "Now she's a real Abruzzo eagle."

Federico also enjoyed tying the meat behind the head of an arrow, using a special knot his father had taught him. At the base of the arrow's shaft, he inserted turkey feathers for stability in flight. He had also built the bow himself from an oak branch. When he drew the baited arrow back as far as he could, the shape of the bow seemed to match the curve of the sky. When he loosed the arrow, Maya would catch it as it hissed through the air.

Federico and Vincenzo had different reasons for being captivated by Maya.

Federico was intrigued by the flight, the glides, and how the currents carried Maya. He imagined himself flying with her and being able to realize one of man's oldest dreams: flying. Above everything, even his difficulties, to see them getting smaller and smaller as he climbed higher and higher and to feel the freedom of the sky.

Vincenzo was consumed by the acuity of the eagle's eyesight, perhaps because he was losing his own. He was fascinated by knowing that Maya could see an ant from the tenth floor, a coin from one kilometer, and a hare from three.

He still had his arm in plaster after the Pacentro accident, so Eleonora's father sewed him a custom-made leather glove to fit over his cast. Vincenzo needed his other arm to put on and take off the eagle's hood and to give her food.

Eleonora was poised and graceful with the raptors, while Vincenzo and Federico would often flinch when the eagle landed on their arm. Vincenzo used the excuse of his broken bone; Federico didn't know what excuse to take. Eleonora laughed at them, but she had a way of using simple gestures that made everything more manageable, and Federico became better at learning from her.

On the other hand, Vincenzo let his interest in hunting with eagles wane: "I would like to have that hood put over my own head and see nothing of this world, once and for all."

Vincenzo taught Federico which berries could be eaten, which ones set one's teeth on edge, like the cornelian, and which ones loosened the bowels. The doctor's son attended middle school in L'Aquila, and once when he came for a visit, Vincenzo made him eat the laxative berries, telling him they were delicious. The poor boy spent Sunday in the restroom: "My revenge for what his grandfather did to mine," Vincenzo explained.

One day, they brought bread and an omelet to Saint Peter, eating them while looking out over the valley. Vincenzo let his eyes blur as if looking into the void and asked: "Federico, who is your best friend?"

Federico wanted to answer that it was him, Vincenzo. Still, something interfered with his courage, and the words that came out of his mouth were different as if he was ashamed of his affection: "Well, there are several: Giovanna, Eleonora."

Vincenzo didn't wait for him to continue; he turned towards Federico, and this time he looked him in the eyes: "My best friend is you."

Federico swallowed and felt his eyelids tighten. He wanted to recover, but now it would have seemed a lie, a rag.

"I would do anything for you, Federico, anything."

"Me too, Vincenzo. Of course, me too."

On the mountain above Villa Sant'Angelo, he spent that summer, until late September, with Vincenzo, who had broken his arm protecting him. And Federico understood why someone decided to add the word "Friend" to the dictionary.

69. THE TRACTOR

Stiffe, 1981

Vincenzo's older brother, Achilles loved driving the tractor: "When I'm leaning over the mountain, I feel like I'm flying".

He was thirteen years old that summer following the eighth-grade school exams. The safety bar and windshield in front of the tractor had broken off, but he promised to be extra careful. He was plowing the clay-like soil on the hillside next to the Stiffe waterfalls to prepare a nice bed for the beets they would sow in autumn. Now and then, the tractor would get stuck, and Achilles would have to put it in reverse and back up, then climb down and clear whatever was blocking it. Often there would be a large stone, which he had to remove with the pickaxe before the tractor could move forward again. The ground had never been plowed and was full of rocks; it was a continuous process of climbing up and down from the tractor.

When it jammed for the umpteenth time, and rather than climb down again, Achilles tried to force the tractor forward by giving it more gas. The plow made it, but the tractor's wheels, having overcome whatever was blocking the plow, accelerated while the plow blades struck another obstacle.

And then what the safety bar would have prevented happened: Achilles was thrown forward, and for a moment, he flew as he dreamt of, just to land in front of the tractor still moving with the gear engaged. Half a second later, the plow broke free again, and Achilles ended up with his legs under the tractor as it ground forward.

He turned on his stomach and started to drag himself on his elbows before the plow reached him. When he saw its shadow covering his own, he pressed himself into the ground hoping the plow would pass over him. He felt instead the blade strike the inside of his foot and then kept climbing to carve into his calf.

Stuck under the moving machine, he ruptured his lungs, trying to scream loud enough to be heard over the tractor's roar that continued to plow forward.

His screams were heard all over the valley, and even visitors to the Stiffe caves reported that they heard the cry enter the caves and bounce echoes off the walls for an interminable time. They thought a pack of bears was attacking them. Some say that even today if you visit the caves when no other visitors are there and stand still, holding your breath and closing your eyes, you can still hear the scream.

The plow reached his mid-thigh when Achilles closed his eyes and cried for his mother like the lost child he was. He didn't have time to scream even louder before the plow ended up between his legs, cutting off his testicles and piercing his intestines. That was too much for the tractor to overcome, and the engine stalled. Being tilted on the slope, it started rolling downhill with Achilles' body still tangled in the plow and iron chains under the deadly machine.

The parents went mad with grief and began to live for their only remaining son: Vincenzo. Federico was spending the summer in Abruzzo and saw his transformation. The parents began to buy him everything to soothe the despair that had seized him. They indulged every whim. And Vincenzo demanded everything. In his father's heart, there was no room for another pain. His eldest son had died, and he knew the youngest would probably go blind. They could foresee when they were gone, and Vincenzo would be left struggling to survive without a brother and suffering from infirmity. And as time went by, the pain in Vincenzo's heart gave him an anger, a determination that never settled.

But when Vincenzo wanted a motocross, his father pushed back. He was afraid of an accident, given his partial disability, even if he could not bring himself to mention the blindness. But Vincenzo had become so capricious that when he was refused, he pushed his father against the wall and pointed a knife at his throat: "I want the bike. And I want it now."

Vincenzo's father worked miracles, and in the end, no one knew how; he found the money and bought it for him. The condition was that it could be ridden on vacation in Abruzzo, where there was little traffic, and not in Varese, where they lived. The same day the bike arrived, Vincenzo tried it, and while he jumped on it, the rear wheel slid on the gravel of the threshing floor of Vallecupa and turned over the low railing. He smashed against the war memorial, breaking the same arm that had saved Federico the year before.

70. THE EAGLE'S SON

St. Peter, 12 April 2009

On Easter morning, Eleonora and Federico both got up early. Federico had already prepared the coffee in the Moka for three. He divided it between the two of them. Eleonora examined the scribbles while doing her hair tails: "Do we have any solution to the riddle?"

He handed her the cup: "I worked on it a lot last night, but nothing. I feel close to it, so I change a few letters and, with that strange pattern, the value increases or decreases unpredictably."

"Thanks for the coffee. What'd you say, should we fly Maya?"

"Do you think she can get to Fontecchio from here?"

Eleonora answered: "Easy. It's only a few kilometers away. I let her fly much farther."

They freed Maya and flew her in the direction of Fontecchio while they followed her on foot. Maya went back and forth several times, and each time, they threw her back toward the Goats' Drop. When she returned with a coin, Eleonora started to jump with joy and clap her hands like a little girl.

"She's beginning to understand."

"How long will it take to recover it all?"

"If it's a boot like grandpa said, maybe a few days. If we can see where she swoops down, we can locate it. Maybe we can climb up there."

"True, it may not be that difficult with climbing gear and an expert guide. But you need a specific place to look; you're right."

"And I'm not keen on having someone else with us, let alone guide us."

They made Maya do a couple more flights and then decided to return since they didn't want to be gone too long.

As they were coming down the mountain to return to their tents, Federico asked Eleonora point-blank: "Whose child is it?"

"Where did you get that from?"

"You often put your hand on your belly. You don't drink wine. You eat meat only if it's cooked. You stay away from cats and wash the salad with disinfectant."

"So now you are Sherlock Holmes? Am I under investigation, Federico? It's Vincenzo's, but you had already guessed that."

"Are you together?"

"Not really. Nobody knows anything yet."

"Then I will call him the 'Son of the Eagle'."

"A little bit of your blood is in him, too; he will call you Uncle."

"Yes. You and Vincenzo seem to be acting strangely toward each other."

"Vincenzo asked me to abort the child. I decided to keep it. He didn't insist and accepted my choice, but it has not been the same since then."

"The mere fact of asking you changed things?"

"I guess. It's what one wants that makes the whole difference. A man defines himself by what he wants."

"Why didn't he want to keep the child?"

"He never told me. And you, how did it go with your wife?"

"Like the Abruzzese proverb: 'First-year heart to heart, second-year ass to ass, third year—fuck off.'"

Eleonora burst out laughing: "Do you mean it?"

"No, I'm kidding, but maybe it would have been better that way. She was critical of me. She complained that I never defended her, didn't take sides, didn't 'fall in love' with Manfredi, and things like that."

"It's true that it's important to feel that you are protected."

"The problem is that I'm not a fan, and we live in a country of avid fans. If I think a person is wrong, even if she's my wife, I can't defend her."

"Don't you even cheer for yourself?"

"If I'm wrong, no. Once she defended me in front of others, I realized I was wrong. I admitted it publicly ,and she got angry because I went against her. That was one of the worst fights. It also happens to me when a policeman stops me; if I run a red light, I tell him the truth."

"You are right, but do you know what the problem is? When there is a reward for doing right, you don't receive it."

"But I don't do it for reward."

"I know, but ask yourself if this is the best thing not just for you but for others, like Manfredi. Do you think that society works with mathematical rules and that everything balances? Sometimes things may add up in your favor, and you need to start paying more attention to that; you have a child now."

"And now you rebuke me too?"

They laughed again.

"I only said that because I can see you feel bad about it. And anyway, I'll always cheer for you, even if you don't cheer for yourself. Even when you are imperfect and you make mistakes. Wait, you didn't think you were perfect, did you?"

"I had a little thought like that once," Federico admitted.

"When do you think you realize that love is over?" Eleonora asked.

"I have given it much thought. It happens when you go from willing to bother the other person to say 'sorry to bother you.'"

Eleonora swallowed.

Federico returned to the previous topic: "I know Vincenzo. He's now acting as if he doesn't care or as if nothing happened. But I'm sure he cares. He's the most goodhearted man I've ever met."

"That's true."

"I know he needs time. He's emotional and passionate. Everything he does is exaggerated, so also his negative reactions are. Let him digest it, and I'm sure he will again become the shoulder you can put your head on."

Eleonora swallowed again and changed her voice: "How bad is Manfredi? I recognize the symptoms, knowing Vincenzo."

Federico felt a squeeze in his chest, bit his lips, and swallowed: "We don't know. He deceived us by hiding the disease from us, so we wasted time. There may be a cure in Cuba, but it takes a lot of money, which I don't have. The doctor says it's genetic. It happens when you have children between blood relatives; both parents must have the gene that causes it. They can be healthy carriers, but they must both have it."

Eleonora continued: "I told you earlier that some of your blood is in this child, but it's not true. Vincenzo is not your blood cousin."

"Excuse me?"

"Your uncle is not his father. Your aunt cheated on him with her cousin. The gene is in the other family, not yours."

"Vincenzo isn't my cousin? How is that possible?"

"And in addition, I must tell you that Manfredi told me that a boy at school tyrannizes him. I didn't understand how he does it; I think he attacks him in the street and robs him of his snacks. He said: 'I can never see where he's lurking.' I believe that Manfredi's friends also play that game of banging him in the back of the head, and then everyone turns away so as not to let them know who did it. He doesn't react and doesn't say anything, but it's clear that he's scared deep down. He's constantly in fear of being caught. Even if you aren't 'in love' with your son, maybe you should find a way to start a dialogue with him on these issues. Even if not as a fan, at least as a sympathizer. What'd you say?"

Federico felt flattened, almost incapable of receiving that information. He tried to organize his thoughts with logic.

It reduces the central vision of the eyes but not the peripheral vision. It's as if the brain wants to exclude what's in front of it and focus on what's around him. And all just because of a bully? Ah, but speak for yourself, you who ran away for thirty years to avoid Balthazar and his shit. You don't know how to defend yourself, so you don't defend anyone else. Face it; it's not that you're above cheering; it's because you're a coward.

He didn't know whether to be relieved or overwhelmed by those revelations. Vincenzo was still his friend, cousin or not. If, however, the gene was not in his family, then there were two hypotheses: either the doctor was right about his psychosomatic illations—and there was Manfredi's bully to support that—or Stefania had cheated on him with her cousin. The cousin she was now with at the Garda lake for that family reunion in their tradition. They never invited anyone else, only cousins. Federico had always thought it was a weird habit or that Stefania's family didn't like him, but in reality, they didn't invite anyone else, not even their uncles and aunts. Only cousins.

Awkward families.

He was tempted to let his imagination run wild with movies of him taking revenge for all those years she spent humiliating and cuckolding him. Or imagine finding Manfredi's bully and kicking the little tyrant all over Milan while holding him by the ear. He already knew that the ending would be the same: he would do neither one nor the other, which only increased his frustration. He clenched his fists until his knuckles became white. Eleonora approached him and took his hands in her own. They stayed like that for a while until he felt his fingers relax and open again.

When they arrived at the tents, they hurried to tell the others what had happened: "Maya has recovered more gold coins. At the Goats' Drop, there is a treasure of immense value."

"Excuse us if we don't rejoice, but the Tzar saw Maya flying over Fontecchio," Vincenzo spat. "He discovered you; you were stupid to let her fly so many times in the same place!"

"It only works at certain hours of the day; the sun must be at the right angle for Maya to see a glint," Eleonora said in their defense.

"Well, Balthazar had a glint in his eye when he discovered you, but it was cold, not gold," Vincenzo responded.

"Where is Balthazar now?" asked Federico.

And the same thought came to everyone's mind, and without a word, they started to run to Saint Peter.

71. BROKEN WINGS

Saint Peter, 12 April 2009 – Easter

Balthazar and Crocko kicked in the door. The Tzar had protective gardening gloves. The eagle was resting on a perch and looked at them, surprised. She was about to take flight towards the nest when Balthazar slapped her on the head and knocked her against the rock wall. With his boots, he trampled on her claws, took her wings, and bent them backward until he heard a bundle of twigs breaking. Then he threw her to the ground, admonishing her as if she could understand him: "Not an eagle stirs, but the Tzar wills it." As he was leaving, he slammed the door of the aviary and crashed Saint Peter's left door with all its rusty hinges to the ground.

When Federico, Eleonora, and Vincenzo arrived, they found Maya agonizing on the floor. As they approached, she began to jump and tried to grab and hold on to whoever came in range.

"Stop. Move away," shouted Federico. "Vincenzo—go and bring Tonino."

Vincenzo ran to Tonino's house, telling him what had happened. Tonino took a bag from a kitchen cabinet, a pair of welder's gloves, a towel, and a cardboard box with some newspaper. Then went out to the back of the house and collected some chips and sawdust, putting them in a bag.

"Let's go."

Maya was still limping around, half flying, going crazy. Neither Federico nor Eleonora had been able to calm her down. Tonino threw the towel on her and covered her, then blocked her legs with one hand. "Federico put the hood on her as soon as I lift the towel from her head." Tonino lifted just a corner, and Federico put the hood on her. The interruption of her sight calmed Maya. Then Tonino laid her down in the cardboard box.

He examined the situation by bringing her out into the light, straightening her wings, and cleaning her beak and claws. He removed his gloves, opened the bag, and smeared his hands with an ointment he had prepared from some plants he had collected in the high mountains. He used arnica and other healing herbs that he had never revealed to anyone.

He covered the injured parts of the eagle with care and plenty of medication.

"How is she?"

"I don't know; we have to wait. Animals are mysterious when they get hurt. Balthazar doesn't know birds, so the wings don't seem broken. Right now, she's under heavy stress."

Vincenzo noted the obvious: "But we can no longer go to the Goats' Drop, so goodbye to that."

"Not right away."

Eleonora hugged Federico, who at first leaned against her shoulder but then shrugged her off and kicked the last remaining piece of the door. "This time, I swear I'll kill him, but first, I'll torture him. He must go mad, locked in the aviary for months, until Maya heals and tears him to shreds. She will gouge out his eyes while he begs for the pity he will not receive."

Eleonora tried to placate him: "Be calm; it doesn't help us to take justice for ourselves."

"Then let's report it to the Carabinieri."

"You have no witnesses; you have no evidence," pointed out Giovanna, who had arrived with the twins.

"And even if I did, he'd get away with a fine. That's the only thing the law requires, and he doesn't have money problems," commented the twin lawyers.

Federico could not help thinking about the difference between law and justice.

Tonino intervened: "Pretend that nothing happened, don't help him organize his defense. On the contrary, while reorganizing ourselves, we return to help in the tents as if we have no suspicions about him. Resist the temptation, and don't give him anything to respond to until we are ready."

They returned to camp and turned on the TV to see what was happening. There was a report on the 'Running Madonna', the annual event that has characterized the Easter celebration by the inhabitants of Sulmona and Abruzzo for centuries. The mayor said he didn't want to cancel it, despite the earthquake and the risk of shocks during the ceremony, which could have triggered panic. Instead, he tried to send the region and the earthquake victims an emphatic message of rebirth and hope that the tradition had always represented.

Federico thought that the premises of the race seemed even more beautiful that day. The faithful came from having spent nights in the tents or in the open, and Federico could sense the fear and tension that was just waiting to be released during the event.

Canceling the run would have felt even more devastating than the earthquake, as it would interrupt a tradition handed down since the Middle Ages. As with the barefoot race, the festival is in honor of the Black Madonna of Loreto. The origins of the brotherhood of the Lauretans, who are the curators and executors of the tradition, are uncertain. There is no complete documentation about them, partly because some papers that could have told more were lost during the earthquake of 1706.

The service calls for a statue of the Madonna, clad in a black robe of mourning and borne on a platform by a formation of eight Lauretans in green cloaks, to leave the church after mass. At first, the Virgin Mary moves with sorrow toward the center of Piazza Garibaldi. As she reaches the fountain in the middle, however, she "sees" her son, the risen Christ—another statue. Then her black robe flies away, releasing twelve white doves and revealing a green dress embroidered in gold with a red rose. Carried by the Lauretans, the Virgin dashes to her son, waiting beneath the arches of the medieval aqueduct as the crowd rejoiced and wept.

The reunion had always been celebrated with a cannonade of firecrackers, but this year as Federico and the others watched, the fireworks were withheld out of respect for the earthquake victims, and the band did not play the alleluia. This didn't prevent an even more powerful explosion of emotion in the hearts of the faithful, who embraced, often in tears, while remembering friends, brothers, and family members suffering from the earthquake.

After the broadcast, Federico walked around to see what was happening in the world around them. In a nearby tent, a Neapolitan had stayed there through the weekend; he had prepared some babà, the delicious sponge cakes soaked in rum, and offered the treats to passersby. These included two men from a northern civil defense team; their accents reminded Federico of two who had come to perform the foreclosure on his house, but they told him:

"We are from Vicenza; Padua is far from us."

"Thank you for everything you are doing."

The words sounded lame to him; he would have liked to say something more intelligent: "I am from Milan."

"I can't believe it," the Neapolitan interjected.

"Pardon me?"

"You have such a sunny face; you can't be from Milan. They look so serious."

"Well, in fact, I'm from Abruzzo."

"Oh yes, an Abruzzese –" the Neapolitan paused as if considering something. He sighed: "You are all right, just a bit naive and quite crazy."

"You mean we are honest; you Neapolitans are crafty."

"No!" the man said, lifting his finger to the sky. "The Neapolitan is smarter. So, how many of you are there? I will give you a babà each."

"I am alone."

The improvised confectioner began to sing a famous song: "Alone, you are left alone."

Federico appreciated that positive spirit: "There is also my son."

"And don't you have any friends here?"

"Yes, of course."

"Here are some for them," putting some babas in a paper bag. "You seem to have the earthquake in your blood."

"What do you mean?" Federico asked.

"The famous philosopher Benedetto Croce, also from Abruzzo like you, was caught by the earthquake in Ischia, close to Naples."

"I don't know the story," Federico said, somewhat ashamed.

The gentleman began to tell it: "On July twenty-eight, eighteen eighty-three, at nine-thirty in the morning, a mighty shock, of magnitude five point eight, made the fishing and holiday village of Casamicciola disappear.

"The victims were more than two thousand and three hundred. Among those who left us were Benedetto Croce's father, mother, and sister. He was hit by a collapse, lost consciousness, and then when he came to his senses, he realized that he was the only one in the family to survive. He was seventeen years old."

"In his 'Memoirs of my Life', Croce wrote about those few moments before his whole family was taken away from him. He felt remorse for being the only one to be saved and wished he had been disabled after that accident as if it would have been almost a consolation to have suffered at least some damage.

"Those years were the most painful years for him. Going to bed in the evening, he hoped not to open his eyes again in the morning and thought several times even of suicide."

"That's why I'm saying that wherever you go, you seem to bring the earthquake with you."

72. AT ONNA

Onna, 12 April 2009

In the afternoon, Federico and Manfredi were taken by the Marshal to Onna to help out. Federico saw that the Pica Alfieri palace, which the Germans had commandeered during the war, had disappeared. It seemed to have been swallowed by an enormous mouth that the earth had opened and snapped shut. Two days earlier, he had learned from the news that the Germans were returning as friends and were already thinking about how to help reconstruct the country and recover its artistic and religious heritage.

Onna had suffered the most from the macroseismic intensity. Built on the alluvial plain of the river Aterno, Onna's terrain had amplified the motion of the ground. There the earthquake's force was three to five times higher than that experienced by Monticchio, which, though only two kilometers away, had suffered minor damage thanks to the rocky ground on which it was built. The local geology played a decisive role in the devastation caused by the earthquake.

The Marshal left them with the volunteers of Islamic Relief Italia, engaged in setting up the autonomous camp near the civil protection camp. Their main activities were focused on first aid, necessities, and canteen service. Meanwhile, they had also set up a small playground, thanks to donations from mosques in Emilia Romagna. Manfredi went to play with the other children.

There, Federico met Abdul Karim, a Moroccan engineer who had attended schools in Milan. Since childhood, Federico had been curious about the meaning of names. As they moved some rubble to make room to free up access to the village, Federico recalled Frederick II's vision for peace with Islam. He shared that he was named after that Frederick, who was connected to the founding of L'Aquila and had lived in close contact with the Muslim world.

His new acquaintance responded: "Many call me Abdul as if it were my first name and Karim my last name. In reality, Abd-ul means 'servant-of', and Karim means 'Generous'. So, Abd-ul Karim means 'Servant of the Generous'. 'The Generous' is one of the Divine Attributes, one of the so-called 'beautiful names', of God, of Allah."

Federico became curious: "Beautiful names? What kind of names are they?"

"They represent the attributes of God: The Clement, the Merciful; the Light, the Eternal; all beautiful. They come from the Koran. Although there is no defined number, they're traditionally considered to be ninety-nine. One hundred minus one."

Federico paused and raised his head to verify with his ears that he had heard correctly. "Sorry, how many did you say they are?"

"Ninety-nine. Why?"

"Ninety-nine is the number associated with L'Aquila. It's said that ninety-nine castles founded it, one hundred minus one. But now you have made me think of Frederick II and his contacts with the Islamic world."

"Fascinating."

"Some scholars associate the number sixty-six with the city of Jerusalem, a city sacred to all Abrahamic religions. This goes to the idea that L'Aquila was founded deliberately as a 'mirror' of Jerusalem; 99 is, in fact, the mirror of 66. You can also see it from the city plans: Jerusalem was divided into four quarters, and L'Aquila was divided into four. The Cedron and Aterno rivers flow along the two cities in the same position. The pool of Siloam in Jerusalem and the fountain of the ninety-nine spouts in L'Aquila are both adjacent to a city wall in the lower part of the city. The city walls of L'Aquila have twelve gates, like the walls of the holy city. The Basilica of Collemaggio takes up the octagon motif in Jerusalem, as in the Dome of the Rock."

"The Qubbat al-Sakkra. I see what you're getting at; do you think that Frederick II designed it to be a sacred city for Christians, Muslims, and Jews?"

Federico nodded. "Yes. It struck me that Celestino V made his entrance to L'Aquila on the back of a donkey while all the other popes had done it on horseback. I believe this imitated Jesus' entrance into Jerusalem on Palm Sunday. But I don't know why the number sixty-six was associated with God."

"It's easy. In Arabic, we have a code to replace the letters of the alphabet with numbers, where each letter also has a numerical value. God, in Arabic—'Allah'—is written with one 'A', two 'L', and one 'H'. The second 'a' is a short vowel, pronounced but not written, so it doesn't count. The 'A' - alef - is worth one, the 'L' is worth thirty, and the 'H' is worth five; if you add them together, you get sixty-six."

Federico couldn't believe it; he was stunned by such a simple and essential revelation. Abdul Karim continued: "If you are looking for other meanings of ninety-nine, I can tell you some."

"Yes, I'm looking for them. I have been since I was born."

Federico was listening with such a level of attention that he wasn't even thinking so as not to disturb what he was hearing.

Abdul Karim understood this and continued: "The expression of monotheistic faith: '*La ilaha illa Allah*', 'there is no divinity worthy of worship except Allah, God.' In this case, note the form of the written letters without considering the short vowels. For example, the short 'I' is expressed with the alef symbol; the 'a', with a sign underneath to indicate that it should be pronounced as 'i'. So if you wrote the sentence: 'LA A(i)L(a)H(a) A(i)L(l)A ALL(a)H', you would use the same letters that you have already seen: 'A', 'L', 'H'. Look."

He wrote the sentence in Arabic on a notebook with a blue and red mason's pen; in blue, the main letters, and in red, the short vowels. It could be seen at a glance: "We have already seen the numerical value of the word Allah, 66. For the first part of the sentence, we have three times the letter 'L' which is worth 30—then 90—four times the 'A', which is worth 1—then 4— the 'H', which is worth 5. Adding 90 + 4 + 5 we have 99. We see that the value of the expression of faith is 165 given by 99 + 66 mirroring themselves."

Ninety-nine beautiful names, 99 castles, 99 squares, 99 fountains.

Federico stopped to absorb those revelations. He realized that L'Aquila had a history intertwined with the Middle East through the 'Baptized Sultan' Frederick II, whose dream was to bring Christians and Muslims closer and unite them through what they had always had in common. Thanks to people of the highest caliber whom he had gathered at court, of all religions and nationalities, he had introduced even more ingredients into Italian culture than we thought. And if L'Aquila, The Eagle, was the mirror of Jerusalem, it was logical to think that it should also become a holy city in the West for all three Abrahamic religions.

Or maybe it's just a fantasy.

Abdul Karim pointed out what was also happening on the lines of the hand: "There is still a place, and you always carry it with you, where the ninety-nine is manifested."

"I always carry it with me? And I never knew it?"

"Look at your left hand. The lines draw the number eighty-one, which in Arabic characters is written as ٨١." He drew the signs on the notebook.

"While on the right hand, as in a mirror, you see the number eighteen, which, as you can imagine, is represented as follows: ١٨. Their sum gives just ninety-nine. When you put your hands together, the two 'eights' - ٨ - overlap as well as the two 'ones' - ١ - generating with their union the ninety-nine."

Federico was stunned by this information: "That is, the number—written in Arabic—associated with the city of L'Aquila is in the hands of every human being? Another coincidence? Is it possible that the different keys to understanding that number are something that no one had thought of but have always been in everyone's eyes?"

Abdul Karim replied: "I cannot tell you this; only Allah knows more. Do you know that even the Koran contains stories, allegories, and metaphors? In a verse of the Sura of the Light, it's written that 'God guides to His light whoever wants Him and proposes metaphors to men. And God knows more. Remember the story of the key and the light; are you familiar with it?"

73. THE LAND

Onna, 12 April 2009

Federico knew the story of the key and the light, thanks to his grandfather and Uncle Tonino. They told him stories of heroism, stupidity, hidden treasures, and flying carpets. Federico often asked them why they told him all those stories instead of getting to the point. Not that he didn't like them, but it always seemed to him that it took a long time to conclude. Tonino replied that it was so to keep the logical part of Federico's mind focused on the rational aspects of the story and, in the process, get other vital messages contained in the story. The stories were a way to convey specific mechanisms of life indirectly and thus avoided being rejected prematurely by reasoning. His father, uncles, and grandparents had filled his childhood with stories of all kinds.

In remembering the story Abdul Karim referred to, Federico could still picture his Nonno, who would stop and wait for everyone to be silent before starting to tell it. Otherwise, he wouldn't start. Federico could still hear his voice:

'One night, some friends met Bertoldo, walking on all fours under a lamppost. 'What are you doing?' they asked him. 'I'm looking for the keys to get into my house.'

'They all bent down to help him, but after finding nothing, one of them had a doubt: 'Bertoldo, where did you lose the keys?'

'Right there on the floor where I was trying to open the door.'

'So why are you looking for it under the streetlight?'

'Because there's more light here, idiots." Snapped Bertoldo in reply.'

Abdul Karim explained the connection: "You have to look for something where you can find it, and not necessarily where you think it's easiest to look. Just because something is difficult to see doesn't mean that our senses won't detect what is hidden if presented under proper circumstances, which may be unexpected."

Federico mentioned the treasure and asked Abdul Karim what he thought about it. The new friend smiled at him: "You know there is a *Hadith Qudsi*, a holy tradition, where Allah expresses Himself through the Prophet Muhammad—peace and blessing on him—saying: 'I was a hidden treasure and wanted to be known. I created the creation so that he would know me.' God is the only true treasure, and we were created to discover Him."

Federico remained silent in the face of these words. There seemed to be too many elements to consider—indeed, it did seem too challenging to be seen or understood. Abdul Karim continued: "Have you ever read any passage from the Koran?"

"No, although I think at this point I will. But now I am curious: what does Surah 99 say?"

Karim had the Koran with him and said that he would translate it for him, even though the translation was not the pure word of Allah. Karim's father had told him that reciting Surah 99 was the same as reciting half of the Koran. And he always preceded it by saying the words: "Said the Envoy of Allah—peace and blessings upon him: 'Truly man sleeps, it's when he dies that he wakes up.'"

First, he read it in Arabic; then, he pointed out that the Prophet Muhammad—peace and blessings upon him—said that the two verses that conclude this surah are the most terrifying of all the Koran. Then he translated it to the incredulous and frightened ears of Federico:

"Surah 99: The Earthquake
In the name of God, the Compassionate, the Merciful.
When the earth will be shaken by its final earthquake
it will discharge its burdens,
and human beings will ask: 'What is happening to her?'
That day the earth will recount everything,
based on the Lord's command.
On that day, men will go out in groups,
to be shown the results of their deeds.
So whoever will have done
even just an atom's weight of good will see it,
And whoever will have done
even an atom's weight of evil will see it."

74. BAD WEATHER

13 April 2009 – Easter Monday

Easter Monday brought lousy weather to Abruzzo, and a thunderstorm hit the tent city with a shivery icy wind. Although spring had already begun three weeks prior, the temperature dropped to almost zero Celsius. A classic in Abruzzo.

Federico had frozen hands and feet and wondered where his Abruzzo genetics had gone, which should have prepared him for these situations. He had to go to the bathroom, and he peeked out of his tent; in the rain, he could see almost nothing but the nearest tents. He looked down: a quagmire of mud had already formed, enough for him to sink up to his ankle. Giovanna read in his mind: "They have not put the gravel under the tents. They will bring it soon, so at least we will be ready for the next round."

The 'next round'. Federico felt he'd spent his entire life waiting to be ready for the 'next round', but it never seemed to arrive or always took a different route.

Civil Protection accelerated the work to complete the reception facilities and began distributing blankets and stoves to fifty-five thousand evacuees whose teeth were chattering from the cold. The firefighters announced the recovery of a gray dog so small that it could fit in a purse. Its owners had managed to escape from their house, but it had swallowed the dog. They renamed her Pasqualina because on Easter—Pasqua—Sunday, after eight days under the rubble, she had come out of her stone tomb to see the light again.

Following the earthquake, the early news focused on activities related to the immediate emergency, the recovery of the works of art, and the safety of cultural heritage. There were also stories about returning the children to school on 16 April when they returned from Easter vacations. Meanwhile, other engineers from the Fire Department arrived to check the stability of the buildings damaged by the earthquake. By April 13, they had checked about a thousand houses; half were considered habitable; a fifth would have been livable with some interventions; the remaining thirty percent were seriously damaged.

Aunt Cesidia's house wasn't considered fit for habitation, even though it didn't seem damaged, and she had continued to sleep there.

They told her that the problem was not her house but the houses all around her, built one on top of the other, with walls in common with hers. If one of the neighboring houses were to fall, it would have brought the others down too. The same was true for Federico's parent's house, which required some structural intervention.

Eleonora knew her brother Giulio well; he avoided her while she saw him arguing with people in small groups several times. She called him in and brought him to a quiet corner: "I still can't understand how Balthazar has known about the treasure."

Giulio's face went red.

"Do you think this is just like snitching on your sister? Do you understand the implications of what you did?"

"You and that Milanese. The Tzar has all the reasons to hate him. Without that coward, we would have had one of the greatest rugby players that L'Aquila would have ever seen. Maybe we would still have the great successes of the old days. Your friend maimed his foot and ran away. What right has he now to come back and play the savior?"

"It had been an accident caused by Balthazar, and Federico has been exiled; you know nothing about it."

"I know I've seen the Tzar only helping all these years. He regularly donates money to the rugby club. He was able to defend peasants in court and obtain things that otherwise would not have been given to them, even if they were entitled to them."

"He abused his power."

"He did it for a just cause, while we all know why your friend is here."

"And that is?"

"He pursued only his interests for thirty years, and now that he has lost everything, he has come back to steal from us."

"You are my brother. I will put all this aside. We'll talk again at the end of this story."

Federico had some questions buzzing in his head. He had turned every corner in his mind, looking for the answers. Who had hidden that treasure? Who were these people who expressed themselves in code? Why was it essential to be so secretive?

Federico decided to go to his parent's house alone to inspect the cave and the house itself again. Maybe there was some answer. And he still needed to read all the papers they had discovered. He would take these along with him, and maybe without a thousand eyes watching, he could examine them as he wanted to. Perhaps Manfredi could stay with

Eleonora while he was there. He thought Manfredi would benefit from the affection of a female figure. *What a selfish explanation.*

And he focused again: *Stay on target.*

He would wait for the right moment in the early afternoon when everyone would have the food and wine of the banquet in their bodies.

75. EASTER

13 April 2009 – Easter Monday

Vincenzo was rushing to continue the search and retrieve the coins: "Let's go, come on, enough of this talk, let's not wait; it's already nearly noon."

"We have no choice; it's Pasquetta, and there's the picnic. If we don't show up, they'll come looking for us," Federico said.

"They are still doing the traditional outing in this mess?"

"Yes, the Unitalsi Charitas of San Benedetto dei Marsi brought three thousand roasts. And besides, we have no new clues in hand; our word combinations don't seem to give new solutions."

With things on hold for the moment, Federico went to look in on Aunt Cesidia; he found her in the cooking area of the tents, thinning the pasta sheet with a rolling pin. "What are you doing, Aunt?"

"You don't recognize the maccaroni?"

Federico stopped to observe. When the dough reached a thickness of about two millimeters, Cesidia took the strip of pasta and placed it on a frame made of stretched steel wires, parallel to each other, on a beech wood frame: the traditional 'guitar'. She slid the rolling pin over it, and the threads cut the pastry into strips. Then she pressed her index finger on the cut sheet at the base of the guitar, as if she were playing an arpeggio, to make the cut pastry come down completely. She then laid it on the tray to dry.

Meanwhile, she cooked the sauce in a pot; lamb meat beaten thin with the knife and flavored with herbs and tomato. Federico could already taste the sauce that would penetrate the pores of those strips of fresh pasta and adhere to it. A guitar string had broken, and he pointed it out to his aunt, who frowned at it: "It's too bad that the umbrella maker won't pass by."

"Umbrella maker" was an itinerant repairman who would ride from village to village by bicycle with a simple toolbox and shout: "*Ooo-òmbrellaio!*" Federico remembered the intonation of the first 'o' prolonged, as when you do the 'ola' at the stadium, which drew the village's attention, followed by the announcement of the service being offered: 'I repair umbrellas and guitars'. And, of course, he meant the tool to cut the maccaroni. Like many others, the umbrella maker was one of the disappearing itinerant trades.

In Federico's childhood, the job that most intrigued him was the ash collector. He came from La Taranta and passed house to house, cleaning the fireplaces in exchange for the ashes. It always remained a great mystery for Federico: *What do they do with that gray dust?*

He asked his father, who didn't answer him. One morning, when he came to wake Federico up, he pointed out the blanket of his bed: "Observe it well, it's; it's the typical wool blanket of Abruzzo. Every family here has at least one for each family member. It has neither a front nor a back and, therefore, can be used on both sides. Have you seen how vivid their colors are? Look also at the fringes and the creative design."

"Yes, they are beautiful."

"They are hand woven by the artisans of Taranta Peligna. They use ash to absorb and neutralize the dye's acidity, making the colors much brighter."

Federico heard the others call him to help prepare the roasts. He came out of the tent with the light and colors of his memories still in his eyes. He set to work. First, they arranged the 'canala', the long and narrow grills. Its name comes from the fact that once upon a time, it used to be an old gutter—'canala'—that, instead of being thrown away, was saved to prepare the charcoal and bake the roasts. They had the perfect width to support the spit. They seemed to be made on purpose.

The proper grilling of the roasts was a contentious topic. Everyone claimed they could make the embers better than anyone else, just as some believed that the roasts should be cooked to perfection, while others said they should be cooked until they were almost charred. The Abruzzese sometimes miss the concept of 'everyone has their tastes'. There is only one way, suitable for everyone else. Are we surprised that it's the one that the speaker is promoting? Famous saying condensed its attitude. For example, suggesting something different from a voiced opinion would be met with a personal statement: "It's okay, as long as you prefer to use a grater instead of toilet paper."

Or they might say, with a huff: "Fine, if you want to wipe your nose with a shotgun."

Federico had witnessed endless quarrels—he never saw them ending after many years—between uncles who fought over a wall, a field, a hand of cards. Basically: you do things differently from me, so you are wrong, evil, sinister, or any other negative meaning. On the other hand, Federico had developed a sense of relativity, live and let live, which caused him problems with Stefania over time.

It's better to be sectarian in this tribal setting, the Italian family.

Federico looked at the raw roasts, now famous all over Italy as 'arrosticini'. Legend has it that they were invented in the thirties by two shepherds who cut the meat of an old sheep into small pieces so as not to waste food, taking it from areas close to the animal's bones. The meat was then skewered on wooden sticks of a plant that grows wild along the banks of the river Aterno and cooked outdoors. They learned how to alternate meat with fat that, melting on the embers, makes the roasts softer and tastier.

Vincenzo arrived with a gutter that he had recovered from a house destroyed by the earthquake; "There is so much here that is no longer needed." He had cut it and then folded it at the ends so as not to let the embers come out. He placed it on some stones, one on top of the other, to raise it from the ground: "These stones are no longer useful either; let's give them some dignity."

"Here, Federico, your fan," Giovanna said, handing him a piece of cardboard to give air to the embers.

Turning to Manfredi and a small group of children watching, Federico offered smug instruction: "If you prepare the roasts in the open air, remember to ventilate the embers to keep them alive and to distribute the heat evenly."

"There you go, he starts to be the professor again," laughed Vincenzo.

The embers, however, were not burning, so a woman named Maria arrived with a hair dryer and an extension cord of about ten meters: "Step aside, Milanese."

Maria pointed the hairdryer to the gutter, put it to maximum, and the embers became hot in less than three seconds: "Refresher course in how to be a good Abruzzese."

Then they taught Manfredi how to take the skewers and turn them a quarter turn at a time, to brown them evenly on a low flame from all four sides. It's a task made easy by the fact that the meat pieces are cut into cubes: four sides, four turns. The skewer length was designed to have all the meat inside the gutter and the ends of the skewer outside, easy to handle without getting burnt. Not like Stefania used to do when she cooked them on a regular grill or in a pan.

Manfredi ate ten pieces, even while cooking them, and completed the meal with a bit of mixed pecorino cheese. "We won't tell your mother," Federico winked at him.

Giovanna brought the wine, Montepulciano d'Abruzzo: "It comes from the plain of Ofena. I like it because it has the scent and taste of fruit, like eating cherries and berries together. Full-bodied."

"Spoken like a true sommelier," Federico observed, lowering the corners of his mouth and nodding several times.

"Yes, I took a course at L'Aquila before the world collapsed."

The wine also had a story connected with Frederick II. As soon as he ascended the throne, he wrote numerous articles in the Constitutions of Melfi that regulated the wine trade in the Swabian kingdom of Sicily and Apulia, with severe penalties against the hosts who dared adulterate it.

Federico told the little group, while eating and drinking, how the Constitutions of Melfi were issued in Latin and in the form of Ean dict. Even today, they exude impressive moral rigor. The wine trade is but one example. Some provisions aimed to repress tavern frauds, which had become more numerous and a symbol 'not only of leisure but also of the consumption of wine by the popular classes.' Federico reported that the Emperor proclaimed: "We forbid the innkeepers or sellers of any wine to sell watered-down wine for pure wine. So that the frauds of the individual artifacts are not without punishment, we decree that the first time they're caught selling the watered-down wine for straightforward wine, they will be punished by our tax authorities to pay a pound of pure gold. But if he cannot pay, he will be subject to flogging. His hand will be cut off if caught doing this a second time. He, who is caught for the third time acting in this way, faces the danger of death by hanging."

Federico concluded: "This was what happened under Federico II to those who allowed themselves to add water to wine, making it weaker and less full-bodied".

"And we should also put those criminals who water down the cement to death," Peppino, the bricklayer, shouted, raising a full glass.

76. ABRUZZO

13 April 2009 – Easter Monday

And as always, it was time for singing with friends after the meal. Guerrino had the most powerful voice in the whole valley and specialized in singing 'Maria Nicola' during village festivals.

At the accordion, Mimìtt, a big man of one hundred and forty kilos whose greatest joy was selling ice cream to children. The classic Abruzzese accordion is played with two alternating basses on the 'pum' of the 'ta-pùm, ta-pùm, ta-ta-ra-ta-pùm' rhythm. Meanwhile, Dino —'Dean'—had put two spoons 'ass to ass', each offering the other its convex face. He then held one fixed between the index finger and thumb, leaving the other movable between the index and middle finger as if they were flexible pliers. Keeping his fist soft, he banged them on the leg and free hand, producing a 'click-it-ee' sound, perfect for the rhythm of the 'saltarello'.

Guerrino sang, leading the orchestra formed by the few musicians and the choir of the people who answered him. Those who could not sing whistled to keep the rhythm, and everyone clapped their hands. The song began:

"You bought a shiny red skirt; from afar it sends an alert, Maria Nicola."

The fantastic thing about Guerrino was that, when he sang, he changed the verses, adapting them to the people present, innuendo at a relationship between them and the iconic young lady that would receive gifts from them. Federico was dying of laughter now, as he was then.

"You bought a bright yellow skirt; with whom are you going to flirt?"

And then all in chorus while holding back the laughter: *"Maria Nico-o-laaaa."*

Guerrino looked around him until he met the gaze of the delicatessen maker:

"You have bought yourself a fur with the sausage you prefer."

Then he included the spoon player:

"You bought the washing machine with the money of Uncle Dean,"

And everybody answered in chorus: "Maria Nico-o-laaaa."
Then it was the turn of the representatives of the army:

"You got a nice apartment with the money of the regiment."

Then he called the stop of the band's snare drum and the final chorus all together on the extended 'a' of Mariaaaaaaaaaa - drum roll - then Niccoooooooo... - another roll - and then all together for the final chorus:

"Why did you put up with this?
You're such a lovely girl,
Come and marry me
Maria Nicola."

People laughed at Guerrino's ability to improvise the stanzas on his feet, which seemed to have been written specifically for the people he was bringing up. The trust was to use the most recent and relevant information possible, so he began to introduce new words. This time he didn't choose people as he usually did:

"The earthquake made me a rover,
it had knocked my whole house over.
Maria Nico-o-la.
We now live in blue tents,
some of us can spare our rents.
Maria Nico-o-la."

The laughter stopped. The blue tents were those provided by civil protection. One could not joke about the situation now. People scattered, some to get coffee, some to pick up something they had left halfway through.

Guerrino was disappointed: "What did I say? It's the truth."

"Maybe it's better to tell people a few nice-sounding lies now."

Guerrino slammed his hands on his hips, swinging his head left and right: "Oh, well, imagine that!"

Mimìtt didn't give up but continued with the accordion, hinting at some chords and a different melody; Federico recognized it. It was "Abruzzo"; his mother would sing it to him every time they walked in the mountains. Federico began to sing it in a low voice, with Mimìtt accompanying him:

"I climbed on the Gran Sasso; it took away my speech,
It seemed that step by step, the infinite I'd reach."

Then Eleonora joined, and Federico silenced himself; as her voice rose in flight, he felt as if it were soaring from the height of the Gran Sasso itself to glide over the valleys. She had no breath of his own as if he had no source to make a sound. And she described the wonders that could be seen from that peak:

"What a turquoise, what a sea, what beauty, what a quiet.
Even Rome and the other sea could be seen from that height."

The song continued, mentioning other places in Abruzzo: the Maiella, the sea, the mountains, the shepherds, and the countryside.

They all drew near each other as she sang, and Federico started singing again, led by her. That moment united all of them. Mimìtt wiped a tear with his right sleeve without stopping playing the chords with his left hand.

Federico looked at Eleonora, who stuck out her tongue at him, and then laughed. Federico shook his head, and Eleonora approached him and sat by his side. They said nothing.

They left their imaginations to climb to that infinite, one panting after another, one smile after another, one blushing after another.

77. THE ENGINEER'S MANUAL

Vallecupa, 13 April 2009

Federico had made his way through the dusty water with which the rain sprayed the base camp, and after going to the bathroom, he took the opportunity to sneak to his parent's house.

He entered it with caution and scrutinized it. There was rubble everywhere, but the load-bearing points didn't seem to be damaged. It was almost empty; his mother had already taken everything she could. The gigantic bookcase was left, as there was not enough room in their apartment in Milan. He stopped to contemplate it; the last time he saw it was in 1981. He could still hear his father's voice when he caught him leafing through the volumes: "Who knows what you hope to jump out of those books."

He reviewed his technical books. *Solar Energy and its Applications*, by Righini e Nebbia, 1966. He read the first line of the preface: "The Sun continually gives the planet Earth a torrent of energy that could essentially cover the needs of the whole of humanity. *The Industrial Technician's Handbook*, published by Cremonese, also from 1966. And then the large book his father constantly consulted: Giuseppe Colombo's, *The Engineer's Manual, 1965*. The book's preface, dated 1877, said it was the 80th edition.

As he thumbed through the book, a note in his father's handwriting fell from page 706. In that chapter, there was a description of materials such as cement, sand, gravel, and then mild, hard, or semi-hard steel. The book emphasized that sand must be free of organic materials and not muddy, earthy, or salty. He read about iron rods and the dosing of the dough.

His father's notes said the water-cement ratio and curing time were crucial. He had written some notes on the history of cement durability as it was used during the '30s, '50s, and '80s.

Cement has been improving over the years. The problem is that they're using less and less of it.

The book said that if the water-to-cement ratio were too high, it would result in more porosity, thus exposing the cement to internal fractures and external penetrations. In short, 'watered-down cement', as

Peppino would have said, is less solid and less durable. Next, his father had written: 'Bridges, highways, viaducts.'

The book cited that in the '30s, in every cubic meter of construction, there were 350 kilos of cement to 140 liters of water. In 1980, less than 300 kilos of cement and about 200 liters of water in a cubic meter. So, in the '30s, by balancing water and cement, builders had a result with less porosity; it was more compact and, therefore, more durable.

Something similar was written in the manual about sand and gravel: "Normal mix: 300 kg of cement + 0.400 m3 of sand + 0.800 m3 of gravel + 120 liters of water."

The book specified: "It's good, however, to keep a certain water-cement ratio (in weight). At least 0.4." He read the 'however' three times. It was as if the manual knew there was a temptation for human nature.

Federico divided 140 by 350, as it was mixed in the '30s and came to 0.4. He returned to reading. He then divided 120 by 300; the proportions recommended by the manual: were also 0.4. He started to be afraid. He made the ratio of the proportions used in the '80s; 200 divided by 300: about 0.67. Too high. So, the cement can't resist; and not only that, but atmospheric agents also penetrate inside, even if it's outdoors; they weaken it, and if there are stresses, it cannot withstand them. Concrete, if it's well-made, is, in fact, impermeable to water and impervious to sulfates. *If it's well-made.*

Although he didn't think he had become an expert builder by reading only a few lines of a manual, he could understand that the situation was serious, and then he saw another note from his father:

Villette di Santa Chiara: TOO MUCH SAND.
Worse than that, they put in seven rods instead of ten.

The summary was simple: from the '30s onwards, cement had been diluted. And some manufacturers, to save money, reduced its strength even more by increasing the percentage of sand. Last but not least, instead of putting at least ten iron rods in the pillars, they put only seven.

He checked the numbers several times. This time his father had not miscalculated, as he had done with expanded clay.

78. THE TZAR'S TOMB

Federico told Tonino what he had discovered from his father's notes and saw him lower his head, plunging into silence.

"What's going on, Toni?"

Tonino sighed: "You know more and more about your father, and that's good. But you don't know an important part I am infinitely sorry about."

"What are you talking about now, Toni?"

"When building the cottages in Santa Chiara, your father observed that the consumption of cement bags was reduced compared to that of sand. Now they call it 'weakened concrete'. Some builders put in less cement to cut costs or earn more money. He also counted iron rods and saw thirty percent less than needed."

"What did he do when he found out?"

"He told me that he warned the builder and would have gone to Armando's house to give him a detailed report. When your father went there, Armando was still at the bar. His wife let your father in. They had known each other as children. When Armando returned, he found them together and, in anger, killed them both. Your mother, in shame, never came back. You were victims of that warning, and while you were growing up, she was withering, inside and out."

Federico felt a bite in the mouth of his stomach but wanted to know everything. "Could you have done something to prevent it?"

"I wanted to report what happened, but your mother begged me to let it go. She didn't want to face all the problems that would result. And above all, she wanted to protect you, whose father had just been killed. She preferred to take you back to Milan. At the time, the two things didn't seem related, at least not in the way I understand them now, so I didn't insist."

"You followed mother's wishes; you have nothing to reproach yourself for. But how were things related?"

"The more I think about it, the more I am convinced that it was Don Cesare who instigated the wrath of Armando. Perhaps he was interested in covering up the story of the material used in the constructions; perhaps he was also involved. I was so upset at the time that I didn't think about it. You were gone, and so, as not to re-enact the story or upset the balance that had come back into everyone's life after the tragedy, I, too, let it go. The worst thing is that Don Cesare also helped me with the building amnesty for my house and had some irregularities approved. Otherwise, my house would have been torn down, and I didn't have the money to build another one. I hope you will forgive me, though I don't know how to forgive myself."

Federico clenched his fists, thinking about all the tortures he would like to inflict on Balthazar and Don Cesare. He imagined tying them by their feet and dragging them over the sharp rocks above St. Peter until their bodies were filled with cuts and then opening the aviaries and leaving them to the raptors attracted by the blood from their wounds.

He took a full breath, and his mind started to clear: "You didn't kill my father, and I don't think you could have prevented it. I don't have anything to forgive you for. I am happy to have been able to meet you again. You are the person who taught me the most in life."

Federico hugged Tonino, still shaking: "I feel bad for not having told you these facts for all these years."

"Think about it, Toni. In the end, these kinds of people never commit crimes. They instigate, threaten, and apply pressure. But the person who shot my father was Armando. People already hurt themselves through this perverse relationship they have with those in power; there is no need to harm them further. And they vote for these vipers and call them their defenders. They are all accomplices, in a way."

Tonino detached himself from Federico, put his hands on his shoulders, and looked him in the eyes: "I want to see the cottages of Santa Chiara. There are about a hundred houses inhabited by families there. The seismic wave didn't pass near them. But they may not be so fortunate the next tremor, and many people could die under their walls. I must prevent it."

"But now we are the ones under suspicion. The authorities won't believe you."

"If I can't tell the Carabinieri, I'll go and tell the villagers."

"And how will you prove it—by breaking a wall and showing what's inside? And in any case, you will be arrested for inciting alarm."

Federico had no immediate solution to help Tonino get that burden off his conscience. He had to be patient and do what he hated most: take a risk. "Give me a few days. As soon as we gain a few grams of credibility, we will disclose this, I promise you. Let's cross our fingers."

Meanwhile, Balthazar availed himself of Aunt Cesidia's house being evacuated, and at 11:00 p.m., he crept back there in secret. He opened all the drawers, finding only old black and white photos: Carlantonio with his mustache and half-closed eye; his father with hat and cane; his uncle, the doctor, in jacket and tie. There was also one of the Tzar, coming out of mass, looking cheerful, with Federico sulking behind him. A handwritten note said it was in 1980.

While he was trying to move the cupboard to see if she had glued the letter behind it, he felt it slide too easily. He was amazed at his strength—but he soon realized that the cabinet was about to crush him against the opposite wall. He became all too aware of what was happening. At 11:14 p.m., a 5.1 shock made the heavy cabinet fall to one side, toward his damaged foot that didn't have enough strength to sustain its weight. Carried by the shaking and their momentum, man and furniture slid towards the stairs leading to the cellar. He tried to cling to the steps with his hands and lift his upper body above the sideboard as they crashed downward, but then he felt a tearing pain in his legs. Chased by an animal more terrible than those pigs that maimed his foot thirty years earlier, he was borne to the floor of the cellar, his scream unheard over the roar of the earth.

Though covered by debris, he realized he could still breathe, even buried under the collapsed house.

79. THE WOLF

A few minutes before the shock, Federico, who was with the others in the tents, had found another place that could be a solution for the poem's riddle. He was proud to announce: "Climb by Case Isaia, Campotosto. Calculating, twenty-one plus nine, plus ten, plus twenty-one, plus thirty-eight equals ninety-nine."

"'Besides the water sloping with the winds' is the 'wind splitter' on Lake Campotosto,'" exclaimed Giovanna.

"Fantastic! We know where it is." exulted Vincenzo.

"Sloping is not precise, though," the twins pointed out.

"Whatever, it's poetic license. Have you become more finicky than me?" replied Federico.

"They thought to hide it there because those who know the ancient history of the place also know that there, beside the lake, were legendary winds."

"Besides the water, so not underwater?" asked Giovanna.

"That's right, remember that the lake was not there at the time; that's why they suggest climbing," replied Federico.

"If it's so ancient, how do you know it?" persisted the twins.

"The Wolf told me."

The lake of Campotosto is the most important artificial basin in Abruzzo and extends for about fourteen square kilometers. It was created by constructing three dams that, trapping water at an altitude of 1,300 meters, gave life to the second-largest artificial reservoir in Italy. There, the 30 kilometers of the Campotosto-Amatrice fault zone flow. Of course, it's a metaphor because no one wants the fault to move. It's about 160 meters from the concrete and iron gravity dam that, with its 39 meters of height, harnesses the Rio Fucino. On the opposite side, 400 meters away, is the hamlet of Case Isaia.

Federico had been on the lake as a boy when he had taken a trip there, together with Vincenzo, his brother, and his parents. They called 'The Wolf' the old man that had driven them there. They got in his boat, and he told them about his life. He had been a porter in the war of 1918:

'I learned to read in the army from a book that explained how to medicate people with herbs.'

The Wolf continued to treat men and animals. He became so skilled that the sick preferred him to the doctor. The latter saw his role threatened and had him arrested. Of course, the doctor didn't ask himself whether the remedies were effective; it was a matter of social position and power. Eventually, the Wolf was released, although he was prevented from administering any treatments.

In 1924 machines designed to extract peat arrived at the plain of Campotosto, and a large construction site was built that extended over the marshes. There was no dam or artificial lake then. The machines dug trenches in the pastures and laid tracks that devastated the green land that gave food to cows, goats, and sheep.

The Wolf had become like St. Anthony against 'Ju Demonie' of the Abruzzese song. The tradition is that the Demon does all sorts of things to spite and tempt St. Anthony, who maintains a sense of humor and can get by and stay positive, so he defeats him.

In the same way, The Wolf didn't give up; he broke the tracks built by the modern Satan and was arrested again.

Not even half an hour later, the people were already in rebellion. The women tied themselves to the bells and made them ring with their batons. The sky rang as during an experimental artist's concert. On the other hand, the men performed the dry sound of slaps and the duller sound of fists on less willing surfaces. The peasants took their pitchforks and freed The Wolf. They brought him home in triumph as a victorious hero against the evil tyranny of the mining industry.

The Wolf told Federico and his family: "That 'peaty region' is now below us at a depth of thirty meters."

The boat was bursting with its weight, and the engine seemed always to be exhaling its last breath. They saw the ruins of the Madonna Del Piedicino, destroyed by the earthquake of 1703, started by the infamous Campotosto-Amatrice fault. Thousands of people had died.

As they cut the fog and water with the boat's bow, The Wolf named the places passing below them, accompanied by the soundtrack of the engine's rhythm at idle. The Wolf spoke as if they were flying over the same landscape in an airplane before the 325 million cubic meters of water submerged the plain, the houses, the paths, and the mule tracks in 1940.

The shock and screams of a young man from the village interrupted Federico's memories of the lake and brought him back to the present in the tents of the base camp: "The lawyer, the lawyer, has been buried. Help!"

They all went into the square: "Where did it happen?"

"At Cesidia's house."

"Bastard," Federico muttered, holding back a grimace of anger. He released his breath and decided: "Let's get him."

"Leave him where he is. He wouldn't even try to save you," Vincenzo tried to dissuade him.

Federico's tone was peremptory: "It's true: we are different," and he began to walk towards Aunt Cesidia's house.

"Federico, the man who forgives everyone," bemoaned Vincenzo.

"Except himself," sighed Eleonora, exchanging glances with Vincenzo.

Both understood that they wouldn't be able to stop his stubbornness; they couldn't but follow him.

Tonino, however, held Vincenzo by taking his arm: "Wait, not you. You must take me to Santa Chiara."

Both looked at Federico, who nodded.

80. THE RESURRECTION OF THE TZAR

Village of Aunt Cesidia, 13 April 2009 – Tuesday night

The Civil Protection arrived and, before midnight, thanks to Federico and the others, had already cleared most of the rubble around the spot where the Tzar had been buried. Giulio had been zealous, motivated by Federico's intentions: "You are right. We are different".

Giulio took away the last stones and invited Federico, with a raised eyebrow and a smile: "Do you want to greet him?"

Federico nodded and then lowered his head to enter the passage and, with Giulio, guided and helped by the Civil Protection, took Balthazar out.

He didn't have any visible injury and started to walk. He seemed to have his eyes on the hands supporting him, covered with cuts and abrasions. Then looking up, he must have noticed that under all that white dust was his rival, the person he most wanted to erase from his life: Federico. He pushed him away, unbalancing himself, and Giulio had to grab Balthazar around the waist as if he wanted to tackle him so that he wouldn't fall and smash himself again on the broken stones.

They both looked around and saw the group of people rushing to watch the scene in a theater of rubble and ruins. Their faces came closer. Balthazar spoke to Federico and Giulio with a snarling whisper: "Maybe you now expect the Tzar to forgive you?"

"Sure, please forgive me because YOU locked me in the pig pen."

"It was just a prank to scare you."

"And smashing my face against the railing? Were you pranking then, too?"

"You liked Eleonora, my girlfriend. Did you think that I hadn't noticed? Tell the truth; you still like her now."

The response took Federico by surprise. He closed his eyes and raised his eyebrows, chasing the thought away by tilting his head to the left. "How many years do you want to go on with this game of 'It's Federico's fault if the Tzar tried to kill him'? I want to write it down, so I can mark it on the calendar."

Balthazar tightened his lips to hold back a violent reaction; he succeeded: "So, are you proposing to forget about the past, like the song? You're not my lover."

"And what do you suggest instead: 'Warn Federico not to tread on my Abruzzo soil covered with rubble, of which I am the sole master?' Look around you. Who will rebuild all this while you go on living your life with the memories and anger of a child?"

Federico realized that he had repeated the exact words that Eleonora had said to him a few days earlier. Balthazar smiled, shaking his head. When he smiled, his mouth widened in a horrible grimace. They didn't shake hands; they didn't hug each other; Federico returned only a quarter of that smile.

Did they forgive each other? Federico didn't even know what that meant. He thought forgiving perhaps meant living without that constant fear within himself, at least from that moment on. Or, for that matter, without that anxious background chatter towards Stefania or his job. In fact, what is forgiving if not avoiding being conditioned by the fear of what has been, for better or for worse, a controlling element of our life and our character? Is the answer not rooted in the construction of the word "for-give"? When you give something, it's a gift; the term refers to an inner gesture that becomes a present: I will no longer hold something against you. You give the other person the gift of freedom from feeling guilty or fearful. At the same time, you give yourself the gift of being free from carrying the burden of hurt, as if it was a debt that needed to be repaid. Could he give such a gift to Balthazar and an even more miraculous freedom to himself? What about giving that gift to Stefania? And to his boss? To his parents, or even to life itself? Would he be free if he could give the 'gift' to Balthazar but not the others?

There must have been about sixty people around them when the TV arrived. With the spotlight on Balthazar, it was easier to see the whitewashed hair and the wound on his forehead. The interviewer began: "Who was the first person you saw when the rubble was cleared?"

Balthazar looked at Federico and nodded in his direction without answering.

The reporter understood and pressed him: "And what did you think when you saw him?"

"That I was dead, and the Devil himself had come for me."

81. THE CARBONARI

13 April 2009

Federico needed to breathe, to mull things over, and as often the case when he needed to feel better; he took refuge in reading. He shook off the emotions of the recent events and walked in the night to his father's library.

He took the essay by Carlo Botta, the scholar of the Carbonari uprisings. It still had several bookmarks; he began to read in one of those places: "The Carboneria had its origin and showed itself for the first time in the mountains of Abruzzo, where a large amount of coal is made. Many forests, much wood, and much coal." As Tonino had told him.

Their creed was clear: "The Carbonari show a sincere faith in the religion of Jesus as found in the Gospel, freed of all the extraneous elements that theologians have introduced for eighteen centuries." He repeated to himself: *"Free of all the extraneous elements that theologians have introduced for eighteen centuries."*

Reading always transported him out of himself; it allowed him to forget who he was. Refreshing. Concentrating on the printed words, he could build other worlds and better situations, which gave him hope that something higher could be achieved. He knew it was beneficial to his mental health, even if it wasn't real.

His father had many books by another author, and many had the same type of art on the covers that recalled Middle Eastern ornamental motifs. He leafed through them. There was one in particular that attracted him. He saw that it also had bookmarks in various chapters; he opened it to one that also talked about the Carboneria.

He saw some notes in his father's handwriting, and it squeezed his chest to imagine him opening those books and declaiming the key passages, as he sometimes did. The notes were paraphrases of what was written in the tome, with some added context and interpretation:

The Carboneria was born as a society dedicated to doing good and mutual aid while following a spiritual path in line with the great Middle Eastern spiritual traditions—Jewish, Christian, and Muslim—in particular with the Sufi tradition, which is their mystical heart. The great religions connect with threads of different colors, whose weaving gives rise to a beautiful pattern similar to that of a Persian carpet.

Another note followed:

The smallest unit of the Carbonari was called 'Baracca'. 'Baraka' means 'blessing' in Arabic. It's considered the palpable energy transmitted from the master to the pupil or from the saints. In fact, in the countryside, the Carbonari gave their blessing to brides.

They called each other 'good cousins'. Good cousin, in Arabic, is the same word to describe the ancient Sufi, 'muqaribin', that is, 'those who are close'.

The Moor that appears on the banner of the city of L'Aquila is a sign of the presence of the coal workers and a hint of their Middle East origin. One arrow, two targets. The influences of the exchanges with the near east are everywhere. As in Arabic, in Abruzzo, we don't voice all the vowels, and we say "porticàll" to say orange, as in many Middle Eastern countries.

Even spaghetti, called 'maccaroni' here in Abruzzo, was brought from China to Italy via the silk route, connecting Rome with Beijing during the Middle Ages. At that time, it was the Arabs who controlled the route and called that type of pasta 'muqarrani', which means 'resembling horns'.

His father had trusted the hypothesis that Federico was now starting to understand. He didn't yet have the words to describe it fully. His father was giving them to him, thanks to that fundamental book that Federico was also beginning to worship, and that was at the origin of all those notes that were not translations of the book but its elaborations:

The Sufi spiritual tradition has been present and active here in Abruzzo for thousands of years, leaving traces everywhere and continuing to live with subtle methods. For example, thousands of stories and timeless anecdotes seem like jokes and so are regularly told and remain imprinted in mind. By causing a smile, they positively alter the thoughts and thus help correct the mental attitudes mocked in the story.

The figure of Bertoldo, for example, is the wise idiot who embodies the human characteristics to which attention must be paid for one to evolve. He sums up all the attributes of the world's wise, idiotic, cunning, and stupid people.

Strange rites are celebrated in Abruzzo: the barefoot race, the Madonna who runs away, and Cocullo's snakes. I don't know which of them are spiritual and which are not. Perhaps we must discover it for ourselves according to our inner perception. Fragments of the mystical tradition are enclosed within them, thus remaining hidden, and for this reason, protected and able to communicate vital signs to those who know how to read them, even after millennia.

Federico saw himself again as a child one summer evening while attending an itinerant theater show around Abruzzo's villages, staging episodes of Bertoldo's life in the squares of the towns.

Drafting the people of the village as extras and actors, they staged the classic stories that, at this point, Federico understood to be teaching stories. Unexpected endings avoided a univocal reading of the stories. It was necessary to keep a broader space in the mind to maintain as many interpretations as possible.

That evening they staged the story of Bertoldo and the woolly hat. Federico knew it because Uncle Tonino had told him. These stories have existed for thousands of years in Abruzzo's culture and others. Their effect continues to exert a positive impact, handed down from mother to daughter, father to son, and generation to generation. Since they're often entertaining, they have been well-preserved over the millennia. Just as the basket carried and saved Moses, they bring important messages to humanity, hidden in the wicker of entertainment. Here is the story:

Bertoldo was traveling, and after having dined in an inn, he went to bed, asking the innkeeper to be woken up early: at five in the morning. The landlord agreed, specifying that night he would have to share the room with another person who would arrive later and wake up later than him. Bertoldo emphasized that the innkeeper needed not to make a mistake and wake the wrong person because he had a long way to go the next day. The landlord reassured him, saying he would ask the other to put on a red woolly hat when going to bed to ensure he was not making a mistake.

When the other guest returned, the innkeeper told him of the arrangement, but the guest decided to play a joke. So, he put the little red hat on Bertoldo's head while he was fast asleep. When the innkeeper woke him up at the agreed time, Bertoldo got up and went to the bathroom. Lifting his head to look at himself in the mirror, he saw the red hat and exploded: "What an idiot innkeeper. Instead of waking me up, he woke up the other fellow."

Those were stories that often made you laugh because it was Bertoldo who was embarrassed, not you. But if you wanted the story to make you progress, you would have to ask yourself: "How many times have I been an idiot, but I called someone else an idiot instead? Do I need a hat, a title, a profession to be able to recognize myself?"

When he was still in first grade, Uncle Tonino offered him a test: "Even if they promote you to second grade, you still don't know how to hide your thoughts. In fact, I can read your mind."

"I don't believe it," replied a skeptical Federico.

"Go over there, and put yourself in the most awkward position you can think of, and when you are ready, ask me: 'What do I look like?' And I will guess."

Federico ran into the other room, put his arms around his neck, crossed his legs underneath himself, put his head between his knees, and then rolled upside down so that his feet went up on the wall, and then asked:

"What do I look like?"

"Like a salami," replied his uncle.

Federico, literal in his childish understanding, thought that salami didn't hang like that, but then he understood that his uncle meant 'idiot' and blushed even if there was no one there to see him.

He smiled at those memories but then became serious as he thought about what he had left to read in that big book and what it might mean for the papers found in the cave. Before returning to the reading, he drank a sip of coffee from the flask he had brought.

His father's notes commented on a strange coincidence found in the book. Two words in Arabic have almost the same sound: HaYYat, snake, and HaYAt, life. Only the second vowel, 'a', changes from short to long, and the Y in the first word is doubled. Federico read them:

Even in Abruzzo, the snake represents life itself. The name of the goddess Angizia, the divinity worshiped by the Marsi and Peligni, comes from the Latin 'anguis', which means snake. Angizia had the gift of healing, and it was believed that she knew how to use herbs for that purpose and that she transmitted that knowledge to priests and kings.

He remembered the story of Maia and her son, Hermes, who needed a herb, perhaps a flower, which she could not find, so her son died. Angizia would have saved him if only she had known what Maia was looking for.

Awakening snakes in spring is itself the awakening to life.

His brain summoned the memory of Francesco, a relative of theirs who was one of the *serpari*, or snake handlers, who went to the countryside in spring to collect snakes. He said it was easy because they woke up from hibernation as soon as the snow began to melt and were still numb.

One day, Francesco returned from the forest with a bag full of snakes. They were trying to get out in every way, and he kept forcing them back into the bag. People were afraid of those slithering reptiles, but not Francesco and, while saying they were not poisonous, he took one and put its head in the hollow between his thumb and forefinger of his left hand, where there is a soft spot—where Balthazar always squeezed Federico's hand to hurt him. The snake's teeth disappeared into the soft flesh of his hand while the snake bit down so hard that its mouth almost flattened. Then Francesco detached it by widening its jaws: "See?"

After collecting them, he put them in a clay jar: "We'll take these to Cocullo for San Dominic's day," he said, and then sang a couple of lines from the Hymn to St. Dominic Abbot:

The Marsic Spring shimmers and throbs the young sun.
Excited, the vipers are looking for fun.

As with Francesco, other *serpari* went to the mountains yearly searching for snakes. Once caught, they are kept in wooden boxes for two or three weeks, feeding them on live rats and hard-boiled eggs.

One year, at the feast on the first Thursday of May, Federico's family went to Cocullo, located halfway between the Peligna Valley and the Marsica in the province of L'Aquila. The roads were full of queued cars parked as much as two kilometers from the center of the town. While walking to the center, his mother said: "Every year, thousands of people come here from Abruzzo, but many also come from Ciociaria, where Saint Dominic died. It's said that the saint protects from snake bites."

Cocullus was also known for the story of Duke Sarchia. He introduced the 'ius primae noctis,' or the right to spend the wedding night with the brides because he had fallen in love with a girl from the village who had just announced her marriage. The villagers pretended to accept the new rule; they waited for a few days and then slaughtered him just before he could enjoy the benefit he thought he had granted himself.

Francesco had announced: "The snakes are inspired; today there will be a great feast," and then disappeared inside the church with the other *serpari* and their jars full of snakes.

When the Mass ended, Federico and his family waited outside in the hot midday sun. The priest went out with the altar boys and four girls dressed in the traditional costume of Abruzzo. In their hands, they had the typical local donuts prepared for the occasion. Behind them in the procession came the statue of the saint, covered with waving snakes. The live reptiles twisted around his neck and arms; some fell but were picked up and put back on the saint or given to one of the faithful who asked for it and then let it twist everywhere. A woman close to Federico also took one; the snake reached out from her thin hands, and when he jumped backward, it formed a perfect circle around the lens of his father's camera.

The snakes suitable for the occasion are the Aesculapian, said to be the type of snake depicted on the staff of the Roman god Aesculapius; the grass snake; the green whip snake; and the cervone, or so-called "four-line" snake because of the stripes that run along its sides. Their colors range from green to black. The cervone, typical of Abruzzo, is the preferred one. This olive-green snake can grow as long as two meters and is known for climbing, which makes it ideal for adorning the statue of the saint and creating spectacular effects. It was believed that the cervone is attracted by the milk of cows and goats and will approach them, crawling in the grass and jumping up to stick to their udders. Some legends even tell of these snakes licking the milk from the wet lips of newborns. When they're placed around the saint statue, these snakes intertwine and climb as high as possible, passing behind his ears, under his nose and mouth, twisting around his neck, and licking the air while hissing in all directions.

It's difficult to determine how far back in history the celebration began. At least a thousand years before Christ, for sure. Some say that it was born as a pagan rite in veneration of the goddess Angizia and that it took place in May—maio—in honor of the pain of the goddess Maia, whose son Angizia could not cure.

Federico remembered how the statue of the saint, which without snakes looked static, seemed to come to life thanks to those reptiles. The Saint protects not just from the bites of those snakes but also from the evil part of human nature that exists in every human enterprise. The part that everyone has to face and then let go of, the part that metaphorically is associated with the devil. With that protection, one can focus on the positive aspect, the 'wisdom of life,' as confirmed in the notes of Federico's father.

After that regenerating read, Federico was ready to think. He now knew how to frame Balthazar. The following day he would have been up early. He had a crucial visit to make.

82. TRANCE-FORMATION

Villa Sant'Angelo, 13 April 2009 – Night

Federico felt his blood had exhausted all of its oxygen when he went to bed. Instead, it seemed to pump letters and figures through his body and splash them on his mind. All those stirring words, numbers, symbols, and images of the past few days, cascaded in a syncopated rhythm that he couldn't predict as if watching motions illuminated by a strobe light.

Images of digging to save the one who might have killed him, the fierce faces of the brigands, twisting definitions of legality and justice in a kaleidoscope of confusion. His eyes became heavy, and in an attempt to resist falling asleep, he imagined himself making a list of the things he didn't understand, but the words kept falling off the page.

He wrote, "Maya—Maiella", and then, as the letters fell, he replaced them with others: "L'Aquila—The Eagle". And the eagle was sleeping, but its eyes were open. Its eyes were those of an Egyptian sorceress, who was now showing him the three of clubs. She then shuffled the deck to show a rugby match, then a church with its façade covered by numbers, which was shaken as the earth danced, and the numbers became letters that said: "Magic could be found in the past. Perhaps where you are not looking for it."

Magic, or was it forgiveness that could be found? Was it an arcane secret or some divine energy that guided his stumbling steps, and why did each stage seem to lead to something worse? Instead of coffee, it was now his blood dripping on Giorgio's floor, and then his face pressed against the rug in Giorgio's office, where he fainted during the meeting with the HR manager. Up close, he noted a familiar pattern in the carpet, like the façade of Santa Maria of Collemaggio.

And then the scene changed again, and he was flying on that carpet. Next to him was a princess that he didn't recognize until a bright light revealed the tip of her nose, and he knew it was Eleonora. And he was seized with the desire to kiss her with a kiss that would last as long as the time she had waited for him. She was singing, and the song conjured the images of his father and mother in the air ahead of where they were flying. Yet, the closer he flew toward his parents, the harder they became to see. As he reached for them, he noticed his fingers had become feathers, and his arms were wings. His feet felt like talons, and he knew that his eyes and mouth had transformed into those of a raptor and that he could taste a gold coin held in his beak. He sensed he was healing Maya with his energy: every breath made her beak stronger; every heartbeat made her claws sharper; every blink healed and strengthened her wings.

Then, from above, he saw his target. He narrowed his eyes and felt the power of the wings around his shoulders as he dove toward the ground—and woke up.

Villa Sant'Angelo, April 14. Morning

He gulped down two coffees. The first one had been pressed too little in the Moka and came out weak, so he had to make another one. Then he went to see Francesco, wondering if he would remember him.

"Good morning, Francesco."

"Good morning, whose son are you?"

"Riccardo's."

"Good soul. Your father was a badass."

Francesco had collected snakes as he did every spring, though he seemed concerned that the celebration would be canceled because of the earthquake: "I wonder if there will be a feast this year."

"And if there won't be one, what will you do with all these snakes?"

"The same thing I do every year after the celebration is over. I will set them free."

After each ceremony, the snakes were released. Just as the Kazakhs did with their eagles after about ten years of service. Federico thought about Maya. She had been a prisoner for thirty years. She should have been free to fly for at least twenty years. He felt sick; closing his eyes, he thought: *How could I have been so selfish all this time?*

Francesco opened the basket and showed its contents to Federico. The squirming and hissing sent a cold sensation down his neck and slid down to the bottom of his back.

"Don't worry; they're not vipers like the song says."

Francesco, too, had been the victim of Balthazar's harassment. He had a funny habit of converting monetary amounts into equivalents of bulls and cows. Once, when they went to Abruzzo with the new Alfa Romeo, he said to Federico's father: "This car is beautiful. It must cost at least four cows." Even today, he kept those units of measure: "I needed to buy a tractor; it cost three bulls. But I had to give the pension arrears to those pigs instead. And I also had to thank them for it. Bastards."

Francesco, already old, had to continue cultivating the land with his hands and the hoe. The angle between his back and legs was permanently set at ninety degrees.

"Francesco," Federico said. "Would you help me catch the most venomous viper of all?"

83. THE CRACKS

Before going to Campotosto, Federico wanted to check how Maya was doing. It was still early morning, and he went to St. Peter. After returning from Santa Chiara, Tonino had been watching over the eagle the whole night when Federico and the others were busy saving Balthazar.

Tonino told Federico that two cottages had been damaged by that same shake that had trapped the Tzar and sighed: "Thank goodness there was no one inside them at that time."

"Did you say something to the owners?"

Yes, I showed them a pillar that had been damaged. I pointed out to them that there were fewer rods than expected and that the cement was too sandy and watered down. The pores could be seen even to the naked eye, damn it!"

"And how did they take it?"

"They reacted as if I were insulting them; they called me a bad word. Someone also went into the house and came out with a certificate from the lab that had verified the concrete samples. They were perfect. An official document."

A bystander had followed Tonino's reasoning and supported him: "This man is right, don't look at the papers, look at the pillar. Don't you see it has a few steel rods? What is holding it up? And this concrete looks like a sponge."

Tonino reported incredulously: "Yet, the owners looked at me as if I were an alien. In their heads, the certificate had more value than their senses."

Another owner whispered: "That man bought the house later, but we all agreed with Giovanni, who built the whole building complex. Do you know how much money he saved us?"

Federico was no longer surprised.

Accomplices.

"And what did you do, Toni?"

"I pointed out to him that agreeing does not mean being right."

Federico expressed his cynicism: "Well, it depends on how many agree. If there are that many, it's equivalent to being right. As my boss said: 'In our society, it's better to be wrong with the many than to be right alone.'"

"I didn't want to be right at all costs. I was interested in not having deaths on my conscience. While other cottages had been damaged, it was fortunate that at least they had been evacuated."

Tonino had breathed a breath of relief, and some of the emotional weight he had been carrying for years had lightened. Back in St. Peter, he had prepared a bed for Maya. He had also tried to feed her, but she had eaten nothing.

Tonino left Federico alone for a few minutes with his thoughts and then reassured him: "The good news is that the damage Balthazar did was less serious than it seemed at first. He's not clever and more familiar with the weak points of humans, whom he can hurt, than with birds of prey. Maya will heal soon."

Federico felt his heart tighten.

Tonino concluded by looking Federico in the eyes and taking his cheeks with his hands: "A Persian poet that your father loved expressed a concept that I cherish."

"And what is it?"

"When you feel pain and sorrow, stay with them."

"And why so?"

"Because wounds are the cracks where Light enters you."

84. CAMPOTOSTO

Campotosto, 14 April 2009 – Tuesday

When they arrived by the lake, they saw that the access to Case Isaia was closed. The last shock had caused damage to the dam, and the road above it was unusable. A gash had opened beneath the roadbed, allowing the water to rush toward the valley below. The speed of the water was disturbing, yet the only way to get to the other side of the lake was by boat.

Giovanna, meanwhile, had studied how to simulate a metal detector. "We can use a small radio and a calculator. I found them by asking people in the village. All older adults have a portable radio like this. Finding a calculator was a little more difficult, but I did it."

She pulled the small apparatus out of the bag, and Federico could almost hear the voice of the rugby reporters coming through the tiny speaker. The soundtrack of his childhood. Giovanna tuned it to the highest AM band, where there was no station, and turned the volume knob to maximum. The static white noise could be heard. Then she turned on the calculator and placed it on the radio, moving it around a bit until a deeper, darker hum was heard.

"How do you know the noise is the right one?"

"Can't you hear for yourself that the tone is more stable?"

Giovanna took some tape, locked both instruments in position, and then taped the device to a broomstick handle: "Here we go. Do you have a bunch of keys?"

Eleonora took a keyring from her pocket, and when Giovanna approached her, the 'radio calculator' started whistling with eerie sounds, such as in science fiction movies.

Vince was enthusiastic: "You are getting cooler day by day."

Giovanna became severe: "Listen to me because the situation is dangerous. If the dam wall gives way, three hundred and twenty-five million cubic meters of raging water will flow into the valley."

"My God, what would happen then?"

"The water would sweep over the town of Crognaleto, and at the junction of Cerqueto, it will meet the reservoir of the Piaganini dam on its way to Montorio."

Federico walked his fingers across the map he always carried with him: "And from there, nothing will stop it until it reaches the sea."

"Let's hope the dam doesn't give way then," shrugged Vincenzo as he headed towards the moored boats. He recognized a local man who, after a brief exchange, lent him an excursion boat. Federico didn't know what he had said to convince the man. Or maybe he owed Vincenzo a favor. A big one.

The boat was in such a poor condition that it reminded Federico of the one piloted by The Wolf. To venture onto a lake near a waterfall of water flowing at more than twenty kilometers an hour in this old boat was madness. Even from where they were, he could sense the frightening power of the water as it gushed through the gutted dam with a roar, creating a tremor in the surrounding ground.

It was enough to cause one to have second thoughts, and Giovanna did: "It's too dangerous with such a boat. It's not powerful enough; we have to give up."

Vincenzo had no intention of listening to her: "If it had been up to you, America wouldn't have seen the moon even with binoculars, let alone set foot on it."

Federico, as usual, saw the positive side in both giving up and tempting fate. He couldn't take any side.

Giovanna noticed a long docking line on the shore: "If you two have hard heads like donkeys, at least tie the line to the boat, and we can try to keep you safe from shore."

Federico liked the idea: "Excellent thought, Giovanna, but there is no 'you two'..' I go alone; Vincenzo does not even know how to swim. Let's hope that the line is long enough."

Federico fastened the line to the boat and, while the others were holding it, climbed on board with the improvised metal detector, started the engine, engaged the clutch, and increased the engine revs, moving away from shore. He found he could counteract the current.

Maybe it's not as dangerous as I thought.

Vincenzo saw that the boat was holding its own. When Federico approached the shore to say that everything seemed to be working, he jumped on board, tearing the line from the hands of the others who had relaxed their grip for a moment: "Federico, it's you who is afraid here. Give it gas!" and pressed on the accelerator, pulling the boat away from the shore.

"Vincenzo, you can't swim. Do you want to commit suicide?"

"What do you mean? We used to swim in the river all the time, remember? And then there is the boat, and you know how to operate it.

Let's cross to the houses of the prophet Isaiah: can't you see that he's predicting a bright future for us?"

Federico began to think the worst about their plan and slowed down as he let the boat approach the houses, carried by the current. He gave the engine a little gas to ensure the ship could overcome the drift. The houses got closer and closer as the cracked dam. They went right towards the 'wind splitter', the 'V' point of the lake where the rocks form the summit. Before the water created the lake, the legendary winds of the plains were separated there. This was where the wind first passes over the water and then descends—'sloping'—to the valley. As they approached the dam, they realized that even if they accelerated, the boat could, at most, only equalize the current. "Vince, the engine is not powerful enough. I don't feel like taking the chance; let's go back. The treasure will wait; better poor but alive," he said as he turned.

"What are you doing, Federico? This is our last chance," exclaimed the disappointed Vincenzo. "Better dead than beggars, I think you meant to say."

"You are delirious, Vince."

At that moment, Federico heard a distant noise, and looking through the telescope; he saw Balthazar arriving with his gray raft. It was the one he used to ride around Sardinia: four hundred horsepower against the winds, the current, and their miserable boat.

"I told you we should have pierced it," shouted Vincenzo. "When will you ever listen to me?"

85. THE DAM

Federico accelerated towards Case Isaia, the engine roaring and the boat soaring: "Yay," shouted Vincenzo, laughing with his hair fluttering in all directions. Federico shook his head and smiled back as he lowered the engine to idle and turned his back to Balthazar's raft.

Vincenzo became irritated: "What are you doing?"

Federico was peremptory: "Too late, they will reach us soon. I have a countermove in mind. Take the helm and keep the boat on this course."

He began to rummage through the junk inside the hull. He saw the two oars supplied, a stick and then blessed the sky when he found a bit of a three-millimeter line that was the right thickness. He remembered how his father had taught him to splice two branches to create a longer one; he put half the stick next to one of the two oars leaving the other half to extend beyond the oar and wrapped the line around both creating a winding of at least one span and tightening it as much as possible. He wanted it to hold well even in a collision with a pig because that was the animal he had in mind to hit. He formed a ring with the final part of the line and laid it in the furrow created between the oar and the stick. He passed the other free end through the ring and pulled it with force until it ended up under the winding. He closed everything with a flat knot, always keeping the top tight. He finished by wedging a thin piece of wood in the groove to make the lashing faster, so the wood wouldn't shift. Now he had an oar longer than the other by a full meter.

By now, Balthazar was about a hundred meters away. Federico didn't have time to test the effectiveness of the knots; he immersed both oars in the water and left them in the oarlock. They looked identical in the water, two ordinary oars at the sides of a boat. He hoped they hadn't noticed him preparing his surprise from that distance.

Federico saw Balthazar's raft pointing at them, then returned to the helm and gave the engine some gas as he came about heading toward him, ready to turn at the last moment to avoid a collision. However, the Tzar turned to flank him, and even though Federico turned in the same direction, the raft was faster; it completed its turn and drove into the back of the boat.

"Hold the helm, Crocko," the Tzar said as he advanced towards Federico, who shouted the same order to Vincenzo; from his side, he took the ax he had hung on his belt. "Let's pick up where we left off all those years ago."

The two entangled boats were being carried by the current towards the dam, rotating in circles because the thrust of the raft's engine overpowered the small boat's engine. Federico advanced from the helm and grabbed the handle of the standard-length oar. Leveraging it on the oarlock, he cranked it in the direction of Balthazar, who managed to avoid it by taking a step back.

"Nice try," grinned Balthazar. "But weak, as always."

Federico tried again and the Tzar, who had measured the distance, managed to sink the ax into the oar. He detached it from the wood with a shoulder movement and advanced on Federico again, lifting the weapon. It was not quite the proper distance, so Federico waited a bit more.

Half a second later, the boats had made a quarter turn, and Federico saw the Tzar put his hand in front of his eyes to protect them from the sun; it was the right moment. Federico leaped towards the oar he had extended and kicked it downward with the heel of his boot. He felt a twinge; his foot was still hurting from the night on Bald Mountain, but the oar's blade lifted from the opposite side and came out of the water. Balthazar must have seen a shadow of glittering drops emerging; he may have expected the oar to be shorter, just like the other; he opened his eyes wide and tried to pull his head back, but the stick hit him on the temple. He tried to stand on his feet, resting on the damaged foot and then the healthy one, but he fell into the water.

"Ha! Federico bested you again!" brayed an ecstatic Vincenzo. "Will you never learn?"

Crocko had meanwhile already taken command of the raft, put it in reverse, and freed it from Federico's boat. Then he accelerated and made a big figure eight to go and retrieve Balthazar, who was dragged by the current towards the crevasse in the dam.

Federico regained control of his engine and steering wheel, opened the throttle wide, and turned hard away from the broken dam. The engine's roar became a scream, and the boat jumped forward three times as they broke free of the current. They watched Crocko recover Balthazar by dragging him onto the raft, and that was when they heard their engine give one of those high notes that seemed like a glorious opera finale—but the boat didn't move this time. The propeller was no longer turning: "He damaged it when he rammed us, and by accelerating, we finished breaking it. We are going towards the crack in the dam!"

Federico tried to find some makeshift repair. There was no emergency equipment on board or any means of rescue.

Meanwhile, Eleonora and Giovanna had taken one of the other motorboats out to rescue them, but they were still too far away. The current had increased, and they saw Crocko and Balthazar as they were breaking away from its grip. They had a 400-horse-power outboard motor, not a 20-donkey-power like Vincenzo defined it.

Some say that if there is no one to see a sure thing, then that thing doesn't exist. However, if there had been someone on the opposite side of the dam, he would have seen a 40-meter waterfall plunging into the valley. They were getting too close and too fast. The solution was to jump into the water and try to swim to shore before they got swept over the dam. They could still make it but had to act now.

Federico incited Vincenzo: "Vince, we must dive. Otherwise, we will be swallowed by the crack. Jump!"

The command didn't have the desired effect. On the contrary, Vincenzo opposed it: "Don't you see how far the shores are? If I throw myself in, I'll die for sure. You know how to fix this tub. Federico, come on."

The voice was no longer his own; he was out of control. Federico felt his spine melt. Vincenzo relied entirely on him. He had to do something. With his bare hands, he tore the bow cover off to get something that would work as an oar since the supplied oars were now lost in the water. They paddled with the cover and their hands, but nothing happened. They were sometimes able to turn the boat away, but it returned to the current's grip. A thousand ideas crossed Federico's mind; he even thought about knocking out Vincenzo and dragging him to safety. He weighed at least a hundred kilos, however, and he already didn't know if he would be able to save himself. Out of his eye, he saw that the last useful point to throw himself in the water was coming. A few meters farther, the water would be turning too steeply down to the waterfall, and it would have been impossible to make it.

They were down now to the last and final solution: "Vince, we must throw ourselves. Are you ready?"

Vincenzo was paralyzed with terror: "I can't do it."

Federico shook him again: "Vince, how many times have I told you 'I can't make it,' but then I came here following you, anyway. Come on!"

He felt that if he had thrown himself into the water without him, he would have betrayed his friend, but when they were close to the crack, he could wait no longer and shouted: "Now or never!"

He heard the echo of that cry merging with the waterfall's roar.

And he dived.

Underwater, he heard a second thud, not knowing whether it was the roar of the water or his heart exploding in his chest. The water swirled as it was being sucked through the crevice in the dam. He resurfaced to breathe, imagined he had webbed hands, and began pushing the water behind him. The landscape, however, remained still even though he was turning his arms like the blades of his grandfather's mill.

He decided to keep his head underwater so as not to have to see death when it arrived. There appeared to him a scene, as in a dream, faded by the light that penetrated the lake. It was the Palm Sunday that The Wolf had told him about: the people going to the countryside to collect wild roses and placing crosses built with blessed palms in the wheat fields with prayers for a plentiful harvest and then the fireworks of the puppet dance after the harvest. Soon he, too, would disappear as that world had vanished forever. Keeping his eyes closed, he turned his head only to breathe and, in desperation, thought of his son Manfredi, the killing of his father, his mother dying of heartbreak.

He cried, imagining his tears flowing through that crack, followed soon after by his ramshackle life. He turned to see where Vincenzo was and noticed him swimming without conviction until the tear in the concrete swallowed him. He felt an adrenaline rush from his back to his throat, which almost suffocated him; the air almost didn't seem to enter him anymore, but his legs surprised him and accelerated. And in his throat, he felt his heart, big as his beloved rugby ball. He cursed himself for not having been able to resist his friend's urgency, for bringing Manfredi into that apocalypse, for not having been a good husband, for not having been able to pick the right fights on his job. He had been trying to do the right things for years, and it seemed they all turned out wrong.

He was so much into his memories and regrets that he imagined he still felt the pain in his shoulder after the clash with the Tzar thirty years earlier. When he next felt the laceration of a rocky edge on his side, he thought: *Here we are, I'm at the dam, and the reinforced concrete will tear my flesh away as it did to Vincenzo.*

He raised his head as a sign of surrender and looked at the sky for the last time. He opened his eyes and saw Giulio taking him by the armpits and dragging him to the shore. He had not realized that he could now stand up instead of swimming in shallow waters. In anguish and with his eyes closed, he had not even thought about it. He looked to the side and saw that the rocky edge was that of the pebbly beach stone at the corner of the dam. He had swum to the shore. Federico looked up at Eleonora's brother, then down to the blood gushing out of the cut, and fainted.

Giulio carried Federico on his shoulders as far as the beach, where they had all assembled. He laid him down on the back seat of Tonino's car and hugged his sister, who had understood everything by then.

An hour later, the lake level had subsided, the gravel, earth, and debris carried by the current blocked the crack, and the waterfall stopped. No damage had been done to the villages downstream, except for a few centimeters of water, less than what had been caused by the previous storm.

Nothing was found of Vincenzo's body, although the family offered a high reward. The iron of the reinforced concrete, the spikes of rocks, and the forty meters jump had torn him to pieces, even worse than what happened to his brother with the tractor plow.

The family could not even give him a proper burial.

86. YOUR EYES

Federico had regained consciousness; they had dabbed the wound that, in the end, turned out to be little more than an abrasion, with a deeper cut that needed nothing more than a few stitches. He had been taken to the doctor's tent as a precaution, and his vital signs were checked. Only extreme fatigue but no damage.

While they were keeping him under observation, an older woman came in. After half an hour, she told him, "I know who you are. Yes, Riccardo's son. I recognized you from your eyes. Have you come back?"

"Not really."

In Abruzzo, you are known for the family you belong to, for better or for worse. In the same way, Federico knew the older woman's history from the stories his parents had told him since he was a child.

Scientists say that nothing exceeds the speed of light except how fast the news in the valley of the Aterno spreads. She already knew everything: "This story has cost too much. It's madness. But one thing is certain: Vincenzo believed in you more than you believe in yourself."

Federico didn't know if it was meant to be a malicious or encouraging comment. The woman continued: "Sometimes the eyes of others are sincerer than our own in looking at us. Continue the search; if you don't do it for yourself, at least do it for him."

When her son came to pick up the elder, he too joined in the encouragement, which Federico had difficulty accepting: "Your father was a good man. He was killed unjustly. He always helped those in need."

"Thank you." Federico didn't know anything better to say.

"Your grandfather was a righteous man too."

"How do you know?" asked Federico. He started to feel that they were consoling him not because of his suffering but because they saw him and his family as losers. He was leaning more toward considering himself a fool, a naive, as the Neapolitan called him.

The woman replied: "Your grandfather once worked on constructing an important man's house in Venezuela. He had a young laborer who helped him: my brother. Your grandfather was clever in building a pulley that made the work easier, and so they did it in half of the time without compromising quality. When the man paid your grandfather, my brother saw the amount. Your grandfather gave him his payment, and my brother realized it was half what he had seen. He rejected the money, saying that he was just a laborer and that it was thanks to your grandfather that the work was done so well. Your grandfather insisted and gave the money back to him. My brother never forgot it."

She snapped her fingers, then circled her index finger several times next to her temple as she continued: "Those bastard lawyers sow bad seeds. They spread discord among people so that they could make court cases and steal money from other people under an appearance of legality and good service. They are fake. Balthazar's father is an Ass with a capital and bold 'A'."

"And his son?" Federico wanted to have the full take.

"Even the son is evil, but he's an idiot. And you're a fool, too; you're afraid of him. Remember that the apple doesn't fall far from the tree. Nor does a pear. Under the fig tree, a small fig tree is born. But under the oak, also a small oak."

Federico had often considered the difference between the countryside and the big city.

In Abruzzo, everybody knew each other and all their families, going back for generations. The regard a person was held in was the result of what they and their families had done in the past, which everyone knew about. Federico didn't like that this caused prejudices and even self-fulfilling prophecies, but later in life, he saw its practical side.

In a big city, a person who betrays someone's trust may be expelled from a group. But they can change friendships and start again with new people who don't know who they are and with whom they can get along well– until the next selfish gesture or any other harmful behavior. And then they start the cycle again.

Stefania did precisely that. She had recognized the pattern. When the group confronted her about her misconduct, she changed friends, boyfriends, and husbands.

What Federico was looking for was not justice, it now seemed to him, but accountability. People didn't have to change their behavior if they could just change their environment, but in this way, their character could not evolve. In small towns and villages, you are always under observation, for better or worse, leading to better average behavior towards the community and a sense of contributing to the well-being of all.

And, of course, there were exceptions.

Was Balthazar as dishonest as his father? A rotten apple from a rotten tree? Even just by imitation, by learning, more than by genetics. And what did he, Federico, inherit from his family? Carlantonio was so noble that he didn't even go to recover a treasure that would make him rich. But rather than honorable, he considered himself just someone who had flown low and had never had to decide anything essential.

Virtue never attempted is not true virtue.

So far, it has been too easy for him. This was proved by the fact that now he would break the law to gain an advantage.

He thought of the coat of arms of his family, recognized as 'generous nobility' by the Royal Commission of Nobility Titles: three golden stars with five rays on a blue bar on a golden shield. Generous nobility meant that all family members, none excluded, were acknowledged as noble. He found comfort in knowing that since 1948 noble titles in Italy are no longer recognized, according to the provisions of the Constitution. He wouldn't have to live up to those expectations.

He saw Eleonora at the tents. She continued crying and bringing her hands to her face, probably hoping not to see the reality that just happened before her eyes. She snapped at Federico: "Kill the bastard. He killed Vincenzo. You maimed his foot; now kill him. Finish the job you started thirty years ago."

Federico tried calming her: "Do you realize what you are saying?"

"It will never end otherwise. Don't you realize that it's him or you? Even worse, it's him or all of us. Send him to prison or kill him; he has to disappear from our lives if we want to rebuild a future."

She then walked away and disappeared in between the tents.

The small community that welcomed him back so warmly was now pressing him to do something to avenge Vincenzo's death. To end Balthazar's bullying once and for all. Was he up to such a task?

He had always loved that version of "good blood doesn't lie," summarized by the saying about the fig or the oak plant that the old lady just reminded him of.

Good blood does not lie. True.

But as to the quality of his own, he was not at all sure.

87. THE TZAR'S LIES

14 April 2009 – Tuesday

In the tents, Federico heard that Balthazar had recovered from the blow to the head and that he had told his version of the events. He declared that he had gone there to help them, that Vincenzo had gone crazy, and that Federico shouldn't have gotten involved. The water current had made them collide, and he had hit his head. And then the tragedy, with the accidental death of Vincenzo. Even then, everyone preferred that version of the accident, and no one filed a complaint: all guilty, none guilty.

Eleonora didn't lose the opportunity. "Can you see now what I mean?"

Federico didn't answer.

None of them had mentioned anything about Case Isaia, so no one knew why they had gone to Lake Campotosto. The Carabinieri had become suspicious listening to different versions of the accident and wanted to review some details.

The Brigadier and his superior, the Marshal, questioned Federico: "What were you doing near the dam?"

"Vincenzo wanted to take me for a ride to distract us from all this tragedy, and it ended in an even worse tragedy."

"Are you mocking us? Your story is ridiculous; this is not a time for a pleasure cruise on a lake with a broken dam."

Eleonora's good heart overcame her good sense: "Federico is not mocking you; it's Balthazar who lies. Do you believe that Federico is to blame? That he killed Vincenzo?"

"Wait, Eleonora, stop," interjected Giovanna, deviating a dangerous drift in the conversation.

But Eleonora stood up and shouted: "I can't take it anymore. Enough is enough. It's time to grow up and acknowledge reality." Turning, she confronted the Marshal. "Here is some reality: why don't you ask Balthazar how he found the treasure on Bald Mountain? Damn it, why is it that everything he does is always good, and what Federico does is always bad?"

The Marshal reprimanded her: "We are now talking about the death of a man; finding a treasure is not the same thing."

Eleonora could no longer hold back: "It was an accident; how can you even think of another possibility? They were friends for life, even if they didn't see each other for thirty years. Balthazar smashed our engine with his boat. We could see it from the shore. Balthazar is responsible for Vincenzo's death."

She burst into tears, and Federico took her in his arms, surprising even himself because, for once, he didn't hesitate or agonize over deciding about a course of action. Spurred by this revelation, or perhaps by the emotion pouring into his heart from where Eleonora's face was pressed into his shirt, he looked at the Brigadier and, in a low but furious voice, began to vent some pressure from the last thirty years: "I can't take it anymore, either. I don't want to hide anymore, looking for strategies to survive in the darkness. I'll tell you the truth, and let's see what happens."

Federico had faith in the Carabinieri that had been handed down for generations. His great-grandfather had served in the Carabinieri, as had other relatives and childhood friends.

Meanwhile, Balthazar joined them and, hearing himself accused and his name abused, knew he had to deflect: "They are lying. They are here to steal from the poor and the elders; they're jackals."

The Brigadier held up his hand and turned toward Balthazar to stop him. Giovanna took the opportunity to move in and turn Federico away from Eleonora and take him aside. She spoke as not to be heard by the others, between her clenched teeth: "Federico, if you tell the truth, we will never be able to recover any treasure at all."

"It's more likely that we end up in jail, accused of theft and manslaughter. How else do we get out of it?"

Giovanna didn't have a solution and cursed herself: "So, even if we find these treasures, there is nothing we can do about our predicament?"

"If you tell me another way, any other way, I'll follow it."

Giovanna paused but could not answer. She lowered her head and bit her lips.

Federico turned towards the Marshal and the Brigadier. "I no longer have anything, neither a home nor a job. Manfredi is going blind. We are looking for some treasures, and I hoped to find them to have enough money to treat my son's illness. It's my last hope at this moment. Vincenzo wanted to find the treasure to change his life; he was almost blind himself, even if he hid it well and even drove in secret, but he was afraid he could not provide for anyone in his infirmity. The others were pulled into this, but they are not to blame."

Giovanna and the twins were surprised: "Manfredi blind? What are you saying? And who was Vincenzo supposed to provide for?"

Eleonora lowered her head and brought her hands to her face, stifling another sob.

The twins regained their coolness: "Anyway, no law has been broken; intentions cannot be taken to court."

Federico continued: "We have an ancient and encrypted document that indicates three treasures. We had found one, but Balthazar followed and stopped us. Then he staged the discovery."

Eleonora intervened, regaining her composure and her earlier point: "Go ahead, ask 'the Tzar' how he knew about the treasure."

The Brigadier took a step toward Balthazar. He had never liked him, and raising his chin challenged him: "Right, how did you know where the treasure was?"

Giovanna replied: "He followed us and dug it up, but first, he broke the metal detector to stop our research."

Balthazar, instead of answering, argued: "And the documents you are referring to, where would they be?"

Federico puffed his breath, shook his head, and pulled his notebook out of the big pockets on the side of his pants: "Here are the clues for the two missing treasures: one is 'below the tower that heavens seduce' and the other 'beside the water sloping with the winds.'"

"You were in Campotosto for this?" asked the Marshal.

"Yes, but I was wrong; there was nothing at Case Isaia," admitted Federico.

"What?" Eleonora was upset.

"Yes, I know. Vincenzo died there. But the other two treasures are elsewhere. I was wrong."

"Holy God," exclaimed Eleonora as she threw herself onto the chair.

"So, tell us where they are," insisted Balthazar.

Federico handed him a copy of the poem and smiled at him with a sneer: "Why don't you find it yourself, genius?"

Balthazar looked at it. It was still the coded version. He squinted his eyes and felt his mind bend at reading the first letters.

Not even legal documents were so puzzling.

88. THE MARK DILEMMA

The Marshal examined the notebook. There was the coded poem, copied by Federico with the writing instruments found in the cave, and the various calculations of word values corresponding to possible locations in the Aterno valley and Abruzzo: pages and pages of names, geographical places, rivers, and mountains. All with some numbers next to them, and then sums of numbers. Two were circled, the Castle on Mount Cerro and Case Isaia, with their respective sums equaling 99.

Balthazar blurted out: "These are pure inventions; they wrote them; they're fake papers. Do you believe these jackals or me? There must be consequences for those who declare falsehoods. Otherwise, I could also write a fanciful version that will benefit me and condemn them!" Emboldened by his bluster, Balthazar pushed his defense and luck: "If what he says is true, he has to prove it by finding the other two treasures."

Federico realized that Balthazar probably counted on the fact that the possibility that he would locate two more treasures in a short time was remote, given the mistake at Campotosto, even if the notebook was true. And if they found one, discovering both was a practical impossibility.

The Marshal had been studying the pages; at Balthazar's words, he closed the notebook and turned to Federico and his friends: "As our esteemed lawyer has suggested, if what you say is true, then take us to these treasures. If you cannot, I will have you all arrested for perjury and looting."

The Marshal's eyes matched the hard pledge of his words. Balthazar began to grin—until the Marshal turned to him with the same eyes and tone: "But if these two treasures are found, and Federico can explain how he deduced their locations from these documents, then I hope that in that case you, Balthazar, have a much better story to tell about your finding and the accident at the lake." The grin froze on the Tzar's face, neither advancing nor retreating; his face turned pale.

Giovanna was right, however. Any result would be harmful to them. If they could not find anything, they would face a bad trial, perhaps jail, and even if they found some precious objects, they couldn't keep the discovery for themselves so they wouldn't see a single euro. And all of this was without considering that it was still to be seen whether those calculations would lead to treasures or instead to another disaster, as had happened in Campotosto.

To Federico, the situation reminded him of a story his family called 'the Mark Dilemma'. As it often happened, it concerned his great-grandfather. This time it was about a quarrel over the irrigation of the fields. A bully named Mark refused to open the lock to give water to a farmer whose turn it was after him. Carlantonio, then still a Carabiniere, was told of this and joined them to solve the dispute, even though he wore his regular clothes and not his uniform. He lifted the lock by prying it with a pickaxe, and the water began to flow as arranged by the law. Mark, who was further away working in the fields, noticed that less water was coming in. He went to the lock and saw Carlantonio with the pick in his hand. He gave him what sounded like an order:

"Lower the lock immediately."

"You lower it. If you think you can," Carlantonio challenged him.

"Close it now. Don't you know who I am?"

"I don't know, and I don't care."

"I'm Mark."

Carlantonio drew a line on the ground with the pickaxe and made a joke out of his name: "If you are Mark, then pass THIS mark." If Mark had crossed the line, he would have had to step down half a meter to lower the lock, and Carlantonio would have hit him on his back with the pickaxe. If Mark didn't cross it, the water would continue to irrigate the following field.

Every time there was a case in which any outcome seemed harmful, but one had to be chosen, there was someone in the family who uttered: "If you are Mark, then pass THIS mark."

Balthazar had already stepped over that line many times. His family history was one of abuse and bullying of the peasants and poor people.

Would Federico unleash that pickaxe?

Or would Balthazar, once again, continue to irrigate his field undisturbed?

89. SEDUCING THE SKY

Rocca Calascio, 14 April 2009 – Tuesday

Federico couldn't help but accept the challenge. The twins tried to dissuade him; they told him that he could not be accused of anything since he had not infringed any law. Giovanna raised a further problem: "I don't remember any other places and numerical series we found. Can we defend ourselves?"

Federico smiled: "I have discovered another combination. We will find the other one. I have some ideas."

"Then you're an ass," Eleonora told him.

"I was just lucky."

"Look, you still don't know if there's anything where you're thinking of going. At Case Isaia, there was nothing. Then you said you were wrong. Who says you are right now? You shouldn't have accepted the challenge," the twins insisted.

"We have no choice anymore. We go where the tower flirts with the sky."

The group returned to the two Carabinieri SUVs: the Marshal drove the first, with Federico, Eleonora, and Giovanna. The Brigadier followed in the second, with Balthazar, Crocko, and the twins. Federico guided the Marshal without revealing the ultimate destination. He passed by San Demetrio and then went up to Barisciano, whose castle—which was among those involved in the foundation of L'Aquila—overlooked the Navelli plateau and the access to the Gran Sasso. It's a fortified enclosure with an isolated tower, called a donjon, with a pentagonal base. It had suffered severe damage during the earthquake of 1703, and many of its stones were then used to build the houses of Barisciano.

Federico liked, in a peculiar way, this idea that the stones of the old buildings now lived in the houses of the villages. It was like a tradition feeding the present; the lifeblood passed from generation to generation. But with the tremor of April 6, the land claimed its share also of those stones, with interest, adding to its collection from the 1703 collapse of both the west and the church tower, which had been erected honoring the victims of the epidemic of 1526.

After a few hairpin bends that climbed around the mountain, they appeared on the hilltop. Some 1250 meters above sea level, at the site of

Santo Stefano di Sessanio, a jewel included in the "club of the most beautiful boroughs" in Italy. At this point, however, they had to stop and get out of the SUVs; a landslide closed the road.

Giovanna, meanwhile, was already solving the following problem: "I guess we will need a metal detector since Balthazar has now destroyed both of ours. It will take a few days to get one. I have not been able to build another makeshift one."

Balthazar went to the attack: "Don't make excuses. You have to prove what you say, and you have to do it today."

The Marshal agreed and emphasized with authority: "Correct, today is the first treasure, and tomorrow the second. At the latest."

Giovanna came up with an idea: "Maybe Philoctetes—one of those names you only find in Abruzzo—has a metal detector to find archery arrows."

Eleonora seemed surprised: "Of course, that is how he finds them. I always wondered."

Giovanna took the Brigadier's car, turned it around, and drove further down into the valley so fast that the Brigadier was left standing, shocked, looking at the cloud of dust where his SUV had been. The others, meanwhile, thought about the immediate issue: "How do we get through the landslide?"

Eleonora had a proposal: "With donkeys and horses, of course. I will get them."

"Wait," said the Marshal. "No one else is leaving unless I go with you." So, Federico and the Marshal accompanied Eleonora on foot and returned after almost an hour with three donkeys and two horses. Eleonora dismounted from the horse she and Federico were riding and climbed the last part of the road on foot, leading the three donkeys by their halters. Balthazar was the first to speak:

"This donkey seems pleased."

"And why is that?" Eleonora asked.

"Because he's following a beautiful girl."

"I thought it was because he had finally found his long-lost brother Balthazar. I can see the strong family resemblance." As the Tzar's face reddened, Eleonora passed him the halter: "This is for you and Crocko." She gave the second donkey to the Brigadier and the third donkey to the twins. She climbed back up behind Federico. The Marshal had wanted the best horse for himself, to be agile in chasing anyone who tried to run away.

"I'm entitled to a horse," Balthazar protested.

Eleonora wrapped her arms around Federico's waist and replied: "The donkey asked for you, specifically."

"You'll pay for this," Balthazar hissed at Federico between his teeth.

Giovanna arrived with the metal detector, and seeing the others already mounted, she seemed dubious about having to share a donkey with the Brigadier: "Weren't there any extra horses?"

"Not with the money we had," Eleonora answered.

"And we need donkeys to carry the treasures," specified Federico.

With a sigh, Giovanna got up on the donkey behind the Brigadier. They climbed over the crushed ground and reached the clear road again. Balthazar's donkey stopped and started eating some bright purple thistles on the roadside. The other donkeys also took advantage of the opportunity. It was impossible to move them; they were like those people who, when they have a goal, can't think of anything else.

Federico, though, let himself get distracted as his gaze got lost in the hollow below, a valley of such elegant proportions and bright green that he considered it the most beautiful in the world.

"Look, how wonderful," Eleonora said, pointing her finger toward the village of Santo Stefano di Sessanio. Below the architecture of the fourteenth-century crenelated tower and the stone church stretched a plateau of almond trees in bloom. They seemed embellished with white pearls tending to pink. Eleonora loved those places: "On this plateau, the best saffron in the world is cultivated; it's not for nothing they call it 'red gold'".

From here, the ancient *tratturo magno*, the great road of transhumance, used to wind its way like a river of grass as wide as two rugby fields that flowed from the Gran Sasso to the Apulian Tavoliere. It was where tens of thousands of sheep moved from the cold of the mountains to warm themselves together; those masses are replaced today by modern tourists. Some of these sheep were of the Carfagna breed, coveted for their dark wool. It was so valuable that the Medici nobles of the time took steps to ensure their continuous presence in Santo Stefano to control the reproduction and quality of the wool.

Maintaining a steady pace, they followed the path past the Church of Santa Maria della Pietà and arrived at what some consider the most fascinating castle in Europe: Rocca Calascio. At an elevation of 1460 meters, it's one of the highest castles in Italy.

Balthazar made a mocking noise: "Rocca Calascio? Damn, Federico, couldn't you have picked a more obvious place?"

Federico heard himself speaking with Tonino's tone of voice: "Obvious doesn't mean false. Sometimes the truth is taken for granted. With this obsession for originality, the world no longer sees the elusive obvious."

Balthazar never liked lectures: "So that's the magical combination that your genius found out? And now you want to drop philosophical sentences that remind me of what just came out of your horse. How do you know this is the place? And above all, where in the castle will you look?"

Federico was more than happy to deliver his riposte: "It's written with precision in the combination of words that I've found."

90. THE ROCK

Rocca Calascio, 14 April 2009 – Tuesday

Eleonora whispered to Federico: "I noticed you hadn't mentioned the Goats' Drop. I thought that the point where 'the tower seduces the heavens' was the clock tower that could be seen from the mountain, in the 'heavens', above Fontecchio. In this way, all Nonno's stories would have been true".

"Without Maya, it's impossible to reach the drop, at least in the short term."

As they dismounted, Federico looked at Eleonora between her messed up hair covering her face: "Did you also notice that I never mentioned who may have told Balthazar where the first treasure was?"

She lowered her head, and Federico continued: "I thought about it for a long time. But now you understand why I stopped sharing my thoughts. The eight associated with the castle of Sant'Eusanio had never convinced me. I now believe that the number didn't refer to the castle but to the tower where we found the treasure, as you had almost guessed."

Eleonora raised her head and smiled, whispering: "Thank you."
Then she increased her volume to everyday speech: "And no rule of ninety-nine?"

"Under the tower eight, translated in numbers, is twenty-six plus fifteen, plus twenty-seven, plus thirty-one. It equals ninety-nine."

"Indeed, it was the tower corresponding to the box where the eight is found on the magic square. And how would we have found out which castle, though?"

"By decoding the poem. Only one rocky hill with a castle on top divides the river into two branches."

"But in Rocca Calascio, there are just four towers. On which number it's the treasure supposed to be?"

"First, I think that the key of the *quatre de chiffre* of Collemaggio has to be placed where is the entrance door of the Rocca."

"So, this group that hid the treasures also knew about the *quatre de chiffre?*"

"For sure. And if I'm right, this tower is right above the number two box. That is, the southwest tower."

Federico showed the magic square with the key that he had drawn:

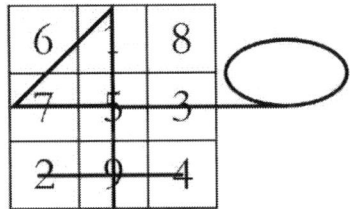

Giovanna had joined them: "Tower on two? What are you talking about? What is the combination of words?"

Federico replied: "Tower above box two, Calascio. Twenty-seven, plus eighteen, plus fourteen, plus thirteen, plus twenty-seven equals ninety-nine."

The castle of Rocca Calascio is built on a ridge of the Gran Sasso d'Italia massif, hovering between the Campo Imperatore and Navelli plateaus. Being at the highest point of the territory, it was a prime military observation point able to communicate with the other strategic points in the region, all the way to the castles and towers of the Adriatic coast. Using lanterns and flashlights at night and mirrors during the day allowed the control of the feudal rule of the barony of Carapelle (literally 'Expensive Skin'). The fort was built both for a defensive purpose and to oversee the routes related to sheep transhumance and the commercial traffic of the Abruzzo's route. The barony was one of the most important pastoral basins in Italy. It included the villages of Carapelle, Castelvecchio, Calascio, Rocca Calascio, and Santo Stefano di Sessanio, all stricken by the earthquake.

His father had brought Federico there several times, sometimes with Uncle Tonino. The view is unique in the world. The plan of the structure, built of white stone, is square, with a tower in the center, also square, and four cylindrical towers at the corners. The towers have deep foundations and make the fortress stable. His father had shown him the apparent signs of the 1703 earthquake that damaged the castle and destroyed the village below. He also pointed out a peculiar effect that was created by that destruction. The white stones of the damaged portions gave the structure a kind of timeless halo as if the fortress had always been there, integrated with the territory as if a naturally occurring part of the harsh rocks and steep ridges on which it remained in magical balance.

And perhaps that timeless feeling was what visitors longed for; a sense that sand had stopped flowing through the hourglass. Federico felt as if he had returned to Mongolia: same plateaus, same mountains, same empty spaces that only an infinite soul could fill. As then, he tried to feel himself a part of this place as much as he could. He took a long breath and thought about how, from up there, contemplating a ruin, one could feel the presence of a superior reality, timeless and placeless.

They walked on the path that climbed to the fortress, and after a few minutes, they found themselves in front of the entrance. Located on the East side, about five meters high was reached in the past by a retractable wooden staircase that was placed on two stone shelves.

"I see it has been restored and reinforced since I was last here," Federico said. Eleonora's thought followed another trail: "What if the places we are looking for are the ones your dad always took you to? The more time passes, the more I think he knows where the treasures are. Your grandfather and great-grandfather must have been able to tell him."

Federico didn't comment; he remembered that he still kept the letter that Tonino sent him when he returned to Milan thirty years earlier. He recalled that on the back he had many postage stamps and there was written 'Francobollo, 22 September 1980—Castelli d'Italia 50 Lire - Rocca di Calascio, in L'Aquila.'

"This place has been visited ninety-nine thousand times," said Giovanna. "If there was a treasure, how is it possible that no one ever found it?"

Balthazar lifted the palm of his right hand, facing upwards, towards Federico's face: "I told you he was a lying scoundrel. He's just trying to buy time by going to lost places. It will end up as it did at the dam. There is nothing up here."

Federico explained further: "Where is it that the mountain falls the most steeply away from the castle? Where is the most challenging point, the one where no tourist ever goes? It's under the tower on box two; let's get there, and you will see for yourself."

"There is also the path around the castle; thousands of people will have walked it," continued Giovanna.

"It's not all around it. On the southwest side, you can't get there easily. See how the mountain goes steeply down to the tower's foundation that extends farther down the mountain?"

They followed the path to the right, but Federico planned to leave it as soon as he reached the back of the castle and go down on the opposite side, turning left to the steepest part. They went near the southwest tower, the one furthest from the bridge, the most distant from the paths, the one with the deepest scarp. Federico understood why it was so called, from the frightening escarpment that fell under the tower.

Now that they were on the opposite side of the castle, he marveled at a vision: his shadow had become gigantic and was projected onto the clouds below, surrounded by a luminescent crown around his head. At his side, the shadow of the castle.

"The ghost of the castle," murmured Federico. "I had heard about it. Or maybe I'm becoming a saint; look at that halo."

"Yes, it's called Brocken's spectrum," Giovanna pointed out, "an uncommon optical effect produced by light reflected from a cloud of uniformly sized water droplets. It happens when a peak is above cloud level, and the area is often foggy. Like today."

"How come you know so much, Madam Engineer?" asked the Brigadier.

Giovanna pointed out the tower they were interested in: "That is the most exposed tower, the one closest to the sky; in fact, it's surrounded by it. The one where nobody goes because it's dangerous. The choice of where to hide something is obvious. Now that we know it."

The tower that seduces the sky, the highest castle in the area, and one of the highest in Italy. It could only be there.

Federico saw that from that height, the valley below was now covered by clouds, and the castle was just above them; it did end in heaven.

Giovanna called his attention back to their task and helped the Brigadier get under the tower's base. She showed him how to operate the metal detector; it was much lighter and easier to maneuver than the one they had found in the cave. He could use it with one hand, while with the other hand, he held on to the rocks or the hand of someone in the group that helped him keep his balance.

Federico suggested: "The ground is rocky; let's probe everywhere, in every crevice. Even where it seems impossible that there could be anything."

When Brigadier put the metal detector under the corner of a massive rock, they heard it playing a sound. They all looked at each other in amazement.

"How am I supposed to move this boulder?" he asked. "And even if I could, it would roll down into the valley and make a massacre in Castelvecchio and Carapelle. They have enough of destruction."

"Let's not move it. Let's dig a hole next to where you heard the sound," Giovanna told him, "and see what is hidden there."

The Brigadier asked for the pickaxe, and in less than ten minutes, he had dug enough to move a buried stone to the side of the boulder. Using the pickaxe as a lever, he moved another stone, stopping it with his foot to keep it from rolling downhill. In the place where the stone had been for years, they could see an old wooden trunk, and another could be glimpsed just behind it. They dug them up and opened them: they were both full of coins and gold objects.

Those who had hidden them had been ingenious. First, digging under the side of a large boulder that was impossible to move, and then pushing the treasure into the space created by the irregular shape of the boulder just below it. The remaining opening had been covered with two heavy rocks that only a strong man could move. Once covered with earth, other small rocks, and stones of the territory, along with the growth of grass and shrubs, it was impossible to guess that something was hidden there or to stumble across them by chance. Those rocks were so stuck together that the earth wouldn't have moved them, even during an earthquake.

Balthazar went pale when Federico stared at him, sneering over his uncultivated beard and from under his rambling mustache: "My dear old friend, are you now ready for the coup de grâce?"

91. BURDENS AND HONORS

14 April 2009 – Tuesday

The treasure was priceless; there were coins, rings, necklaces, and gold jewelry of all shapes and sizes. The Carabinieri seized it to hand it over to the Superintendent. Federico had the satisfaction of mocking Balthazar, drawing himself up in a pompous pose and, in his noblest voice, imitating the Tzar: "I give this treasure to all of Abruzzo for the reconstruction."

He then turned towards Crocko: "See? I'm giving you a hand with the reconstruction, just as you asked."

The Marshal turned back to Federico, impressed but not satisfied: "You spoke of two treasures. One is missing. Is it at the dam of Campotosto where we found you with Vincenzo? Is it where the poem refers to 'beside the water sloping with the winds'?"

"I made a mistake with Case Isaia, Marshal. I've told you; the slope is not there."

"And if you remember, we had pointed out that your guess on the word combination was inaccurate," said the twins.

"I know," Federico replied somberly. "I can't believe I made such a big mistake and that Vincenzo died for it."

"Sorry, we didn't mean to make that reference. However, we want to remind you that Balthazar struck your boat of his own volition. It's not your fault."

Balthazar thought it best to change the focus of the conversation: "So, where is the second treasure?"

"The water that comes out of the earth and goes down—'sloping'—when it comes out into the air—the 'wind'—is in Stiffe."

"In Stiffe? And where exactly?"

"In the Cave of the Brigand."

Balthazar replied angrily: "I have never heard of this cave. It's not in the caves of Stiffe. He's babbling."

"Enough, lawyer," the Marshal intervened. "All of the babble so far has come from you. We have an agreement. Let's all respect it."

Federico clarified: "It's true; it's not 'in' the caves. It's 'above' the caves, besides the waterfall. It's a minor cavity, never visited by tourists."

"How do you know it's that one? Did you find the numerical matches?" prodded Giovanna, almost more interested in solving the riddle than in the treasure's location.

"I have changed my approach. Eleonora's comment that my father knew where the hidden treasures were made me think. And I looked at the past. Once, as a child, I was trying to remove a screw from a toy. No matter how I looked at it, I could not understand how to do it since it had another piece in front that prevented me from reaching it with the screwdriver. My father noticed me struggling: 'Don't ask yourself how you can take it off; ask yourself how they put it there.' That comment was enough to show me the structure of the toy in a new way, and I understood how to take it apart."

"So what? Mamma mia, you are starting to talk like Tonino."

"And so instead of going crazy with numbers, I first thought about where they could put the three treasures and where my father took me when I was a child. Then I looked at the numbers for verification. I thought of places in my childhood where you have the impression that there have been many people, where everyone has already looked. Still, nearby there are inaccessible or underestimated places. The tower in the ravine of Rocca Calascio and the Brigand Cave, with a touch of irony, in Stiffe. As a child, my father took me there. I entered only once, but I remember where it is."

"And the numbers?" insisted Giovanna.

Federico was taking some satisfaction in feeling professorial: "I haven't checked it; do you want to try it? You should find it immediately if you heed what I said."

Giovanna took pen and paper and calculated the numbers corresponding to words like Stiffe, caves, brigand, waterfall, above, side, mountain, etc. After a few minutes, she came out with one correct sequence: "Brigand Cave, Stiffe's side. Thirty-seven, plus thirteen, plus twenty-nine, plus one, plus nineteen, equals ninety-nine. Your fifteen minutes of celebrity are over."

"Almost right, although I got a different combination."

Balthazar tried to discredit them: "What a pathetic story, his father and the little toy? I'm starting to cry."

"We have set out the rules. Let's follow them," the Marshal said. "And go to Stiffe."

92. THE BRIGAND CAVE

14 April 2009 – Tuesday

Driving down the shortcut to Stiffe, they passed through Castellana, watching the plain of the Aterno covered with rhombuses, squares, and diamonds of green meadows, brownfields, and ochre-colored geometries divided by the serpentine of the river. On the left stood the mountain showing a giant hole—the Campana pit—and just above the village, the majestic split. Here, hidden by vegetation, are the caves of Stiffe, underground karst carved out by a subterranean river that courses along the seven hundred meter length of the caves before exiting through a cut in the side of the mountain. As the coded poem stated, one would see "the water sloping with the winds."

Federico's father told him how he and his friends had discovered the caves about ten years after the war. He had been about eighteen years old, and they had gone to catch some shrimps in the stream generated by the waterfalls. The motivation that drove them to wander in the countryside was not the spirit of adventure but sheer hunger. The water that came down in some periods of the year was relatively consistent. It had been redirected to a small power station that generated enough energy to move the mill wheel and illuminate the village's few homes.

Federico's father told him that one summer, he and Tonino noticed that the amount of water had decreased and left a small space between the rocks. Their curiosity to see what was beyond was overwhelming, so they swam underwater and against the current for three or four meters until they found themselves in a large cave sprinkled with blocks of stone. The visibility was poor, and they could see only thanks to sunlight that came through the small gap between the water and the overhanging rock. They heard several sounds and realized that there must have been an empty cavern above them.

The next day they returned, equipped with flashlights, and could admire beauties whose existence they had not even imagined. Only later did they learn that the names of those natural sculptures were stalactites and stalagmites. A little farther ahead,they noticed a small recess formed by the erosive action of the river that showed archaeological traces of primitive men: "Riccardo, some people made this place their home," Tonino said.

The two had entered the cavern as they crossed the threshold of an enchanted world. The limestone walls were so white that they seemed covered with snow. Higher up, two dark bands extended parallel inside the cave. They were metallic oxides deposited by the river in its millenary action.

His father told him that his senses were heightened by the cool temperature—the opposite of the summer they had left outside—the light bouncing and flickering off the rocks and the sound of the bubbling water, which would disappear under the earth and then reappear further away. The muffled rumble of the flowing water returned the cave to its most intimate, primordial essence.

Continuing exploring, they entered a gigantic hall, where the river could not be seen or heard anymore as it flowed under them. Total silence fell. After admiring some stalactites, they entered a majestic room where the water, falling with a thunderous waterfall, gave them a show they would never have the creativity to imagine.

What attracted them was the vastness of the environment, all inside the mountain and invisible from the outside. It was a great sounding board for the murmur of the waterfall: an extraordinary reverberation of all kinds of echoes.

On the way to Stiffe, Tonino completed the discovery account: "Your father wanted to spread the news and began the speleological explorations."

"What did you want to do instead?"

"I would have enjoyed them some more by ourselves. When we were there, we felt something special, mystical. Instead, a team of speleologists placed nails and rope ladders to explore as far as possible. The archaeological remains that your father had seen among the rocks were also discovered."

As he approached those caves, Federico felt the intense and profound bond he had with that land growing even more; it was one of the most beautiful places in all of Abruzzo and was equidistant from his mother's and father's village. On one side, his gaze swept over the basin of L'Aquila, just below the Gran Sasso; on the other side, it climbed steeply to the rocky wall about a hundred meters high, overlooking the entrance to the cave, made invisible by the intense green of the foliage.

Their little procession of Carabinieri SUVs, now followed by media trucks and the curious, arrived, parked, and everyone began walking towards the main entrance, which had been closed to visitors due to the earthquake. In any case, they wouldn't be entering that way; their destination was higher up, where there were other natural cavities, and among these, set in a gully on the right, would be the Brigand Cave. Federico and his friends, along with the Carabinieri, Balthazar, and Crocko, started up a steep, narrow path. Tonino turned to the media and the other followers. "It's too steep for someone my age. I will stay here, but I am excited to tell you a story about the history of this place." As he spoke, a rock the size of a melon was dislodged by Balthazar's foot and tumbled down the path to land at their feet. The men carrying the cameras decided Tonino's offer was a valid alternative, as did the followers; they were, after all, curious but not suicidal.

Federico's group made their way to the gully that he said would lead to the Brigand Cave. The path they needed to take looked arduous, and the access was too narrow for an adult. *Ideal as a refuge and to hide treasures*, thought Federico.

"Visitors don't go here," Federico said. "They are attracted by the main caves, which are easier to visit, and contain many beauties. This way, moreover, is not safe." Then, turning toward Balthazar, he added: "As Vincenzo might have told you, treasure hunting can be dangerous."

The Marshal gave the Tzar a dark, thoughtful look. "Perhaps most of us should wait here in case we need to ask for help."

"Good idea," said the Brigadier, who then volunteered to go into the gully first.

"I'm coming too," said Giovanna, whose curiosity was stronger than that of any cat in the whole of Abruzzo. Federico concurred with the plan; the last thing he wanted at this point was to leave Balthazar unattended with the Marshal—or the media—to make any speeches.

The path the Brigadier and Giovanna took was like a series of small gaps that were less inaccessible than the rest of the surrounding terrain. To steady themselves, the treasure hunters laid their hands on the untouched mosses that covered the stones above the Stiffe ravine. The intense green of the moss seemed almost phosphorescent in the dim blue of the mountain's shadow, which had covered that slope for millions of years, preventing the full strength of the sun from ever reaching it. They arrived before a narrow crack that appeared to lead into the mountain.

Giovanna stuck her head in it; there were huge, hairy spiders and dangling cocoons. Turning toward the Brigadier, she bowed and extended her hand toward the crack: "I offer you the '*ius primae cavernae*'. After you please."

The Brigadier smiled, swelling his chest. "Does this mean 'Go ahead, I'm not brave enough?'"

"On the contrary, I am just a medieval Amazon. The female version of an ancient knight. I defer the honor to you."

The Brigadier crawled into the crack full of cobwebs and turned on the flashlight to not rub his face against the walls. The light awakened the spiders asleep in the small holes in the rock, which were now a few centimeters from his eyes; he disturbed them and felt them close to his face, hands, and nose. He felt them walking on his neck, but he crawled inside anyway.

"They are not poisonous, don't worry," Giovanna comforted him. Then she tightened the laces to the sweatshirt's hood so tightly that only her glasses were free, and she entered the narrow passage too.

They found themselves in a small room. The Brigadier scanned the cave with the flashlight and saw other small spaces. A giant spider ran along the walls, and a flock of bats flew past them. An insect that looked like a transparent grasshopper with long legs startled the Brigadier and made him jump back.

"Holy crap! Who knows what that is?"

"It's called Dolichopoda," remarked Giovanna.

"Such a clever amazon. Even the scientific name disgusts me."

Two small black eyes looked at them for a moment before a hedgehog turned and took an uphill path they had not noticed. The Brigadier pointed the flashlight in that direction and saw a secondary chimney: "Look—who knows where it goes? Maybe there is easier access at the top of the mountain."

They continued, and the way became even narrower. They looked at each other, undecided on what to do. Giovanna tried to be logical: "The bats passed by, so there must be another room behind this bottleneck."

Turning sideways, they squeezed through—and entered the famous Brigand Cave.

They examined it: "There's nothing here," noted the Brigadier. Giovanna went towards a rock, but the Carabiniere warned her: "Stop, you can't touch the stalactites."

"What you see here is a stalagmite because it rises from the floor."

"Don't try to be funny: it's illegal anyway."

"We are looking for treasure hidden by brigands. Do you think they worried about what was legal?"

The Brigadier grimaced, shook his head, and then went over to help Giovanna with a little more leverage. The stone moved and revealed what looked like an animal's lair. Inside, a shabby ancient chest that seemed to have come out of a junkyard store had been pressed into the hole.

It was closed by an even rustier lock.

93. IN BLACK AND WHITE

14 April 2009 – Tuesday

Everyone looked stunned when they came out with the chest and the story of its discovery.

"I can't believe it!" said Eleonora. "Is it possible that no one has ever moved that rock all these years?"

"We have to acknowledge the obvious: there must have been speleologists in this cave, but they were looking at something else, or maybe they would rather not touch anything so as not to break it."

"And we dared to break the egg, just like Columbus," said the Brigadier.

Federico took the chest in his hand. "The lock is old and rusty. We may need to break it to see what's in it, and we have no tools up here. Let's return to the parking area; maybe someone will have something we can use." Then, looking at Balthazar, he added, "And besides, perhaps the Tzar will want to claim another treasure for the people." The sudden look on Balthazar's face indicated that he was already thinking of a way to turn this discovery to his advantage.

When they came back with the chest, the crowd gathered around them. The local TV camera alternated between zooming in on the object and panning around for shots of the people around it.

"Another treasure; how many are there?"

"It's too small to hold a treasure."

The Brigadier wanted to open it: "We need a wire cutter. Does anyone have one?"

The growing excitement was frustrated as no one appeared to have brought such an unlikely item.

Then they saw Carlone walking back from the pigsty with a bag full of sheep skewers, the 'arrosticini'. A cry went up: "Carlone will have those tools."

Carlone from Stiffe was famous for having once declared: "For those who like a smell, it becomes a cherished perfume." The occasion he coined the saying was questionable, but it became a proverb of the area and one that was needed.

"Carlone, can you please lend us a wire cutter?"

Carlone couldn't wait to use his tools, of which he was proud: "What for?"

They described the problem to him.

"I don't have a cutter," he said while passing the bag of skewers to Giovanna and unhooking a hatchet from his belt: "Is this okay?"

Federico looked at Balthazar sideways and muttered under his breath: "I don't like hatchets".

The Brigadier took the casket from Federico's hands and pushed it forward with the lock away from him. Carlone gave the lock a blow, which broke it away from the casket in a single lump, solidified by fifty years of rust.

They looked into it. There was no treasure. There was instead a letter. Giovanna turned away: "Let's hope this is not another puzzle."

The Brigadier reached in and took the letter. Puzzled, he said, "It's addressed to Cesidia, and the sender is the firm of the lawyer Balthazar and his father." Federico imagined he could hear the Tzar's heart stop beating.

The Brigadier passed the letter to the Marshal, who opened it and read it aloud. His face became dark, and he wheeled to Balthazar for explanations: "What are you doing? Extorting defenseless old women?"

"It will surely be proven a fake."

The Marshal slammed the back of his hand on the letter several times: "It's in black and white, Balthazar". At the least, you are disbarred from the order and then a trial. There is your signature; I recognize it."

The Brigadier asked the obvious: "Who brought this chest here? The brigands had nothing to do with it."

Federico spoke: "Vincenzo. I had him deliver it before we went to Case Isaia. Aunt Cesidia wanted to show the letter, but only in front of many witnesses."

Then he advanced towards Balthazar and, with a grim smile, said, "I think it's more than just your foot that has been caught this time."

The twins interjected: "And the legal warning against Federico has not been found; perhaps it was another of your frauds. An investigation will be opened about your work and your father's, and you will not come out of it well. Everyone heard the words of the Marshal, and there was the TV to film the scene. This time you won't cover it up."

The crowd was meanwhile growing angry. Voices were heard saying, "They asked me for the pension money, too. He and Don Cesare." Another shouted, "He also told me that it was thanks to him that I had the arrears!" The crowd seemed to grow as more people gathered from the village.

The Brigadier wanted to be precise and ask for details: "Who told you this?"

And the same answer came from many voices: "Don Cesare."

The pensioners were all ready to testify. A popular uprising had broken out. The cameraman turned the camera to try to film as much as possible. Balthazar looked for Crocko but had already slipped beyond the crowd and rushed down the road. Instead, Balthazar hid behind the Marshal, who feared lynching, and intervened, in his most authoritative voice: "We declare you arrested!" and motioned to the Brigadier to put handcuffs on Balthazar. Then, leaning close to the Brigadier, he whispered: "I'll take him away before they crush him like a bug. You collect the evidence."

The Marshal took the chest in two hands and pushed Balthazar towards the truck. The sun's heat had meanwhile warmed the chest and awakened its contents. The bottom fell off, dropping a writhing mass of snakes at Balthazar's feet; he jumped backward as the snakes started to climb on him as if he were the more famous St. Domenico. With his hands cuffed behind his back, the only other thing he could do was scream, and the sharp sound of it echoed against the cliffs of Stiffe. But it wasn't just an echo; everybody heard more cries coming from the sky. Eleonora recognized them: "It's Maya. Look!"

The eagle was rising over the battered houses of the village on a thermal current.

"So she can fly," said Giovanna.

"She's not so confident in her movements."

"It looks to me like she's flying all right."

As she got closer and closer, Federico realized that Maya hadn't eaten since the day Balthazar attacked her. With a sudden inspiration, he took a handful of raw skewers from Carlone's bag that Giovanna was still holding and called Maya with the sound she knew while shaking the skewers. The eagle saw them and changed direction as Federico ran towards Balthazar, positioning himself so that, along an imaginary line, Balthazar was between himself and the eagle.

"Are you crazy?" cried Eleonora.

The eagle turned and started to fly toward him. As she did, Federico stopped the call and lowered his hand holding the roasts; Maya followed with her eyes and saw the snakes waving on Balthazar's chest and around his neck. Instead, she fixed her gaze on these, closed her wings, and swooped down. She landed with her claws on the snakes writhing on the Tzar's chest and unbalanced him with the kinetic energy of the impact.

With her tired wings and claws extended, Balthazar thought Maya was trying to rip his heart out. Having his arms tied by the shackles, he tried to duck to one side, but his lousy foot found the side of the mountain, and he stumbled. At that moment, the eagle released its claws, and the Tzar fell, sliding along the ridge of the hill and tumbling along the rocks, brambles, and stones, like the *Zingari* of Pacentro. Perhaps he thanked the sky when, unworthy of its status, a simple ornamental plant stopped him before he had built up too much speed, saving him from a crash.

Maya tried to fly back up with two snakes between her talons, but they were twisting around her legs and wings, as in the statue of Laocoon. A snake managed to block one of her wings, and the eagle lost lift, stalled, screwed to one side, and crashed to the ground. The snakes didn't hesitate, and as soon as they touched the grass and felt the talons loosen, they shot away from her grasp.

Federico ran to get Maya and, even without his glove, wrapped her in his vest, covering her head and turning his back to all the people: "Stay away!"

The Brigadier, Giulio, and others made a human chain, and thanks to some ropes that Giulio retrieved from the 4x4, they recovered Balthazar from the slope and took him to the hospital in the truck. An hour later, Don Cesare would also be arrested on extortion charges.

Giovanna approached Federico: "Why didn't you tell us anything? Your ploy might not have worked. And the code, how could it have fit?"

"Because someone was listening to us. The same person who told Balthazar about the first treasure. Don't ask me who it was. And it wasn't me who came up with the ruse. I was lost and didn't know how to close the match. I had to ask for help."

The twins seemed amused: "Yes, and we all know how difficult it is for you, the invincible Federico. And by the way, you are not even that clever. We couldn't be sure if any of the authorities were on Balthazar's side and might have helped him cover this up if it came to light. We were also not sure about who the spy was. We suggested that the letter be revealed in the most public way possible—especially if we didn't find the third treasure in time."

Federico continued: "To be safe, I had also scanned the letter and sent it to myself by email. Vincenzo took the chest and the letter in the cave, knowing there would be no visitors these days."

"Vincenzo avenged himself in advance."

"Yes."

"What do we do with the traitor?"

"We will forgive him. He thought he was protecting you and your territories."

Giovanna was curious about the strange object: "That case looked like an old padlock; where did you find it?"

"In Aunt Cesidia's cellar. I detached and reattached the bottom of the chest and locked some snakes that Francesco gave me as long as I would have set them free. Everyone focused on the padlock and ignored the bottom. But that part was just for fun, drama, and revenge. Did you enjoy the look on Balthazar's face as much as I did?"

Eleonora hugged Federico: "It's a revenge too subtle for my taste, but I am so happy that you listened to my feelings."

Federico felt the warmth of Eleonora's cheek close to his, only to realize that the heat was coming from his redness.

94. A HIPSTER'S BEARD

14 April 2009 – Tuesday

That evening, Federico received a call from Milan, offering a job interview. The woman on the phone was kind and told him his LinkedIn resume was perfect for the role they were looking for. They had also read in the news about the discovery of a treasure and the donation of the same by him to help the earthquake victims in the reconstruction. He shared the news with Eleonora, who looked him in the face, then took his head in her hands, tilting it to the left and right. Smiling, she shook her head: "You need a fix; you look like the proverbial griffin."

"The proverbial griffin" refers to a man so unkempt and disheveled that he looks like a griffin bird. He thinks that he looks fabulous, however.

In the tents, they found a retired barber of Corbellino: Di Francesco. He had been living in Canada but had returned a month earlier to visit his homeland.

"Now the beard is in fashion, and those who wear it are called 'Hipster'," the barber said. "Do you want a modern cut?" Federico didn't like his beard at all, and every day he thought of shaving it. He agreed to have it trimmed just to try it out: "Let's see if I like it; there's always time to shave it."

As he worked, the barber told them his story. Federico asked a thousand questions: "I live in Toronto, even though my father wanted to emigrate to America and join his uncle in Ohio. We made a stopover in Canada to wait for the permits. We were supposed to stay there for three months and then go to the United States. But my father died in an accident during those months. I had neither the money to return to Italy nor a permit to go to the US. So I started working in Toronto, in the Italian neighborhood of Woodbridge, as a barber."

Di Francesco was proud to have sent all his three children to university. His son was his oldest child and was an engineer; his middle daughter was a doctor, and his youngest daughter was a lawyer. He was happy to have dedicated a life of sacrifice to achieve the dream of independence, economic freedom, and above all, to have seen the end of poverty.

Federico thought that he, too, should have studied law, engineering, or medicine instead of an obscure subject like mathematics. Maybe then he wouldn't have gotten into trouble. He wondered if it was the right advice to give Manfredi or if the world was changing so radically that even those certainties were reduced to rubble by life's tremors.

Di Francesco told him the stories of the immigrants and the funny way they spoke English, '*Amma haangree*' - I'm hungry; 'Shes a nowork'- it doesn't work; '*Amma no-beeleev*'- I don't believe it. He told them how, in America, Italians had often been referred to derogatorily as 'wop', which stood for 'With-Out Passports' because they usually arrived in America without documents. Hundreds of thousands of people from Abruzzo emigrated to the United States and Canada.

Federico knew that it was a false etymology, but he didn't feel the urge to correct him, a skill he had learned the hard way. Wop originates from the Southern Italian 'guappo', pronounced as 'wahpp', and indicates a showy, cocky, well-dressed man.

Di Francesco stepped back and admired his work: "Look how handsome you are. By the way, you don't want to go to Milan wearing these rags, do you? It would dishonor your mother and your father. Don't you have a business suit?"
"Yes, in the hut in Milan."
"In the hut, you said?"
"It's a long story. Just forget it."

Federico couldn't leave without returning to his parent's house; he wanted to collect an old, framed photo of his great-grandfather. He took it in his hand, studying the old image that had been one of the first photos ever taken in the village.

Tonino had told him a story about the early days of photography; he had a story for every occasion. One woman thought her husband cheated on her with a woman in San Demetrio. She sought evidence of his infidelity everywhere until searching some drawers, she found a small, oval mirror. They were so poor that she had never seen anything like that before. She thought to herself: *It must be that thing everyone is talking about: photography. It must be a picture of her. He keeps it here to come and see it in secret.* When she lifted the mirror, the woman didn't recognize herself and exclaimed: "Oh God, at least he could have chosen a more decent one!"

The glass protected the photo of Carlantonio in the frame. He had a beard and a mustache even longer than the beard itself. His expression: stern and challenging. Here was a man whose deeds he had heard of through the stories of the family but whom he was only now getting to know as if his genetic code was shaking and claiming more and more space. Carlantonio was the son of Fernando, whose progeny was so feared that in all the houses of the village when the rosary was prayed, it ended with a litany:

"A Lord's Prayer to all saints, as we hold this sacred string:
Save us from all constraints and Fernando's offspring."

He held up the picture and looked that older man in the eyes. His image was reflected in the glass and superimposed on the charcoal brigand, the lover of justice and truth, looking at him from the other side. His old eyes squint, and the corners of his mouth bent downwards. Was it in disappointment?

95. BACK TO BUSINESS

15 April 2009 – Wednesday

"Federico is entitled to a reward," claimed Eleonora.

She was referring to the treasure of Rocca Calascio, the only one they had found. But the question was controversial. The twins consulted the '*Legislative provisions on cultural and environmental heritage*' and made a summary of the relevant articles.

"In essence, when speaking of fortuitous discoveries—and especially of things of archaeological interest—by anyone, and in any way found, underground or on the seabed, the discoveries belong to the State."

"But it was not accidental."

"Ah, wasn't it all a stroke of luck?"

"No, you knew where to go."

"Should I have lied and staged it, then?"

"In the case of occasional discoveries," the twins went on to read, "the discoverers have, therefore, the obligation to report the discovery of the immovable or movable property indicated in article ten, within twenty-four hours to the Superintendent or the Mayor, or the public security authority, and to provide for their preservation, leaving them in the conditions and in the place where they were found. The Superintendent will also inform the Carabinieri responsible for protecting the cultural heritage of the discovery."

"And we did."

"Well, even more than that, we had the Carabinieri present."

"To the fortuitous discoverer who has complied with the obligations provided in article ninety, the Ministry shall pay a reward not exceeding a quarter of the value of the found items, subject to their estimate."

"There, see?" rejoiced Eleonora.

The twins had not finished: "Beware, no prize is due to the discoverer who has entered and searched the property or possessions of others without the owner's consent."

"Should we have asked for permission then?"

In the end, once again, and as usual, the only possible solution was to forget everything. No permission had been requested. The Brigadier and the Marshal, while they were officers, they were also part of an expedition that had not been authorized.

They all agreed.

Eleonora then asked: "What about the other treasure?"

"I don't know," Federico replied, as he had when the Marshal asked the same question. "Maybe it was at Case Isaia, and someone found it before us. Or perhaps we need to look for some other number combination. For now, I don't have any other ideas."

Eleonora interrupted Federico: "Let's take a break. You go for the interview, it's your future, and you can start over. Manfredi can't stay here for long because he must return to his mother and school. You'll see that it will all turn out well."

"How can I leave all this? Didn't you say that you and Vincenzo called me because now I was finally in trouble as you were? And what about you and your baby?"

"You left 'all this'—and us—for thirty years, and we made it ourselves. We will make it this time, too."

"It seems like thirty centuries."

"Just promise you'll come back and visit us."

"I would have invited you to my hut in Milan, but...."

And they had a great laugh.

96. THE TASTE OF BLOOD

Abruzzo - Lombardy, 15 April 2009 – Wednesday

Federico had confidence in the doctor who had treated him after the dam accident. He had known since they were children, so Federico told him about Manfredi and disclosed that he was ill. The doctor seemed to have different ideas from the psychologist they were still supposed to meet in Milan: "Forget those theories; they're more metaphors than anything else. Even the body gets sick, and the mind may have nothing to do with it. It's certainly a genetic condition. Either Manfredi is not your son, or she's not your wife's. Maybe this is what YOU don't want to see."

He proposed a DNA test to check whether the gene responsible for Stargardt's disease was in his chromosomal kit: "I'll have it done urgently. I'll call you tomorrow."

Maya was exhausted but constantly agitated, and since she remained calm only in the presence of Federico, he decided to take her with him. *So much space in a hut. An eagle can stay with me there.*

Federico loaded the car, said goodbye to everyone, and, with Uncle Maurilio driving and Maya and Manfredi in the back seats, began the long drive to Milan. They were not yet out of Abruzzo when Manfredi noticed that his uncle was hesitating to speed up, so he asked him: "Why are we going so slowly?"

Maurilio replied, with a sad half-smile: "You see, the car doesn't want to go. Look, I have my foot on the accelerator, I press hard, but she won't go."

He had not yet told his wife about Vincenzo; he had not wanted to do it on the phone. Better in person to support her when she would have fainted and gone mad with grief over the loss of her son for the second time. They had also decided to leave Aunt Cesidia behind in the places that were familiar to her. She had found a balance, and taking her to a place she didn't know and that would be immersed in the darkness of mourning wouldn't have been a good idea.

Aunt Cesidia, as was her custom, had again cried when they were saying goodbye. This time, Federico understood why.

When it was Federico's turn to drive, Maurilio sat in the back to get some sleep, and Manfredi sat in the front seat. Federico looked for the right moment to bring up the subject of the boy who was bullying him, but he couldn't find any moment suitable enough. When he made a rather direct reference to people who are perhaps scary and aggressive, Manfredi denied any difficulty. He had almost thought of confessing his fear of Balthazar, but he couldn't. He thought then he would tell Stefania. Maybe Manfredi would have talked more openly to his mother.

After all, I don't even know if he's my own son.
Of course, he's my son; that is why the thought of him going blind is so scary.
How can he not be my son? We wanted him so much.
The probability that Stefania has that disease in her genes is low.
Yes, just like the probability of losing your job or an earthquake destroying your home.
Indeed he's my son; what else?

He saw from afar the colossal smog dome over Milan as they approached the large city and saluted it. He lost a few seconds looking into the setting sun on their left as the number of cars around them increased. Uncle Maurilio was again sitting in the front seat while Manfredi continued sleeping, leaning on Maya's cage. His uncle remained silent, as always, the kind of silence that left Federico in a state of apprehension.

Maurilio broke that silence like Federico would have least expected: "I know it's rumored that Vincenzo was not my son."

"Uncle, what are you saying?"

"Don't worry; everyone knows by now. And it's the truth. At least the first part of it. Nobody knows that the second part is even truer: Vincenzo has become my son. From the times I used to put my hand next to his face so he wouldn't bump into an edge; to the nights he would ask me to lie in bed with him and his brother after I had told them a story. It happened each time I tried to comfort him, every cry after a disappointment; every time he put me between himself and that which scared him. It happened that time he fainted in my arms when he saw his brother's ripped body, as well as every time I showed him something that amazed him, and he smiled at me. While I did not even realize it, he had become, day after day, and forever, my son."

Federico felt the saliva become dust in his throat and blew out a slow breath like the swamps of the river Po they had just left behind.

"Federico, do you believe belonging to a family is measured by a genetic test? Do you know how much hate can be nested between the genetic chains that bind people?"

Federico nodded: "Is that why we fall in love with someone whose genes are so different from ours?"

Maurilio looked out the window. Federico thought of his wife, the mother of his children, both now dead, and the dull pain he was bringing with him again from that torn region. He looked at his uncle for a second and then returned to stare at the road. Yes, he was an orphan and had lost a friend only a few days after meeting him again, but his uncle had lost his brother and two sons. He reflected that when someone loses their spouse, they become widows. If they've lost their parents, they're orphans. But what is the word for parents that had a child who died? And what about the parents who have seen all of their children die? It's such a grievous experience that no word has ever been found that could include so much pain.

They arrived in Milan towards the evening. Maya had remained covered in the cage; she could not see the outside world, and the outside world was unable to see her. It was the only way to keep her quiet. Stefania met them as they got out of the little gray Panda, hugged Manfredi, and reproached Federico:

"What happened to you? Are you limping?"

Federico didn't even look at her while he was unloading.

"Manfredi will tell you."

Stefania urged him: "You don't want to talk to me anymore? By the way, you should have been here already."

Federico agreed with her: "Yes, I know. I had a setback; then I miscalculated the time; in Abruzzo, the Easter vacation doesn't end until tomorrow."

"So now Abruzzo rules the world?"

Manfredi was smiling, impatient to tell her about the heroic deeds they had accomplished and the wonders they had seen: "Mom, you know we found a treasure."

Stefania considered it a joke: "Yes, of course, Freddie."

Federico continued to unload the car, and with his voice strained as he lifted a bag, he threw a little dart at Stefania by saying to Manfredi: "Mom doesn't believe you," and then he leaned down towards his son and whispered in his ear: "Those who don't share our blood, cannot taste its flavor."

Manfredi tried to get his mother's attention and doubled his enthusiasm: "Look, Mommy, look at the coins we found," taking them out of his pocket and showing them to her.

Stefania smiled at her son: "How beautiful, Freddie."

And how stupid that we're back to that nickname.

Stefania changed her voice as she turned to her ex-husband: "Is this some more of your usual crap? Where did you get these?"

He remained calm; he just wanted to go to the hut, read the rest of the papers he had found in the cave, and prepare for the interview: "Yes, that's right—just a piece of crap. Don't worry; it's just a game. Just a game."

When he opened the back door, Federico smiled and took the blanket off the cage with a single gesture, like a magician, to surprise her, wondering how she might react.

"Oh God, and what is this?"

Manfredi smiled enthusiastically: "It's Maya, Mamma."

Stefania had made two leaps backward and brought her hands to her face: "An eagle? Oh God, not even a balcony is as far out as you are."

Manfredi continued: "It's Dad's eagle, the one from Mongolia; all his stories were true."

The surprises didn't end: "O Holy God, what is this other thing, a rifle?"

Federico took it in his hands, opened it, and closed the bolt with a double shot, as in the movies, to make a scene: "A 'magnum' rifle."

Stefania was incredulous. "You don't even have a gun license."

Federico put the rifle back in the trunk: "It shoots, all the same, so be careful."

He also could not refrain from a further tease: "And don't you think you are mentioning the Supreme Divinity too many times, you who profess to be an atheist?"

"You are also slimmer, and you have a harder face. I didn't notice it under that long beard."

"Yes, there have been some adventures. And how did it go with your cousin?"

"My cousin?"

"Weren't you at the lake with him?"

"With the whole family, including all cousins. Why did you mention him?"

Federico let it go: "Just curious". *Let's wait for the genetic test.*

After unloading the suitcases, he said goodbye to Manfredi: "See you during the weekend; I'll call you tomorrow night at nine."

"Ciao, Papi. You keep the coins, so they're safer."

"All right. They remain with the family."

"Are you staying with Antonio?" Stefania asked.

"No, his wife is back. I found a hut."

"A hut? Then you must be stupid."

"Even more so. I'm a sucker. And anyway, in Abruzzo, which rules the world, they say: 'Better a hut where you laugh than a castle where you cry.' Tomorrow I also have a job interview; maybe I can start a decent life again. However, I must say that I have everything I need in the hut. Or almost. It would perhaps take another heart to be perfect."

"You have the eagle's, Papi. And when I come to the hut, you'll have mine, too."

"Sure, Manfredi, you will come and visit me at the weekend."

"And Maya, will she be there too?"

"I don't know yet. Maybe the time has come for her to live a new life. Away from us crazy human beings."

97. SEVEN FRIENDS

15 April 2009 — Wednesday

Uncle Maurilio left Federico just outside the hut. Federico thought about him and how he would have found a way that was just not there: how to tell his wife about Vincenzo and best cushion the crash that would happen in an hour and a half.

"One day, I will come to see you, Uncle. We are close."

"Sure, Federico. Bye, take good care of yourself and Manfredi."

Federico entered the hut, put the aviary in a corner, unloaded the few things he had brought for himself, and lit the lamp on the worktable. He moved nails, screws, and various tools and laid a blanket over it. He opened the suitcase that Eleonora had lent him. Opening the two halves of the case was as if he were opening a seashell; he was stunned by her scent, as if first her thin legs appeared and then the entire Goddess Venus, lowering her head with class so as not to get her hair caught in the valves of the shell.

He imagined her smiling at him, wrapped in a transparent light:

"Mysterious Hamlet: I miss you, my man."

He heard in his mind the rhythm of the decasyllable and the five 'm's', each punctuated with the dip of the tip of her nose. He was dazed, looked up, and realized he was smiling at the tools on the wall.

He blinked twice, took out the leather folder, and closed the suitcase. After placing the papers on the soft blanket, he rushed to read the story he had started but could not finish. While promising himself that he wouldn't stay up too late since he had his interview the next day, he put his hand in his pocket and felt the coins, his mother's ring, and the keys to the house in Vallecupa.

He leafed through the papers he had found in the cellar. They were handwritten in sepia, black ink on high-quality paper. Federico scanned them with his eyes, dwelling on the passages that seemed most dense in meaning.

It was the account of seven Abruzzesi born in Alexandria of Egypt. A weaver, a pharmacist, a bricklayer, a boilermaker, a builder, a carpenter, and Carlantonio.

I didn't know this about my great-grandfather.

He remembered his father telling him that before the Second World War, a large community of Italians—"as many as the inhabitants of L'Aquila"—lived in Egypt. Half of them lived in Alexandria alone. It wasn't an accident that Giuseppe Verdi's opera "Aida" had been set in Egypt, commissioned by Cairo's Khedivale Opera House, and debuted there in 1871.

The seven friends met in Alexandria. Each of them was there for different professional reasons of their families of origin, as it was for the vicissitudes of each one who returned to Italy and reunited to create a brotherhood inspired by the charcoal works. They all studied Western history and symbolism similar to that found in Egypt, such as the emerald plates of Hermes Trismegistus. They were looking for a bridge between different cultures.

So, they chose Frederick II as their inspiration because he had immense knowledge without geographic or cultural limits. And because he had been involved in the foundation of L'Aquila.

Federico flipped through the pages. There was a note on the succession of colors of the alchemical development of the Great Work.

Citrinitas, Rubedo, Albedo, Nigredo, Viriditas. The path begins with yellow and goes from red to white, black, and green.

In the book his father treasured, there was a similar reference. The order of colors was the same, and the position of the colors was indicated as points of mental concentration placed on the human body. They were in the same points touched by the great sign of the cross, with which Federico marked himself before entering a church: from forehead to stomach and from shoulder to shoulder, ending with his hands joined in front of himself.

His father had written a note about the succession of these colors in the history of L'Aquila.

After the earthquake of 1703, L'Aquila changed the city's colors from red and white—rubedo and albedo—to black and green—nigredo and viriditas, thus indicating the new spiritual phase that had begun.

His father's notes referred to the Carbonari, the black color, and the Moor on L'Aquila's banner. Federico understood that the Moor's rose in his mouth is a play on words in Arabic between rose—'ward'—and spiritual exercises—'wird'. The rose also appeared in the hands of the running Madonna of Sulmona.

He consulted the book that his father treasured so much. Those practices, symbolized by the rose, are devised to provoke the awakening of the perceptive faculties that reside in the heart and mind of man. In the same chapter on the charcoal works, he had already read about the parallel between black and wisdom and was surprised to find this connected to Baphomet, who was also present as one of the masks of the fountain of the ninety-nine spouts. Scholars believed that Baphomet was a kind of pagan idol or a demon, but the text he had in his hands said that it could instead be a corruption of the Arabic word 'abu fihamat'. The term means 'father of understanding'. In Arabic, 'abu'—'father'—is also used for 'source, the main seat of'.

The book pointed out that the word knowledge, or understanding, sounds similar to 'black' and 'coal man'. Baphomet is then nothing but the symbol of the 'complete man', the spiritually realized man. He found confirmation that the dark brown head, as it appears in heraldry, is a word in the jargon of the Crusaders that refers to this type of knowledge.

Also related to the color black, the book referenced the Black Madonnas, which are common in Europe. Their meaning would therefore be 'Wise Virgins'; an example is Loreto's Madonna. To her are dedicated the barefoot race and also the Easter of the 'running Madonna'. The color green is the color that follows the black also in that ritual: the Madonna first wears the black dress, then she loses it to show a green one. Green—viriditas—is the color of initiation, nature, truth, and immortality. Here it seems that the message is: "Wisdom and knowledge lead to truth and immortality."

The Lauretan monks, worshipers of the black Madonna of Loreto, wear a green cloak, a white robe, and a black cord as a belt.

A black cord. A black snake. The 'wisdom of life'.

Federico looked throughout the book for his father's notes, and it seemed almost like his father had done much work. There were bookmarks of various colors: red, yellow, green, white, and black. He had copied a Persian proverb that said: "Pidar natawanad, pisar tamam kunad. If the Father does not succeed, the son may bring it to completion."

Father, how much did you leave me to complete?

He came out of the hut, took a long deep breath, and looked around, absorbing every detail. He didn't understand what he was experiencing. He felt one with the whole creation. As if there were no separation between him and what was around him. He was inside it, but it was also inside him. He could hear the waterway behind the hut, and Eleonora's perfume was still lingering, soothing his sense of smell. He hadn't yet realized that the magnolias and the azaleas were blooming around him. A motion in his heart sent him new questions:

How is it that all of THIS exists?
How can a 'thing', any 'thing', exist?

He was surprised for the first time in his life that there is such a thing as existence. That something is there. That it actually exists.

Not the fact that there is life on earth but that anything exists at all.

He paused and smiled.

And enjoyed not only life but the miracle of existence itself.

98. KNOWLEDGE

15 April 2009 – Wednesday

Federico was more and more fascinated by all his new learnings. With the help of Michele Scoto—Magister, an Arab-Latin translator, philosopher, encyclopedist, astrologer, and scientist—Frederick II came into contact with Jewish scientists in Spain and Provence. They gave him access to Islamic and Greek philosophy through a network of cultural relations in the Mediterranean and between Europe and the Near East. Many Greek classics were known in the Islamic world through translation into Arabic, Hebrew, and other Eastern languages. Frederick II welcomed astrologers, alchemists, philosophers, doctors, and scientists to his court, following the tradition set by his father, Roger II. Once again, "a son who brings to completion what his father began."

Federico returned to the book, interspersed with his father's notes. An entire chapter was dedicated to St. Francis. Federico had himself read a biography of the Saint, inspired by Igor Stravinsky's "Chronicles of My Life". In Genoa, the Russian composer was attracted to a book stall where he found a biography of St. Francis in French. He read it that night. What struck Stravinsky was how St. Francis—when he wanted a solemn language, for poetry, for prayer, for special occasions—expressed himself in the Provençal language.

Francis of Assisi was baptized as John of Peter of Bernardino and became "Francesco, Francis" thanks to his youth spent in France, in direct contact with the French poet-musicians, the troubadours. Many of these artists went to live at the court of Frederick II, "The most Muslim of Catholic kings, the most Catholic of Muslim kings."

Italian poetry was formed at his court through contact with Muslim poets and troubadours, influenced by Andalusian musicians from Spain.

Even the Italian hendecasyllable verse was born from Provençal influences. Jacopo da Lentini, the poet of the Sicilian school at the court of Frederick, wrote one of the first poems in Italian that had that meter: "Io M'aggio Posto in Core a Dio Servire", "I have put in my own heart Servicing God."

Following Stravinsky's example, Federico, during a trip to Assisi, had also found and read the "Life of St. Francis" by St. Bonaventura.

Some passages that at the time seemed incomprehensible now made complete sense. When Francis went to Rome to meet Innocent III, the

Pope met him and his companions. They were miserable and barefoot and came to propose a new monastic rule. He rejected them. But the Pope later had a remarkable vision: a palm tree grew little by little at his feet to become a tree, big and beautiful. He understood that that palm represented the spirituality proposed by the poor man, so he called Francis back for an audience and listened to him again.

Everything was written in the book, while his father punctuated it with notes about Italy and Abruzzo, Lombardy, Sicily, and Piedmont.

For example, St. Francis told the Pope the parable of a wealthy king who, with great joy, had married a beautiful and poor woman and had children who had the same physiognomy as his father and were therefore raised at the same table as the king. It meant that the heirs of the Eternal King would never have to worry about their livelihood. This story is also found in the Sufi tradition, told by Attar and then Jalaluddin Rumi. Federico was struck by such a coincidence that could only be explained by acknowledging the existence of a common level of spiritual communication.

A similar principle was followed by St. Francis of Assisi and Frederick II. Both traveled in the East and met at different times, Sultan Kamil Al Malik. San Cesidio da Fossa—after whose name aunt Cesidia was christened—went as far as China. He was also a Franciscan missionary; he prayed for a long time in the nearby Convent of S. Angelo in Ocre and was killed in China during the Boxer Rebellion.

And speaking of Franciscan journeys, Federico remembered the discussions with his American colleagues when he told them that San Francisco had Italian origins. They didn't believe him; it didn't ring true. But in fact, the Spanish Franciscans founded the city in honor of St. Francis, and Los Angeles was named in honor of Santa Maria degli Angeli. From that small village and the church that you can spot when looking above the valley from the village of Assisi had come the names, and the spiritual energy, of two cities of the modern world where the movement of troubadours resurfaced in the love songs, the lifestyle and the pacifism of the flower children.

Federico felt an increasing love for his land: Abruzzo, a region of stone castles, wolves, bears, and golden eagles. The Abruzzese, rustic like wild boars, run until they break their feet in Pacentro; and in Cocullo, they put the snakes that would bite them around the neck of the saint. He thought of the Marsi, who resisted the Roman army, Duke Sarchia lynched by the people, and The Wolf, standing against the modernity of industrial exploitation. The people of Abruzzo refused the title of Pope —as did Celestino V—preferring the mystical solitude of a hermitage.

Or perhaps the people of Abruzzo are some kind of madman. He felt that that thought contained a pinch of vanity. Crazy, in the sense of original, unique. He regretted that thought, even if perhaps a bit of madness in life is needed if it pushes us to challenge the reality that everyone considers normal, or to reject the accepted definition of success, for example.

In his mind echoed the words of the Neapolitan who sold the babas under the tents: "You Abruzzesi are good, just a bit naive and quite crazy." He had been being 'good', but not just a bit naive—he had been foolish. Yet, nobody would have said that he was crazy. At least not until that moment; he was beginning to feel that seed of madness already blossoming in him.

But first, he had to deal with the domesticated captivity of a job interview and the wild freedom of a golden eagle.

99. EAGLES DON'T FLY IN FLOCKS

16 April 2009—Thursday

For the first time in his life, he went to a job interview with a beard. It was not his style; he shaved every day, even on weekends. He felt uncomfortable when he got out of the car that Antonio had lent him and walked in the streets. He regretted that he had not cleaned his face. But he realized—as when you buy something, and then it seems that everyone has it—that around him, many young men, if not all, had a beard.

Either he had never noticed, or maybe a new fashion had broken out; the one the Toronto barber told him about. Long beard, tight-fitting clothes, and pants shortened at the ankle. They all seemed to have a woodcutter's physique, but Federico was sure they had never split a log. Most had never even held an ax in their hands, let alone heard one whistling behind their backs and biting into a rotten wooden door.

He checked his phone and saw a notice that the festival of the snakes in Cocullo would not take place this year. Given the severe damage to houses and churches, personal and public safety was preferred. On the one hand, he was happy that Francesco wouldn't regret giving him the snakes.

He put the phone back in his right pocket and examined his reflection in a store window. Di Francesco had carved him a perfect beard. It covered his scar and emphasized his jawline, making him feel more robust. The lapels of his suit were perhaps too broad, and his pants were too long and broke with a crease above the ankle. It was the best he could do, considering that he had neither money nor home and had slept in Ranieri's hut. He admitted the lie to himself; the truth was that he hadn't updated his dress style for years. He imagined those young people he saw on the street competing with him for the job. They would beat him mercilessly.

And just then, one of these young people approached him. The first thing Federico noticed was that the man had an aquiline nose; beneath it was a mustache, curled and frozen by wax, and a short beard was well cared for. He was wearing a tweed jacket and had longer hair at the top of his head, combed to the left, with short hair on the temples and behind the nape. He reminded him of an English gentleman of the nineteenth century. With kind and elegant manners, he asked Federico the most absurd question he could have imagined at that moment: "Good morning. Excuse the unexpected and inappropriate interruption of your noble thoughts. I wondered if, thanks to the extravagances of chance, you might know a man willing to sell or acquire ancient coins?"

Federico remained speechless and squinted his eyes. *Is he making fun of me?* He thought, and then stammered: "No ... no ... no."

With the corner of his eye, he checked the store window to see if it reflected anyone else approaching or nearby. He imagined someone was following him to rob him of his few coins. Maybe they had known about the brigand's boot and perhaps believed that he had a significant amount of valuable coins. The young man smiled and gave him a business card: "If you should hear of someone, please let me know. There is also a commission for those who can put us in contact." And with a formal bow, the young man walked away.

The dream-like nature of the exchange unsettled Federico. He took a few moments to consider the card the young man gave him. *The Vase and the Coin. Ancient Numismatics.* He put it in his pocket, where he had his mother's ring and the few coins he had recovered from the Goats' Drop. He jingled them as if to give himself an alarm clock and shrugged off the awkward encounter.

The interview was too important; with a regular salary, he could pay rent, find a cure for Manfredi, and return to normal. Still looking in the window, he rehearsed all his best interview faces: the determined look, the mouth with an intriguing smile, the mysterious look of the visionary.

With a final adjustment of his suit coat, he walked the remaining distance to the office building. He gave his credentials to the receptionist and was directed to the top floor.

They welcomed him with kindness, "Would you like a coffee?"

He didn't feel like it: "No, thanks." *When had he ever refused coffee?*

The headhunter waiting for him seemed beyond aesthetic perfection as if she had come out of one of those lawyer movies set in New York. She showed Federico a newspaper page with a spreading story about him and the treasure he had found and donated: "You have a real story to tell; you will become famous, and people will recognize you. It will be easy for you to sell these apartments at CityLife. We want to make a great start with people who care about other people like you do."

The situation became more evident to Federico; he had no competitors, no younger men who were better dressed. They wanted him for what had happened in the days before.

"Thank you; you are too kind."

She pointed him toward a model of the buildings. "A year ago, it was rubble, and now it rises like a new life."

Rubble.

He was reminded of the houses of L'Aquila, the churches, the historic buildings smashed by the earthquake, demolished by natural causes. He was reminded of Vincenzo's smiles as a boy when he could pass the ball to him and send him into the goal. He was already beginning to be unable to see but hadn't said anything to anyone. Out of shame or resistance to admitting that circumstances were already getting the better of us. Vincenzo had tried to fight those circumstances.

Who knows when L'Aquila will be rebuilt?

The villages where he had spent his childhood would have to disappear to make room for 'provisionally permanent' housing modules.

He heard the lady continue with what now seemed to him a teleshopping script: "Experts say that there are three important indicators to evaluate a property. Do you know what they are?"

Federico thought about it, but the lady didn't let him think long and answered herself: "Location,"—and paused.

"And the other two?"

She smiled at the opportunity he had given her to score a point in her favor: "Location, and location."

Federico liked the technique she had just used and cursed himself for not being able to get it in advance.

The presentation continued: "The crisis will end, and the most important business center in Italy will arise." The headhunter turned towards a model of the new area of Milan: CityLife. "There will be new skyscrapers like in other big international cities."

At the center of the model stood the three towers—the Straight, the Crooked, and the Curved—that the woman said would belong to large international financial institutions: "Look, here there will be the largest urban shopping center in Italy, with an area of 32,000 square meters, containing more than a hundred stores. The second-largest park in Milan will be inside the complex, with an area of about 170,000 square meters. Once the crisis is over, this area of Milan will expand, and you will rise with it."

The more the woman spoke, however, the more the words began to seem to be coming out of an old radio. Those with a knob, even older than the one used by Giovanna to simulate the metal detector. He heard the phrases moving further and further away, like strips of words coming out of the window and going up into the sky, dispersing. The image of the perfect woman became smaller and blurred until she looked like an announcer in one of those small black TVs that some people keep in the kitchen.

"Excuse me, may I use the bathroom?"

"Sure, it's down the hall to the right."

Federico got up. Instead of going to the bathroom, he went towards the exit, handed the badge back to the receptionist, and left the building. He walked among a flock of pigeons eating corn seeds thrown by a woman. They were frightened by him and flew in every direction, regrouping behind Federico's passage.

When he arrived at the parking lot, he got into the car and set out for the second thing he had planned to do that day. He drove out of the parking lot, passed Largo Domodossola, and turned left into Corso Sempione, heading towards the outskirts.

And so, he turned his back to Milan and the famous daily bread promised by the city's economic power.

Stopping at the red light, he heard the roar. In the rearview mirror, he saw the dust of the explosion rise and blend in with the gray clouds. He felt a new sensation. He smiled. He had refused an unrepeatable opportunity, as had Celestino V. He had done so to follow an internal urge. Would he have succeeded? He didn't know. And for the first time in his life, he didn't care.

He felt real, just as everything around him now seemed to be, especially when compared to the fictitious world he had pretended to live in, where he had always tried to meet the expectations that others had of him.

The phone rang; it was his friend, the doctor. He went to the point:

"He's not your son."

Federico had to stop the car.

"How? And whose son is he?"

"A relative of your wife. Or they swapped him in the cradle."

"I mean, am I paying a monthly check for someone who is not my son? Am I here to risk everything for a child she had with someone else?"

"Yes. But you love him."

He was reminded of yet another story his uncle used to tell him. A fellow countryman left for the war and, when he returned, sat down at the table with his family. He saw an extra little boy.

"And this?"

"This? Well, this is that."

And nobody ever mentioned the innuendo again.

Federico found the gut to answer: "I do love him. I thought he was my son until now."

"I have one more thing to tell you. I have inquired about available treatments. There is a doctor who is discovering new and interesting ones. Saffron seems to have a beneficial effect on degenerative eye diseases, even like Stargardt's disease. Some people who couldn't see well enough to read can now do so, thanks to a saffron-based preparation. It's incredible but true. It appears that the only saffron that works is the variety from Abruzzo. I would rather not give you false hopes, but I would give it a try. Call me back in a few days, and I will be able to tell you more."

Saffron from Abruzzo cures degenerative vision problems?

He arrived at Ranieri's old hut, changed his clothes, and put on the leather glove. He saw on the table the color schemes, full of keywords, and the accounts he had made to understand how to start a new business and if it could give him a living. They didn't work all the way through. Next to the coffee machine was a photo of Manfredi. He checked once again, as if to verify their actual existence, the two round-trip tickets to Cuba, one for Stefania and one for Manfredi, which he had bought in the morning.

Vincenzo's face returned to his imagination to admonish him: "You should have gone there. We gave you the money, and you send her?" He laughed from his nose and felt Vincenzo's presence in the corners of his smile. It was true. Money had been lent to him by Eleonora, Tonino, Giovanna and uncle Maurilio.

He opened the aviary and removed the bandages from Maya's beak and claws. She had recovered well; under the broken beak, another was already sprouting, and new talons were forming. The wings moved almost entirely. She had lived too long in captivity, and Federico knew inside himself that the time had come to free her, respecting the ancient Kazakh tradition. He had already thought about it many times, and he knew what he had to do. He put Maya back in her cage, then into the car.

He got behind the wheel and drove towards Bergamo to reach the Orobic Alps.

When they arrived, he took her out of the car, and Maya jumped on the glove. He still hesitated—perhaps the new talons were not yet strong enough? He took off her hood and looked at her. He didn't have any powerful sentences of great speeches; he had never had them. He was confident, however, that the eagle would understand freedom. "What'd you say, shall we give it a try?"

Maya seemed to catch his eyes before they both turned and admired the mountains: light and space opened up on the crown of the surrounding Alps. Maya swelled her feathers, loaded her legs, and spread her wings. She went higher and higher towards those peaks still covered with snow. Federico saw her getting smaller and smaller; he swallowed, squeezed his lips together, and passed his hand over his eyes. Once, like thirty years before, he had left her behind without a thought. And now, he was crying like Aunt Cesidia, thinking about this loss.

He turned around and started towards the car with his head down. He took a crumpled piece of paper from his pocket: 'Goats' Drop, just below the bell: $17 + 26 + 7 + 21 + 15 + 13 = 99$.' Right where his grandfather had always said. Where a gap opens between the rocks, the only place from that part of the mountain where the church bell tower can be seen. Look down; it's buried there.

What the father could not finish, perhaps the son will complete.

Federico sighed.

Maybe. Maybe not.
Sorry, Dad, but I feel that it's too much for me.

He saw a trash basket and crumpled the note in his gloved hand with force as if the noise it made could erase its contents and legacy. The sound was overwhelmed by the screams behind him. He turned around and saw Maya gliding, getting bigger and bigger in his field of view as she approached him.

Federico stopped and stretched out his arm, resting his knee on the ground to better withstand the impact. Maya spread her wings, steered with her tail, and braked, landing on the glove he brought to his chest. Federico felt his heartbeat against one of her wings. He looked at her, smiling, and caressed her head: "It will be for another time, then."

The eagle turned her head, staring at the sky. Federico felt he was the biggest idiot in the world but then thought that was a sign of vanity and let it go. The laughter started from below and reached his mouth first and then his eyes. He turned to Maya as if she could understand him or perhaps understand his wild side, the one reflected in the lake's icy waters on the plateau of Campo Imperatore, 'the mirror of the Gran Sasso.' This time the reflection took the form of a golden eagle showing him her own diagonal eyes, curved beak, claws, and wings while she filtered through her feathers all his false excuses.

"Right. You're right. Forgive me for the moment of weakness. We have a house to fix, some saffron to collect, and some hidden treasures to find."

Printed in Poland
by Amazon Fulfillment
Poland Sp. z o.o., Wrocław
21 October 2022

f6487e60-a9d9-4f8b-ad64-9c5ae0e5cfc0R01